BETWEEN HATE AND DESIRE

BROOKE FOX

Dear reader,

Between Hate and Desire was originally published as a duet: Baby Mine and Baby Yours by Kennedy Fox in 2019. It's been re-edited, re-titled, and merged into one longer standalone. If you'd like to listen to the audiobooks, you can search them up by the original titles on all retailers.

Between Hate and Desire is recommended for mature audiences only due to sensitive subject matters, open door sex scenes, and adult language.

This book contains the death of a partner and best friend (on page), living with grief, and the healing process. This book shows pregnancy from the early stages through delivery and topics of infertility are discussed. This is an angsty, slow burn romance between two people who found friendship and love through a tragic situation and ends in a happily-ever-after.

If you'd like more detailed information or specific chapters of events, feel free to DM me on Instagram @brookewritesromance or email me at brookewritesromance@gmail.com.

Happy reading!!
-Brooke

And there goes my mind racing
    And you are the reason
    That I'm still breathing
    I'm hopeless now

I'd climb every mountain
    And swim every ocean
    Just to be with you
    And fix what I've broken
    Oh, 'cause I need you to see
    That you are the reason

You Are The Reason
Calum Scott

PLAYLIST

Listen to the full playlist on Spotify

I Can't Fall In Love Without You | Zara Larsson
The Feeling | Travis Atreo
Mercy | Brett Young
Enemies | Lauv
Naked | James Arthur
Lifeline | We Three
Baby Mine | Alison Krauss
See You Again | Wiz Khalifa, Charlie Puth
Power Over Me | Dermot Kennedy
Thru These Tears | Lany
Only Want You | Rita Ora
Can I Be Him | James Arthur
Already Gone | Sleeping At Last
Heaven's Not Too Far | We Three
You Are The Reason | Calum Scott
With Love | Christina Grimmie
I'm a Mess | Bebe Rexha
Dancing On My Own | Calum Scott
Be Alright | Dean Lewis
Wait for You | Jake Miller
Ruin | Shawn Mendes
Forget Me | Lewis Capaldi
Remind Me to Forget | Kygo, Miguel
The Reason | Chelsea Cutler
Say You Won't Let Go | James Arthur
Pillowtalk | Conor Maynard

PROLOGUE
HUNTER

For the past four hours, I've been running around behind the bar, getting people's beers and making cocktails nonstop. Spring break means the bar stays insanely busy, especially with California State University ten minutes away.

"Dude, Hunter," Brandon hollers. Over my shoulder, I see him standing at the opposite end of the bar. "Need a refill, man!" He shakes his empty beer bottle as if that'll encourage me to hustle. Considering he doesn't tip, his pretty boy ass can wait.

"I'll be right over!" I reply, shaking my head. It'll be his fifth beer in the past few hours, but I know he's taking full advantage of our last semester in college. In a couple of months, we'll graduate and be in the real world—hopefully not still bartending, though. I'm getting my degree in engineering and don't plan to use it making drinks.

Brandon Locke is my roommate and one of my best friends. Though we grew up hating each other in high school since he was the kicker for my school's rival team, we moved past that when we played football together at CSU Sacramento. He's one of the most dependable guys I know, and though he tries to keep up with me and our other buddies, he's more of a straight arrow. Tonight, however, he seems to be bending.

"Locke, you sure you want another?" I ask when I'm in front of him.

"Don't make me jump over this bar and punch you," he threatens, then slaps down a five-dollar bill, making me chuckle.

"Oh, big spender. Fine." I grab a cold beer from the cooler and slide it over to him. I take the five and put it in the drawer. "But don't think I'm holding your hair back when you puke your guts out later."

Brandon chugs away while holding up his middle finger. "I don't need a sitter, *Dad*. Besides, Mason and Liam will make sure I get home safely."

That makes me snort, and I shake my head. "They aren't much better."

"True." He shrugs, giving no fucks.

This last semester has been hard on us. These final months before graduation have been a mental head game as we focus on the future and job hunting. Bartending pays the bills for now, and I don't mind it, but on nights like this, I wish I were hanging out with my friends instead of serving them. At least being the sober one keeps me entertained because they're a bunch of idiots when they're drunk.

"Manning!" When I hear my last name being yelled across the room, I know it's Mason. As the loud and obnoxious one of the four of us, he's always ready for a party. Hell, he *is* the party.

He squeezes his way through the crowd until he's standing next to Brandon. His lazy grin tells me exactly how drunk he is.

"You better slow your shit down, Holt. I'm not gonna get a fine for over-serving your ass," I warn, cleaning up a beer spill from the person he bumped into when he barged over to the bar.

"Dude, I'm totally fine. Look…" he tells me, aiming for his nose with his finger, but he misses and gouges his eye. "Well, I'm not driving anyway, so hook me up."

I slide open the cooler door, grab him a PBR, and hand it over. "I don't know how you drink that shit." I take his money off the bar. "Should charge you extra for making me serve it to you."

"You don't know what's good." Mason takes a long swig.

I scoff, ignoring him.

"Smells nasty as fuck too." Brandon leans over and makes a face. "Probably why he likes it. Just his type."

"Where's Evans?" I ask, realizing I haven't seen Liam in a while and look through the crowd. He's not as rowdy as Mason, but he's been known to get thrown out of a party or two. Kinda ironic considering he's a bouncer here and usually the one breaking up fights and kicking drunks out on their asses.

"Saw him heading toward the back with a redhead," Mason explains. Liam isn't on duty tonight, so that can only mean one thing—closet sex.

"Fuck," I mutter, shaking my head. I'm not about to hunt him down just to see something I'll need to bleach from my memory and eyes. This wouldn't be the first time he's banged some girl at work and probably won't be the last.

"Hunter!" Greg, the other bartender, shouts and gives me a look to keep moving down the line.

"Yeah, yeah," I murmur, waving him off. He's in his thirties and always on my ass. If I didn't need to pay half the rent and bills, I would've left months ago.

"Alright, man. We'll let you get back to work. Be back for a refill shortly," Brandon tells me, tapping his knuckles on the bar. He drags Mason away with him, and I get back to serving drinks to the dozens of people waiting.

As I'm grabbing beers and making cocktails, the bar continues to fill and grow louder. Music blares, couples dance, and I wouldn't be surprised if a mosh pit broke out soon.

"What can I get ya?" I ask a blonde whose hair covers half her face. The moment she looks up and her blue eyes meet mine, all the air is sucked from my lungs. Her smile widens, and she tilts her head slightly as if she's examining me. Her gaze slowly slides across the tattoos on my arm before she meets mine again.

"What would you recommend?" The sweetness of her voice

has me licking my lips and swallowing hard. She's stolen my thoughts with one question.

"Uh…um…well…" I stutter because I can't form a cohesive sentence. She blinks, waiting patiently. "What're you in the mood for?"

She pinches her lips together, moving them from side to side as if she's truly contemplating. Then she taps her fingertips on the bar. "Something dangerous."

Good God.

Considering I work in a bar where the ladies parade their asses in short skirts and low-cut tops, I see beautiful women all the time. But this woman—the word beautiful doesn't seem sufficient to describe her. A mesmerizing light surrounds her, and as ridiculous as it sounds, I'm half-tempted to ask where the hell she came from. She's stunning, and something about her makes me want to get to know her—everything about her.

"Technically, that could account for ninety-five percent of what's behind the bar, so…" I try not to stare, but honestly, it's impossible. She has a sweet, charming vibe about her, but at the same time, mysterious. "You like straight liquor?"

"As a matter of fact, I do," she replies with confidence.

Fucking hot.

"I'm gonna make you something, sweetheart. Sit tight." I point at her, making sure she doesn't go anywhere.

"Should I be worried?" she taunts, lifting a brow when I grab the bottle of 1800 tequila.

"Yes," I tell her. "Yes, you should…" I linger, hoping she'll tell me her name.

"Lennon," she announces. "What's yours?"

"Hunter." I point at where it's embroidered on the left side of my shirt.

"Ah, yes. I see it now." Lennon smiles wide, and it's pure heaven. "What're you adding in there now?" She leans over slightly when I pour some vodka, gin, and rum. "Are you trying to get me drunk?"

I finish mixing her drink and place it in front of her. "Yes, I figured that was your intention." I smirk. "Hold on." I hold up a finger so she doesn't take a sip yet. Grabbing a cocktail stick, I stab a couple of cherries onto it and gently place it in the glass. "Alright, now."

Lennon grins with an arched brow. She takes a hesitant sip, then goes in for another.

"Strong enough for ya?" I tease when she makes a sour face.

"Yeah, that definitely does the job." She blinks a few times. "What's it called?" She brings it back to her lips.

My smirk deepens. "The Leg Spreader."

Lennon quickly covers her mouth before she spits out her drink. She's holding back a laugh, and it's impossible not to laugh with her.

"You asked for dangerous," I remind her, smirking.

She swallows and nods. "And you delivered."

Our eyes stay locked as she finishes her drink, not even flinching at the extra liquor I added. Impressive, to say the least.

"Don't forget your cherries." I nod toward the cocktail stick.

She stands, setting the glass on the bar, and grabs it. "I wouldn't dare." Her voice is sultry and seductive, and if this stupid counter weren't in the way, I'd close the space between us.

Once she slides them off and swallows them down, Lennon takes a step back, then stops. "Thanks for the drink, *Hunter*."

"My pleasure." I shoot her a wink, and she blushes before walking away. My heart pounds at the way my name sounds on her lips. I swallow hard, trying to stay focused, but Lennon has knocked me off my axis.

For the next couple of hours, I keep tabs on her as she and her friends dance around the bar. After a while, they come up for shots, and I happily hook them up. She's cute and flirty, and it's so damn hard to focus when she's near that I almost slap myself.

"So what brings you girls out here?" I ask when she and a friend order another round.

"We're on spring break," her friend answers.

"Oh, so you're from Sacramento?" I ask while I help make a fuck ton of margaritas for Greg so I don't stare aimlessly at Lennon.

"A few hours away," Lennon responds. "We attend CSU in Fresno."

My heart drops because she's not a local, but that doesn't stop me from wanting to take her home and kiss every inch of her delicate skin. Something simmers between us, and I know she feels it too by the way her eyes study me. She's intense and hot, setting my rapidly beating heart on fire.

"We're here visiting friends for the week. They're the half-naked ones on the dance floor with those guys who can barely stand." She giggles as she points at the center of the bar.

When I look over her shoulder and see the girls she described surrounded by Brandon, Mason, and Liam, I grin. Of fucking course. I haven't served them in the past hour and have wondered where the hell they went.

"Careful," I warn, nodding toward them. "They're as plastered as you all are, considering I've served them all night too."

"I already called the beefy one," Lennon's friend singsongs. "I hope he doesn't get whiskey dick, though."

I chuckle at the thought of Liam with a limp dick. I'm sure he'd have some asshole comeback at the mention of it.

"I think you're safe. He can drink anyone under the table. He's a bouncer here."

Her eyes light up like a kid in a candy store. "Oh really? Well, don't mind me then…" She trails off before slowly walking away and waving bye to Lennon.

I nod toward her empty glass. "You want another?"

"No, I shouldn't." She sets it on the bar, and I reach for it before her fingers release. Electricity buzzes down my spine the moment her skin is against mine. Her eyes focus on where we're touching, and she swallows hard. I pull away, and I almost see the immediate loss on her face. Damn, this woman could have come straight from my dreams.

"I have to start cleaning up soon, but can you come back in about thirty? Things will slow down, and I won't have to rush around," I say, hoping she gets the hint. I want to ask for her number or, hell, even sit and talk with her until the sun rises.

"Sure." She flashes a sexy grin.

As she's walking away, Lennon glances over her shoulder and winks before going to her friends. The smile that fills my face might be permanent, and she's definitely to blame.

Forty-five minutes fly by, and I finally have time to breathe. I look around the nearly empty place for Lennon but don't see her anywhere. My heart drops at the realization that she's gone.

Fuck.

The announcement for last call is made, and the lingering patrons order their last drink before leaving. We don't close for another fifteen minutes, so I hang on to hope that she'll reappear before then.

By the time I make it home, it's well after 3:00 a.m. I'm bummed and almost feel numb that Lennon never came back. Whether it was her way of brushing me off or she left with someone else—and both options make my blood boil—I'm pissed at myself for not asking for her number when I had the chance. Considering she's only visiting and not from here, I may never get the opportunity again.

The lamp casts a dim light in the living room when I enter the apartment. I know it was off before I left for work, so hopefully, that means Brandon made it home safely. The moment I notice his shoes haphazardly thrown on the floor, I don't bother checking because it's confirmation he did.

It always takes me a while to wind down after a busy shift and even more so tonight because my mind is reeling over Lennon. Rather than going to bed right away, I take a shower and wash the night off me. It's hard to think straight when her face is all I see and her voice is all I hear. She was something special, one of a kind, and no woman has ever had that effect on me. I'm kicking myself and wonder if it was for the best, considering she doesn't live here. Still, I can't seem to shake the feeling, gnawing me to the bone.

Once I'm clean and in bed, I toss and turn. I'm unable to fall asleep, but it's not the thoughts of her keeping me awake. Rather…

Thump. Thump.

Moaning.

Thump.

What the fuck?

"Yes! *Yes, yes, yes!*"

"Oh, come on." I groan to myself.

Brandon brought some chick home, and now they're fucking at nearly four in the morning. I wouldn't give a shit, but his room is right next to mine, and I can literally hear every damn pant and movement.

The headboard slams against the wall we share, and I want to pound my fist against it and tell them to keep it down, but since I've done the same to him, I let it go. Instead, I grab my headphones and turn on some music. It helps for about thirty seconds until his bed pounds and rattles so hard against the wall, I'm certain it's going to come through the drywall.

Now I wish I'd waited to take a shower and was in the bathroom right now. I have plans in the morning and have to be up in five hours, so I don't have time to waste not sleeping.

I do my best to drown out the noise, but the walls are paper thin, so it's no use. Part of me wants to give him a high five for pleasing this girl so well—if her screams are any indication—but considering they're both probably drunk, I'm impressed with how long this continues. Guess I won't be calling him "Limp Dick Locke" tomorrow.

"Fuck!" After one final loud thud against the wall, the apartment goes silent.

About goddamn time.

Rolling over, I shut my eyes and attempt to fall asleep. Ten minutes pass, and I'm still restless.

"Fuck it." I decide to get up and grab something to drink. Maybe chugging three beers will help me pass out.

Without turning on any lights, I walk down the short hallway and see a glimmer of light coming from the kitchen. I turned off the lamps after my shower, so Brandon must've got up and I didn't hear him.

Stepping into the kitchen, I notice the fridge door is open with an almost bare ass perked up in the air. She's wearing an oversized T-shirt and thin panties while digging through our food.

God help me.

Apparently, Brandon's date is raiding our fridge now. Decent ass, though.

Leaning against the counter, I cross my arms over my chest and loudly clear my throat. "What're you—"

Before I finish my sentence, something flies through the air, and I don't dodge it quick enough before it grazes my right nut.

"Son of a bitch." I barely get the words out and hunch over, holding my junk in my palm.

"Oh my God!" the girl squeals. "I'm so sorry! You scared the shit out of me!"

I'm ready to curse her out, but I can barely breathe as I squeeze my eyes tight, trying to regain my composure. "You...*hit*...me!" I hiss.

This is what I get for being thirsty.

"It was an accident!" She kneels, trying to console me.

"Don't touch me," I warn when a lock of blond hair lands on my arm. "I just...need a minute."

Feet pad against the floor, and a light switch flick on.

"Jesus, what the hell did you do to my roommate?" Brandon asks.

"I threw the bottle of Reddi Whip at his nuts," the girl explains cautiously.

"Fucking hell." Groaning through the pain, I squeeze my eyes.

"I didn't mean to! I didn't hear him approach, and then I heard his voice, and it was instinct," she rambles a ridiculous explanation that has me seeing red.

"You okay, man?" Brandon tries to muffle his laughter as he pats my shoulder and offers me a hand.

I inhale a deep breath and swallow down the discomfort. Taking his hand, I stand and try to get my bearings before I chew her out.

"Sorry about that. She was thirsty and wanted some snacks," he explains like I'm an idiot and didn't hear their entire fuck session.

"Whatever, it's fine." I pinch the bridge of my nose to regain my control.

My vision finally clears, and it's then I see the woman Brandon has his arms wrapped around, swatting her ass.

"Lennon," I croak out, blinking, hoping I'm imagining her in front of me, standing in my kitchen with my best friend. My jaw tightens and my nostrils flare at seeing her pressed against him. What in the ever-loving fuck is she doing here?

"Hunter." She says my name so softly I almost don't hear it.

"You know each other?" Brandon asks, pulling her tighter as he looks at her like she's the most beautiful woman he's ever laid eyes on.

Because she is.

"From the bar," Lennon quickly explains.

I can't seem to form words at the moment. The air in the kitchen grows thick, and I wish it were only my nuts that felt numb right now. I look back and forth between them, watching them together, and know deep down inside that Brandon isn't going to let her go after tonight. He's not a wham-bam-thank-you-ma'am type of guy. He fucked her senseless and claimed her as his. Brandon has the ability to give her everything she could ever need or want, but I, on the other hand…

"He made me a special drink," she adds, pulling me from my self-deprecating thoughts.

The Leg Spreader.

How fitting.

"Oh, right." Brandon smiles, having no fucking clue what this is doing to me. Of course he has no idea. I didn't even get the chance to say anything or make it known I was attracted to her. But this answers my question as to why she never came back.

Fuck my life.

"Certain he makes all the pretty ladies *special* drinks. That's how he gets the big tips." Brandon chuckles, tilting Lennon's chin up until their lips collide. And I'm out.

"I gotta get up in a few hours, so I'm gonna head back to bed," I say casually, pretending my heart isn't being gutted.

I turn to walk away when Lennon calls my name. "Hunter." The sound of her voice makes my jaw tighten and my hands ball into fists.

When I turn, she's behind me and smiles when I look into her eyes. Goddammit, why does she have to be so gorgeous?

"Water?" She offers as if she's trying to make peace.

Blinking, I look down and see she's holding a bottle.

"You said you were thirsty," she confirms.

As I stare at her, my lips move into a firm line, and I ignore her offer. Is it possible she didn't feel what I did? Was it all a figment of my damn imagination? She came up to the bar at least a half dozen times, and I never asked for her number. *Fucking moron.* Did she think *I* wasn't interested and found someone who made it clear he was? My roommate, to be exact.

Without another word, I walk away with my bruised nuts and defeated dick between my legs.

CHAPTER ONE
LENNON

PRESENT DAY

THE ANNOYING BUZZING causes my eyes to pop open, and I reach over to turn off the alarm on my phone. My boyfriend, Brandon, stirs and pulls me close to his warm body. We fit perfectly together like puzzle pieces, and even after all this time, I can't get enough of him. If I didn't have a meeting at the school with the principal this morning, I'd stay in bed a little longer and enjoy his hard body pressed against mine. He hums against my neck, and I smile. Since I moved in eight months ago, me waking up early and him trying to lure me to stay longer has become our morning routine. There's never enough time.

Brandon holds me tighter, and I'm tempted to stay but still need to shower and dress. I turn around and face him, brushing a soft kiss against his lips as he throws an arm over me. "I have to get up. I can't be late for work. Principal Orson will have my ass, and I'm still trying to get on her good side," I whisper.

"I know, I know. You're so warm and comfy," he quips in a husky tone before I slip from his hold with a smile. Waking up next to him is the best start to my day.

I lean over the bed and place another kiss on Brandon's lips before I rush into the bathroom and turn on the shower.

A smile fills my face as I think about how far we've come these past couple of years—well, *almost* two years. It's hard to believe it's been that long already, but at the same time, it feels like only yesterday when we first met.

Though it started with a friendly hello and flirty banter, I instantly knew he'd be more than a random hookup. After we danced a few times, he asked for my number, which I willingly gave to him. Brandon knew what he wanted—me—and I couldn't deny I wanted him too. There was something electric between us, something that pulled me to him and made my heart race. Though I'd shown interest in Hunter earlier, the way Brandon gave me his full attention drew me closer. Random women walked up and tried to steal him away, but he politely told them he wasn't interested, and he never took his eyes off me. The way he looked at me that night made me feel so damn special.

By the following morning, we'd shared so many personal details about ourselves that I felt like I'd known him for a lifetime. He understood me on a deeper level than some of my closest friends. I'd never felt a connection like that with any other man before, and Brandon still holds that record.

Although we didn't take things slow right away, my feelings for him were almost immediate and have only grown stronger. I wasn't the type of girl who went home with a random guy, and I'm not one-night-stand material, but with Brandon, it was different. Hell, I'd only ever had one serious relationship before him, and we've been inseparable ever since.

Since I still had one year of college left and lived three hours away, we dated long distance, staying exclusive and taking turns traveling back and forth as much as possible. During my final semester, I applied for elementary schools in Sacramento and some of the suburbs. I wanted not only to be close to him but close to my older sister, who moved here as well. As soon as I was offered a position as a music teacher at Hillsong Elementary, I moved in with him and his roommate, Hunter. The apartment is small and quaint, but we make do with the space since it's within all of our budgets. Eventually, Brandon and I will get our own place, but until that happens, I'm forced to tolerate Hunter and all his asshole antics.

I hop in the shower and wash my body and hair. As I scrub, I sing the Beatles songs I grew up listening to. Considering the Beatles released over three hundred songs, I have an almost unlimited morning repertoire. Just as I finish up the chorus to "I Want To Hold Your Hand," hard banging echoes against the door.

"Shut up! And hurry your ass up, Lennon!" Hunter shouts, beating his fist on the door, which only encourages me to sing louder. I'm practically belting out the words by the time I'm rinsing the conditioner from my hair. I honestly don't know how Brandon sleeps through this every morning, or maybe he's immune to it. At this point, Hunter and I argue worse than a brother and sister.

After I scream out the Broadway-worthy grand finale of my vocal performance, I turn off the water and hold back my laughter. Hunter hates it when I sing, especially early in the morning. He's always a grump before eight, and getting a rise out of him is fun. It's payback for all the times he purposely annoys the shit out of me. I've sung in the shower since I was a little girl, so I'm not changing that for anyone, especially not him.

Stepping out of the shower, I grab a towel and dry off. Hunter pounds on the door again, startling me, and demands I hurry for the thousandth time. As I brush my teeth, I think back to when we first met. Most assume we met after Brandon and I started dating, but that's not the case. Hunter was bartending that same night, and we'd shared a moment at the bar before Brandon and I started talking.

At first glance, he gave me heart palpitations, but he was a total sweetheart and the cute way he flirted made me comfortable ordering from him. I remember his tattoos and how they intricately covered his forearm and wondered if he had more. I was in a different town on spring break and wanted to let loose and be reckless. We exchanged side glances and smiles, and as he poured different liquors into my glass, I couldn't keep my eyes off him. But neither could every other woman in the bar. Nervous exhilaration coursed through me when he spoke. Hunter's charismatic and charming vibe lured me right into his web.

I went back to my friends and kept the electrifying moment to myself as I tried to find the courage to go back to the bar and get his number. When I looked at Hunter, a handful of women desperately vying for his attention surrounded him. He happily obliged, smiling and flirting with them just the same. They were all gorgeous, leaning over the bar to touch his muscular arms and laughing as if he'd told the best joke. Though I didn't have much experience with men, I still wanted a week of fun and spontaneity. However, my insecurities got the best of me, and I knew I wouldn't be able to satisfy a guy like that, not even for one night.

My fears and self-doubt kept me from going back to the bar alone for the rest of the night. I played it safe, staying within my comfort zone, and kept my friends nearby. After seeing the way he bantered with other women and they clawed at him, I convinced myself what we shared was nothing more than him working hard for his money. Considering the bad attitude and rude comments he continues to throw at me, I know with certainty there wasn't anything special between us that night.

The first summer after Brandon and I started dating, Hunter had a different woman over every other weekend I was there. He couldn't even remember their names half the time and had no qualms about openly bragging to his guy friends for being able to "bag and shag" any girl he wanted. If he wasn't bragging about his conquests, he'd go on about how hot or how built he was. Hunter's muscular, there's no denying that, but his appeal was lost after hearing him talk about it for the tenth time.

Since he no longer works at the bar, the number of women he brings home has slowed down, though he's still superficial and still acts like a womanizer. "Bartender Hunter" was nothing more than a façade, a made-up gentleman my imagination created. "Real-life Hunter" is a smart-ass jerk who complains about my singing, lives like a slob, and has a revolving bedroom door.

Once my hair is dry and I'm happy with my appearance, I go to my bedroom where Brandon is still sleeping.

I look through the closet and slip on a skirt and a comfortable blouse. Before leaving, I carefully lean over the bed to give Brandon a kiss goodbye when he suddenly grabs me and pulls me on top of him.

"Sure you don't have time for a quickie?" he playfully asks as I straddle him, feeling his thickness beneath me. Brandon sits up, palms my breast, and releases a small groan of desperation. I slightly rock on him as he arches his hips, feeling his arousal but knowing we can't start something right now.

"Babe, if you make me late—" I start as he moves his hands to my ass and squeezes, pushing me harder against him.

"Then I'll get to fuck you for the next hour?" The morning sunshine barely lights the room, but I see his cocky smirk.

"You're the ultimate tease. You know I'm gonna be thinking about this all day now," I admonish as I climb off, squeezing my legs together. He knows damn well I have to get going.

Brandon chuckles. "Have a good day, my little sex kitten."

"Shut up," I mock before telling him goodbye for real this time.

As I walk down the hallway, I spot a pair of red lacy panties on the floor that *aren't* mine. I look down at them, and my nostrils flare. I try to ignore it until I walk into the kitchen to find cabinets open, half-full beer bottles on the counter, and dirty dishes piled high. A loud groan releases from my throat when I notice a bowl in the sink with dried cereal on the bottom.

Goddamn him.

I turn the water to a scalding temperature to soak the bowl. He knows I hate this because the cereal becomes rock hard and essentially superglued to the glass, which makes it nearly impossible to clean without scrubbing. Hunter walks past me to place another dirty-ass bowl in the sink that's full of what looks like old macaroni and cheese. When I see the random noodles stuck to the bottom of the bowl that's clearly been in his room for days, maybe even weeks, I almost lose my shit.

I turn around and glare. He's shirtless, wearing pants that hang off his hips, and has his normal no-fucks-given attitude. If he weren't such an asshole, maybe he'd be able to find a woman to help take care of him because he's obviously unable to do it himself.

"Are you serious?" I ask, trying to keep my tone level. "Are you incapable of using the dishwasher?"

He shrugs, opens the fridge, and lifts the gallon of milk to his lips, taking a drink directly from it.

My eyes widen, and my mouth falls open as I gag. I make a mental note not to have any milk until we buy more or maybe not ever. "What the fuck, Hunter? Have you lost your damn mind?"

He places the jug back in the fridge and slams the door shut. Glaring at me with deep brown eyes, he finally responds, "I lost my mind when you moved in."

I growl, unable to keep my frustration buried inside. "God, you're such a freakin' slob!"

Hunter walks away and his door closes. My heart gallops in my chest as I look at the mess, and it angers me to no end. Each night before I go to bed, I clean the kitchen until it's spotless. Then I wake up and find different articles of women's underwear scattered on the floor and dirty dishes filling the sink. I'm no one's maid or babysitter, especially not his.

More empty beer bottles and chip bags litter the coffee table in the living room. The cushions are haphazardly thrown around, which I hate. It looks like a fucking tornado went through here last night. I close my eyes and suck in a deep breath, hoping I find the restraint not to walk into Hunter's room and strangle him to death because he deserves it right now.

Before I leave for work, though I don't have time for this shit, I have to clean up the mess, or it will bother me all day. I quickly throw the random trash away, situate the couch cushions, and pick up until the place looks semi-normal. Hunter enters the kitchen, fully dressed this time, and places two slices of bread in the toaster.

"It's a new year. Think you can start cleaning up after yourself? New year, new you?" I ask, hopeful, but the sarcasm isn't lost on him.

"That's what we keep you around for." He shoots me a snarky smile, and I'm two seconds away from slapping it right off his smug face.

I huff, seeing red. "Why are you so insistent on being like this? No wonder you're single. No one can stand you once your clothes are back on."

Hunter places a hand on his chest over his heart and gives me a fake pouty look. "Oh man. That one hurt. What will I ever do with myself?" He makes the extra effort to roll his eyes with so much exaggeration, I'm afraid they might get stuck. "Try again, Lennon. Your jabs have become as old and worn out as you."

I narrow my eyes. "You're gonna be single forever and die alone."

"Better than being stuck with someone bossy and always nagging—like *you*." His toast pops up, and he sets it on the counter with no plate, scattering the crumbs everywhere as he spreads peanut butter over both pieces.

"You're impossible!" I glare at the mess he's making where I cleaned. "If you weren't Brandon's best friend…"

"Go ahead. Say it," Hunter says over his shoulder. "I *dare* you."

Ignoring him, I grab a protein shake out of the fridge. "I don't have to because you already know what I was gonna say."

"That you'd kick me out?" He releases an evil chuckle. "As if you have some sort of power over him. Hate to break it to you, honey buns, but Brandon does whatever he wants. Just because you two are fuckin' doesn't mean shit. I've known him for longer than you and know him better than you ever will. Your magical pussy won't be able to make him bend to your will forever, sweetheart."

I let out a sarcastic laugh, refusing to let his words get to me. "You're so vile and immature. You need to grow up. Acting like this at twenty-four isn't cute anymore."

"Oh, so you thought I was cute at one point?" Hunter taunts and takes a bite of his toast, crumbs falling on his clothes and the floor this time, but he doesn't seem to care.

I narrow my eyes. "I *never* thought you were cute."

"Liar," he says matter-of-factly, smacking his lips. "I know for certain you did."

My blood pumps at a much faster rate, and I know if I don't walk away, I'll say something I'll regret later. So I choose the high road like any mature adult would. If only he'd act like one every once in a while.

Though it pains me, I allow him to have the final word. Turning on my heels, I grab my bag and leave with the door slamming behind me. As I walk down the stairs, I try to take in deep, calming breaths, refusing to let him ruin my day.

Brisk air brushes against my cheeks, and I can't get to my car fast enough. Winter in California is bearable and much different from Utah where I grew up. There's no snow here, but sometimes the cool air chills me to the bone. Once I'm inside, I set my things on the passenger seat and inhale a deep breath as I start the car. The thought of toast crumbs on the floor and counter has me twitching, so before I leave, I text Hunter, unable to let him get away with this.

LENNON

Please, if you could, pick up the kitchen before you leave. I'd appreciate your help with this.

HUNTER

New number, who dis?

LENNON

Why do you insist on aggravating me all the time?

HUNTER

Not sure what you're talking about. And the answer is no, honey buns. I'm walking out the door and can't be late. Have a NICE day.

Ugh! He knows how much I hate that nickname, yet he continues to say it. Ever since the first time I made Brandon cinnamon rolls, Hunter has called me that, but I know he's being condescending by the way he treats me.

I type out a rude message but decide to delete it. Reminding myself I'm the bigger person, I tuck my phone into my bag and try to push the thoughts of him away. Hunter's been dead set on treating me like an inconvenience since the first night I came home with Brandon. After eight months of living together, I don't know why I'd expect him to change.

Sighing, I reverse and pull onto the road and drive toward the school. I hate being this worked up in the morning and can't wait until Brandon and I get our own place. When we're more financially stable, we will. I've only been working for the school since the fall and haven't completed my first year yet. Brandon has been at his job since he graduated, but he has some student loans to pay off because his football scholarship didn't cover everything. Even though Hunter acts like an ass most of the time, I can put up with him as long as it means I get to live with my love and not struggle to pay the bills each month. Small sacrifices, I suppose.

Hardly any traffic is on the road on the way to work, which is a miracle. Depending on what time I leave in the mornings, it can be a smooth sailing or bumper to bumper, another reason I like being early. Soon I'm parking and grabbing my bag, then crossing the parking lot. I walk to the office to meet Principal Orson. She's strict and scary, how most kids imagine principals, and has worked in education for over twenty-five years. I respect the hell out of her, but it doesn't make me any less nervous when we're having a one-on-one. She's the type of woman who will chew a person up and spit them out with only a few words.

"Sit," she instructs, barely glancing up from the papers in her hand when I enter her office. I take a seat, dropping my heavy bag on the floor.

"I saw you submitted a budget proposal for the spring concert," she says, her dark eyes finally meeting mine.

I swallow hard. "Yes, ma'am. I'd like to be able to buy a few new microphones and instruments for the kids to play at the concert. We have a large supply of recorders but are missing several percussion instruments like hand drums, claves, and even a bass drum," I linger nervously. "The tambourines aren't in the greatest condition either as you can imagine with the kids smacking them around."

"Lennon, this should've been submitted before the school year started." The sternness in her voice isn't lost on me. She sets down the paper, and I notice it's a printout of the written budget I made to show where the money would be spent. It took weeks of research for this request over winter break, and I made sure all the numbers were accurate.

"I understand and apologize. I applied for several grants to purchase the extra equipment, but we weren't accepted as I had hoped. I thought the kids could do the spring program with what we had, and while we can, I think they'll learn more if we could purchase new rhythm instruments," I explain.

She looks at me but doesn't say anything. I'm growing more anxious as each second passes, and it's so quiet I can hear the ticking of the second hand on the wall clock. "I've decided to approve five hundred dollars, which is within my limits of authority. I know this is your first year, and you probably didn't realize what you would need, but next year, proposals are due before the first day of school. Understand?"

I nod, my heart pounding at the prospect of having my

contract renewed next year, which is overly exciting, but I don't allow it to show. "Yes, ma'am. Thank you so much. I appreciate this." Flashing her a grateful smile, I add, "I won't let you down, promise. It's going to be the best spring concert the kids have ever done."

"I like you, Lennon, and I like your drive. Keep up the good work. Remember this first year of teaching and how passionate you are. I hope you never lose that. After years of teaching, too many educators lose that spark and only clock in to earn a paycheck," she tells me as her phone rings.

"I will. Absolutely! Thank you again." I stand, see my way out, and walk toward the music room with a little hop in my step. She didn't outright say I'd have my contract renewed, but she always chooses her words carefully.

Unlocking my classroom door, I step inside, feeling elated that I'll be able to teach the kids new things. I stop for a moment and look around the room. Taking it all in, I focus on the fire to teach music inside me right now. The child-size chairs surrounding the piano in the center of the room will soon have eager children who want to sing and learn sitting in them. I'm living my dream.

Glancing at the clock to see how much time I have until the bell rings, there are twenty minutes left, so I text Brandon about the little sexy stunt he pulled this morning.

Before I click on his name, I find an unread text from Hunter and a picture of our sink stacked full of dirty dishes that have been in his room for only God knows how long.

My nostrils flare, and now I'm worked up and raging all over again.

Bastard.

CHAPTER TWO

HUNTER

I CAN'T HELP but chuckle as Lennon stomps around, huffing and cursing me out like she does every morning. It's our own little fucked-up routine, but without the make-up sex afterward.

When we met almost two years ago, I knew she was special. Call it instinct or maybe fate—I don't know what it was—but I felt it right down to my bones that Lennon Corrigan was meant to be in my life. The way she looked at me, our flirtatious banter, the electricity that soared between us—it all made me come alive. The fact I'd never felt instant chemistry like that with anyone before her had me wanting to get to know her.

Imagine my shock that night when I saw her standing in my kitchen after fucking my best friend. As much as I wanted to be happy for Brandon, I was slowly dying inside. I still am, and I've wanted to ask her *why* so many times.

Why him?

Why not me?

Why didn't she give *us* a chance?

I've concluded the moment we shared at the bar must've been one-sided. She'd flirted to get a free drink, and that's all it was. She came up a few more times with her friends but never made it clear she had felt what I did. Of course she returned for more drinks, but I clearly spun it in my head into something it wasn't, which made me a goddamn fool.

She chose Brandon, and I refused to stand in the way. However, that doesn't make it easy to see them together, even now. You'd think I would've gotten over it, considering nothing happened between us, but the more I saw her on the weekends and the days she'd sleep over during the summer made it impossible for me to forget her. We shared something special at that bar, or at least my heart fed me that lie anytime she was close. I quickly decided the only way to deal with her constant presence was to get under her skin and frustrate her as much as I could because that was what she did to me.

It was all fun and games until eight months ago when Brandon announced she'd be moving in permanently. Lennon found a job at one of the schools here so they'd no longer have to date long distance. It was easy to see how happy he was about it. I could've said no, made an argument about how there wasn't room for her in our tiny apartment, or even mentioned how I didn't approve of their relationship. However, I'd never put our friendship at risk by making him choose between me—his best friend—and the woman he loved.

I refused to be that guy. If the tables were turned, I knew he'd wish me luck and give me his blessing. So that's what I did and continue to do.

Now hearing her sing in the shower each morning, watching her dance in the kitchen while she makes coffee, and doing her stupid yoga in the living room have tortured me for the past eight months. Everywhere I turn, there she is—invading my space and creating dirty thoughts in my head that I'm always pushing away.

It's been fucking hell.

The only way to erase the thoughts of Lennon from my mind is to find someone else. Or that's what I keep telling myself, at least because I've tried many times and failed miserably. Something's obviously broken inside me because no matter what I do, those feelings for her don't go away. I know she doesn't reciprocate them, and you'd think my dick would get the memo and stop getting hard anytime she's in a tight skirt or low-cut blouse. You'd think my heart would stop racing each time she's near. You'd think after hearing them having sex and her screaming his name, I would stop obsessing over my best friend's girlfriend.

But no.

I'm fucking broken.

Nothing in my head works right when it comes to her, and even screwing random girls to erase the thoughts that haunt me hasn't worked so far.

Though it doesn't stop me from trying.

Once Lennon leaves for the day, slamming the door behind her, I let out a breath of relief. I still have thirty minutes before I have to leave for work, and since I showered the night before, I drink my coffee in silence without distraction.

I didn't always shower before bed. Normally, I'd do it before work every morning or after the gym, but Lennon blamed me for hogging the bathroom and making her late for work. I prefer to shower before bed now—I've come to like it—but hell if I'd ever admit that to either of them. During those early days when Lennon first moved in, we'd fight over who showered first in the mornings, which led to a lot of shouting and toilet flushing sabotage. Needless to say, Brandon begged me to compromise so the three of us could live together in peace.

For the sake of my best friend, I did, and once again, Lennon got her way—the bathroom is hers in the morning.

"Sounds like you two got off on the right foot today," Brandon says, slowly making his way into the kitchen. With eyes half closed, he reaches for a mug and pours himself some coffee. Then he adds creamer and sugar before meeting me at the kitchen table.

"Not my fault she's wound so tight," I say into my cup before taking a drink. "She gets pissed over the smallest things."

"Probably doesn't help that you egg her on before eight in the morning," he kindly reminds me as he's done dozens of times before. He takes a slow sip and releases a deep breath. "She likes routine."

"Doesn't mean she has to force her ways on everyone," I tell him. "If my dishes are dirty, I'll clean them when I feel like it. She gets her panties in a knot because I don't do them on her watch." We have this same conversation every few weeks, and you'd think he'd learn by now that I won't change my ways for anyone, especially *her*.

"It's your funeral, man. This fight is between you two." He shrugs, surrendering. Brandon knows this apartment is as much mine as it is his, and he can't force me to do anything as long as I keep up with my half of the bills and chores. I hate putting him in the middle like this, but if I bow down to her every demand, she'll never stop. Considering I already hate having to see her every day and live in this agony, she'll have to deal with me the way I deal with her.

Before Lennon moved in, we'd clean once a week, and that was enough. Between working full-time jobs and mostly ordering out food, there wasn't much to keep up with. Now, Lennon cooks for Brandon every night, does their laundry twice a week, and tells me when it's "my time" to vacuum and dust the apartment. After enough nagging, I do the chores she assigns, but only when I'm ready.

However, vacuuming up her panties and cell phone charger got me thirty minutes of scolding and a lesson on checking the floor beforehand. When she found out I used bug spray instead of furniture polish to dust the apartment, she stomped her foot and screamed at me for being an idiot.

Safe to say, I made my point on how I felt about her assigned "chores."

"Nah, don't worry, man. It's how we show affection," I reassure him, chuckling and finish my coffee. "If she hates it that much, maybe she'll go live with one of her sisters or friends or something, and we can get our bachelor pad back!"

I stand and walk to the sink, where I set my empty mug. A few of my cereal bowls that Lennon soaked in soapy water are still there, and I shake my head at how she tries to control everything.

"If she moves out, you know I'm going with her," Brandon tells me softly. "She's the love of my life, and you're my best friend, so I'd hate to even have to pick, but she's my future. However, moving out is the last thing I want."

His words have my jaw tightening at how pussy whipped he is. I know he loves her, but fuck. I miss the days when it was just us. We'd play video games, order pizza, and head out to the bars. In college, we were so broke that we'd take advantage of all the happy hour 2-for-1 deals so we'd have enough money to buy a drink for a girl or two. Mason and Liam would always be there to fuck shit up. Through thick and thin, it was always the four of us, and there was a strict no girls tagging along rule until Lennon came along.

Brandon's one of the good guys, and deep down, I know he deserves to be happy, but I can't help feeling like he stole something from me. It's unfair to say, considering he had no idea how I felt about her, and once they hooked up, I knew none of it mattered. Even if it'd been nothing more than a one-night stand, Lennon would always be off-limits. Bro code and all that shit. You don't dip your toes where a buddy has already been. The second he claimed her, my chance was shot.

"I know, man," I finally say, grabbing my bowls and emptying out the water.

I don't want to have these feelings for her. Hell, I'd do anything *not* to have them. The only thing that seems to work, even if only temporarily, is pissing her off. She'll scream, tell me how immature and irresponsible I am, curse me out until she's red in the face, and for a split second, those feelings of lust dissipate.

Approximately thirty seconds later, she'll do something adorable like shake her ass as she stomps away or force a smile in my direction to pretend she's not seething, and those stupid feelings quickly rush back.

Heading to my room, I grab the last of my things that I need before I leave for work. I spot three more bowls, a glass, and silverware on my desk and carry them to the sink.

Brandon's already finished his coffee and left the kitchen by the time I return. Knowing this will piss Lennon off, I place them next to the other dishes I left her this morning, and a smirk hits my lips.

My cell phone beeps, and as soon as Lennon's name flashes across the screen, I know it's going to be a passive-aggressive comment. When her message is what I thought it'd be, I reply like I always do—with anything to set her off even more. When she doesn't respond to my last text, I take a picture of my dirty dishes and send it to her, knowing it'll have her steaming. Nothing satisfies me more.

To be honest, I don't know why she even tries anymore. She'll text me with a simple request, and I always do the exact opposite, so you'd think she'd learn by now.

Her messages are usually along the lines of:

I'm making Brandon dinner tonight, so don't bring food home for him or he won't be hungry later.

Or…

I have to stay late at work, and my sisters are coming over right after. Do you think you could sweep the kitchen when you get home since you're the one who made the mess?

Or…

It's your turn to do laundry. Don't forget the towels in the bathroom this time!

Of course I brought home a six-pack of beer and two large pizzas. Instead of sweeping, I walked around in my work boots caked with dried dirt and stones from the worksites. And I did do laundry that night, just not her towels. Hearing her scream my name the next morning when she realized the linen closet didn't have any was totally worth it.

You think she'd understand she can't boss me around like a child. She's living in *my* apartment, so maybe I should start giving *her* a to-do list. Hell, the lease has my name on it, not hers.

Except she makes Brandon happy. That's the *only* reason I put up with her shit.

As if she read my mind, she sends another text.

Before I head out, I double-check I have everything I need—phone, keys, wallet. I slip on a jacket since it's a tad chilly, even for California in February, because I'll be visiting the jobsite today to check the progress and get a status update from the contractors. I yell to let Brandon know I'm leaving, but he's already in the shower. He's a lucky asshole who doesn't have to be at work until nine. As an accountant, he has the coveted banker's hours. Meanwhile, I have to be out of the house by eight as a project manager at a construction company. Typically, I do a lot of the bitch work since I only graduated two years ago, but I was recently assigned my very own project to oversee.

Being in charge and making sure we stay within budget, on schedule, and have limited fuckups only add to my list of growing responsibilities. On top of managing a major project, I have business meetings with owners, subcontractors, and team members, plus a mountain of paperwork on top of that. I travel between the office and jobsite daily, and even though it's busy and stressful, I love the complexity of it. Engineering and technology were always my strong suits, and working in the construction field during the summer while I was in high school helped pave the way to where I am now.

Once I'm in my truck, I stick my Bluetooth in my ear and get the day started. Liam and Mason like to give me shit for how much work crap I keep in here, but it's my mobile office.

By the time I'm on the highway, I'm already on a conference call as I drive out to the building site. Four large units with eighteen apartments inside, along with unattached garages, are being built. On top of that, a community recreational center with a tennis and basketball court will be added. We're only four months into the project and have six more months until it's complete. Of course the owner wants it done as soon as possible to fill it with renters, so he's already on my ass about getting ahead of schedule.

"Hunter Manning," I say, answering another call.

"Where the hell are you?" my boss, Phil, hisses, and I can tell he's already in a mood. "I'm ready to look at these plans, but I need you here."

"Okay, I'm three minutes out. I'll be right there."

After hanging up, I press my foot down on the gas pedal and book it. Once I pull into the gravel driveway, I park. Grabbing my work boots from the back, I quickly put them on along with my hard hat and safety glasses. Since I have to be on the jobsite one minute and in a meeting the next, I always dress professionally for work but also have a change of clothes and shoes in the car.

"Morning, Phil," I greet once I find him.

"Hunter," he replies flatly.

I flash him a confident smile, which he ignores.

After an hour of going over the plans, walking the jobsite, and proving to him I'm in control of the project, I'm on my way to the office to catch up on emails. I have a meeting at eleven, then another one at two, and after that, I'll work on my computer until I leave for the day.

By the time evening rolls around, I'm emotionally and mentally exhausted and more than ready to go home and relax. Once I finally reach my apartment, I park in my assigned spot and groan when I see Lennon's car next to it. Technically, it's Brandon's, but the moment she moved in, he gave it to her and now parks on the road. *Pussy.*

My phone rings just as I gather my things from the back seat.

"Hey, man," I answer. My older brother, Hayden, is as busy as I am these days, which means we don't get to chat much. It also doesn't help that he lives in New York now, and our time zones are different. "What's goin' on?"

"Not much," he replies. "Just thought I'd check in on my little brother and see if he's staying out of trouble."

Laughing, I take what I need from my truck and shut the door. I glance at Lennon's car and frown, annoyed she's home already.

"Always," I tell Hayden. "Just getting home. What're your plans tonight? You and Sav doing okay?"

He's been dating Savannah since last summer and moved to be with her. It was shortly after Lennon moved in, and my life took a turn for the worse.

"That's what I wanted to talk to you about." The nervousness in his tone makes my heart race.

"What? You two break up?" I panic, knowing what it took for them to get back together after being apart for ten years. I'd be devastated for him if that were the case.

"No! Hell no. I'm not letting her out of my sight again," he says, laughing.

"Whew. Scared me there for a sec, man."

"I'm planning to propose to her. I've always known she's the one for me and want to make her my wife."

I'm smiling so big at his news. "Hell yes. I'm so fucking happy for you, Hayden. And honestly, about fucking time." I let out a laugh as he sighs in relief.

"I haven't told our parents yet, but I've designed and ordered the ring. I wanted it to be one of a kind—just like her—so now I have to find the right time to pop the question. It's not all planned out yet, but I'm nervous as hell."

I almost make a remark about how lovey-dovey he is, but I'd rather see this version of him than the hollow person he was without her.

"Don't be. You know what her answer will be. And honestly, who cares what our parents or anyone else say? You know this is right. So do I. And I'm not a bit shocked." I take the steps two at a time as I listen to Hayden's plans. After I enter the apartment and drop my shit by the door, I hear Lennon singing in the kitchen and walk that way.

She has her headphones in, and she's bobbing her head back and forth and shaking her hips. Either she hasn't heard me come in yet or she's ignoring me, so I walk past her, open the fridge, and grab myself a beer. Then I see a sandwich on the counter.

"You made me a PB&J sandwich?" I taunt Lennon and grab it off the counter before she can stop me. "My favorite!" I take a huge bite and shoot her a wink.

"Hunter!" she squeals, slamming her hand down. "That was the last of the bread!"

"Good thing you're going to the grocery store," I say around a mouthful, walking into the hallway.

"Fucking seriously?" She's seething, which has me smiling from ear to ear before I take another bite. "I wasn't planning to go to the store yet!"

"Guess you have an excuse now," I retort, not looking over my shoulder. I'm sure she's glaring or giving me the finger. That's her usual go-to move.

"Who're you talking to?" Hayden asks.

"Satan."

He bursts out laughing, knowing who I'm referring to.

"You two still fight like brother and sister?"

"Pfft. Worse." I step into my bedroom and shut the door behind me, finishing off her perfectly made sandwich.

"When are you gonna get over your feelings for her? Don't you think you've made both of your lives hell for long enough? Learn from my mistakes, bro…"

Hayden is only five years older than me, but I swear he's an old soul. We're the only two kids in the family. Our parents didn't bother trying for a third after me, and it didn't help that their relationship was always in the spotlight. My dad's a piece of shit, but in public, he acts like Father of the Year.

As a California state senator, he has a picture-perfect image to uphold. I was the wild child who had him running to the doctor's office, begging to get snipped. Though as I got older, I figured out it was so he couldn't knock up any of his mistresses.

Hayden was more of a father figure to me than our dad ever was, and he tried to keep me grounded when I acted out for attention.

Needless to say, I never claimed to be an easy person to live with, and Hayden knows how I get. It doesn't help that Lennon brings out this bitter side of me, and I want to make her life hell for forcing me to see her every goddamn day. I couldn't give her what Brandon can anyway. For most of my life, I never met my father's expectations with my grades, sports, and choices, and after living here and listening to her constant nagging, I know I would've never met hers.

It's more than obvious that I would've never measured up to Brandon and his unconditional love for her since the very beginning. I pussyfooted around and didn't make a move while he didn't think twice about it. My hesitation came back to bite me in the ass, and now I have to live with that choice every day.

Brandon also eventually wants a family, and I have my own commitment issues to work through, which have only gotten worse since Lennon moved in. Though it fucking sucks she didn't choose me, it's probably for the best, or at least that's what I keep telling myself. It could've ended badly with me hurting her, though I'd like to think I wouldn't have. She's a constant reminder that I'm not good enough and how I'll never be.

"There are no feelings." Lies.

"Yeah, and Donny's my secret life partner," he replies, cackling. "You aren't fooling anyone, especially not me."

Savannah's gay best friend, Donny, insists on calling me Beefcake. At first, it was insulting, but now I know it's a compliment coming from him.

"HUNTER!" Lennon slams her fist on the door. "Do you have to be an insensitive asshole?"

"Oh fuck." Hayden laughs hysterically. "You really pissed her off this time."

I roll my eyes as I take a swig of my beer. "What else is new?"

"Gonna let you deal with that. Call me later."

"Will do."

We say goodbye and hang up. I open my door with a shit-eating grin and wait for her to speak. Her face is beet red, with eyes narrowing in on me.

"Would it kill you, just *once*, to be a decent human being? I was starving and wanted that damn sandwich!" She's seething, and fuck if that doesn't make me hard.

Tense as ever, I take a pull of my beer and watch her over the bottle. "Oh, was that sandwich for you?" I furrow my brows as if I'm genuinely confused. "Thought you were making that for me." I shrug, knowing how angry she already is, but hell, I don't care.

"Argh! You're the literal worst, Hunter Manning!" She turns, her hips shimmying as she walks away.

"Well, feel free to leave anytime. Don't let the door hit your ass on the way out!" I shout my usual retort whenever she's freaking out about something. A nice little reminder that she can leave any goddamn time and no one's stopping her.

"You need to grow the hell up!" she shouts after I shut my bedroom door. The walls are thin, so I hear every word that leaves her lips. She's muttering curse words, calling me every name under the sun, and I smile in victory. Getting her worked up is another step toward getting her out of my damn head, though sometimes it feels like hot foreplay.

Better to be under her skin than fantasizing about her being on top of me.

CHAPTER THREE

LENNON

MONDAY AND TUESDAY FLEW BY, but today drags. Seconds feel like minutes, and minutes seem like hours, and all I want to do is go home and be with Brandon. At lunch, I look over my salad, not feeling very hungry as I think about everything left to complete for the spring concert in a couple of months.

Over the past few days, I taught my students two new songs on their recorders, and they were enthusiastic and seemed to enjoy learning. I want this concert to go off without a hitch because it's my first big program since I graduated and became a teacher. So much rides on its success, and it could determine if my contract is renewed or not, which is a big deal. I try not to think too far ahead in the future and live in the moment, but it's hard when there's so much to do in so little time. Being stressed at home because of Hunter and the dumb shit he constantly puts me through doesn't help either.

As I take a bite of my salad, I think about how every grade from kindergarten through fourth will be performing together on the stage. I have to choose the songs for them to sing as well as music for them to play on the instruments, and I need to have it finalized by the end of the week. After Principal Orson approved my budget increase, I ordered the percussion equipment for the older kids, and thankfully, it'll be delivered by the end of next week so we can start practicing. Once I'm finished eating, the bell rings, which means recess is over and my classroom will soon be full of little bodies. As I walk down the hall, I unlock my phone and see a text from Brandon.

BRANDON

I love you, sweetheart. Hope you're having an amazing day!

I instantly smile.

LENNON

Love you too, baby. I wish you were here with me so I could sneak kisses.

BRANDON

Mmm. You're making me miss you even more right now.

LENNON

You have no idea how much I wish we were home and in bed. Or that you were here so we could christen the instrument closet

BRANDON

So my naughty teacher fantasy might come true?

LENNON

Ha-ha! Class is starting. Only a few more hours left until the day is over! Love you!

Shortly after I enter my classroom, a group of kindergartners comes inside for their lesson. I smile at Mrs. Jenson, who escorted them over, before she waves and shuts the door.

Their attention spans are so short that I have to work hard to keep them occupied for the class period. Though it can be exhausting, I still love it. They keep me on my toes.

"Good afternoon, class!" I greet, smiling wide.

"Hello, Ms. Corrigan," they say in their cute little voices.

"So the spring concert is in a couple of months. Do you know what that means?" I ask, meeting their gazes.

Some of them shake their heads and others nod, while the rest are too busy picking their noses to care that I'm even speaking.

"It means we're going to perform for a bunch of people, including your parents. This year, Disney is the theme!"

Several of them are so excited they stand and start dancing around like I fed them pure sugar. Disney, to kids, is an instant trigger word, which is why I chose it.

"Jewel and Lacy, please sit, okay? So today we're going to learn a new song that many of you probably already know. It's called 'Zip-a-Dee-Doo-Dah,' and you'll be singing it with the first and second graders. Have any of you heard of it before?"

David stands up and starts belting out the chorus before I can stop him, but he has a family addicted to all things Disney, which I learned when I met his mother at parent-teacher night. I made the mistake of commenting on her adorable Mickey Mouse shirt and listened to her go on for ten minutes about the five trips they take each year.

"Very good," I tell him, and he proudly sits down.

I have the class stand and do stretches, then we go through the scales to warm up their voices. Once they're ready, I teach the main chorus of the song. We sing it slowly at first, over and over, and I add in a few hand movements. Repetition is key with children this young, but I'm beaming with pride when most of them get the basic concept down. They're quick learners, and I'm overjoyed that we're already making headway.

After we've gone over it at regular speed, the bell rings, and all the little bodies swarm to the door and follow their teacher out of the room. I have just a minute to breathe before the first graders rush in to fill the chairs. Once everyone settles, I make the announcement about the spring program, and they're ridiculously excited about the news. It's official: Disney is a win with the kids.

After I pass out the sheet music, we practice the song all the way through. They catch on much quicker than the kindergarteners, and not long after, I add in the hand movements for them to mimic. Before the class ends, we start at the very beginning again, and I'm pleased when they get most of the lyrics and choreography. This concert is going to be so cute, and ideas for other songs start flooding in.

"Great job!" I clap my hands, continuing, "You all make me super proud. We'll have more songs to learn, so take your music folder with you and practice at home. I can't wait to see how great you are next time!"

The second half of the day passes quickly, and by the time the final bell rings, I'm more than ready to get home to Brandon. Being with him melts away all my worry and stress.

As I walk to my car, I pull my phone from my pocket, and a smile fills my face when I see an unread text message from my little sister Madelyn. She's four years younger than I am but moved from Utah to California to be near our older sister Sophie and me. The three of us have always been close, so being within driving distance of each other is something we've always wanted.

For Maddie, staying with our parents during high school was difficult because she felt so alone without us. It was an adjustment when Sophie left. A year later, I followed, and Maddie was basically an only child without us there. She's been here for a year now, though it feels like only yesterday since we haven't been able to spend a lot of time together due to our conflicting schedules. She's such a talented dancer and received a full-ride scholarship to CSU in Sacramento.

Sophie left after high school to attend CSU Fresno, which is why I applied there too. After graduation, she moved to Sacramento, and I followed the next year. I wanted to be close to her and to give Brandon's and my relationship a real chance since he lived there as well. During my last semester, I applied for teaching jobs and was fortunate enough to find one right in the area.

Sophie now plays the violin in the Sacramento Philharmonic &

Opera, and when she's not practicing, she's performing side gigs for weddings or special events. She's often fully booked, but when she has downtime, she teaches music lessons on the side for extra money.

Music played an important part in our lives growing up. It was all we knew. Ingrained in us from the day we were born, it paved the path for our chosen careers. I just love that we're here together now and can hang out as much as we want when our schedules don't clash.

I unlock my phone and read my message from her.

MADDIE

Sis! Guess what? I received an invitation to an exclusive audition for a ballet company for their summer show. I AM SO EXCITED!

She's been dancing since she could walk and is obsessed with ballet and lyrical dance. This is a huge deal, and it's not lost on me how important this is to her. She's worked hard over the years to perfect her skills, and I'm so thrilled for her.

LENNON

Oh my God! That's amazing! When's the audition?

MADDIE

In two weeks, which means I'll have to practice my butt off until then.

LENNON

You'll do fine! Are you ready?

MADDIE

I'll make sure I'm ready! Sorry, I know you're probably on your way home from work now, but I had to tell someone before I walk into practice. Love you! Oh, tell Brandon I said hey!

I grin at her last comment. My sisters love Brandon so much. Their support means everything, considering my parents still don't know we live together or how serious we are. My sisters know my secret, and while it's been hard to keep it from my parents since I hate lying, I know they'd never approve. Their rules were always so strict when it came to relationships. Couples don't live together before marriage, and they surely don't have sex either, simple as that. I love my parents so much and have always wanted their approval, so having to lie hurts more than I'd like to admit.

Living in a conservative, religious household wasn't always easy. My dad is the pastor of a large congregation in Park City, and my mother is the daughter of one as well.

Growing up, the three of us kids sang in the praise and worship choir. When we got older, Sophie and I played in the church orchestra. She played her violin, and I played the organ, which was always fun, but it consumed so much of our time when all we wanted to do as teens was hang out with our friends.

My parents had stern rules in place until the day we left for college. We had an eight o'clock curfew, and we dedicated Wednesday nights and Sunday mornings to service. Dating was never allowed, and we were expected to get straight As in school. Though they were tough, they raised us with wholesome values and a distinct moral compass and taught us compassion. We know they love us wholeheartedly, but after high school graduation, we were ready to leave the nest and do things our way.

Disappointing them would be one of my greatest regrets, and that's why it's important for me to keep my relationship with Brandon locked tight. Although I don't always stay within the lines they've drawn, I'll never admit it to them because it would hurt them too much.

Moving closer to Sophie gave me the freedom I desperately craved. The way she talked about California made it sound like paradise. I knew from the moment she left that this was where I wanted to be and so did Maddie.

Love you too! I'll send the message along. Have fun!

After I get in my car and buckle up, I pull out of the parking lot. I can't wait to put on some comfy clothes and start dinner before Brandon gets home. Sophie calls me while she's driving and tells me how her private lessons are going so far. She didn't want to teach but decided it was nice to make some extra money.

"There's this one student who refuses to practice at home, and the only reason she takes lessons is because her mother is living vicariously through her." Sophie groans, releasing a frustrated breath.

Shaking my head, I pull into my assigned parking spot. It's Brandon's, but after I moved in, he insisted I take it, and he now parks on the street.

"Well, we didn't always want to practice music either, but Mom and Dad made it fun, remember? And now look. You play professionally, and I'm a music teacher."

"Ugh, yes." She sighs. "But still, I don't know how you're patient enough to teach. I love kids, but their parents can be devils. Hell, sometimes the kids are devils too." She chuckles, though I know she's being serious.

Laughing with her, I grab my bag, then exit the car and make my way down the sidewalk toward the apartment. "I know. Every morning, I wake up and tell myself it's a new day, and each kid has a fresh slate. Most of them aren't old enough to know they're being little shits."

"You're right. Wise beyond your years." I can tell she's smiling by her tone. "Are you home yet?"

"Yep. Walking up the stairs now." I need to work out because I'm almost out of breath after taking the two flights.

"Alright! I'll talk to you tomorrow. Tell Brandon I said hey, sugar pie."

"Sugar pie?" I ask with a giggle.

"'Cause he's a *sweet*heart," Sophie adds before we say goodbye and hang up.

I unlock the apartment door, set my bag down, and head to our bedroom. I change into leggings and a sleeveless shirt, then go to the kitchen where the dirty dishes are piled in the sink. *Of fucking course.*

"Asshole," I mutter, turning on the hot water and filling the bowls that have dried food in them. As if the ones he left me Monday weren't bad enough, these dishes look months old, and I'm tempted to just throw them in the trash instead.

Once that's done, I pull out the ingredients to make spaghetti and meat sauce. Trying to push my frustrations aside, I fill a large pot with water and wait for it to boil. Just as I put the hamburger meat into the frying pan, the door swings open, and I light up with a smile that fades when I glance over my shoulder and notice it's Hunter instead of Brandon.

When I focus back on the stove, the laughter begins, only enraging me further. With as much willpower as I can muster, I ignore him, which is nearly impossible as the booming sound grows louder.

"What in the hell are you wearing?" he asks the moment he enters the kitchen.

I flick my head toward him and watch as he pulls a beer out of the fridge. He twists off the cap and tosses it on the counter, regardless of the trashcan being closer.

"None of your damn business. Keep your comments to yourself." I don't feel like arguing, though it's inevitable when we're in the same room. If I didn't know better, I'd say he has a man crush on my boyfriend, and he's jealous. The thought has me cracking up inside.

Hunter leans against the counter, watching me intently. More than likely, he's judging me as I stir the meat. I'm sure by his standards, I'm somehow doing it wrong.

"Don't you have *somewhere* to be or *someone* to do?" I ask, thinking about the red lacy panties I found on the floor earlier this week. There's venom in my tone, and I refuse to look at him.

Before Hunter can open his big mouth with a rebuttal that would've most likely been rude as hell, I hear the door swing open again. When I glance over my shoulder, I'm relieved and thrilled to see Brandon. He's wearing a sexy button-up shirt with black slacks and grins the moment our eyes meet as if he remembers our little exchange this morning.

He crosses the room, spins me around, and pulls me in closer. Our lips collide, but we break apart when Hunter makes a loud, obnoxious gagging sound. I scowl before he walks away.

Brandon thinks it's hilarious, which annoys me even more. I wish he'd have the balls to stand up to Hunter and tell him to mind his own business instead of laughing it off.

"Don't let him get to you, baby. He's probably had a stressful day at work with his project," Brandon reminds me, then gives my ass a squeeze. It sends shivers down my spine whenever he does that and causes me to smile even though a certain roommate has soured my mood. I try to take Brandon's words into consideration as to why Hunter has been more of an asshole lately.

Behind me, the meat sizzles, so I spin around to stir it before it sticks.

Once it's fully cooked, I drain the water and add the sauce.

"You're distracting me," I tease when his hands snake around my waist, and his mouth feathers kisses from my shoulder up my neck. Brandon takes my earlobe between his teeth and growls, causing me to moan.

"Mm, baby. You're the distracting one wearing those tight little pants that leave nothing to the imagination, and I have a pretty damn good imagination."

His comment makes me giggle, almost blushing. I love that he can't keep his hands off me and that we're still in the early honeymoon phase. I cover the pan and put it on low heat.

"I wear them for you, babe." I turn toward him, wrapping my

arms around his neck, and pull him in for a kiss. "Plus, I like your hands on me when I do."

His head drops as he releases an animalistic groan. "And now I need a cold shower." Brandon presses his groin into my lower stomach, letting me feel his hard cock. Feeling how badly he wants me makes me want to skip dinner and drag him into our bedroom.

"I mean…we could shower together?" I taunt, waggling my brows. "Conserve water and all that."

"Hm…I like the way you think." He places a quick kiss to my nose. "But your delicious dinner would go to waste, and we can't have that."

I laugh, knowing we won't last much longer after we eat before we're jumping each other. "I'm going to change, and uh… take care of this situation here," he tells me with a frustrated groan. "Smells so damn good."

"It does, doesn't it?" I gush.

"Well, I *was* talking about you." He winks, then backs out of the kitchen, keeping his gaze on me until he reaches the hallway. My heart flutters, and I swallow hard, wishing I could follow him into the bedroom and take him right now.

I pull plates from the cabinet and put a loaf of garlic bread in the oven. Minutes later, Hunter enters the kitchen in athletic clothes and grabs a bottle of water from the fridge. Of course he doesn't return with his beer bottle, which means he's added it to the collection of trash piled in his room.

"Do you wanna eat with us?" I ask him, not wanting to be completely rude, though he deserves it, considering the way he treats me.

"Nah. I'm going to the gym." He makes his way to the door. It slams shut moments later and I let out a sigh of relief. At least tonight, Brandon and I can eat alone without any of his snarky side comments.

Brandon returns to the kitchen dressed in a T-shirt and gray joggers. I take longer than needed to gawk at him because damn, I love him in those pants. They ride low on his hips, and his shirt is snug around his waist. The oven timer beeps, making me jump from my daze. I quickly pull the garlic bread out as Brandon scoops food onto our plates.

"How hungry are you?"

"Ten out of ten," I tell him while I cut the bread. He laughs and adds more to my plate before placing them on the table.

Brandon pulls two wine glasses from the cabinet and fills them with my favorite Merlot before we take our seats.

"So I hate to bring this up again, but the way he's treating me seems to be getting worse, and I don't know why Hunter hates me so much." I twirl my fork around my plate. "I didn't even do anything to him except ask him to clean up after himself, and he acts like I'm asking too much."

Considering how things have been lately, I don't feel very welcome in my own home. He was edgy around me before I moved in, from the night Brandon and I hooked up, but for months, it's gotten worse. I think he lives to be an asshole to me.

"He doesn't hate you," Brandon says with certainty, smiling. "It has a lot to do with his job and all the added stress it's putting on him. Knowing Hunter, he probably finds it funny to get you riled up. He's a good guy, but his childhood fucked him up a bit. Honestly, I think he likes getting a rise out of you because it's so easy. You two bicker like brother and sister, and he probably sees you like one." Brandon shrugs as if that explanation should make me feel better. I don't want to be picked on like a younger sibling, considering I'm a twenty-three-year-old woman and very much *not* his sister.

"Getting a rise out of me and acting like a total asshole are two different things," I tell him, defeated. "I don't pick fights with him just because I have a lot going on with school. Coming home to him being a dick is the last thing I need. I'm stressed enough as it is."

His eyes meet mine, and he releases a slow breath. "I'll talk to him. I want you two to get along because I love you and he's my best friend. Hunter's going to have to work through his issues without being a douche to you. He's like a brother to me, and if he's being an asshole, then I'll call him out on it. I know he has trust issues and has never had a long-term relationship, but I also know he has a big heart. I wouldn't be best friends with a total dickhead."

I give him a pointed look, and we both laugh.

"I just wish I understood what I do to set him off all the time," I say. "Except maybe take you away from him? Whatever the reason, it's creating tension between us, and I hate that."

"I'll talk to him." He gives me a small smile.

I hate putting him in the middle because Brandon is too sweet to talk shit about his friend, but I wish he'd knock some sense into him regarding how he acts around me.

"So how's the spring concert preparation going so far?" he asks, changing the subject.

I light up, thinking about it. "Great. Disney is going to be a hit, just as you said it would be. The kids were thrilled by the mention of it."

"I don't wanna say I told you so, but..." His hazel eyes meet mine, and he gives me a genuine smile.

I try to talk around a mouthful of pasta. "I wuv you." I giggle.

"I love you too, baby." Brandon looks at me as if I'm the most gorgeous woman on the planet. Even though my hair is pulled up into a messy knot, my makeup has worn off, and I'm wearing comfy clothes, he still manages to make me feel beautiful. There's something special in knowing I'm with the man I'm supposed to be with forever.

After we finish eating dinner, Brandon clears the table, and I put the remaining food in containers for lunch tomorrow. I even make a plate for Hunter and stick it in the fridge, though I know he won't be a tad grateful or even say thank you. Sadly, I've gotten used to it over the past eight months I've lived here, so I don't expect anything less from Hunter. Sometimes what I do is a thankless job.

After I wipe down the table, countertops, and put the dirty dishes in the dishwasher, Brandon and I settle in the living room and turn on the TV. We're not even watching whatever reality show is playing because the moment he lies on top of me and our legs intertwine, we're only interested in each other.

"Keep that up, baby, and I'm hauling your ass to bed right now," he growls against my lips, arching his hips against mine to show me how hard and thick he is for me.

Wrapping my legs around his waist, I moan loudly so he knows that's exactly what I want.

"Mmm. I like the sound of that," I admit as the front door swings open.

My legs drop from his waist, and Brandon sits up, pulling me up with him. We look at Hunter with guilty faces, though mine is mostly filled with annoyance. He stares at us like he's disgusted, which seems to be his normal look, so I pay no attention to him at all. I should be mad, considering I'm all worked up now and he barged in at the worst fucking time possible.

"What's up, B?" Hunter asks Brandon and gives him one of those manly head nods, completely ignoring my existence. He looks like he just ran a marathon by the amount of sweat covering his body.

"Just watching TV," Brandon answers, which makes Hunter scoff. He knows damn well we weren't. "There are leftovers in the fridge if you're hungry."

Hunter acknowledges it with a shrug, then walks away.

I pull Brandon back to my mouth, wanting to pick up right where we left off before we were rudely interrupted.

The sound of dishes crashing in the kitchen and the fridge opening and closing echoes throughout the apartment. Hunter comes into the living room and sits on the love seat with a bowl of cereal. He smells like he ran a marathon.

"Valentine's Day is this weekend," Brandon reminds me. "I have something special planned for us, so clear your schedule." He leans forward and places a sweet, lingering kiss on my lips, not caring that Hunter is eating as loudly as possible. My heart flutters at the mention of Valentine's Day, knowing he'll make it special for us.

"Oh God." Hunter snorts, ruining our moment once again.

I let out a sigh. Sometimes I just want to slap him. No, *most* of the time.

Brandon turns to him. "Do you have any plans? Gonna find a lucky lady maybe?" Brandon's tone is filled with hope and encouragement.

With an eye roll, Hunter shakes his head. "Nah. Valentine's Day is lame as fuck. Unless Lennon wants to share her Valentine with me, I'm riding solo." He forces a wide, giddy smile at us, clearly making fun of the whole concept.

I let out a fake yawn and stand. "I'm tired. I think I'm going to call it a night," I announce, hoping Brandon gets the message. He lifts an eyebrow and smirks, and that's all I need to know he does.

Because Hunter's always trying to get a rise out of me, I look directly at him and say, "Make sure you soak that bowl, okay? That means add water to it. Think you can manage that, or should I draw you a diagram with little stick figures?" I taunt in a high-pitched voice, purposely talking to him like one of my five-year-old students. Of course he doesn't appreciate it, scowling and narrowing his eyes. If he wants to be treated with respect, he's gonna have to show some respect first.

"I wouldn't quit your day job if I were you. Jokes are pretty stale," he retorts with a mouthful.

"Sadly, for you, that wasn't a joke, considering you don't actually know how to soak a bowl." I flash him a go-to-hell grin and walk out.

Once I'm in the bedroom, I light a few of my favorite scented candles I keep on the dresser. The ambiance of the warm glow reflecting off the wall sets the right mood. A few moments later, Brandon enters and gravitates toward me. Our mouths crash together, and I instantly melt into his warm body. Without missing a beat, we greedily remove our clothes. His strong hands memorize my body, every curve, every inch that's his. Moments later, he's lifting me in the air, and my legs instinctively wrap around him. His skin feels hot against mine as we stumble to the bed, and he takes me, *all of me*. I need him more than I need air, feeling as if I can never get enough.

"I love you, Lennon," he murmurs, trailing kisses combined with bites over my heated skin that's burning for more of his touch.

"I love you too. So damn much," I whisper.

We get lost in each other, and I never want to be found.

CHAPTER FOUR

HUNTER

Work was a total shitshow today. After going through bids for the pool added by the owner yesterday, I realized the project might go over budget, which he didn't like hearing. Because of the tantrum he threw, I was late for two different meetings and didn't have a chance to eat lunch. Thank God I keep shitty protein bars in my truck as backup because, without them, I would've starved today. Though it might've been better than eating what tasted like play dough mixed with rubber chocolate chips.

I drive across town, sit in traffic for nearly forty-five minutes, and by the time I make it home, I'm so damn irritated that I find it hard to concentrate on anything.

After parking, I grab my laptop and head to the apartment. Brandon's sitting on the couch with his feet propped up on the coffee table, drinking a beer and playing on his phone. He always leaves early on Fridays. He gives me a head nod and a smile when I enter.

"Hey, how was work?"

"Sucked," I admit. "I need a drink…or ten." I go to the fridge and pull out a beer, then join him on the sofa. Though I know I should eat first, I don't care at this point.

"Where's your other half?" I ask, wondering where Lennon is because it's nearly dark.

"She's with Sophie and Maddie until ten." He lifts his beer and chugs it. "So I have a favor to ask."

Although I already have an idea about what, I say, "Sure, what's up?"

"Can you go a little easier on Lennon?"

I narrow my eyes, wondering how hard he's going to be on me this time. Not that I'm a bit shocked. Lennon looked like she was about to blow a gasket yesterday.

"I think you're really hurting her feelings," he continues. "I mean, I know you don't like her living here very much, but she's stressed with work, and you constantly picking on her makes things miserable for her. Plus, I want you two to get along. You're my best friend, and she's my girlfriend. We're going to be in each other's lives for a long time. I know it takes two to argue, but you fight like brother and sister. Honestly, you both have so much in common, it's kinda sickening. You'd probably be good friends if you gave her a chance."

I swallow hard, realizing what I've tried to accomplish has come to fruition. I've wanted her to feel the same as me, and now she does.

"Okay," is all I offer. I don't deny my hatred for her, though what I feel in my heart is far from it. The fact he says we could be friends and have things in common is a punch straight to my gut.

"Plus, you're kinda killing my sex life," he adds with a chuckle, taking a big swig of his beer, nearly finishing it.

I let out a stifled laugh. "I seriously doubt that. We share a wall, remember?" I nod toward his nearly empty beer. "You're gonna be trashed by the time she gets home if you keep up that pace, and it'll be your limp dick killing your chances tonight." I want to change the subject, but Brandon empties his bottle and slams it on the coffee table, then goes to grab another. "Get me one too," I shout, thankful for the moment alone to compose myself.

He comes back and hands me one. I twist off the top and press the bottle to my lips. The cool liquid goes down so easily, and I finish my second beer in no time.

"Dude," Brandon says, laughing. "Remember when we used to do some of the stupidest shit in college?"

I laugh at his random comment. "Yeah, like sneak into the sorority house to steal girls' panties so we could hang them on a clothesline at the frat party."

"Fuck! I forgot about that. I'm surprised we didn't get suspended." He shakes his head.

"I'm surprised we graduated." I chuckle at all the memories we've shared.

"Oh yeah, I almost forgot. So about Valentine's Day…"

"Yeah, what about it?" I ask, grabbing another beer because I'm going to need it for this conversation.

Just another day commercialized to hell and back and often comes with the price tag of selling your soul for flowers that'll die within a week. It's a sickening reminder that I'm alone and may never have a solid relationship.

I've dated plenty in the past, even tried a stupid dating app after Lennon moved in because I was sick of not only hearing them all night long but having to see it every damn day too. Work keeps me busy, so going out to meet girls isn't as easy as it was in college. However, those often ended in one-night stands or waking up with regret. In fact, that's how most weekends went as I tried to forget Lennon and push her out of my head, but it didn't erase her. Every second date I went on ended with me avoiding them shortly after. If my own father could betray a woman as amazing as my mother, how was I even capable of love? Where was the trust? What was the point of giving your heart away? When Hayden lost the love of his life, I saw what it did to him. It shattered his heart, and I remember that dark time like it was yesterday. I don't blame him, of course—he was only eighteen years old—but I never want to put myself in a position to feel that kind of pain. The risk doesn't seem worth it.

Until I met Lennon.

You can't fake that kind of chemistry, as instant as it was, and I swear she felt it too, though I've tried to convince myself it was one-sided. I've replayed it dozens of times in my head, but it doesn't matter. Brandon's like another brother to me, and his happiness matters more to me than my own. I'm glad he's found someone who makes him happy and truly cares for him, but I can't help feeling a tinge of regret, a tinge of bitterness that I should've done things differently.

If I could go back to that night, I would've asked Lennon for her number right away. I should've pushed my self-doubt away and listened to my heart. We shared something special, and I allowed my insecurities to stop me, leaving the ball in her court. She never returned. Hell, I should've chased after her.

It's in the past, though, and all I can do now is accept what is and move on, even if I'm failing miserably.

"Well," Brandon lingers, and I wait for him to ask me to get lost for the night so they can spend Valentine's Day together alone. "I kinda wanted to make sure we had the place to ourselves. Don't want my headboard slamming against the wall and interrupting you or anything." He sets his beer on the table and grins, telling me exactly what I predicted.

I cough out a pained chuckle, already done with this conversation. That reminder that I'm alone repeats in my head again. "I can disappear. No problem."

"Thanks, man. I owe ya one. Let me know when you want Lennon and me to give you some privacy, and I'll make sure it happens."

I nod. "I might take you up on that soon."

I wake up and head to the gym to release my frustrations. When I return home, Lennon's standing in the kitchen in the tiniest jean cutoffs, cooking her and Brandon a late lunch. She might as well be bottomless with the way they show off her ass cheeks. Her slender legs go for days, and they're distracting as fuck. It's annoying how she flaunts herself around here as if I don't exist.

Last night, I stayed awake staring at the ceiling, wondering what I could do today to stay out of the apartment for their stupid special Valentine's date. Just as Brandon said, Lennon came home right at ten. I heard her muffled voice on the other side of the wall, and I wished she'd just go away. Out of sight, out of mind, right? I know living together isn't forever, so I'll deal with her for now even if it slowly kills me.

Eventually, they'll move out, or I will, and we'll go our separate ways. Maybe then I'll be able to get over it without having to see her or smell the sweetness of her skin. All I want right now is for her to hate me—hate me so much she won't look in my direction or talk to me. By what Brandon said last night, I think I'm on the right path. After eight months of pushing her to the limit, she's still so goddamn relentless it's exhausting, but eventually, she'll crack.

I don't give her another glance as I walk down the small hallway leading to my bedroom. Before I take a shower, I text Liam and Mason and ask them if they want to meet up at the bar.

Every Valentine's Day is "singles night," and it'll be the perfect distraction. I'm going to try to walk into the place with an open mind, and whatever happens, happens.

After my shower, I read their responses, and we decide to meet up at five to pre-game. I'll more than likely make myself disappear sooner because I don't want to get in the way of whatever the hell Brandon has planned.

I go to my room with a towel wrapped around my waist, and Lennon stops walking toward the bedroom when she sees me. I notice the way her eyes linger on my body and trail across my tattoos and abs, just as they did that night at the bar, but the fantasy vanishes as soon as she rolls her eyes. *Perfect*. Glad I can get that kind of reaction from her. Makes being around and living with her that much easier.

Shutting my bedroom door, I change into some jeans and a nice shirt. Once I'm dressed, I walk into the hallway and hear Lennon and Brandon laughing in the living room. Instinctively, I groan.

"I'm heading out," I tell them, grabbing my keys and not looking in their direction.

"Got a hot date tonight?" Brandon sounds hopeful, considering I haven't dated anyone in years. At least not anything serious.

I nod with a grin and feel Lennon's eyes boring into me, but I don't give her any attention.

"Don't wait up for me," I tell him with a forced laugh as I walk out of the apartment and head toward my truck. The downtown bar sits in a heavily trafficked area on a strip surrounded by restaurants and nightclubs. Considering it's a Saturday and a fake holiday, I drive over early and look for parking. It's usually a clusterfuck, and tonight will be worse than normal.

I park on the street a few blocks away and walk to the sports bar where I'm meeting Liam and Mason in a couple of hours. I'll have to pace myself even though all I want to do is lose control. Instead of texting the guys and letting them know I'm here, I go inside and sit at the bar. Since I didn't eat earlier, I order food and a beer. Bernie, the bartender on duty, has been working here for as long as I can remember.

"Can't believe you're here alone on this special holiday," he says, his sarcasm not lost as he wipes down the countertop. He's in his mid-thirties and is as single as I am. When I worked at the club a few buildings down, I'd often come over here and hang out before my shifts.

I let out a small laugh. "Surprised you're surprised, honestly."

"With a track record like yours, though?" He smirks.

I roll my eyes, wanting to change the subject. "Can I get another beer?"

Bernie pops the top of the bottle and slides it across the bar. He picks up my empty plate and carries it to the back. My phone vibrates in my pocket, and when I grab it, I find a text from Liam.

LIAM

I'm gonna head that way. Want to meet up early?

I grin and send him a picture of the current situation. Me with my second beer.

LIAM

You bastard. Shoulda texted me.

HUNTER

I had to get out of the house so Brandon and Lennon could bang on every flat surface we have.

LIAM

The visual…gross. I'll be there in fifteen.

By the time I finish my beer, Liam walks through the door wearing a shit-eating grin. He sits on the stool next to me, and Bernie comes around the corner carrying a tub of margarita mix. Three more bartenders arrive to help prep for the busy shift they're about to endure. I don't envy them whatsoever. Though my job can be stressful, I'd rather do it over bartending any day.

"Hey, man. Two shots of whiskey," Liam says.

I glance at him, noticing he's starting with straight liquor. "Tonight's gonna be interesting, isn't it?"

Sometimes when he and Mason drink, they go wild and crazy. We're supposed to be mature adults now that we've graduated from college and have real jobs, but I don't see that happening for a long time. At least not until we're all settled down, and even then, I'm not so sure.

When the shots appear in front of us, Liam slides one over to me. "It's always interesting when the three of us are together. I texted Mason, and he'll be here within the hour." Liam and I take our shots, and it burns going down. Considering I was a bartender at one of the hottest clubs on this side of the state, I know how stupid it is to mix my alcohol, but I can't find it in me to care.

I check the time on my phone. It's barely four in the afternoon, and in just a short few hours, we're gonna be a trio of hot fucking messes.

"So," Liam says, "how's living with the happy couple these days?"

I groan. "Miserable as ever."

He orders us another round of shots. At this pace, we won't make it until Mason shows up. "I'm sure it's not that bad."

"Oh, it's fucking bad. Lennon nags all the time about every little thing. I miss the simple life when it was just Brandon and me," I admit because it's true.

"You just need to get a girlfriend and have her move in." He barely finishes his sentence before he laughs at his own words.

I shake my head. "The apartment is too small as it is. I'd probably just move out and let them take over the lease. I have a feeling things are getting pretty serious with them, considering the constant fucking I have to listen to and the sickening lovey-dovey nicknames they have for one another. But who knows?"

Our next round of shots appears in front of us, and our names are called behind us as we take them. This time it doesn't burn, which means I've officially drunk too much too fast. Liam and I turn around and see Mason. I realize they're both dressed in dark blue button-up shirts and dark wash jeans.

"Look at you two, dressed like twins. You call each other and agree to match on purpose?" I ask, giving them as much shit as possible.

Mason looks at Liam and chuckles, though Liam doesn't seem too impressed.

"Who knows, maybe your periods will sync this month too," I tell Liam as Mason sits on the other side of me. They've been roommates for as long as Brandon and I have and can basically finish each other's sentences at this point.

"Are you two assholes already drunk?" Mason asks before ordering.

Liam shrugs. "Traveling on a one-way street toward Wastedville."

"If you keep it up, you're gonna have whiskey dick and be crying for your mama." Mason takes a pull on his beer as soon as it's set in front of him.

We continue drinking until it's dark, and I haven't laughed this much in weeks. Hanging out with them is exactly what I needed. By the time we leave, we've had so much to drink, we're essentially invincible. Stumbling out, we weave through the happy couples filling the restaurant and walk the few blocks to the club, but all I can think about is taking a piss.

Most of the people working still know Liam and me since we worked here throughout our college years, so we don't have to pay the cover charge and go right in. The club is jam-packed, and I wouldn't be surprised if the fire marshal shows up to shut the party down. People crowd around the bar, and I tell the guys I have to make a pit stop first. I move across the club, making my way through hordes of bodies to the bathroom. I have to stand in line, which is annoying as hell, but thank God it's not as long as the women's bathroom.

As I lean against the wall, I open my Facebook app and see pictures of the flowers Brandon got Lennon for Valentine's Day, along with the giant red velvet heart full of chocolates. Stupidly, I give it an angry face emoji and continue scrolling through my feed to pass the time.

"Hunter?" a female voice calls my name.

I look up and see Jenna Crosby wearing a low-cut shirt that leaves no room for the imagination and a skirt so tight it looks as if it's painted on.

"Hey, you." I grin, and she gives me a hug.

"It's so good to see you!"

The line moves, and it's my turn to walk inside. "Can you hold on one second? I'm about to piss myself."

She nods. "Yeah, I'll wait right here for you."

I hurry and go, wash my hands, and walk into the dark hallway where Jenna patiently waits. She's a pretty girl with dark brown hair and blue eyes. When I worked here, she was a cocktail waitress. I figured she had a thing for me by the way she flirted with me, but I never allowed the idea to cross my mind. She had a boyfriend, and though she was a freshman in college, they seemed pretty serious. She's a few years younger than I am, but tonight, she looks like a woman who knows exactly what she wants.

"I haven't seen you since I quit," she says. "How's life been treating you after college? Did you ever get that dream job as a project manager that you wanted?"

We walk down the hallway and head toward the bar area while making small talk. The loud music means I keep having to bend down to hear her.

"Let me buy you a drink," I offer, placing my hand on the small of her back.

"Sure, let's get this party started." Jenna smirks, her eyes laser focused on me.

I flag down the bartender as soon as we make it to the end of the oval-shaped bar.

With a grin, I ask, "What would you like?"

"Tequila," she answers matter-of-factly.

I lift an eyebrow. "Tequila is *trouble*."

"So am I," she taunts, and I have no doubts about that. I order our shots, and moments later, they're in front of us. We shoot them down and suck on our limes.

"How're you and what's his name? Was it Chris?" I ask her once the fiery burn fades.

"Craig," she replies with an eye roll. "We broke up. He's a cheating bastard, so I'm better off without *that* in my life. I graduated and recently got hired at the hospital, so I'm focused on my new job, staying busy with friends, and doing what's best for me for once."

"Nursing, right?" My eyes meet hers, and she gives me a sweet smile and a nod.

I'm sure she didn't think I'd remember, but I'm not a complete douchebag, regardless of what Lennon thinks.

"Wanna dance?" Jenna asks as the mood in the room changes.

"If you want." Not sure if my drunk ass can handle it right now, but I'll sure as hell try.

By the look on her face, dancing isn't all that's on her mind tonight.

"I'd love that," she tells me, and I take her by the hand.

We're two single people in a sea of others trying not to feel so lonely as we move together. Though I've never felt anything toward Jenna, she's the perfect distraction.

I place my hands on her small waist and pull her closer, allowing the alcohol to lead and take control. My inhibitions are down, and after a few more songs, our lips crash together. We're breathless, and at this moment, I want her as much as she wants me.

"Where the fuck did you go?" Liam asks from behind me, interrupting us. My friends are both wasted, dancing with two pretty girls.

"They're twins," Mason whispers with a drunken chuckle as he points toward Liam, and sure enough, the girls they're with are identical.

Laughing, I shake my head because he thinks he's being inconspicuous, but he's practically yelling. Dressing the same played in their favor after all.

The song changes, and Jenna hooks her fingers in the loops of my jeans and pulls me closer. Her chest rises and falls, and the look in her eyes gives her away. I know what she wants.

Standing taller, she pulls my ear down to her mouth and whispers, "Wanna get out of here?"

The alcohol makes the decision easy. "Fuck yes."

Jenna pulls my bottom lip into her mouth, then speaks confidently. "I'm a freak in the sheets."

"How could I ever forget that rumor?" I tease as she takes my hand in hers and leads me through the crowd of people. Her boyfriend, Craig, used to sit at the bar and talk about how kinky Jenna is in bed, and soon, the rumors spread among the staff. After dancing with her, I believe every word the man ever said. She knows how to rock her hips and move that ass.

Though time has passed since we worked together, I probably shouldn't do this. It's obvious she's always been attracted to me, but I don't want to give her the wrong idea because we're not two strangers who just randomly met up. However, I came here tonight for a reason, and now that reason is Jenna.

As we walk out of the bar, she schedules a ride because neither of us is sober enough to drive. Moments later, we slip into the back of a car, and as we head toward her apartment, I give no fucks about my decision.

CHAPTER FIVE

LENNON

Last year, Brandon went out of his way to make Valentine's special for me. He proves how much he loves me every day, and I know tonight won't be any different.

After I get out of the shower, I blow-dry and curl my hair, then slip on a slinky black dress and high heels. I meticulously apply a smoky look to my eyes and contour my face. I smile in the mirror when I finalize the seductive look with a coat of deep red lipstick.

Before I walk into the living room where Brandon patiently waits for me, I go into the bedroom and pull out the strand of pearls he gave me during our first year of dating. I grab my clutch and tuck my phone inside.

As soon as I enter his line of vision, Brandon stalks toward me.

"Fuck, baby," he says, running his gaze down my body with a smirk. Placing his hands firmly on my ass cheeks, he pulls me in close for a kiss. "You look so damn beautiful."

Butterflies swarm inside me, and I blush, and the only thing that breaks our gaze is my phone vibrating in my clutch.

"Shit. Hold on," I tell him and see it's a FaceTime call from my parents. "I have to take this."

"It's fine. We have plenty of time." He swats my ass and steals another kiss before I answer.

I accept and see my parents sitting next to each other, grinning wide.

"Happy Valentine's Day, honey!" Mom singsongs.

I've loved this holiday for as long as I can remember. Something was always so fun about bringing handmade cards and candy to school and handing them out to my classmates and teachers. It was the best day of the entire school year because there was always a party with juice boxes and cupcakes. Now that I'm on the opposite end of that, I kept that tradition going with my students by treating them yesterday.

"Happy Valentine's Day!" I smile, and Brandon comes into their view when he stands behind me.

"Brandon!" They both squeal. It's sweet how much they adore him. They haven't met in person yet but have talked plenty on FaceTime.

"How've you been? You two look nice. Are you going on a special date tonight?" Dad asks in his deep, commanding voice.

We're both grinning from ear to ear.

"Yes. He just came over to pick me up, and we're about to head out."

"Such a gentleman. There needs to be more men in the world who meet their dates at the door," Mom praises. "You've got yourself a keeper there, Lennon." I wonder if she can see the pulse in my neck going haywire like it does every single time I lie to them about us living together.

Brandon nods, his smile never fading. "Always," he tells my parents. "I'm never late either."

I hold back my laughter, knowing he's just trying to get into their good graces as he plays along with my story.

"Okay, we'll let you two go on your date. Going to call Sophie and Madelyn and wish them an awesome evening. We love you," Dad says.

Brandon waves as we simultaneously say, "Love you too!"

I hurry to end the call and place a hand over my heart. Twisting me around to face him, he gives me a pointed look.

"Why do you keep doing this to yourself? You're a nervous wreck every time you talk to them." Brandon searches my face as my breathing steadies.

I let out a long breath. "Dad's a pastor. Mom's the daughter of a pastor. Ringing any bells?"

"But don't you think it'd almost be easier to just tell them the truth, considering how long it's been since you moved in?" He wraps his arms around me and pulls me against his chest.

I look up into his eyes and shake my head. "You know what kind of household I grew up in, babe. Sometimes, and in this case, what they don't know won't hurt them. It's my life, and I want to live it how I want, but they don't see it that way and never will."

He nods, twisting one of my curls between his fingers. "I understand your decision, sweetheart. One day, I want to make you my wife, and I want your parents to be there because I know how much they mean to you. Whatever you think is best, okay?"

I wrap my arms around his neck and kiss his cheek. "Thank you."

"For what?" He chuckles.

"For understanding me. For loving me. For being everything I've ever wanted in a man," I admit.

He leans forward and kisses me, then reaches around and grabs a handful of my ass. "I should be thanking *you* for giving me a chance to prove how perfect we are together."

I paint my lips across his and moan into his mouth. "If you keep kissing me and touching me like this, we'll never leave the apartment." I giggle.

"Oh, I almost forgot." He heads to the kitchen and returns with a huge bouquet of red roses. My mouth falls open.

"Flowers?" I ask, taking them.

"And chocolate," he says, going back and grabbing the biggest heart box of candies I think I've ever seen.

"You sure know how to make a girl feel special." I smile, biting my lower lip. "Thank you so much." I bury my nose in the petals and sigh. "I love the smell of fresh flowers."

"Does that mean I'm getting lucky tonight?" he taunts, smirking.

"We'll see," I singsong. After grabbing a vase from one of the kitchen cabinets, I place them on the table. The fragrance fills the room. I take a quick photo and post it on Facebook, tagging Brandon so both of our families can see.

He takes a few steps forward and cups my cheeks. "You are so special to me, Lennon. You're *everything* to me." Pulling me close, he slides his tongue against mine. I'm lost in the moment and don't want him to stop. I am so damn lucky.

By the time we pull away, I'm completely under his spell. Laughing, he checks the time. "We should get going because if we don't, I'm going to fuck you against every wall in this apartment."

I lift an eyebrow and bite my bottom lip. "That might not be a bad thing."

Brandon adjusts himself and swallows hard. "Dammit. Don't tempt me." He winks, grabbing my hand and leading me outside.

"Maybe we should take the bike?" He looks over his shoulder and smirks as we pass his motorcycle.

"And mess up this perfect hair? No way. Also, I'm wearing a dress."

"True. I don't want any guys looking at my girl's ass. That's just for me." Brandon grunts, opening the car door for me. "Always a gentleman," he adds, repeating my mother's words.

"Shut up!" I snicker, shaking my head as I buckle up, and he climbs into the other side. He loves that damn thing so much and would ride it every chance he got if he could. I go with him occasionally, but it makes me nervous with how other cars don't see us. Not to mention, my butt gets sore, my face gets windburn, and it sucks to sit in the traffic.

We drive across town, and I soon notice we're leaving the city. "Where are we going?"

"It's a surprise that I'm not letting you ruin…"

He merges onto the highway as I try to figure it out.

Eventually, we take the exit and head toward the bay. He parks at the harbor, and I notice a small yacht illuminated with lights.

"Is that for us?" I gasp.

"Thought we'd do dinner on the water tonight." Brandon grabs my hand and kisses my knuckles. "Come on, babe. Let's go. Unless you'd rather christen the back seat instead?"

I burst out laughing as Brandon leads me across the parking lot. Thankfully, the cold weather we had a few weeks ago has passed, and it's sixty-five degrees outside. So far, everything is perfect. He leads me onto the ramp of the yacht and to the upper deck where a table is set up with candles and more flowers.

"You've completely outdone yourself, baby," I tell him when he pulls out my chair for me.

"Anything for my girl." He winks, taking the chair across from me.

A man dressed in a tuxedo walks up and fills the empty wine glasses and hands us two menus. Only six items are listed with no prices, but I can only imagine how much they cost.

"Bonjour, ma belle," the waiter greets in a thick French accent.

I grin from ear to ear and glance at Brandon, who's watching me.

"Welcome to Navire D'Amour. Please look over the menu, and I'll return for your selections soon." He quickly bows before walking away.

I have to pick my jaw up from the ground. "Are you serious right now?"

A laugh escapes him. "So you're surprised?"

I nod, unable to contain my excitement. "You could say that."

The yacht leaves the harbor, and we cruise over silky smooth water. I walk over to Brandon and sit on his lap. He wraps his arms around my waist and kisses me deeply, so passionately, I almost forget we're outside on a boat. We break apart, and I look up at the moonless sky and see stars, which is something I miss being in the city. As we're looking up, one shoots across, leaving a greenish trail behind it. Brandon squeezes me tighter.

"Make a wish," he says just above a whisper.

"I'm already living my wish right now with you." I lose myself in his lips, but before things can go too far, a throat clearing interrupts us. We break away, and I shyly stand and walk back to my seat.

"I apologize for the interruption, but have you decided what you'd like?"

Brandon nods. "Chef's choice."

"I'll have the same."

"Perfect choice. Chef Ardoin will not let you down." He grins, picks up the fancy, silk-papered menus, and disappears.

The smile on my face is permanent as I sip the sweet red wine. The space of the table between us feels too far. As if he can read my mind, he reaches forward and takes my hands in his.

"I love you so damn much."

"I love you too. Actually, I love you *more*," I add with a grin.

"No way. Not even possible." He gives me a wink, which always sends a shiver down my spine. The boat stops moving in the middle of the bay, and a set of footsteps approaches from behind me. I turn to see two violinists taking a seat in two empty chairs I didn't notice when I walked to the table.

I turn to him with wide eyes. "There's more?"

Brandon playfully shrugs and stands as they begin playing. He holds out his hand. "Wanna dance?"

I nod, then grab it. He holds me close as we dance under the starlit sky. I'm not sure what I did to deserve such a good man. He's unlike anyone I've ever met, and there's no doubt in my mind he's *the one.*

I rest my head against his shoulder as we sway on the small dance floor. I want him so fucking badly, I can barely stand it. After several songs, the waiter arrives with two silver platters of food. Brandon leads me back to the table, and we take our seats. When the waiter removes the covers, we both laugh when we're served the biggest lobsters either of us has ever seen.

"If you need anything else, please do not hesitate to let us know," the man says, giving us privacy. The violins continue to play softly in the background as we eat buttery lobster, steamed broccoli, and some fancy potato dish. I'm not sure if it's cheese or Alfredo sauce, or what's on top, but I could eat it every day for the rest of my life. It's insanely delicious.

Once we finish eating and the plates are cleared away, Brandon takes my hand and guides me to the front of the upper deck. He takes off his suit jacket and wraps it around my shoulders as the boat moves effortlessly on the glass-like water.

We stand in silence, looking up at the stars with my body pressed against his. Everything about tonight has been perfect. When the yacht makes it back to the dock, I'm almost sad it's over, though I'm more than ready to get home. Before we leave, he pulls me into his arms and kisses me one last time, and as I breathe him in, I know I'll never get enough of this man.

"Happy Valentine's Day, my love."

I wrap my arms around him and squeeze. "Thank you. I loved everything. You spoil me way too damn much."

"And I will for the rest of our lives." He brushes loose pieces of hair behind my ear and presses a light kiss on my lips.

"That's a promise?" I ask with a hopeful smile, loving how he talks about forever with me.

"You better believe it." He takes my hand in his. The entire crew thanks us as we walk off the boat and head toward the car. I feel as if I'm dreaming as we practically fly to the apartment, but I blame the bottle of wine I drank.

As soon as we walk up the stairs, Brandon unlocks the door, then picks me up in his arms and carries me to the bedroom. He lays me down on the bed and carefully removes the black dress that's hugged my body all night, and all I can think about right now is how much I want and need him.

The next morning, I wake up naked, tangled in the sheets. Brandon sleeps soundly next to me, and I watch him before getting up. Sundays are our lazy days, and after our night of lovemaking, I need rest, lots of it.

"Morning, beautiful," he says in his sexy sleepy voice, pulling me to his chest.

"Morning, baby. Sleep good?"

His eyes wander down to my exposed breast, and I laugh. "You're insatiable. But I gotta pee, and I'm thirsty. I'll be right back."

He watches me as I quickly slip on some clothes.

"Hurry back to me."

I shoot him a wink and rush to the bathroom for sweet relief. After I wash my hands, I look in the mirror and see how swollen my lips are. Our night of passion has left my hair a mess and my makeup smeared. I wash my face, then head to the kitchen and grab a bottle of water. As I twist the top and take a huge swig, the front door swings open and closes. Walking out of the kitchen, I make eye contact with Hunter, who has regret painted on his face. He looks like he had a rough night, which causes me to laugh.

"Oh, look who's doing the walk of shame," I taunt and take another sip of water.

At first, he ignores me, but he stops and turns on his heels, taking a few steps toward me and closing the space between us. "It's no different from when you did the walk of shame almost two years ago. Actually, it is, because *I* lived here, and you didn't." The annoyance in his tone is thick and harsh. He breaks our eye contact and walks to his bedroom, then slams his door.

Sometimes he says things to be hurtful, and if I didn't know better, I'd say he really hates me, regardless of what Brandon says.

I shake my head and think back to that night that forever changed my life. Sure, I'd spoken to Hunter first and felt the attraction then, but it didn't matter.

In retrospect, I don't think Hunter ever mentioned it because it didn't mean anything to him. I was just another pretty girl at his bar who refused to be a notch in his bedpost. I was in a toxic relationship before I met Brandon. My ex made me feel less than, like I would never be good enough for any man, and I often wore my insecurities on my sleeve. I push the thoughts away and grab another bottle of water for Brandon to take to our bedroom. Soft snores fill the space, and I crawl back into bed and wrap my arm around his waist.

"I love you," I whisper in his ear as my eyes flutter closed, and soon I'm falling asleep again.

CHAPTER SIX

HUNTER

THE MOMENT I wake up and smell the sweetness lingering in the air, I grin. Fucking hell.

Lennon makes the best damn homemade cinnamon rolls, and if I weren't trying to keep her at a distance, I'd stroll right into that kitchen and snag myself one. Shit, I just might anyway.

She normally makes them on the weekends, but I remember tonight is the start of their anniversary celebration. Valentine's Day feels like it was yesterday, and now we're already halfway into March.

Groaning as I think about their special weekend, I slide out of bed and put on some gray joggers so I can face the reality of my unfortunate life.

"Mmm, babe. These are delicious." I hear Brandon moaning as I round the hallway into the kitchen.

"Oooh, thanks, baby," I mock his sickly sweet tone. "I made them just for you, big boy."

When both of them face me, Brandon chuckles, and Lennon flashes me the death glare I've become so accustomed to. I lick my finger and circle it around my nipple, making kissy noises. "I have somewhere you can put that thick cream." I wink at Brandon, and he shoves my shoulder, laughing and shaking his head as he makes his way to the table.

"What?" I ask Lennon as she continues to scowl. "Not a fan of the cream, huh?"

She rolls her eyes, grabs her mug of coffee, and walks away. "Grow up, Hunter."

"You first, honey buns." I toss a grin over my shoulder just in time for her to look at me.

Without asking, I take one of the cinnamon rolls and shove half of it into my mouth. I take a drink of milk and inhale the other half.

I overhear Brandon telling Lennon he's going to take a shower and head to work. Then he'll be able to leave early so they can go to whatever prissy-ass place he's taking her.

As I lean against the counter to finish my second cinnamon roll, Lennon returns to the kitchen. She walks past me to rinse their plates and load them in the dishwasher without saying a word.

"Well, at least you didn't bother dirtying a dish since you clearly don't know how to clean one."

She loves getting under my goddamn skin. Good, because I love returning the favor.

"Fuck, you're a damn good baker. No wonder Brandon keeps you around. All this time, I thought it was because of your sweet pussy. Guess I was wrong." I push off the counter to walk away.

"What'd you just say?" Her voice is venom, and I'm begging for more of it.

"You heard me loud and clear."

"Don't make me junk punch you. I'll do it without a second thought like that first night," she threatens, which is adorable, considering I'm twice her size, but then she had to go and mention the night I found her in this very kitchen after hooking up with my best friend.

My scowl deepens. "Ooh, don't threaten me with a good time, honey buns." I shoot a wink over my shoulder and keep walking.

She bangs around some dishes and groans loudly, making me smile all the way back to my room.

After I get ready for work, I walk down the hallway to get my keys and immediately regret looking into the living room.

Lennon's in her yoga clothes or, rather, yoga scraps since what she's wearing isn't considered clothes. A sports bra and tight-ass spandex shorts hug her tiny body. She's on the stupid mat in front of the window, and her arms are out as if she's soaring into the wind.

I swear she does this just to shove it in my face that she's not mine and never will be.

"What the hell are you doing?" I bark, and she nearly jumps.

"Do you mind? I was in the zone!" she snaps back before changing positions to one where her ass is straight up in the air. Just fucking kill me already.

"Aren't you going to be late for work?" I check my watch, and she's definitely not supposed to still be here.

"Not that it's any of your business," she says in a bitter tone, "but there's no school today. Don't mess up my downward dog."

I roll my eyes. Of course there's not.

At least they'll both be gone by the time I get off work tonight, I remind myself.

I leave without another word and inhale a deep breath. As soon as I'm in my truck, I'm already thinking about having the place to myself this weekend. It's been a month since Jenna and I first hooked up, and while those few times were fun, it's the furthest thing away from being serious. Considering she was in a long-term relationship not too long ago, I hope that means she doesn't mind keeping things casual.

Before putting it in reverse, I text Jenna and change that.

HUNTER

I have the apartment to myself tonight. Wanna hang?

The jumping dots appear, and I wait for her response before pulling out of the parking lot.

JENNA

Just so happens I'm free. Count me in.

"Oh my God," Jenna squeals the moment she enters. "Your place is so nice."

I notice she's carrying bags. What the hell? I didn't ask her to come over for a damn dinner party.

"Thanks," I say, closing the door behind her. "Not really my doing." I shrug. It was pretty simple and bland before Lennon moved in and sprinkled her girly crap around like fairy dust.

"So," Jenna says, walking toward the kitchen and finding her way through the apartment with ease. She drops two bags down on the table and smiles. "I brought Chinese, which I hope you like because if not, that could be a deal breaker for me."

I raise my brows, wondering what the fuck she's talking about.

"And of course, beer," she continues, holding up a six-pack. "I'll get us some plates and forks." She moves through the kitchen like she owns the place and opens a few cabinets before finding what she's looking for.

When the hell did I say to bring over dinner and beer? Right, *I didn't.*

However, I don't want to be a jackass to her, considering it's a nice gesture, and I'm starving. I'm just worried she has the wrong idea about us. I invited her over to mess around, not to play house.

"So how was your day?" she asks, setting the plate in front of me and unpacking the containers of food and chopsticks. Before I can respond, she continues. "Mine was fucking nuts. The only thing that got me through it was knowing we were gonna hang out tonight."

"Mine was fine. Busy as usual." I shrug, giving her the bare minimum. I don't typically share my workday with anyone except Brandon and only if he asks. Sometimes I tell Mason and Liam if we hang out afterward, but work is work. I love my job, but I also love leaving it behind when I clock out for the day.

Once our plates are made, Jenna suggests we eat on the couch and watch a movie. I don't argue and let her pick something on Netflix.

"Who's Lennon?" she asks before clicking on my name.

"My roommate's girlfriend," I reply dryly before taking a swig of my beer.

"She has her own profile?" she asks, scoffing as if she's jealous.

"Yeah, she lives here too."

"Ohh." Her voice goes up an octave. "That makes more sense. I wondered who the yoga master was." She chuckles, nodding to the mat Lennon left out this morning.

And fuck, now the images of Lennon's ass as she practiced the downward dog pose are back in my head.

"Yeah, ironic she left it out," I mutter to myself. She gets on me for having anything out of place, yet she somehow "forgets" to put her shit away. She probably did it on purpose.

But you'll miss it when she's gone, a voice in my head says, but I shake it off.

"So you said your roommate's girlfriend. You don't consider her your roommate too?" Jenna asks, thankfully pulling me from my thoughts. She finally clicks on a show and puts her feet under her ass, getting more comfortable.

"No. She moved into his room last summer. Her name isn't on the lease. However, I really wasn't given much of an option if I didn't want to lose Brandon as my roommate," I tell her honestly and shrug. "It's whatever. I ignore her most of the time."

"You don't like her? That's a shame. She made your place look so cute," she says in an annoying baby voice as she digs into her food.

I *do* like her.

That's the goddamn problem.

I fucking like her a lot.

Pushing myself up, I grab Lennon's stupid, distracting mat and walk down the hall to their bedroom. Flicking on the light, I glance around and see how different it looks. I haven't been in here since she moved in, nor had a reason to be, but I know for a fact Brandon didn't have a houseplant in the corner, candles on his dresser, and all this frilly pink shit everywhere.

I scoff with a chuckle and put her mat on the back of his desk chair. There's a collage on the wall of photographs I've never seen before. All pictures of Lennon and Brandon hanging out, hugging, *kissing*. They look stupidly happy together.

Flicking off the light, I walk back to the living room and dive into the plate of Chinese food I no longer have an appetite for. I don't know why seeing those pictures affects me so much, considering I'm tortured with their unrestrained PDA every damn day. Brandon's like a brother, and his happiness is important to me, so maybe I need to try harder to get over my feelings for his girlfriend. I can't resent him just because he got the girl, regardless of how much it eats at me every time I see them together.

"Another beer?"

"Huh?" I snap my eyes to Jenna's, realizing I've ignored her the whole time she's been going on and on about this movie.

"Would you like another beer? I was just about to get a refill." She smiles, eagerly.

Grabbing my bottle, I chug the rest of it and hand it over to her. "Sure, that'd be great. Thanks." I grin, showing my appreciation even if inviting her over tonight was a dick move. Clearly, I'm not in the right headspace, but she's all too ready to give me whatever I want.

Fuck, I'm an asshole.

Jenna's a decent girl. Can't say I know much about her other than what the old rumor mill at the bar had on her and the few nights we've spent together. Not that we talked a lot either.

"Here you go, babe." Jenna hands me the bottle and rounds the coffee table, then snuggles up next to me. "Your arms are huge, Hunter. They feel like bricks when I lie on you." She giggles, and I'm not sure what kind of comment that is, but I brush it off. She's trying, and I should appreciate her compliments, but my heart isn't in it.

After twenty minutes, I still don't know what this stupid movie is about. I can't concentrate for shit and feel all sorts of fucked up for leading Jenna on. While part of me wants to fuck my feelings for Lennon away, the other part of me knows it won't solve a damn thing. I've been trying to forget her for the past two years, and if it's even possible, she's more in my head than before. She's under my skin, and each day I have to be around them drives me closer to finding my own place and moving out.

However, the selfish part of me can't let go.

This is my apartment. Brandon and I were friends long before they met, and there's no way I'm letting anyone get between us. I'll continue—or, rather, try—to push my feelings aside. Eventually, they'll go away.

They have to, right?

"If you don't have any plans tomorrow, there's a great farmers' market downtown. I try to go a couple of times a month." Jenna looks at me when I don't respond, a crease forming between her brows as she studies me. "Would you wanna go with me?"

Unable to get my thoughts together, I scrub a hand over my face and blink a few times.

"I usually just get myself a fresh bouquet and some veggies," she continues as if she thinks that'll convince me.

"Uh, what time are you thinking?" I finally reply.

"It's from six to ten, but we can go around nine?" She takes a swig of her beer. "We could walk downtown after. There's a great café that serves the *best* homemade donuts and cinnamon rolls."

My eyes widen at the mention of cinnamon rolls. *Fuck.*

"It'll be a little chilly, but we can snuggle up to each other. I bet you're like an oven with all that muscle." Jenna flashes me her bedroom eyes, and it's obvious where she's going with this.

"Another beer?" She stands, holding out her hand for my nearly empty one before I can even reply to her previous question. She's so damn eager to please me and spend time with me that it's hard to get annoyed about it.

"Yeah, thanks." I give her a small smile, and she shimmies her ass to the kitchen.

An hour later, we're out of beer, and she's straddling my lap, her mouth fused to mine. Jenna moans my name, and for a little while, I'm lost.

Lost in the movements.

Lost in our bodies.

Lost in a world that makes sense when I'm not thinking about *her*.

CHAPTER SEVEN

LENNON

THE ONLY WORD TO describe this perfect weekend is *bliss*. Having uninterrupted alone time with Brandon is just what I wanted, what we both *needed*. We get each other on a different level than most and being able to have a couple of days alone has cemented that.

"This weekend was a dream," I tell him when he cages me against the car door after I get out. Wrapping my arms around his neck, I pull him in for a sensual kiss. "I wish it didn't have to end." I pout, sticking out my lower lip when he leans back to study me.

Brandon chuckles and dips down for a quick peck. "Don't worry, babe. We have plenty of time for more anniversary getaways."

I smile. "Promise?"

"Yes." He winks. "Now let's go make sure Hunter didn't burn the place down." He reaches around and squeezes my ass, causing me to squeal.

At the mention of his name, I frown. With our getaway officially over, it's time to go back to the real world.

The moment we walk into the apartment and I smell bacon, I

know Hunter isn't alone. He's too much of a food freeloader to cook for himself.

"Dude, that smells good," Brandon says.

"We just ate," I remind him, laughing.

He spins around, wrapping his arms around my waist, and pulls me to his chest. "Yes, and you were fucking delicious."

Brandon's growl has me chuckling, and he tickles my neck with his lips.

"You must be the roommates!" a woman's voice says, and I want to claw her throat for interrupting our moment. Rude.

We face her, and Brandon plasters on a wide grin as he takes in the half-dressed brunette. I know he's used to Hunter's weekend flings, but I think it's tasteless, considering he strings them along.

I doubt he'll find *the one* or settle down. Not when the parade of women he brings around are never anything more than a fling.

"Yeah, we are," Brandon replies.

"I'm Jenna." She saunters in wearing nothing more than a T-shirt and panties.

Wait.

"Is that my shirt?" I blurt without thinking. I narrow my eyes as she lifts the hem and stretches it out.

"Oh, yes. I hope you don't mind?" She meets my harsh gaze. "Hunter's shirts are *way* too big for me. The sleeves went past my hands." She giggles as if it's funny, but I'm not laughing. Hell, I don't even crack a smile. "I promise to wash and return it as soon as possible."

I roll my eyes, walking past her. "Don't bother. Keep it."

Or *burn* it.

I march down the hallway and go into our room, dropping my bag on the floor. That freaking asshole. His guests prancing around in their underwear is one thing, but allowing her to wear my clothes is pushing it too damn far.

"Babe," Brandon says the moment he steps inside our room and shuts the door. "Why were you so rude?"

"Are you kidding me?" I narrow my eyes. "She's wearing my clothes! That's not cool!"

"You're mad over a shirt? You don't even wear that one anymore. Probably why Hunter grabbed it."

I'm shocked he's so casual about this.

"So is this just something you guys did before I came along? Your flings leave clothes around, and you hand them out to the next flavor of the week?" I cross my arms over my chest.

Brandon steps toward me with his hand out. I step back, holding my stance.

"Lennon, you can't be upset over this. She probably didn't have anything else to wear." He continues to move forward until the backs of my knees hit the edge of the bed, and he pulls me to his chest. "Are you jealous?" he asks with a hint of amusement.

"Jealous?" My brows shoot up, and I pull back to look up at him. My heart races with anger. Of course I'm not jealous. "Of *what*?"

"Jealous of Jenna…the single life…random hookups. You want to be *my* weekend fling?" He waggles his brows, taunting me.

"You're insane," I say, hesitantly laughing. "I'm not jealous. Especially not of her. Or the single life."

"You sure?" He palms both of my ass cheeks and squeezes, grinding our bodies together. "You wanna role-play, baby? Be the random girl at the bar where I pick you up, take you home, and have my way with you?" Brandon leans forward and takes my bottom lip between his teeth, and I moan at the aggressive way he handles my body. The same way he handled it all weekend long.

I laugh at his attempt to settle me down with sex. "Pretty sure that already happened. Two years ago, to be exact." I smile at the memory.

Shit.

I was Jenna two years ago. Woke up in Brandon's arms, gladly wore his baggy T-shirt during breakfast, and didn't need it for most of the day while we stayed in his bed.

"Yep, except I decided you were a keeper." He winks, making me snort. I realize how unfair I'm being toward Jenna because we have more in common than I want to admit. Maybe Hunter will fall madly in love, and they'll move out together.

Wishful thinking.

That'd mean Hunter would have to stop going through women like torn up socks and form feelings for one of them. Though she is his type—brunette, thin, and pretty—just like all the other girls he's brought home.

Brandon's plan to calm me down worked, as usual. There aren't many instances when I get heated, but it's usually because of Hunter and his antics.

"I was thinking of calling my sisters to meet up later," I tell him as I start unpacking my bag.

"Okay, babe. I'm gonna check some work emails. Then maybe we can go for lunch in a bit?"

"Sounds good." I smile, piling my dirty laundry into the basket. "I should probably do a load of clothes too for the week."

Walking into the hallway, I hear Jenna giggling in the kitchen, and when I round the corner, I'm nearly blinded by Hunter's bare torso and messy hair. He runs his fingers through it and grins at Jenna. It's the first time I've seen him show this much interest in a girl, and it has my stomach in knots. Usually, he kicks them out before the sun rises.

"Oh, hey." Jenna turns and faces me, popping her hip. "Again, I'm sorry about snagging your shirt. I promise to wash it, and it'll never happen again. Next time, I'll keep an extra outfit in my bag." She looks up at Hunter and bites her lip as she waits for a response from him. He shoots her a playful wink and squeezes her hip, which makes her smile widen. "Anyway, we have plenty of food if you're hungry."

I blink, unamused by how comfortable she's making herself in my home. Last I checked, we didn't even have bacon, which means she either brought it or they went out shopping together.

I'm not sure why that thought bothers me so much. Maybe it's because Hunter's made my life hell the past nine months and now he's letting this girl prance around like she owns the place. Hunter wraps his arms around her and pulls her close. I notice how his fingertips gently graze her arm and see the way she reacts to him.

"Oh, no, thanks. We're going out for lunch in a bit, but…" I turn my gaze to Hunter with my lips in a firm line as he pinches her ass. Jenna squeals and laughs along with him, and I hold in an annoyed groan. "I'm gonna put in a load of laundry and wondered if you have any towels in your room? I'll probably do a load of those after my clothes."

"Oh, I can grab them. There are quite a few in his room from this weekend," Jenna interrupts our stare down, giggling as she walks past me to the hallway. From her devilish expression, they're probably stiff as a board too from all their wild sex. Ew.

"Never mind. You can do your own nasty laundry." I groan, rolling my eyes. Just as I'm about to spin around and walk away, Hunter grabs my elbow and pulls me back.

"Too bad you weren't here this weekend to hear my headboard bang against the wall every night. We could've had a competition." He draws his words out lazily and ends with a slow, shit-eating smirk.

"You're disgusting," I hiss.

"Oh, don't even pretend to be a prude." Hunter cackles. "We share a wall, remember? I know all your moans by heart, honey buns."

I inhale sharply, reminding myself he only does this to get a rise out of me, and force myself to walk out of the kitchen and back to my room without giving him the satisfaction of a response.

After confirming dinner plans with my sisters, we meet up at the Coliseum Bar that doubles as a restaurant. It's a fun place to hang out because we can sit, eat, and chat in the main room, then play darts or pool in the side room where it normally gets loud and rowdy.

"Oh my God," Maddie squeals the second she sees us and plops down next to Sophie in the booth. "The Uber driver drove like crazy, and I thought I was gonna die!" She releases a breath and holds up her purse. I take it since I have room on my side.

"Why didn't you tell me you needed a ride? I thought you said you'd get a ride from your roommate," I ask, reaching for a chip and dipping it in the salsa in the middle of the table.

"Because she flaked on me at the last minute, and I didn't want to bother you on such short notice," she says, grabbing the menu. Maddie lives on campus, which is the only way she could afford to move out here after she graduated high school.

I look back and forth between my sisters—Sophie, the oldest, and Maddie, the youngest—and see how similar their features are. Both have dark hair and a slender build. I'm the only one with blond hair, and as kids, they used to tease me and say I was adopted. It makes me laugh now, of course, but as a kid, it pissed me off and hurt my feelings. If I didn't look exactly like a younger version of my grandmother, I might've believed them.

"What the hell is that?" My eyes snap up to Sophie grabbing Maddie's wrist. "You got another tattoo?"

I hold back a chuckle because Maddie already sent me a picture. I'm the less judgy sister and don't mother her quite as much as Sophie does. Our parents would never approve, and I'm certain it's why she does rebellious things in the first place. I got it all out during my college years—partied, drank, and had fun before meeting Brandon—but Maddie is super focused on dance, so she acts out in phases.

Such as tattoos, knowing our parents would two hundred percent disapprove.

"It's a butterfly!" Maddie yanks her wrist back and smiles down at it. "Isn't it cute?"

Sophie purses her lips, clearly not agreeing. "Mom and Dad are gonna murder you."

Maddie scoffs, then laughs. "Mom and Dad aren't here, and last I checked, it's my body."

"You see this?" Sophie asks me.

I shrug, wanting to stay out of it. "It's cute."

"You knew," Sophie accuses, reaching for her lemon water.

"Only after the fact!" I confirm. "You and I both know Maddie is gonna do whatever the hell she wants, so we might as well be supportive of her decisions."

"I hope you got a tetanus shot." Sophie groans, and fortunately for Maddie, the waitress shows up.

We all place our orders, and I continue eating chips and salsa.

"Someone's hungry," Sophie says with a chuckle. "Brandon forget to feed you this weekend, or were you two just too *busy*?"

Maddie's eyes light up with realization. "Oh yes! Tell us all about your anniversary! Was there a lot of sex?"

"Maddie!" Sophie and I simultaneously scold her, except I'm laughing and Sophie's cringing.

"What?" The corner of Maddie's lip tilts up. "I need to live vicariously through you in that department, so no skimping on the details."

I give them the PG version of our time together and how perfect it was. They swoon and tell me how jealous they are. I beam proudly, happy to be this damn happy. Soon we're eating and laughing about other random things. "Brandon's gonna meet us here in a bit. Wanna grab a drink and go to the side room? Maybe let me kick your ass in darts?" I ask after we pay the check.

"Well, I'll have one drink," Sophie starts. "Maddie can have a virgin-something." Sophie turns her head so she doesn't get caught laughing.

"Really…virgin jokes?" Maddie chuckles, not even fazed by it anymore.

"I'm just saying!" Sophie shrugs. "You can't drink alcohol. Legally."

"Unless my big sisters wanna buy me a drink?" she asks as we grab our things from the table.

"Nice try, Mads." Sophie wraps an arm around her shoulder as we walk over to the bar side. "You'll have plenty of time to experience puking your guts out all night and waking up with horrible hangovers."

I snort, and both of them turn to look at me. "Oh, come on. Like Soph ever did that stuff. She's all proper and modest. Look…" I point at her sweater that's an inch away from being a turtleneck.

"Hey! It's chilly out, thank you very much." Sophie pulls the sweater tighter against her chest, and Maddie and I both laugh.

"Point made," I quip and she rolls her eyes.

She's the firstborn and always wanted to please our parents. Even after she moved away, she needed their approval. I can't say I blame her. A part of me wants that from them too, which is why I don't tell my parents the truth when it comes to Brandon. What they don't know won't hurt them, so I only share necessary things.

"Lennon went to college and teaches, and I'm always working out and practicing my routines, so your excuse is invalid," Maddie mocks, walking right up to the bar as if she can order.

"What can I get you ladies?" the bartender asks, placing three napkins in front of us.

"I'll have a Jack and Coke. She'll have some kind of light beer." I snicker, pointing at Sophie, who gives me a fuck-off look. "And she'll have a ginger ale." I shoulder bump Maddie, who grimaces.

"Gee, thanks, *Mom*." Maddie groans.

"I know your dietary restrictions, and I'm pretty sure it doesn't include alcohol, so quit your whining. I'm doing you a favor." I wrinkle my nose and taunt her. I know Maddie has a show to prepare for, and I'd rather her eat her calories than waste them on booze.

"I thought I moved out here to get away from *rules*," Maddie quips.

"We're your big sisters," Sophie interjects. "We'll always look out for you even when you don't think you need it."

Maddie smiles and pretends to be annoyed with an over-the-top eye roll. "Fine." She grabs her drink and pushes off the bar. "Get ready for me to whip your asses in darts since I'll be the only sober one."

A half hour passes before Brandon finally arrives. He catches me off guard and wraps his arms around my waist just as I'm about to throw a dart, making me miss the bull's-eye.

"Damn you," I say, chuckling against his lips after he spins me around and pulls me close. "You're supposed to want me to win!"

"Baby, you've got *me*. You've already won." He winks, which makes me laugh and playfully groan at the same time.

"That was so lame, it was borderline cute," Maddie interrupts our moment with an exaggerated aww.

"Should hear what I said the first night we met." Brandon smirks, tightening his hold on me. "She loves all my cheesy lines. Especially the ones about her falling straight from heaven."

Maddie pretends to gag, but she's smiling. She's only giving him shit, but I think he likes it.

"You by yourself tonight?" Sophie asks once she throws her dart and completely misses the board. She's so bad at this, especially when she's distracted.

I turn to Maddie with a knowing grin and find her smiling. Sophie would never admit it, but she has a crush on Mason. Since Brandon and I started dating, Mason and the guys have hung out several times with my sisters. Since I moved in with Brandon, the group of us go out more, but Sophie is too shy to make a move on Mason. She's friendly and outgoing when she has to be, but when it comes to relationships, she's on the timid side.

Another side effect of having parents who didn't let us date.

"The rest of the guys are on their way. I told them to stop jacking off and get their lame asses out here. Maybe we'll team up and play pool. Whoop your asses." Brandon smirks, smacking my butt. "I'm gonna grab a beer. Need a refill, babe?"

"I do!" Maddie slides over with a sweet and innocent look on her face.

"Nice try, Tinker Bell." He bops her on the head with a grin. "I'll be happy to get you a Shirley Temple, though."

"Hilarious. But yes, that sounds good." She spins around, and I'm dying with laughter.

Moments later, Mason and Liam come waltzing in like royalty. You can almost hear them from a mile away with how loud and rowdy they always are. The fact that they live together humors me because I can only imagine what their place looks like, especially after a weekend of partying.

Sophie lights up and acts friendly, which has me laughing internally. Maddie's ready to cozy up to anyone who'll buy her a drink.

Looking around, I can't help but smile like a fool at the people surrounding me. My sisters, boyfriend, and two of his guy friends who don't annoy me every chance they get.

"Checkmate, assholes," Maddie shouts twenty minutes later at the pool table while we play guys versus girls.

"Uh, wrong game there, Mads," Sophie tells her, and I snort.

"Potato, *potahto*. We're still kicking their asses," she says. Mason and Liam's jaws hit the floor at Maddie's expertise playing. Dancing isn't the only thing she's talented in.

"Alright, Tinker Bell. Show me whatcha got," Brandon taunts, but I already know it's no use. Maddie lives for competition.

"I'm only sorry we didn't place any bets." Maddie calls her pocket and looks up at the guys with a devilish smirk. She angles the cue stick, then shoots the solid ball, and it smacks the eight ball right into the corner.

"Yeah!" Sophie and I squeal when it drops in. We throw our arms up and bombard Maddie with hugs. She's a damn pro.

"Now who's buying drinks?" She pops a brow at Liam and lives to torture him with her sex appeal. He pretends to be annoyed by her antics—has mentioned it to Brandon a few times now—but I think he secretly likes it. As the youngest, Maddie can be a bit much sometimes, but he likes to act as if she's too obnoxious for him to handle. I think it's his way of pushing her away, but if he knew Maddie at all, he'd know it only encourages her.

"C'mon, Hulk?" She pops a brow at Liam, who she's nicknamed The Hulk because he's huge and beefy, similar to Hunter. It's probably why he used to be a bouncer.

Liam grunts, hating the name.

"You won fair and square, so I guess it's earned." Mason intervenes, pushing off the wall. He doesn't seem to mind Maddie, or he just feels bad that Liam dismisses her. Either way, I think it's sweet he acts like a big brother to her.

"Non-alcoholic!" I shout, pointing my finger at him as he follows Maddie to the bar.

He nods and waves me off. Looking at Liam, I notice the way his eyes focus on Mason wrapping his arm around Maddie's waist as they walk away. Mason's easy to befriend, and Maddie's a natural flirt, so if her goal is to make Liam jealous or to get his attention in any way, it's working.

"Look at these motherfuckers!" My body stiffens the moment I hear Hunter's voice.

He walks up to Brandon and Liam, smacking them both on the back as they hug each other. Then he goes to Sophie, hugging her and telling her how good it is to see her again. *What the shit?* Mason and Maddie return, and of course my little sister, who's desperately trying to get anyone to buy her a drink, makes herself known in Hunter's presence.

Moments later, he leaves for the bar, and I grip Maddie's upper arm and pull her over to the other side.

"Ow, what the hell?" Maddie rubs her bicep as if I actually hurt her, but she's practically made of steel from dancing.

"What're you doing?" I narrow my eyes.

"Um, being friendly. What's your problem?" She folds her arms over her chest, frowning.

"Hunter's an ass who's only after one thing, and since that *thing* of yours isn't up for grabs—especially for him—you need to stay away," I tell her coldly. Hunter can fuck with me all he wants

—ruin my day and parade his one-night stands around the apartment—but I won't let him spread his toxicity to my sister.

"Why would you assume I'd give it up to him?" She peeks over my shoulder and smirks. "I mean, I wouldn't be opposed…"

I slap her shoulder, bringing her attention back to me. "Mads, not funny. He doesn't date or have serious relationships. I've only ever seen him have flings. In fact, the girl he had over this weekend while we were gone was prancing around the apartment in a shirt and panties when we got back."

"So? It's his apartment too." She shrugs, obviously not understanding the amount of hatred Hunter and I have for each other.

"First, it was *my* shirt." I pause when she bursts out laughing. "Second, he's a player, and you deserve better than that. Got it?"

She slowly inhales a deep breath before bringing her eyes back to mine. "Calm down, okay? I'm not even interested in him that way. He's just fun to flirt with and beg for free drinks from. Or in my lame case, non-alcoholic drinks." She rolls her eyes, which makes me laugh. So eager to grow up when life doesn't get any damn easier.

"Just be careful, please. Hunter knows how to sweet-talk and get his way." I look over my shoulder and see a girl approach him. He leads her to the bar for a drink. "See?"

"Stop worrying. I'm a big girl. Plus, guys usually run far away once they find out they aren't getting to home base." She shrugs, but I notice that same embarrassed look on her face as before.

"Waiting to experience it with a guy you love makes it that much more special. Trust me." I pull her in for a side hug. "Plus, no booze or sex during training."

"Something I'm actually mastering." We both laugh, then walk back to the group.

We play pool and darts for the rest of the night, and Hunter prances over with his new friend. I decide since I have nothing nice to say, I won't say anything at all. Besides, he makes it a point to talk to all his friends and my sisters, yet deliberately ignores me. I can deal with his asshole remarks and digs at me, but acting as if I'm invisible somehow makes me even madder.

Hunter glances in my direction once, his lips in a firm line, eyes unmoving, then shifts away just as quickly.

His silent fuck you makes my jaw clench, and I'm determined more than ever to forget his entire existence.

CHAPTER EIGHT

HUNTER

ALMOST TWO WEEKS have passed since that night the group of us played pool and darts together. I can't shake the way Lennon looked at me with disgust as if she were reading my most personal thoughts about her. I want to sleep all day, but I'm pulled awake. My eyes pop open, and I check my phone. It's barely past nine, which is late for me on a Saturday. My internal alarm clock goes off at seven each day since I have to get up so early for work.

Once I roll out of bed, I open the curtains and look out at the cloudless blue sky. I can't believe it's already April, and in a blink, it'll be summer. Since I'm outside most of the day at work, I notice the weather because it affects everything I do.

After I use the bathroom, I walk into the kitchen and grab some food. I crack open a couple of eggs and begin to scramble them when Brandon goes to the fridge and pulls out a gallon of milk. He drinks it straight from the jug, which makes me laugh. If Lennon saw him do that, she'd shit bricks.

"Oh, you're making me breakfast too?" He wipes his mouth with the back of his hand and grins.

I snort. "Isn't that what your woman is around for?"

"She went shopping with Maddie and Sophie today. Apparently, the outlet mall has some sale, and I took a hard pass."

"I'll cook for you, baby," I taunt. "But I'm not putting out."

He bursts into laughter and pulls two plates down from the cabinet. I scoop the first serving for him, then grab more eggs.

"No bacon?" he asks.

I roll my eyes. "Beggars can't be choosers." I start cracking them into a bowl and mix them before pouring them into the skillet.

Brandon opens the fridge and looks inside but doesn't find any bacon or sausage. Actually, there's zero meat in there. All that's left is canned tuna in the pantry.

"Thank God Lennon's going to the grocery store when she's done hanging with her sisters. The fridge is practically empty."

"Did you give her a list?" I ask as he leans against the counter and eats his food.

"She knows what we like," he says around a mouthful.

A few minutes later, my eggs are done, and I turn off the stovetop before I slide them on my plate. I grab a fork and walk to the table. Brandon follows behind me, and we both take our seats.

He looks at me as if he has something else to say but hesitates.

"What's up?" I finally ask because he's being weird as fuck.

Sucking in a deep breath, he runs his fingers through his hair and pulls his phone from his pocket. I wait for him to speak up while I finish eating.

"I want to talk to you about something," he begins, his breaths uneven and shaky.

My heart pounds, and I hope he's not about to blindside me and ask me to move out or something. The last time he looked like this was less than a year ago when he told me his girlfriend was moving in. Different scenarios rush through my mind.

"I want to propose to Lennon."

Dagger meet heart.

He scrolls through his phone and flips it to show me a photo on the screen. "This is the ring I picked out. Do you think she'll like it?"

My brows rise, shocked. I look at the picture, and my eyes go impossibly wider. "It's stunning. She'll love it," I manage to choke out.

"It's a princess cut diamond ring on a white gold band. Exactly what she wants," he says nervously, looking at me. He's waiting for some sort of approval, so I smile.

Jealousy washes over me, but I push it away, forcing those feelings to step aside because right now, I need to be supportive of my best friend. "It's perfect."

A wide grin fills his face, and happiness radiates from him. "Thanks, man. I'm fucking nervous. But since I started at the firm, I've been saving money so I can get her the ring she deserves. I love her so damn much, and I'm ready to take our relationship to the next level. Being with her the past two years has been…well, everything, and I know without a doubt she's the one. You know when you just feel it?"

I nod, my heart lodged in my throat. "When you know, you just know."

"That night we met at the bar, it was special. Within the first five minutes of chatting with her, I knew she was the woman for me," he continues.

That familiar feeling returns. How's it possible for me to have felt the same way about the same woman on the same damn night? But Lennon made her choice, and regardless of the chemistry between us, Brandon was her best choice, *is* her best choice. He's a good guy. I know he'll give her the world and everything she'll ever want. I'm a selfish bastard sometimes, but as hard as it is to say, even I'm man enough to admit I can't give her what she needs. And that's what matters in the end.

"Yeah." That's all I offer.

"I was gonna ask her on Valentine's Day, but her parents are conservative, so I thought when we visit them over the Fourth of July weekend, I'll pop the question then. We just had our two-year anniversary, and I haven't met her parents in person yet, so I think it'd be a sweet way to propose so her family can be involved. I might fly her sisters in too because I know how close they are and how Lennon would want them there. The logistics are a little overwhelming, but I'm gonna figure it out."

Brandon looks down at the photo on his phone, smiles, then locks it. I can see the sparkle in his eyes and know how fucking happy he'd be spending the rest of his life with Lennon. "I haven't told anyone yet, not even my parents, so you have to promise not to let it slip around Lennon."

Ever since I saw her in my kitchen that night, I knew this wouldn't be easy. I just didn't realize as time passed, it would only get harder.

I smile and let out a chuckle. "I won't tell her. I'll take your secret to the grave. Also, if you need any help with anything, I'll be happy to do whatever you need. I'm here for you." It's a response that's expected even if I just want this conversation to be over so I can drown my feelings in a bottle of beer.

"Well, I wanted to ask you something. I know it's probably early for this, but I want you to be my best man. You're my best friend. You've been with me through everything, and I can't imagine you not standing up there beside me as I marry the woman of my dreams. I imagine it'll take a while to plan the wedding, and the earliest it would be is next year, but—"

"I'd be honored." I cut him off and swallow hard.

Brandon stands, and so do I, and we exchange a tight hug. "I'm happy for you. You deserve it, man," I tell him, genuinely meaning it.

As we break apart, I grab my plate and place it in the sink. He does the same. "Thanks. Appreciate it. Now to grow some balls and get down on one knee and pray she says yes."

I chuckle. "She's going to automatically say yes the moment those words leave your mouth. Shouldn't even be a concern."

"Hope you're right. I never imagined I'd find someone like *her* —gorgeous, sweet, strong values—and she'd be interested in a guy like me. We never would've met had you not guilted me into going out that night. When I think about it, she's more your type. Well, based on the girls you dated in college. I never dreamed I'd even have a chance, but I felt something almost immediately, and there's no way in hell I'm letting her go now."

The knife in my chest drives in deeper as if that was possible. "You don't give yourself enough credit. Lennon wanted you, or she wouldn't be with you."

That's been fucking clear since day one.

Brandon nods and watches me rinse off our plates. "I know you two have this weird sibling rivalry thing going on, but you'll both have to learn to like each other or at least get along. We're going to be a big, happy family," he says, snickering. "The wedding, then hopefully buying a house and starting a family. You two are gonna have to set your differences aside so I don't lose my damn mind. That or Lennon will eventually cut your balls off once and for all."

At least my façade is believable. The last thing he needs to know is how I feel—how I've always felt—about his future wife.

"Yeah. It'll be fine." Grimacing, I wipe my hands on a towel.

Brandon chuckles, knowing damn well it's not going to be that easy.

"I think I'm gonna go to the gym," I tell him, needing to release the weight of the pain bubbling in my chest. I'm fighting an internal tug-of-war I know I'll never win.

"Cool," he says. "I gotta stop by the office. I left my laptop there yesterday."

"Working on the weekend? Damn." I walk past him, forcing a chuckle.

"I won't make partner within the next decade if I don't show initiative," he sarcastically responds.

I go into my room and change into my workout clothes, grab my keys, and tell Brandon bye before I head out.

Once I'm inside my truck, I sit there with the engine idling, trying to catch my breath as I hold the steering wheel with white knuckles. I knew this day was coming. Their relationship has always been serious since day one but even more so since Lennon moved in. The part of my heart reserved for her knew this was inevitable. The sinking feeling takes over, and the guilt of wishing she'd chosen me instead of him practically strangles me. I need to work through my demons and be genuinely happy for them both.

I drive to the gym, but after I park, I call my brother before going inside.

"Hayden," I say as soon as he answers.

"Everything okay?" he instantly asks. I know I don't sound like myself because I certainly don't feel like myself.

I try to find my words because I don't want to be a little bitch about this, but Hayden knows the truth—the full story. He's the only one who does. "Brandon just told me he's gonna propose to Lennon in July."

The line goes quiet, and I have to look at the screen to make sure our call didn't drop. Apparently, cell reception in New York sucks because of all the buildings.

"Wow, man. I'm sorry." He sucks in a deep breath. I'm sure this was the last thing he expected me to say. "What're ya gonna do?"

I release a sarcastic laugh. "Be his best man and give him all the support I can. I'd never do anything to ruin their relationship. She hates me anyway, which I've purposely made happen these past two years, but—"

"But it doesn't make it hurt any less," he says somberly.

"Yeah." I don't even know what to say, and I don't know why I called him.

I'm losing my fucking mind.

"I don't have any life-changing advice for you, Hunter. I wish I had something to say that'd fix everything for you, but I'm at a loss. Maybe it's time to move out and make a real effort to get over her for good. Perhaps date someone for more than a weekend? What was it you told me that one time? Have a one-night stand, wake up in someone's bed whose name you don't remember, bathroom sex? Yeah, do *all* those things." He chuckles at the memory.

I think back to that time in his apartment last summer when he was still hung up on his high school sweetheart, Savannah. After ten years, he never got over her. I draw in a deep breath and exhale.

"I already did those things, remember? That was part of my sex bucket list to get over Lennon in the first place. But hell, maybe I need a new and improved list."

One that can numb the goddamn pain.

"You know what they say. The only way to get over someone is to get under someone else, right?" Hayden's being overly encouraging right now.

"How'd that work out for you?" I ask, reminding him about his own past. "Okay, that was a dick move. Sorry, I'm just frustrated right now."

"I get it. Don't worry about it. Anyway, I gotta go. I have a conference call in five minutes, and I want to be prepared to deal with these assholes today."

I look at the gym and all the people spending their Saturday on the treadmills. "Alright. I'll call you later if I need to be talked off a ledge."

"Sounds good." He pauses, then adds, "You have a lot to offer a woman, Hunter. Don't be discouraged. You'll find her someday."

Before I can argue that I've already found and lost her, we say goodbye and end the call, and I make myself get out of the truck. Once I'm inside the gym and find a treadmill, I run until my chest burns, and my lungs beg for air. I don't give myself time to rest before I'm lifting weights and can barely move. All I want to do is break my body down because I shouldn't feel this way. I'll continue to force a smile and be supportive just as Brandon would do for me because I owe him that much. If I could kick my own ass right now, I would because I deserve it.

Considering I didn't bring an extra set of clothes with me, I drive home drenched in sweat. As soon as I pull up to the apartment, I see Lennon's car next to mine. I notice she's slowly walking up the stairs with several plastic grocery bags in one hand and a paper bag in the other, but I pretend as if she doesn't exist as I stride past her.

"Seriously? You're such a dickhead!" she shouts, and I chuckle as I climb the stairs two at a time. My legs feel as if they'll break as I take the top step. I unlock the door, walk in, and kick it closed behind me.

Once I'm in my bedroom, I take off my shirt, grab a clean towel, and place it in the bathroom. I grab a bottle of water from the fridge, feeling dehydration setting in. Moments later, Lennon enters, slamming the door behind her, and drops the grocery bags on the counter. Her hands go to her hips, and she glares, but I catch her studying my shirtless body. I arch a brow, wanting to tell her to keep her eyes to herself. She must realize what she's doing because she shakes her head and the scowl returns.

"What the fuck, Hunter? You saw me struggling. The least you could've done was help me bring everything upstairs because this food is for *all* of us, not just me. I'm not sure what crawled up your ass and died the past few months, but maybe it's time to grow the fuck up?"

My eyes meet hers, and I shrug. "Sorry. I didn't notice you out there." I smirk, which infuriates her further.

She groans so loud it reverberates through the apartment. "Why do you hate me so much? What did I ever do to you to deserve to be treated this way? I've lived here for nearly a year now, and we still can't seem to get along. Why do you think that is?"

"Hmm. That's a really great question." I pretend to ponder it before I walk around her and go to the bathroom. I close the door and lean against the cool wood, trying to shake the sadness on her face that I've caused. This is what's best for everyone. Making her hate me is easier and the way it has to be, especially now that Brandon wants to propose. If I let my guard down around her, I don't know that I could hold back my true feelings. Being friends would only hurt worse, so maybe Hayden's right—I need to make a real effort to move on. Even if it's going to be hard.

I need to let go of my feelings and stop torturing myself with what I'll never have. I need to wake the fuck up and pull myself together. Even if it seems impossible right now.

I jump in the shower and wash off my workout, hoping one day I'll be able to look back at the ridiculousness of this and laugh. I can't decide if fate is an angel or if it's really the devil because this whole situation is fucked up.

I've never believed in love at first sight, but Lennon changed that, only to torment me with her presence every single day. *Maybe I'm only hung up on her because I can't have her?* Fuck, I know it's more than that, but I'll take any excuse to validate how I feel.

After my shower, I change into some clean clothes because I need to get out of this house tonight. I look through text messages on my phone and notice an unanswered one from Jenna. The last time we hooked up, she stayed the whole weekend, playing house and making it obvious how much she liked me. I kept things casual between us and made it clear I wasn't after anything serious. I could tell she was disappointed, but she seemed to understand at the time.

Deciding it's now or never, I take the plunge and send Jenna a message, asking her to go out with me tonight. If I'm going to try to move on, I need to make a real effort. I don't want to have these unrequited feelings for someone who isn't mine, and maybe if I wasn't so stuck on Lennon, there'd be room in my heart for a woman like Jenna.

She immediately responds, sending me smiley emojis and heart icons. Jenna's a gorgeous girl, and she's fun, so maybe I can try this time with someone who wants me.

I only hope I can reciprocate those same feelings.

The next morning, I wake up with a major headache. Jenna's body presses against mine, her arms snaked around my waist as my dick comes to life. Last night, we met up at a bar, danced, and drank until all my inhibitions were gone, and I ended up in her bed. I want to feel something for her, something *more*. I focused my attention on her all night long, making actual conversation to get to know her on a deeper level as I waited for that spark. There's no reason I shouldn't have feelings for her, but I'd be lying if I said I did. She's a brunette bombshell—all tan legs and perky tits—so any guy would be lucky to have her attention. I kissed her on the dance floor as if my life depended on it. Cupping her face, I poured everything I could into a deep, sensual kiss that left me feeling like absolute shit. As she moaned against my mouth, her arms wrapped around my waist and tugged us closer together. My cock felt it, but my heart? It was dead.

Carefully, I slip from under the sheets and pull on my jeans and shirt. It smells like beer and sweat, but I don't have any other options at the moment. I sit on the edge of the bed and grab my shoes to put them on. Jenna rolls over and looks up at me, smiling with anticipation.

"Last night was *so* fun," she purrs. "You should stay for breakfast. And we can do it all over again." She bites down on her lower lip, and my heart drops. She deserves better than this—better than me. I should've stopped when things escalated last night, but I kept hoping something would spark inside me. That I could let Jenna in and have some emotional response besides our physical connection. But I realize now that's not in the cards for us. I can't keep leading her on to think we'll be something more.

"No, I can't," I tell her, standing. "We shouldn't have done this."

Her face drops, and I feel like shit for hurting her. I know how she feels too because having feelings for someone who doesn't return them hurts like hell. I don't want to do that to her.

"You're cutting me off again, right? Is this how things are going to be between us?" She sits up, pulling the sheets over her bare breasts. "You text me when you want some and bail on me the next day? We only meet up when it's convenient for you." The pain in her voice makes me feel like a dick.

My eyes soften. "I wish I could like you the way you like me, Jenna. It's not you. You're everything, the whole package, and I don't want to lead you on. I'm in this fucked-up place, and it's not fair to you. I tried and thought I could let you in, but—" I shrug, feeling defeated and even a little vulnerable that I'm sharing this with her.

Jenna frowns, reading between the lines. "Who is she?"

Shaking my head, I refuse to acknowledge that Lennon is the reason. "No one."

"You know, if you keep lying to yourself, you're just going to end up hurt and alone. If this 'no one' doesn't have the same feelings for you that you do her, then why are you still hung up on her? I'm here, ready to give you anything you need. I like you, Hunter. A lot."

"I know you do," I admit, squeezing the back of my neck because the tension is building between my shoulders. "That's why I wanna be honest with you. I thought I was capable of forcing myself to move on, but I realize now I can't." I release a deep breath, partly relieved to get that off my chest and partly terrified.

"Let me help you move on," she says with a seriousness that has me feeling like a piece of shit. "If that's the only way I can have you, Hunter, then I'll take it until you get over her. Okay? I'm fine with it."

"You deserve more than that, Jenna. More than being a second choice." The irony of this whole fucked-up situation isn't lost on me. "And at this point, I'm not sure I'll ever get over her," I admit honestly before leaving. I schedule an Uber and wait outside, thinking of all the ways I'm fucked. Jenna doesn't give up easily, and I wish I could give her what she wants and needs, but I'm tired of pretending.

I think back to my sex bucket list I told Hayden about and wonder if that whole thing is what got me into trouble in the first place. I can't fuck around to get over my feelings for Lennon, and I was a fool for ever thinking I could.

CHAPTER NINE

LENNON

"Mmm, why do you always smell so good?" Brandon hums as he buries his nose in my hair. His arms wrap around my waist and slide under my shirt as I rinse the dishes in the sink.

I arch my neck, smiling when his palm grabs my breast and squeezes. "Maybe because none of my students threw up today." One of my students is always sick, so I consider that a win for a Monday.

He chuckles against my skin and presses a soft kiss under my ear. "What do you say we go for a joyride tonight? It's gonna be a nice evening. Maybe we can ride up the coast, grab some dinner, and watch the sunset?"

"Brandon Jude Locke…" I singsong, drying my hands on a towel. "That sounds awfully romantic." Suspicion rings in my ears.

He spins me around and cups my cheeks. "Do I need a reason to be romantic for my amazing girlfriend?"

I bring a hand up to his forehead and brush the hair off his face. With a wide smile, I pull his lips to mine. "Of course not. Let me go change real quick, and we can go for a ride."

He arches a brow with a devilish smirk.

"Not that kinda ride. Down, boy," I tease, dropping my eyes to his crotch. He wraps an arm around my hips and smacks my ass, then takes a handful in his palm.

"But you make it *so* hard." He winks, and I burst out laughing.

"You're relentless." I push him back slightly, creating space between us before his sex-filled brain takes over, and we never leave.

"You like it."

I slip out of his grip, laughing, and walk to our room. I change into a pair of jeans, a sweater, and put on socks and boots. It can get chilly on the back of his motorcycle, especially once the sun sets.

Just as I'm about to tell Brandon I'm ready to go, I get a phone call and see it's Sophie.

"Hey, what's up?" I answer.

"Lennon." Her voice cracks, and I instantly know something's wrong.

"Soph, what is it? Are you okay?" I panic.

"Yeah, I-I'm just having some roommate issues. Figure you were the best person to talk to about that."

I snort, nodding in agreement, though she can't see me. She knows all about my troubles with Hunter.

"What kind of issues? I thought you and Maria got along great." They've been roommates for the past few years, and she's never complained about her.

"We are, we do. It's…well, she's asking her boyfriend to move in with her. With *us*." I hear the struggle in her voice.

"Carter?" I ask.

She gets along with him as well as I get along with Hunter.

"Yep. I don't know what I'm going to do. Or can do rather. The lease is in her name. She took me in, so it's not like I can say anything. Him moving in here is going to make my life a living hell, and I do *not* have time for his bullshit. I'm swamped with private lessons and orchestra practice as it is. The last thing I want is to come home and deal with his lazy ass."

"Sounds all too familiar…" I groan. "What about getting your own place?"

"I can't afford it right now or in the near future. Not when they'd want the first and last month's rent along with the security deposit up front." Her voice softens, and I know she's defeated.

"Want me to come over? Brandon and I were going for an evening joyride, but I can have him drop me off instead. We can drink wine and eat ice cream."

She releases a choked laugh, which makes me smile because I was hoping that suggestion might lift her spirits a bit. "I don't want to ruin your date night."

"No, it's okay. We can do it another night. I'll come over, and we can talk," I insist, and she finally agrees. "I'll be over in twenty."

Once I explain the situation to Brandon, he's understanding, as usual, and tells me it's no problem. We hop on the bike, and he drives us to Sophie's apartment. Once we're there, I swing my leg over and get off the back. The engine continues to run as I take off my helmet, then strap it to the back and give him a big smile.

"Sophie will bring me back home. I have a feeling we're going to be chatting for a while, so I might not be home until late."

Brandon takes off his helmet and pulls me close, smiling against my lips. "You girls have fun. But not too much fun," he says, giving me a wink.

Leaning forward, I steal another kiss. "Don't worry. I need to get her mind off potential asshole roommates, so romantic comedies and junk food it is since I might know something about that."

When I give him a pointed look, he chuckles.

"I love you, baby. Have fun." He wraps a hand around my neck and pulls me in for one last deep kiss.

"I love you too." I hum against his lips. "Be careful on that thing. I'll see you when I get home."

"Always am." He winks, replaces his helmet, and revs the

engine. I wave as he drives out of the parking lot and slowly turns back to the road.

I walk to Sophie's apartment and knock. The defeated look on her face when she opens the door has me giving her a big hug.

Moments later, we're on the couch watching *10 Things I Hate About You* with a bottle of Merlot and a pile of snacks.

"So things are still rough between you and Hunter?" Sophie asks after our second glass of wine.

I groan loudly to emphasize my point. "Yep. Every damn day. He's a slob, disrespectful, arrogant, selfish, and rude. All of the above."

Sophie chuckles, then sips her drink. "Still blows my mind, considering he was hitting on you that first night you guys met." She waggles her brows, and I playfully shove her shoulder.

"Stop. It was nothing. He was hitting on half the bar. Brandon swept me off my feet, and I'm supposed to be with him, and I'm happy!" I reassure her.

"I know you're happy, which makes me happy! I just can't help wondering if you hadn't dated that asshole who cheated on you in college, you would've pushed your insecurities aside and pursued Hunter?" she asks, and it takes me by surprise. "You told me all about spring break week afterward and mentioned him but then ended up dating his roommate. I mean, that's why you chose Brandon, right? He was a nice guy and the safe choice?"

"What?" I furrow my brows. "No! I mean, yes, Brandon's nice. But it wasn't like that. Nothing happened between me and Hunter, so it's not like I chose between the two. Hunter's the total playboy cliché—panty-melting looks, knows exactly what to say to seduce you, and flirts like you're the only woman in the world. He charms the panties off any woman to get them into his bed. He's a player, and I think my heart knew that. It also knew Brandon was the one."

Sophie laughs. "Always the hopeless romantic."

"So even if my ex didn't cheat on me, I wouldn't have wanted to date a guy like that. It had nothing to do with choosing between the two because the moment Brandon and I met, I was captivated. Yes, I was attracted to Hunter, and we had chemistry, but I've been attracted to other guys before. You know how Mom always said to find a guy you can see a future with? How we should date *with* purpose? That's what I saw in Brandon." My thoughts are all over the place, and I blame the wine for that but continue anyway. "His ridiculous pickup line had me cracking up, and it was easy to see he was a genuine guy. It made me feel like giving him my heart was right and that he'd take care of it and never break it, if that makes sense." I take another drink to stop myself from rambling.

"I'm glad it worked out," Sophie says with a dazed look in her eyes. "He looks at you like you're his whole world," she adds with a goofy grin. "Which is kind of sickening for us in the single girls' club."

"He really does," I agree, smiling. "Even if I'd pursued Hunter, I can guarantee you it would've ended in heartbreak by now, considering the way he acts. I don't think I could've handled his mood swings and attitude."

"Well, when a guy like Hunter looks like he could barge through walls and lift anyone over his head, he's bound to catch some attention," Sophie says with a laugh.

"Yeah, playing football all those years and going to the gym religiously helped make him so muscular, and he knows it. I'm surprised his brain hasn't exploded from how big his ego is."

Sophie and I both giggle, and soon, we're laughing so hard tears fall down our cheeks. We continue drinking and cracking jokes, and by our fourth glass of wine, I know she's no longer worried about Maria's boyfriend moving in. Though she can't do much about it now, I'm glad I could offer some comfort and distract her, even if only temporarily.

I realize it's getting late, and I should go home since I have to work in the morning. "My first spring concert is this Friday, so I need some sleep since it's going to be another hectic day. We're practicing in the auditorium tomorrow, and then Thursday is the stage rehearsal. I'm super nervous."

"I'm so proud of you, Lennon. I'm positive it'll run perfectly!" She smiles sincerely. "I wish I could come and watch it."

"I know you do, but you're also busy, so don't even sweat it." I lean over and give her a hug. "I'm going to call an Uber since you're a little tipsy."

She giggles, agreeing.

"Brandon's probably passed out already, so I don't wanna bother him," I explain, opening the app, knowing he doesn't stay up super late during the week. I put on my shoes and jacket and tell Sophie goodbye. "We'll chat again soon, okay? If it becomes unbearable, I'm sure Brandon wouldn't mind you crashing on our couch while you look for another place."

"Thanks, sis. I doubt it'll resort to that, but thanks for the offer."

Thirty minutes later, I'm back at the apartment and look for Brandon, but the light is off in our bedroom.

"You fall in a wine cellar? Damn." Hunter's loud voice makes my ears ring. I turn and see him lounging on the couch without a shirt.

"Can you keep it down? Brandon's sleeping." My head pounds, but I don't admit that to him.

"He's not home. I thought he was with you."

Hunter's words have me frozen in my tracks. "Are you sure? He went for a motorcycle ride like four hours ago. He dropped me off at Sophie's before he took off."

"I've been home since five," he explains. "Did you call him?"

"No, I figured he'd be in bed already." I pull my phone from my pocket and call him. It rings five times, then goes to voicemail. "Hmm. No answer."

"Let me try," he says, shifting his weight to one side and grabbing his phone.

"You think he's going to ignore my call but answer yours? He's probably still out cruising, lost track of time, or doesn't feel his phone vibrating," I say but wait to see if Hunter gets through.

"Nada."

"He did say he wanted to watch the sunset, so he probably went for a longer drive." I shrug, making my way down the hall to my bedroom. I change into some leggings and a tank top and decide to make myself something to eat, hoping it'll soak up the wine.

"I see you finally figured out the dishwasher," I call out when I'm in the kitchen and see the sink isn't full for once.

"No, I just put everything back in the cabinets."

"You better be joking!" I scold, instantly opening the doors to call his bluff.

His feet pad against the floor as he makes his way into the kitchen. "I'm not completely incompetent. I had a date over. She did it."

I slam the door I left open and avoid his gaze. I can't tell if he's messing with me, but if his dates want to do his chores, I'm all for it. "Well, whatever."

Opening the fridge, I grab the ingredients to make a sandwich. I think back to the conversation Sophie and I had about Brandon and Hunter and how she's basically going to be Hunter in her situation—the third-wheel roommate.

I'd feel bad for Hunter, but he's the reason things are so tense between us. If he didn't make my life a living hell, maybe help out a bit, and stop being an arrogant bastard, we'd get along just fine. Part of me wonders if he acts out because he feels I stole his best friend from him. Or that I invaded his space. Whatever the reason, it doesn't merit acting the way he does.

"Where's the deli meat?" I ask, digging around where it usually is.

"Uh…" Hunter stands close behind me, and considering he's almost a foot taller than I am and shirtless, I don't dare turn around. "In my belly."

I glance over my shoulder to scowl when he rubs a hand over his stupid abs.

"I literally bought two pounds of turkey last week," I say between gritted teeth, slamming the door.

"Guess you'll learn to buy double next time," he says smugly.

"Ugh!" I crash into him as I walk by, but it doesn't even faze him. But damn, it makes my shoulder throb.

"I don't know what you're getting so worked up about. Untwist your panties and chill." He strolls back to the couch and plops down, spreading his legs out like an animal.

"Because I'm hungry, and you eat everything!" I shout. "Perhaps we need our own shelves, and you can buy your own food since some of us are children and don't know how to share!"

His chuckling only angers me more. I wouldn't be so damn pissed if I weren't starving, with a bottle of wine swirling around in my empty stomach.

"Fuck it, I'm ordering food," I mutter mostly to myself as I open the delivery app on my phone.

"Sweet. Where're you ordering from? I could eat."

I slowly glare at him so hard I'm sure my eyes will pop out of my face. "Are you fucking kidding right now?"

Hunter holds up his hands in a mock surrender. "Fine, geez. Someone needs to get laid."

Taking a seat on the chair, I ignore him as I scan through my food options, then finally pick something.

"Speaking of laid, my date and I were on that chair earlier."

I leap up so fast, I nearly lose my balance. "You're a goddamn pig."

He's sitting on the other side of the couch, and when I walk past, I smack him in the head and don't even feel bad about it.

"What the hell was that for?" He rubs it as if it actually hurts.

"For having sex in the living room! Don't you have any decency? What if Brandon or I walked in when you were naked and…" I shudder, unable to finish my sentence, and walk down the hallway to my room.

"For the record, I wasn't naked! Blow jobs don't *require* nudity," he shouts.

I want to scream, but instead, I go into my room and slam my door. I can't wait until Brandon and I move out, and if it's not sometime in the very near future, I might choke Hunter in his sleep. Hell, knowing him, he'd probably think it was foreplay and enjoy it.

Thirty minutes later, the doorbell goes off and I'm relieved my food is finally here.

"Our dinner is here," Hunter singsongs, rushing toward the door and beating me there.

"Fuck off." I push him with my hip, and he chuckles, backing out of my way.

"C'mon, you're the one who said we're supposed to be *sharing*."

"I wouldn't share with you even if we were the last two people alive during an apocalypse." I scowl, grabbing the door handle.

"You know then I'd just eat *you*," he taunts. "And not the pussy kind of eating either."

Rolling my eyes, I mutter, "Go away."

When I finally open the door, I'm stunned to see two police officers instead of a delivery driver.

"Hello, I'm Officer Fisher, and this is my partner, Officer Schmitz. We're looking for the family of Brandon Locke." His tone is flat, and the second he says my boyfriend's name, my heart stops beating.

"We're his roommates," Hunter answers before I can get out any words. I hadn't even realized he was still standing behind me.

"I'm his girlfriend," I finally speak. "What's wrong? Did something happen to him?"

The officer briefly looks down before making eye contact with me. "I'm sorry to inform you of this, miss, but Mr. Locke's been in a serious motorcycle accident. The paramedics were unable to revive him."

CHAPTER TEN

HUNTER

I CATCH Lennon before she collapses to the floor. There's a loud gasp and she's hyperventilating, unable to catch her breath. I'm on my knees, holding her up when the officer's words repeat in my head. They don't seem real. They can't be. I saw him this morning before work, and now he's...*gone.*

My throat threatens to close, but I push back the feeling. With Lennon falling apart in my arms, I try to be strong for her.

"Lennon, breathe," I remind her softly as she gasps for air. She's going to pass out if she doesn't.

After a moment, she relaxes in my arms, and I look back at the two men.

"What happens now?" I ask him. "His parents...do they know?"

"He's been transported to the medical examiner's office, and someone there will notify his next of kin. They'll discuss with them what happens next."

"Wait. I should tell them. They're like family to me, and Brandon was their only child."

The officers look at each other again but don't argue with me about it. "We can't tell you not to call them, but the staff may have already. The family will need to properly ID him and make arrangements from there."

I nod, but that's not going to stop me. They give us their sincerest apologies and condolences before leaving.

Lennon buckles over with her hands covering her face. I manage to shut the door, then I hook one arm under her knees, the other behind her back, and pick her up. She wraps her arms around me, burying her face in my neck as I carry her to the couch and carefully set her down.

"Lennon…" I whisper, brushing blond hair away from her face so I can look at her. "I need your phone to call them. Mine's dead."

After a few seconds, she reaches into her pocket and hands it over. She unlocks it, and I start going through her contacts, looking for Mr. and Mrs. Locke's number.

"Do you want to speak to them after?" I ask softly.

She shakes her head as tears roll down her cheeks. "I can't," she chokes out.

"It's okay. I'll be right back." I don't want to leave her, but I also don't want her to overhear the conversation, so I walk to my room where I can speak to them privately.

Everything inside me is numb, shocked, *devastated*. How could this happen? My best friend. He's too young to die. He had so many dreams and aspirations, with a full life ahead of him. Why the hell did he have to go? *Fuck*.

I don't know how to make this phone call. I've met his parents dozens of times at barbecues, celebrations, and have even attended family dinners. How the hell am I supposed to tell a mother her son is dead? I wish I could, at least, do this in person, but I can't leave Lennon right now, and the medical examiner's office could be calling them any minute.

Choking up, I try my best to get my shit together before I call. It's late, and they're going to know something's wrong the moment they realize it's me and I'm calling from Lennon's phone.

I manage to push my feelings down so I can hit their number, but the doorbell rings again.

Assuming it's the delivery guy, I ignore it. He'll get the hint and leave the food at the door. But then I hear shouting.

Lennon.

Shit.

Rushing out of my room, I sprint down the hallway and wrap my arms around Lennon's waist and pull her away. She's screaming at the guy and saying he forgot her soda and that he's a fucking moron. The poor man is frozen in place, and I don't take the time to explain before grabbing a hysterical Lennon and shutting the door.

"Can you believe that guy?" she says the moment I set her down on her feet. She waves a hand in the air and scowls. "How hard is it to bring what I ordered? Idiot."

My brows rise as I try to make eye contact with her. She's muttering about her food order moments after she was a sobbing mess.

"Lennon…" I tread carefully. "You're in shock. Let's go sit." I reach for her hand, but she yanks it away.

"You haven't been nice to me since the day we met. No need to start now," she hisses, taking her bag of food and going to the living room.

Holy fuck.

I brush a hand through my hair, trying to figure out what to do. Before it gets any later, I need to call his parents, so I do.

"Hello?" Brandon's mother answers in a sleepy voice. "Lennon?"

"No, Mrs. Locke, it's Hunter. I'm using her phone," I explain.

"Oh, Hunter! Hey, kiddo. Why are you calling so late?"

She doesn't know that in about three seconds, my words will change her entire life. I don't want to be the person to deliver the news no mother should ever have to hear, and it's going to destroy me. Brandon was an amazing guy, and he came from incredible parents, something I've always been envious of. Neither deserves to be given this kind of bad news.

"It's Brandon," I start, inhaling deeply so I don't break down before I get the words out. "He was in a motorcycle accident."

I hear the rush of air she sucks in before she responds. "Hunter, please tell me my son is okay." Her shaky voice rattles through me, and I hear the fear in her tone. "Please, Hunter," she pleads, begging to hear positive news that I can't deliver.

I squeeze my eyes shut. "I'm so sorry, Mrs. Locke. I wish I could."

Pinching the bridge of my nose, I force back my tears. I'm trying to be strong for his mother right now, but I can't handle hearing her heart-wrenching sobs.

I stay silent for a few minutes and listen to her wake her husband. She cries that her only son is gone. This moment between them is gut-wrenching as I hear Mr. Locke choke up. I can't find the strength to end the call, not wanting to leave them in this state.

Once she returns to the phone, I tell her that the examiner's office will be contacting them to discuss the details.

"How's Lennon doing?" she asks shortly after, and I can tell she's trying to compose herself.

"I'm not sure. We found out less than an hour ago. I'll take care of her, so please don't worry." Even if Lennon doesn't want me around, I won't let her push me away when I know she'll need me just as much as I'll need her. We won't be able to get through this alone or by arguing with each other.

"I appreciate you telling me as soon as possible, Hunter," she says between sniffling. "Once I hear from them, I'll let you know what we find out."

I can't even fathom having to watch my best friend's parents bury their child. This can't be real.

"I'd appreciate that. I'm here to do whatever you guys need, okay? Don't hesitate," I tell her, meaning every word. It won't be easy for any of us, but we need to stick together during this time.

Once the call ends, I head back to the living room and find Lennon curled up in a ball on the couch. She's crying into a pillow. No words I can offer will make her feel better, so instead, I grab a blanket and cover her. Even though I should make some phone calls, I don't. Instead, I get another pillow and blanket and lie on the floor next to the couch so I can be close to Lennon. Her cries are the only sound in the room, and I know tonight will be a sleepless night.

It's after two in the morning when Lennon stops trembling and her sobs quiet. I reach up for her hand and rub my thumb over her knuckles. The fact she doesn't pull away or punch me in the face tells me she's finally fallen asleep.

I've lain here for the past four hours with my mind in overdrive as I think back to when I first met Brandon, and I'm slapped with the reality of never seeing him again. Mason, Liam, Brandon, and I have been a foursome of friends since our freshman year of college, though I've known Brandon since high school. Mason and Liam are from SoCal, but Brandon and I are both Sacramento born and raised. His parents became my family and always welcomed me with open arms. I didn't just lose my best friend—I lost a brother.

At sunrise, I decide to get up and make a pot of coffee. Lord knows I'm gonna need it today. Hell, I should add a bottle of vodka to it.

Unsure of where to start or what to do, I decide to text Hayden to see if he's awake. Since he's on the East Coast, he's three hours ahead of me and should be available. I need to get with Mason and Liam. More calls I don't know how the hell to make.

"Hey, what's up, bro?" Hayden answers with a smile in his voice after telling me he was free to chat. "You're up early. Or did a girl keep you up all night?" He chuckles at his own joke, and I wish I could laugh with him.

"It's Brandon," I respond, but it comes out rougher than I intended. "He died in a motorcycle accident last night."

Just saying the words aloud has my heart pounding harder, almost as if it'll beat right out of my chest. My breathing quickens as the anxiety of what this means and how my life will forever be changed hits me.

"Oh, Hunter. God. I'm so sorry," Hayden softly replies. "Fuck, I don't even know what to say. I can fly in this weekend if you need me to."

"Maybe. I don't know. I'm not even sure when the funeral is or any of the details yet. I had to tell his mom over the phone and hearing her break down nearly had me in tears," I tell him, my voice cracking. I try to keep it together for Lennon's sake because I know she's going to need it, but I know I can talk to my brother about anything without judgment. "I can't believe he's gone."

Hayden stays on the phone with me for over thirty minutes, listening to me ramble and getting my juggled thoughts out of my head. He reminds me that he's here for me, and if I need him close, he'll fly home anytime. I appreciate him so much. Once again, he's proven to be the only true relationship I have within our family.

After hanging up, I pour a cup of coffee and sit at the kitchen table. My mind's too cluttered to think about how I'm going to handle all this. We'd been so close, hung out all the time, especially on the weekends, but things noticeably changed when Lennon moved in. His happiness was all I cared about, so I understood when he ditched our guy nights for date nights. It wasn't as though I didn't find other company to keep me occupied.

I'm lost in my thoughts until I hear Lennon rustling in the living room. I walk over and see her dragging her feet down the hallway, then enter the bathroom. She slams the door shut with unnecessary force, and I head into the living room and see her phone's still on the coffee table.

Remembering I need to get Brandon's work number and assuming her sisters need to know too so they can be here for her, I grab her phone and walk to the bathroom.

"Lennon," I call, tapping my knuckles on the door. "What's the code to your phone?"

She doesn't answer, but a second later, she whips it open and stares at me with an unreadable expression. "For what?"

"I need Brandon's boss's number. You should call Maddie and Sophie too, but I can do that for you if you want," I tell her.

Lennon narrows her eyes, her hair a wild mess. Her skin is blotchy, and her eyes are red from crying. I feel a strong desire to pull her close and hug her, let her know it's all going to be okay, but I don't.

"It's your number," she murmurs, walking past me and down the hallway again.

"Huh?" I ask, thoroughly confused. She heads to the kitchen and pours coffee into a mug.

"6-6-6." She spins around to face me with a deadpan expression.

"Lennon." I step toward her, but she puts up a hand to stop me from coming any closer.

"Like I said," she says with harsh emphasis, "you haven't been nice to me in two years, so there's no reason to start now. Give me my phone, and I'll forward you the contact info. I can call *my* sisters."

Lennon holds out her palm, and I reluctantly deposit her phone into it. I can't even argue with her, especially now. I've been a grade A asshole to her, there's no denying that, but she doesn't understand the circumstances of why I had to be—why I had to push her away.

I walk away without responding, not wanting to say anything I'll regret later. She's not going to let me in easily, but regardless, she'll need all the support she can get over the next few weeks, months, hell, maybe even years. We still live together, after all.

After taking a shower and getting dressed, I decide it's time to do the inevitable and tell Mason and Liam. They're probably both working, but I can't let more time pass without letting them know.

HUNTER

Brandon was in a motorcycle accident late last night. Can you two come over today?

I don't want to tell them via text or over the phone, but I don't want to tell them in person either. Seeing their crushed faces will be hard.

MASON

Shit, man. He okay?

LIAM

Told that dumbass he couldn't ride for shit!

HUNTER

Just come over, okay?

MASON

I can be there within the hour.

LIAM

Same.

I swallow the tight knot in my throat and am already dreading the rest of this fucking nightmarish day.

By the time I make it back into the living room, Sophie and Maddie are on the couch with Lennon. No one's talking, but Lennon's sisters sit next to her. I feel better knowing she's with family and am glad they can give her some comfort.

I text my boss around seven to explain the situation and let him know I won't be in. Then I think about Lennon's job. She's so dedicated, but there's no way she's going to be able to work in her emotional state. I hope she's not stubborn and takes the time off. She's going to need to process everything.

I call Brandon's boss and go through the same emotional roller coaster once again. He gives me his deepest apologies and asks me to inform them when and where the funeral will be held.

Speaking of which, I decide to call Mrs. Locke to see if anyone has contacted them yet.

"He's really gone," she says with uneven breaths after confirming with the medical examiner and sharing the details. "I don't know how to survive this."

I do my best to tell her we'll get through this together and that I'm here for whatever she needs. His parents shouldn't plan his funeral alone, so I offer to meet with them tomorrow at the church to discuss the details.

Shortly after we end the call, there's a knock on the door, and I dread having to tell my two other best friends. I open the door and let them in. They look at Lennon and her sisters and then at me.

"Dude, what's going on? Locke okay?" Mason asks.

"Is he at the hospital?" Liam glances around me.

Shaking my head, I lower my eyes. "He didn't…make it, guys."

"What?" they both shriek.

I'm sweating when I look at them. "Died at the scene. Officers showed up late last night to tell us."

"*Fuck*. Are you joking?" Liam scrubs a hand through his hair, visibly upset.

Mason shakes his head in disbelief. "No way."

I frown. "Serious."

They're both distraught, and I lead them to the kitchen table to sit so we don't upset Lennon any more than she already is.

After moments of silence, Mason clears his throat. "Do you know what happened?"

"Yeah, Mrs. Locke spoke with the medical examiner and officer this morning. But last night, all I knew was what Lennon told me, which was that he went on a solo joyride."

As I say it aloud, it hits me. Lennon told me they were supposed to go cruising together, and she ended up changing her plans at the last minute when she went to Sophie's last night. Holy fuck.

Not only is Lennon dealing with this news, but she's also probably thinking about how she was supposed to be with him. Hell, I honestly don't know what she's thinking, but I can only imagine the grief and anger she's experiencing. The same emotions rush through me.

I repeat the information Brandon's mom told me about how the investigation is still ongoing, but that a semi-truck hit him at sixty miles an hour. The driver claimed he didn't even see him, and that Brandon flew off the bike and landed in a ditch. Even though he was wearing a helmet, nothing could've saved his life at that speed. He was dead before the paramedics arrived on the scene.

He was only twenty minutes away from home.

The visual and realization have me rushing to the sink and emptying my stomach.

"You alright, man?" Liam asks after a moment, handing me a towel.

"Fuck if I know." I wipe my mouth and the cold sweat off my forehead. "I can't believe he's gone."

"I know." Mason claps his hand tightly on my shoulder and squeezes.

Lennon's sisters and the guys stay through the afternoon, but soon they all have to go, leaving the two of us in a silent apartment. Neither of us has eaten all day, and I know if we don't, we'll lose our strength to get through this.

I don't bother asking Lennon if she's hungry because I already know what she'll say. So I order comfort food, and when it arrives, I plate it for her and bring it to where she's lying on the couch—the spot she hasn't moved from all day.

"No, thanks," she mutters, staring off into space.

"You need something in your stomach, Lennon." I push it closer toward her.

"You don't know shit about what I need," she says, her voice a bit louder this time.

"Look, I know you're pissed. I know you're hurting. I know you're angry. I get it. If you need to use me as your emotional punching bag, then I'll let you. But I'm not going to let you starve." I tell her firmly.

She finally turns and looks at me but remains silent.

"Just try to eat a little," I say, softer this time. "I ordered your favorite."

Lennon blinks, then looks down at her plate. "How'd you know this is my favorite?" She eyes the lobster and shrimp mac 'n' cheese.

I swallow, looking down at my own plate of the same thing. She thinks I don't listen when she talks, but she's wrong. I'm always listening, especially when it comes to her. Not for any particular reason, but I hear what she says all the same.

"I just do."

She sits up and takes the plate, placing it on her lap. "Thank you."

The TV's been on all day as background noise, but neither of us talks or watches what's playing. We sit in silence and eat, and though I have no appetite, I scarf it down. Lennon moves her food around with her fork before she finally takes a bite.

Nothing either of us can say will make the other feel better or change things. As much as Lennon wants to hate me, I'm here to stay and help her through this—help us both through this. Even though I don't want to admit it, I need her as much as she needs me. She's the only person who was as close to Brandon as I was and can fully understand the never-ending grief I'm feeling. I know I've wanted to hate her and have her hate me this whole time, but Brandon dying has put everything into perspective. Life's too short and unpredictable to be a dickhead. I know he'd want me to look after her the best way I know how, even if she'd rather push me away.

"Are you done?" I ask when she abandons her barely eaten food and lies back down.

She nods.

Pushing myself up, I grab our dirty dishes and go to the kitchen. I rinse and put them in the dishwasher, a skill Lennon always thought I couldn't figure out. Except who does she think did them before she moved in? Though before she insisted she buy new china, we used paper plates and a mismatched set we'd bought from the thrift store.

Once I've cleaned up and put the leftover food in the fridge, I head back to Lennon and see her knees up to her chest with her arms wrapped around her legs. I wish I could take her pain away even though I'd never be able to.

"Going to bed?" I ask, grabbing the remote to turn off the TV.

"I'm sleeping here," she says. "I can't sleep in there."

Lennon pinches her eyes shut, and I can see her lip visually trembling, so I don't push her on it.

"Okay," I say, setting the remote back down and grabbing the pillow and blanket. I place it on the floor next to her just like last night.

"What're you doing?" Her sad eyes meet mine.

"I'm not letting you stay out here alone," I tell her. "Want another blanket?"

She blinks up at me. "Sure."

Once I grab one, I drape it over her body. Then I turn off the living room light and settle into my makeshift bed. Lennon hasn't broken down since her sisters left hours ago, but now as the silence and darkness surround us, she tries to keep her tears and emotions at bay but can't.

God. Hearing her cry is fucking ruining me. If I hadn't been such an asshole toward her during the past two years, she'd trust me to comfort her. The pain she's feeling is bound to be on a level greater than even I can understand. We both loved Brandon, but she was *in* love with him. I can't begin to fathom losing the love of my life, and my heart fucking aches for her, for what she no longer has, for what she lost—a good man, best friend, a future husband even.

The last part punches me straight in the goddamn gut as I remember the conversation Brandon and I had not too long ago. I push the thoughts away, hoping I don't lose my dinner because I'm so fucking sick over it that I might.

"Tomorrow's a new day, Lennon. We'll get through this, okay?" I tell her, hoping it'll calm her and me too.

I hold on to tomorrow like a candle in the darkness, a light that will guide us into the morning as I close my eyes and try to think of nothing. Only time can heal this pain, but the seconds feel like minutes and minutes like hours as the past day continues to play on repeat. *We'll survive this, won't we?*

Lennon speaks up as if she's read my mind, but she's only responding to my last comment.

"We have to. There's no other option."

CHAPTER ELEVEN

LENNON

I'M LIVING in my own personal hell, a nightmare I can't seem to wake from. Shock and anxiety have become my best friends and never leave my side. They're determined to swallow me whole and smother me until I'm no longer here. One moment, I'm okay. The next, I'm so lost and broken I feel as if I'm dying from the inside out. My heart hurts, and heaviness weighs on me while I drown in emptiness. No one understands this from my perspective. How could they?

I've cried myself to sleep the past two nights at the reality that I'll never see him again. I try to remember his voice and think about how he'd make sure to tell me good night before we went to bed. The past few mornings have been the worst, though, because I dream of him and wake up to a new day without him in it. The smell of Brandon is already fading, and though it's only been two days since the accident, I already feel as if he's slipping through my fingers. The thought of my love becoming nothing more than a memory causes tears to well on the edge of my lids. I'm surprised I have anything left.

The last conversation I had with him plays on repeat in my mind. One of the last things he said before driving away was how much he loved me. Every chance he had, he told me how much I meant to him, and I wish I could see him or kiss him or hold him again. Just one more time.

I sit up on the couch, careful not to step on Hunter. He hasn't left my side because I can't find the courage to sleep in my bed.

Brandon and I were supposed to get married, have kids, and grow old together. We were going to have a million grandchildren and spoil them rotten. We dreamed big, and it always included each other. I believed with every fiber of my being that he was the man I'd be with for the rest of my life. This was supposed to be the beautiful beginning of our love story, not the fucking end. *Not the end.*

But it *is* the end…

I gasp and feel as if I can't breathe as the weight of it all comes pounding down again.

Tears threaten to pour out, but this time, they're accompanied by anger. I force myself to stand, to walk around Hunter's body to the bathroom. My movements are robotic as if I'm on autopilot because essentially, I am. I eat and breathe because I have to, not because I want to. The hollow shell of me goes through the motions of living, but I don't know how I'll ever move on from this.

The only thing that keeps me going is the fact that my kids at school need me. I hold on to that like a life jacket, and right now, it's saving me from drowning.

I turn on the light and look in the mirror at a zombie version of myself, with puffy eyes and a red nose. I'm in a constant state of sadness, but somehow, I force myself into the shower. I turn on the water as hot as it'll go, hoping it will steal the place of the constant pain inside my heart, but it's no use. For the first time in my life, I shower in silence. I lean against the wall and allow the stream to fall over me, to snap me out of this, but it's no use.

The water goes cold, the only indicator I've been in here long enough, and I step out of the shower and dry off. I put on a dress and some flats, an outfit I've worn for class a half dozen times. After I blow-dry my hair, I pin it back so I look somewhat put together. Though I try, no amount of concealer will cover the dark circles under my eyes or the redness on my face, so I give up.

Walking into the kitchen, I find Brandon's mug on the counter and tears flood my eyes. Grief is a bitch and slaps me in the face as the memories of us drinking coffee together flood in.

I try to hold back my emotions as best as I can so Hunter doesn't hear me. Ironic considering he's heard me crying the past two days. He's the only person who understands the loss I'm feeling. My sisters came over to comfort me, but I had nothing to say, so we sat in awkward silence. No words can describe how broken and lost I am. I'm unrepairable.

A soft hand lands on my shoulder, and I jump. Turning around, I wipe the tears from my cheeks and try to dry them up, though it's no use.

"Lennon," Hunter says softly. "I don't think you're ready to go back to work already. You need time to heal, to process everything. I'm sure the school would understand considering what happened." He looks like he didn't get any sleep either. It's been a rough two days for us both. I can tell he's emotionally angry too, but he's better at hiding it than I am. Instead of crying like me, he holds it all in, but if he doesn't release it soon, he's eventually going to snap.

"I know…" my voice cracks and when tears fall, I wipe them away again. "But my students need me. The concert is on Friday, and they've worked so hard for this. Only three more days and I'll be on spring break and can process it all."

I can tell he's choosing his words carefully by the way he stares at me. "I understand, but just know that no one would blame you if you changed your mind. If you show up and feel as if you can't do it, it's okay to admit it."

I don't know how long Hunter plans to take off work, but I know he's meeting with Brandon's parents today to help with the funeral arrangements. Part of me is glad I won't be there because I wouldn't be any help, but I'm also appreciative that he's being strong and doing this so Brandon's parents don't have to do it alone.

Nodding, I feel numb but am grateful I have this concert to keep me moving forward. I don't feel like singing and pretending to be happy, but I will for my students. Grabbing my bag and keys, I head to work, hoping I can make it through the next three days without breaking down in front of the entire school. I have to be strong for them or at least try to be.

The school concert goes off without a hitch. It was the perfect distraction, and the kids sang their little hearts out. Many of them asked what was wrong because when they'd sing, I'd cry. While I didn't want to lie, it was easier to say someone I cared about passed away and explain how proud I was of them. So damn proud.

After the performance, Principal Orson congratulated me for a job well done and gave her condolences. I think she knew I was in a fragile state of mind and left it at that, though I've heard the whispers about me being at work so grief-stricken. For the most part, everyone was extremely understanding or at least acted like they were. But now it's Sunday, a day I've been dreading for the past week because today's the day I'll put my love to rest.

Some people say funerals give closure to the soul, but to me, it only makes it real that Brandon's never coming back. I wear the same black dress as on our Valentine's Day date, and I don't know how I'll ever put it on again after this. Once I'm ready, I suck in a deep breath and sit on the couch, wishing I could sink inside the cushions and disappear.

Hunter walks into the living room, dressed in a sleek black suit. "Do you want to ride with me?"

I hear him talking, but I'm too lost in my head, thinking about this funeral and what it means once it's over.

He walks farther into the room and kneels in front of me so we're at eye level. "Lennon. Do you want to ride with me?"

Blinking, I look at him, meeting his gaze. "Sure."

"We should probably get going." He stands and walks away. But I don't know if I'm ready. I stand, and I lose the control I thought I had.

"I'm sorry," I tell him. I try to stop crying but can't seem to find the faucet to turn off the tears.

Hunter takes a few steps forward but maintains some distance between us. "Hey, hey. Don't be sorry."

I feel stupid each time I burst into tears around him. I know he doesn't like me, and he's only being nice because I'm so emotional right now. As difficult and impossible as it seems, I'll eventually have to find my own place and try to move on with my life.

I inhale a deep breath and wipe my face.

"Ready?" Hunter lifts his eyebrows and gives me a small smile. The truth is, I don't know if I can do this, but I know I have to.

I grab my phone and tuck it into my clutch, then follow Hunter outside. He walks beside me, and neither of us speaks. We get into the truck and drive across town to the church Brandon grew up attending. After we park, Hunter turns off the engine, and we sit and stare at the double doors that lead inside. His breathing increases and tears well on the edges of his eyes, but they don't fall.

"I always imagined this'd be the place we'd get married," I say aloud, but more so to myself.

Hunter stills, and a ragged breath escapes him.

"We should probably go inside." He finally speaks after the silence awkwardly draws on too long.

I nod, get out of the truck, and force myself to walk across the parking lot and up the stairs. As soon as I enter, the scent of fresh flowers hits my nose, making me nauseous. The smell of roses used to bring me so much joy, and now the sweet smell seems so pungent. I look inside the chapel and see the black casket sitting at the front. My feet feel as if they're glued to the floor, and as much as I want to move, I can't.

Liam and Mason walk up and give Hunter a hug, then give me one as well.

"I'm so sorry, Lennon," Mason offers. "If you need anything…"

I wipe tears from my cheeks, and Liam hands me a handful of tissues. "You might need these."

I let out a choked laugh, then look at Hunter as Liam and Mason walk back inside.

"I can't do this," I tell him. It's wrong. This all feels so wrong.

His eyes soften, and he gently places his hand on my shoulder. "We'll go in together, okay?" His words are comforting as he takes my hand.

I tuck my lips inside my mouth and look up at the ceiling, trying to find what little strength I have left. Water fills my eyes, and I can barely see as I walk through the entrance and down the aisle. It's all too much, and I want it to be over right now so I can be alone.

"We don't have to go up there if you don't want," Hunter tells me. I know I'm expected to, though I'm not sure I can keep it together long enough to do that.

A slideshow plays on the big screen with the saddest fucking music I've ever heard, and when pictures appear of me and Brandon together, I turn into a complete mess. Instead of walking, I sit as quickly as I can and let it all out, not caring who sees me.

Soon someone sits next to me and wraps their arms around me, and when I look up, it's Brandon's mother, Mrs. Locke.

"Oh, sweetie. I am so sorry."

I hold her tighter, and when I finally pull away, I apologize when I notice my tears have spilled onto the shoulder of her dress.

She waves it off and studies me, asking with her eyes if I'm okay, though we all know the answer to that one.

I sniff and wipe my nose with the tissue Liam gave me. "I don't know how I'm going to go on without him, Mrs. Locke."

She rubs her hand against my back and gives me a small smile. "You'll have to do it the same way I am—one minute, one hour, one day at a time—and continue to live the life Brandon would want you to live. He loved you so much, Lennon, and above anything, he'd want you to be happy."

I open my mouth, but no words come out, just a ragged sob.

Hunter gives Brandon's mom a side hug, then sits next to me, but he doesn't say anything. Eventually, people come up to speak to Brandon's mother, and she gives me one last hug and walks away. I stare at the slideshow, seeing all the photos of Brandon as a kid, pictures of him and Hunter, Liam, and Mason, and us when we first started dating. As soon as it ends, it repeats itself, and I watch it five more times before I feel like I can breathe again.

"I'm ready," I tell Hunter, then stand.

My shoes are made of concrete as I walk forward. Brandon's dad stands by the casket and speaks to people after they pay their respects. When I realize I'm next, my heart races and pounds so hard in my chest, it echoes in my ears. I step forward, but when I see Brandon lying there, I lose my fucking mind.

For the last week, I tried to imagine this moment. I imagined what it would be like to see his lifeless body, and as I look at him, it's not how I thought it would be.

Makeup on his face covers the bruises and gashes from the helmet, but I can still see it all. I overheard Hunter talking to the guys about how much blood was at the scene, and thinking about it makes my stomach turn. This is not him. That's not the love of my life. My heart aches, not understanding why such a good person was ripped away from me.

All I can hope is that he didn't feel any pain, but after seeing how broken he is, I'm not so sure. I hate knowing he was alone when he died. My body begins to tremble and shake, and Hunter places his hand around my shoulders and squeezes, bringing me against his body for comfort. If I could crawl inside and be buried with Brandon, I would.

For the first time in my life, I truly understand how Romeo and Juliet felt, not wanting to live without the other. And if I'd joined him on that ride, who knows what my own fate would've been or if any of this would've happened at all. As I kiss my fingertips and place them on his lips, the lips I've kissed for the past two years, I know I'll never be the same. At least we had that, but whoever said it's better to have loved and lost is fucking wrong.

"I love you, Brandon. I love you so much. Save a place for me up there, baby," I whisper, thinking how unfair this all is. I'm suffocating as I somehow break away from him, knowing it's the last time I'll ever see him.

Brandon's dad says something while he gives me a hug, but I don't retain any of the words.

As I walk back to my seat, Hunter isn't behind me, and when I turn around, he's still at the casket with tears falling down his cheeks. It's the first time I've seen him break down since we found out, and I realize how much it's destroying him too. He's been putting on a brave face, but right now, he's releasing it. We're two broken people who will have to somehow find a new normal, though I'm not sure one exists. Mason and Liam join him, and they stand there together, saying goodbye to their best friend.

As I watch them, a voice behind me grabs my attention and I see Maddie and Sophie walking toward me. They pull me into their arms, and I'm so grateful my sisters are here. My parents wanted to come, but Dad had to speak at a funeral service for a longtime member of the church, so I told them it was fine and meant it. My sisters tell me how much they love me and are here for me, and I don't ever want to let them go.

Maddie grabs my hand, and we go to a pew close to the front. They sit on each side of me and hold me tight. Being in this room makes me want to jump out of my skin.

Soon the service starts, and it becomes a blur as the pastor officiates. It's a beautiful service, but I can barely focus on anything that's said.

Brandon's mother allows me to stay with the family to say my last goodbyes, but I hardly remember it because shock takes over.

Hunter, Liam, and Mason, along with Brandon's cousins and childhood friends, were asked to be pallbearers. They lift the casket and carry it to the hearse.

Brandon's mother asks me to ride in the limo with them to the gravesite, so I do. During the drive over, I stare out the window, trying to process everything. The car eventually slows, and I get out, following behind Brandon's family. They carry him to the tent set up by the burial site, and I somehow walk toward it.

It's funny because at this moment, I notice the clouds moving across the bright blue sky and how time keeps ticking, regardless if my world has stopped. Stepping under the tent, I hear sobs escape from Brandon's mother, and I worry I'm going to faint, so I find an empty chair to quickly sit on.

The pastor says a few words as I stare at the shiny black box in front of me. Memories of us together flood in, and for a moment, I hear his voice in my head, telling me it's going to be okay. The minutes feel like hours, and yet within a blink, it's all over, and everyone walks away.

I take a single rose from the flower arrangement draped over the casket before they lower it into the ground. A scoop of dirt lands on top of the box and then another until my Brandon is fully covered. Then, just like that, it's over, and I'm left to pick up the pieces of my broken heart alone.

Maddie and Sophie say their goodbyes. I hug Brandon's family and walk to Hunter's truck. We drive back to the apartment in silence and once we arrive, I numbly walk in and sit on the couch in a daze.

As I stare at the blank TV screen, I realize this is what true loneliness feels like. And I think it might be here to stay.

CHAPTER TWELVE

HUNTER

THE HARDEST THING I've ever had to do in my life is bury my best friend. For the past six years, since we were freshmen in college, we've been inseparable. From playing football together, then becoming roommates, he'd been one of the only constants in my life. Through hard times, he always had my back and supported all my decisions, even if they were stupid. The only thing that could separate us was death itself—nothing could've gotten in the way of our friendship.

As I roll over and turn off the alarm on my phone, I think about how pissed I am. I told him not to buy that fucking motorcycle so many times, and he did it anyway. I wish I could go back in time and stress how bad of an idea it would be. Not that he would've listened to me, but I could've tried harder. Once Brandon made up his mind, nothing could change his decision, but I should've done more to persuade him. The guilt of that alone has me clenching my jaw, anger finding its way back in.

I sit on the edge of my bed and rub my hands over my face. I'm still numb from the funeral yesterday, and while I don't want to go to work, I have to. Last week, I left early on a few days because I felt as if I were crumpling. My mind hasn't been right since the day the officers delivered the news. A piece of me died with Brandon.

At first, I thought it had to be a mistake, but as the reality set in that he was in an accident, I've experienced a whirlwind of different emotions, and watching Lennon suffer through this hasn't helped. I've tried to help her, though she's not asked for anything.

Since she's moved in, I've treated her like shit, and now things are awkward between us because neither of us knows where to go from here. I don't know what to talk about, but I try to make sure she's eating and gets off the couch some. What kills me the most is how she's completely stopped singing since the accident. I used to nag her about it so much, but now it's all I want. She's not herself, and who knows if she will be again.

Though I admit I haven't been myself lately, either. I'm short with people at work, and I want nothing more than to be alone to process my thoughts. I haven't done that yet, and I'm not sure when I'll be able to.

I force myself to stand and go through my morning routine. After I dress, I walk to the kitchen and turn on the light, then brew some coffee. I'm not ready for the day or to deal with the emptiness that blankets me. The coffee maker beeps, pulling me away from my thoughts, and I fill my to-go mug. As I snap on the lid, I feel someone behind me. I turn and see Lennon and give her a small smile. She smiles back, but it doesn't meet her eyes the same way it used to.

"Do you want me to make you some breakfast?" I ask, knowing I don't have time, but I'll be late for her if that means she's eating something.

"Thanks, but I'm not hungry." She opens the fridge and grabs a bottle of water, then leaves the kitchen. I follow her into the living room, where she's determined to sleep every night.

And most of the day.

"Lennon, if you need anything while I'm at work, please call me."

She lies down and pulls the blanket over her body and turns on her side, facing away from me. I hate that she'll be alone like this, but I have to go.

"I will," she mutters, and I know the conversation is over. It's basically how we communicate lately. I'd much rather have her curse me out and tell me how much of a dick I am than see her like this.

After checking the time, I decide to leave and get on the road before I get stuck in traffic. As I pull up to the office building, I call Sophie.

"Hunter?" she asks when she answers the phone.

"Hey. Yeah. Sorry for calling you this early, but I'm worried about Lennon. If you have any free time throughout the week, can you stop by and make sure she's eating, maybe get her out of the house or something? Maybe Maddie can help too if she has time?"

"Yeah, sure. I've been trying to reach her, but she's been unresponsive," Sophie says, defeated.

"I know. She's been like that with everyone lately. I know it's going to take time, but I'm concerned. And I know if she needs anything, she's too stubborn to ask anyone, especially me."

She chuckles. "She is." The line sits silent for a moment. "How are you doing with all this, Hunter? Are you okay?"

"As okay as I can be considering the situation. But hey, I'm walking into work, so I gotta go." I try to get out of talking about myself, and we end the call. I have her sisters' numbers in case I need them for things like this, which, so far, has come in handy.

After my morning meeting, I give my boss a status update on the apartment complex project. I spend the next few hours calling different contractors to go through the upcoming milestones and deadlines along with approving payments for the completed work. Before lunch, I let everyone in the office know I was going to the jobsite to do a walk around. After that's done, I stop by a local taco shop that Lennon loves and pick up her favorite burrito.

I drive across town to the apartment, and when I walk in, I'm surprised to see she's not on the couch. The water is on in the shower, and when I set the food down on the table, it stops. Moments later, she's stepping into the room towel drying her hair, and when she sees me, a terrifying scream escapes her.

I hold out my hand. "I'm sorry. I thought I'd bring you lunch. I got your favorite burrito from Taco Ranchero."

"Hunter." She tilts her head as she tries to catch her breath. "You don't have to take care of me, okay?"

My eyes meet hers. "I know that, but Brandon would want me to."

"That doesn't make me your responsibility," she blurts out. She stops in her tracks and swallows hard. "I'm sorry. I—" She shakes her head, bringing her fingers up to her temples, and I wish I hadn't said that because I notice how much it upsets her even though it's partly the truth. I want to take care of her for selfish reasons too. I hate seeing her this distraught, and considering there's nothing I can do about his death, I can be here for her in every way possible.

"No, *I'm* sorry. I just know he'd want me to make sure you're eating and taking care of yourself, and that's all I can do right now. If I'm overstepping my boundaries, tell me, and I'll stop."

"Hunter…" Her bottom lip trembles. "You don't have to apologize. I truly appreciate everything you've done for me even if I haven't shown it."

She shakes her head.

"I don't feel like myself. I'm so fucking sad that I don't know what to do or how to act. Time stands still, but goes by fast at the same time, as if I'm living the same day in hell over and over again."

Tears stream down her face, and I want to hold her, tell her it's okay, and comfort her even if I don't know how. But instead, I stand there feeling like the biggest piece of shit in the world.

"Lennon…" I murmur. "Come sit. It's okay. I shouldn't have said anything. I know what you're going through. It's not easy, and I don't know how I'm going to get over this either. It's the hardest thing I've ever experienced, and the only person who understands that right now is you."

She sits, and I take the food from the bag and hand her some napkins. I ordered the same thing because it's my favorite too.

We unwrap our food, and neither of us immediately eats. Before it gets cold, I take a bite, and she follows. I haven't had an appetite for the past week and haven't felt like going to the gym, though I know it'd probably be good for me to release some of my anger and frustrations. Every waking moment has been spent worrying about Lennon and making sure she's moving forward, as difficult as it is. She's the only reason I've been able to get out of bed in the morning.

"This is so good," she says, taking another bite and sending me a gentle smile. "Sophie's coming to pick me up in thirty minutes. We're getting pedis and manis. I didn't want to go, but she's relentless, so I agreed to shut her up."

My heart bursts with joy at the sound of her little laugh, and I'm glad I called Sophie on the way to work to get her out of the house.

After we eat, a knock taps on the door. Sophie smiles wide when I answer it, and I whisper a quick *thank you*.

"There's my favorite sister!" she calls out, walking over to Lennon and wrapping her arms around her.

"I'm telling Maddie you said that," Lennon teases.

"It's okay. I tell her she's my favorite too, so she won't believe you." Sophie shoots Lennon a wink, then leans over and steals a bite of the burrito that's barely been touched. "Oh mah gah." She moans around a mouthful, taking another bite.

"Hey!" Lennon says, genuinely smiling.

"If you don't finish eating this, I'm gonna," Sophie threatens with a snort as she goes in for another bite.

Lennon shakes her head and stands. "I'm going to change real quick and brush my teeth. Gimme five minutes?"

Sophie nods, and Lennon walks away.

"Thank you," I tell her again, knowing I can go to work without worrying about Lennon wasting away alone.

"Anytime. It took some begging, but she eventually caved when I told her I was coming to pick her stubborn ass up regardless if she wanted me to or not." Sophie laughs and looks around the apartment. The last time she was over after the accident, everything was hectic, and her attention was on Lennon.

"My sister girlied the place up, didn't she?" Sophie stands and makes small talk. The photos of Lennon and Brandon still hang on the wall, and she looks over them as she waits. The reality of my best friend being gone practically punches me in the stomach. The sadness comes in unexpected spurts when a memory is triggered. Thankfully, Sophie doesn't mention the photos scattered all over the place, and when Lennon enters, she turns around and puts a huge grin on her face.

"I hate how pretty you are without even trying," Sophie tells Lennon with a pout.

Shaking my head, I laugh. "You have the same genes."

"Yeah, but she got all the good ones."

Lennon rolls her eyes. "Okay, well, that's what you get for telling me I was adopted for all those years." She smirks. "We should get going."

Sophie heads toward the door and walks out, and before Lennon follows her, she stops and looks at me. "Thanks, Hunter. Right now, you're my only saving grace. And I know you're making Brandon proud."

Though the sparkle in her eyes is gone and the smile is vacant from her face, I know she means it, and that's enough for me. "You're welcome," is all I'm able to get out before the door clicks closed.

I put her half-eaten burrito in the fridge and head back to work. I turn on the radio to drown out the memories of Brandon flooding my mind. The one that keeps popping into my head is how he wanted to propose to Lennon, to spend the rest of his life with her, and it's not fair that opportunity was stolen from him.

Though jealousy consumed me over the past two years, I never wanted this. If I could trade places with him, I would do it in a heartbeat. He had so much to live for.

I go back to the office and basically make calls for the rest of the afternoon. It's annoying to have to talk on the phone so much, but I'm managing this project, and if something goes wrong, it's my ass on the line.

I want to go above and beyond so I can prove myself to my boss. Too many people expect me to fail, so I'm trying to stay focused on completing the job efficiently and effectively without any huge setbacks or disasters. This project is the only distraction I have at the moment. Well, and Lennon.

Soon, the day is over, and as I'm walking to my truck, my phone vibrates in my pocket. Considering I've told Lennon to call me whenever she needs something, I hurry and pull it out, only to see it's Jenna. I swallow hard, exhale, and reject it.

When she found out Brandon died, she texted me to give her condolences, and I thanked her. She's texted me several times since, but I haven't had the strength or been in the right mindset to reply. I made it clear the last time we hung out that I couldn't give her what she deserved and that her feelings weren't reciprocated, but she hasn't given up.

Even if I did feel the same way, I'd need to work on myself before I jump into a relationship because right now, I'm all sorts of fucked up, and it's going to take time.

As I climb into the truck, my phone vibrates, and I find a text from her.

JENNA

I miss you. I hope you're doing okay.

I know she's trying to be nice, but I lock my phone and throw it in the passenger seat instead of replying. I cannot deal with her insistence right now. The drive home is uneventful, and when I walk into the apartment and instantly smell vanilla in the air, I know it's one of Lennon's candles. Anytime she'd burn them, I'd complain about how they reeked, but now I welcome the smell.

As soon as I set down my bag, she looks at me from the couch. "Welcome home."

She's in higher spirits, but considering how grief works, I know it might be short-lived.

"Hey." I give her a smile.

Her phone vibrates on the coffee table, and she leans forward to check it. As I pass by, I notice her parents' picture on the screen, but she rejects it. Instead of asking her about it, I go to my room, grab some clean clothes, and take a shower.

All I can think about is how Lennon will have to spend the next six days in the apartment alone while she's on spring break. Though she made it through one day, I worry how she'll make it through the others.

After I dry off and dress, I walk back into the living room and sit on the opposite side of the couch from her to watch TV. It's some stupid reality show, but she seems to be into it. Her phone rings, and I notice it's her parents again, but just like before, she ignores it.

I look at her and lower my voice. "Lennon."

"I don't feel like talking to anyone. I've done enough socializing today," she says before I can get another word in, leaning her head back on the couch to stare at the ceiling.

"You can't avoid them forever. I'm sure they're worried about you."

Her eyes wander back to the TV, but I know she's not paying attention.

The third time her phone rings, I stand and snatch it before she can reject the call. Her mouth falls open, and her eyes go even wider as I answer it.

"Hello?"

"Hi." I smirk at Lennon, who's frowning.

"Is this Lennon's phone?"

"Yes, it is. But I wanted to answer so you don't have to continue to worry about her. My name is Hunter, and I'm—"

Lennon quickly mouths, "Do *not* say roommate."

"—her friend. And I've been checking on her to make sure she's okay. And she is."

"Thank goodness she has someone looking out for her other than her sisters," her mother says, releasing a relieved breath.

"I make sure she eats and gets out of her apartment. But anyway, she can't come to the phone right now. She's not feeling like herself, but I didn't want you to worry that something was wrong." I smile, hoping she can hear my sincerity.

Her mother is very appreciative and sends her love before I end the call.

Lennon stands with both hands on her hips. "What the fuck?" she scolds in the same tone she used to curse me out in.

I shoot her a grin, though she's not happy.

"You have no idea what you could've just done." She snatches her phone out of my grip when I take my seat.

I'm confused by her statement, so I narrow my eyes. "What do you mean? And why didn't you want me to say roommate? That's what we are."

She lets out a huff and mutes the TV, then turns toward me. As she looks at me with annoyance and anger on her face, all the air in the room evaporates. I wait for her to tell me what the hell is going on and why this is such a big deal.

"My parents didn't know Brandon and I lived together," she explains.

"You never told them?"

"You don't understand how they are, Hunter. They're extremely strict and have very outdated beliefs. I wanted them to love Brandon as much as I did, and if they found out I was living with him, they wouldn't have accepted our relationship. They're extremely religious, and a man and a woman don't live together until they're married. Also, I'm still a virgin."

I burst out into laughter, realizing she's not amused.

"They really believe that?" I wonder if she's joking, but by the serious look on her face, I know she's not.

"Sometimes it's easier not to tell them every detail of my life. Their opinions won't change anything, so it's best to keep my secrets tucked away. Now, I guess it doesn't matter."

"But it does…because *we* still live together."

"Yeah. But *we* aren't dating."

She closes up, building her walls again, and I know she's thinking about Brandon.

"My mother tends to ask a lot of questions. I've already received so many calls from people at church sending their condolences, so I know right now, I'm the talk of the community. I guess that's what happens when your father is the pastor of a megachurch. With the way I feel right now, it's best I don't chat with my parents. I don't want to say something I'll regret or snap at them for no reason. The last time I talked to her, she told me to come home and move back to Utah."

"Are you?" I eagerly ask.

She pauses for a moment and smirks. "Hell no. As long as my sisters are here, I'll be here. I have no desire to be told what I should and shouldn't be doing. I had eighteen hard years of that, and if I moved back, regardless of my age, it'd continue, and I can't. Plus, I love my job. California is my home now, and I don't ever plan on leaving."

My heart pounds hard in my chest. Knowing she's not running away when it would be so easy to do causes a smile to touch my lips.

"Okay, good."

"I do have a trip planned to see them in a couple of months after school ends. Plane tickets are already purchased. Brandon and I were going together." She pauses for a moment. "He was the only person I ever told about how strict my parents were growing up. He understood me on a deeper level."

I want to reach out to her, but I'm on one side of the couch and she's on the other, and it's best if I don't. But when she's in this fragile state, I want to hold her close and keep her together so she doesn't shatter into a million pieces. My only job right now is to be the glue that keeps her whole as best as I can. I almost tell her about my childhood and how fucked up it was but decide to keep it to myself for now. It wasn't easy, so I understand.

"I miss him too," I offer. I miss our Friday afternoon beers and all the shit he'd give me when I was being a total asshole. He'd listen to me talk about things that didn't even matter. I feel guilty for never telling him how much his friendship meant to me, though I hope after all these years he knew.

Lennon unmutes the TV and continues watching this ridiculous show, but as I glance over in her direction, I realize how happy I am that she's here. Neither of us is the best company as broken, hollow shells of ourselves, but at least we have one another in some fucked-up way.

My phone vibrates in my pocket, and it's Jenna again. I reject it and act like I'm watching the most interesting conversation and get lost in my thoughts. When it buzzes again, Lennon looks at me as if I'm interrupting this shitshow.

"If you don't answer it, I might," she taunts but looks serious. "After you answered my mother's call, I kinda owe you one."

The thought of her talking to Jenna has me pulling my lips into a firm line. Before Jenna can call again, because she will, I turn off my phone and stuff it into my front pocket. I feel Lennon's eyes on me, but I don't dare meet them.

CHAPTER THIRTEEN

LENNON

It's been two weeks since Brandon's death, and I'm trying to find my new normal without him. I promised everyone I'd take spring break to work through what's happened, but I didn't. I floated through the week with no concept of time. The days and nights blended, and instead of being twenty-four hours, they felt never ending. As if I were in my own personal prison. I'm in a constant state of sadness, and while the random bouts of tears still come, I've been able to maintain a sliver of control.

I talked to Mrs. Locke last week, and we reminisced about all the good times Brandon and I had over the past two years. She talks about him as if he's here with us and just went on an extended vacation or something. If I didn't know better, I'd say she's in denial, but I get it because it's easier to think about it that way.

I'm up before my alarm goes off as usual. My back aches from sleeping on the couch, but I can't lie in our bed, the one we've shared for almost a year. A fucked-up part of me even wants to leave his dirty clothes and shoes on the floor from when he changed to go ride. Loose coins from his pockets are scattered on the nightstand, and everything is exactly how it was the last time he was here. It's a time capsule of our life together, and I don't want to disturb it.

I've been sleeping on the couch and only go into our bedroom to grab clothes, but otherwise, I avoid it as much as possible.

The apartment is dark as I stumble down the hallway. As soon as I open my bedroom door, I turn on the lights and hurry to grab the things I need before going to the bathroom. As I stand in the shower, feeling the streaming water fall over me, my emotions start to bubble. Every morning, I used to sing as loudly as possible to start my day. However, I haven't felt like it lately. Though I'm sure Hunter is thrilled since he hated it so much. Singing always made me so happy, but right now, there's nothing to be happy about.

After I dress, I walk into the living room and realize how early it is. It dawns on me how clean the apartment is too, which is odd, considering I haven't been keeping up with it. Hunter always had a disaster waiting for me in the mornings, and now he's cleaning up after me.

The sun hasn't risen yet, so I snatch my phone from the floor where I left it last night and see it's barely past six. Instead of sitting around in a dark room, I decide to grab my bag and go to work early. Hopefully, today will go by fast, though I couldn't be so lucky.

I arrive at school an hour and a half before my first class and keep myself busy by reorganizing the instruments we used in the spring program. The last time I was here was for the performance, so my classroom is a complete mess. I'm grateful it keeps me busy until my students arrive. Since school will be ending within the next few weeks and summer vacation will begin, I planned to teach them the history of some of the greatest composers to ever live like Mozart, Beethoven, and Bach.

The day passes by quickly, and when I take lunch, I feel the stares of the other teachers, and all I can do is pretend nothing's wrong and smile. When I heated my leftovers in the teacher's lounge, I could've sworn I heard someone talking about me outside the door, and as much as I wanted to confront who was gossiping, I decided it wasn't worth it. After I finish eating—or try to, considering my appetite is nonexistent—it's time for class to start again.

I feel as if I'm on a stage, putting on an act for each of my classes as we talk about eighteenth-century composers, but I'm grateful I don't have to sing right now, or I might burst into tears. Soon, the day is ending, and I'm relieved to be in the confines of the apartment. After I park and climb the stairs, I sit in the same place I've been sitting every single day. I lean my head back and close my eyes.

For a moment, I think I hear Brandon calling my name. My eyes pop open, and I look around. My blood rushes and pumps through my body, and I try to calm down, realizing I must have dozed off because I'm so damn exhausted, but it sounded so real. Before I'm able to get too lost in my thoughts, my phone rings, and it's Maddie.

Each time she calls me, a picture of us when she first moved to California flashes across the screen. It brings a small smile to my face, and I hurry and answer the call before she's sent to voicemail. There aren't many people I want to talk to right now, but I'll always answer the phone for my sisters anytime they call.

"Hey!" Her excited voice makes me smile.

"Hey, what's up?"

She barely lets me get my words out before she's squealing in my ear.

"I was picked! I got the part!" She shouts so loud, I pull the phone away for a split second.

"Oh my God, Maddie!" I shout right along with her. "I'm so happy for you! I'm so sorry, I forgot about your auditions."

"Lennon. You've had a lot on your plate lately. But I had to tell you because we talked about it not too long ago."

"I'm so proud of you, Mads. Seriously, you have no idea. If anyone deserves this, it's you. You're always pushing yourself to the limit and rehearsing all the time, and it's paid off."

As she continues talking, the smile in her voice is contagious. I can't stop from grinning.

"And guess what? They're even paying me!"

I chuckle. "Because you're a pro! So happy for you."

"Oh my gosh." She sounds out of breath now. "I need to call Sophie. Then Mom and Dad. I think I need to celebrate. Maybe we can go out soon and do that?"

"Definitely. You've got it. I'll let you go so you can tell the masses. Love you."

"Love you too, Lennon. Bye!"

I end the call, and it's the first time in a while I've felt real happiness, and it seems almost foreign. Eventually, I close my eyes and find myself drifting off again, but this time, I welcome it.

A strong hand on my shoulder gently shakes me awake.

"Brandon," I mutter, half-asleep, but when I slowly blink my eyes open, it's Hunter, and his face floods with sadness.

"I'm sorry," I whisper, sit up, and smell Italian food.

Hunter makes sure I'm eating every day even when I tell him I'm not hungry. My life has become routine, and today is no different. He graciously brings me food, and I barely speak to him, though he seems to be okay with just my company. Never in a million years did I ever think we'd be able to even sit in the same room without strangling one another, and now we're having meals together.

"It's okay. I picked up chicken fettuccine Alfredo and got some of those rolls you love," he says, smiling.

I appreciate how sweet he's being, but I wonder when this will end, when he's going to get sick of me and push me away.

We sit across from each other and eat in silence like usual.

Hunter plays on his phone, and I realize how awkward this must be for him to eat with his dead best friend's girlfriend every night.

"I'm sorry I'm not better company," I blurt without thinking.

He sets down his phone and looks up at me with the most genuine expression. "I think your company is perfect." He shrugs, moving his fork around his plate. "You don't force me to talk about what happened or how I feel. You accept me how I am, and you have no idea how goddamn refreshing that is." He pauses before adding, "Okay, well, maybe you do."

I nod with a half-smile and move the chicken around on my plate, not eating. "I don't want all this to be pretend, Hunter. That you're forcing yourself to be nice to me when you wanna tell me to get the fuck out and move on with my life." My voice cracks, and I suck in a deep breath, trying to get ahold of myself. "Without Brandon here, there's no reason you should have to live with me. You didn't choose me as a roommate, and I don't want to be a burden. I was thinking before summer ends, I'll look for a place of my own since this is your apartment."

He slams down his fork, and when his eyes meet mine, he stares into my soul, seeing all my truths, my faults, and the raw, vulnerable version of me I hide from everyone.

"There's no way in hell that's happening. You're staying here, Lennon. This is your home as much as it's mine. And listen to me very carefully," he says firmly, searching my face. "Brandon was like a brother to me, and I knew everything about him and could probably finish his sentences if I wanted to. We were inseparable. Practically grew up together in college. And the least I can do is what he'd want, which is to make sure you're taken care of. He wanted us to get along and had asked me a million times over the past year not to keep fighting with you. But most importantly, he'd want us to lean on each other during this because he was important to both of us. I lost my best friend, but you did too, okay? No one, let me repeat, no one is forcing me to do shit."

His words linger, and my heart threatens to beat out of my chest as I process his words. Hunter's the type of man who says what he means and means what he says. But I can't help but feel like a burden to him, and maybe I'm not right now, but I will eventually be when he's ready to move on. Our situation isn't a perfect one, but it's ours, and I guess we'll cross that bridge when we get to it. I'm grateful he's not kicking me out on my ass because the thought of leaving right now seems impossible. It's something I've thought about while on spring break even if I can't afford to live alone on my teacher's salary.

I swallow hard, keeping his gaze. "Thank you. I want us to get along." My voice comes out fragile and soft, but I don't have the energy to try harder. I don't know what else to say. My words sound so insignificant compared to his.

That earns me a relieved smile. "Good."

After we're finished eating, Hunter puts my remaining pasta in the fridge as he does every night, then we sit on the couch and watch TV, though I can't pay attention to anything that's happening. He flips through the channels, and soon, I'm yawning over and over.

Hunter tilts his head, giving me a worried expression. "Lennon." His voice is just above a soft whisper.

When he looks at me with gentleness in his eyes, it brings me back to the first night we met at the bar. The Hunter sitting beside me is the man I met two years ago, not the asshole I've been living with for the past year.

"You can't continue to bunk on the couch. It's not comfortable, and I know you're not getting any rest. You're always tired and going to burn out. You need a real bed."

I shake my head to argue. "I can't…I can't sleep in that bed, Hunter. With his side empty. It's cold and bare without him. The sheets still smell like him. It's painful enough to walk in there in the mornings. I…"

For a moment, he watches me, then sucks in a deep breath as if he's contemplating something. Taking me by surprise, he places his hand on top of mine and squeezes. "You can have my room. You have to get some sleep."

I'm shocked he'd even offer, but he's been surprising me a lot lately. "I don't want to lie in the same bed a hundred other women have slept in," I say, trying to break the tension in the room while cracking a smile.

Hunter removes his hand and sticks up his pinky. "What if I swear to put clean sheets on for you?"

I twist the corner of my lips, pretending to think about it. "And flip the mattress?" I ask, with raised eyebrows.

"Damn, girl," he says with amusement, dropping his arm. "You're a tough negotiator."

I give him big puppy dog eyes, and he rolls his.

"Fine, if that's what you want, Lennon. I'll even spray Lysol and light one of your girly candles if that's what it'll take for you to finally get a good night's sleep."

When I don't answer right away, Hunter stands and crosses his arms over his broad chest. "Well?" He looks even larger when he towers over me, making me feel small and fragile. Though I'm sure that's how most women feel around him. His muscles alone could crush me if he wanted to.

I study his hard expression, realizing he won't take no for an answer. I bite my lower lip as I try to imagine myself in Hunter's room. In his bed. As weird as it is, I know he's right. The couch fucking sucks. "Okay."

"Thank God." He releases a relieved breath, which makes me smile. He does care. "Never had to persuade a woman into my bed before. Thought you were gonna make me go on my knees and beg for a minute there," he teases, which quickly eases the tension.

"And for a minute, I thought you were being a gentleman," I fire right back, though I'm chuckling at his exaggerated relief.

"I very much am." Hunter winks before he takes off down the hallway. I gather my pillow and blanket from the couch, then hear him flipping the mattress, which makes me laugh.

A few more moments pass before he returns. "It's all yours," he says, waving his hand out to gesture for me to walk ahead of him.

Once we reach his room, I open the door and glance around. I realize I've never been in here longer than it took to throw in the random bras and panties I found lying around the apartment.

Relief floods over me that I might actually get some rest. I'm exhausted from trying to get through everything while sleeping on the most uncomfortable couch of my life. Not that I'm surprised. They probably bought it cheap while they were in college since it's been here the whole time I've known Brandon.

"Let me know if you need anything else." Hunter turns with his pillow and blanket to walk away, but I reach for his arm and stop him.

"Thank you, Hunter," I genuinely say, hoping he sees in my eyes how much I appreciate him.

With a nod, he gives me a little grin. "Anything for you, Lennon. Good night."

He shuts the door behind him. I fan my blanket out on top of the freshly made bed and slip under the cool sheets with my pillow. For the first time since Brandon's death, I relax enough to almost instantly fall asleep, which is a miracle in and of itself, and the only person I have to thank is Hunter.

CHAPTER FOURTEEN

HUNTER

I DON'T EVEN KNOW how to describe these past two months without Brandon. Our normal routines of hanging out on the weekends, hitting up the clubs, or fucking around at home feel like a distant memory now, but at the same time, it seems like only yesterday.

Now the reality of him never coming back or seeing him again hits me over and over every morning I wake up in his room. It's a fucked-up situation, to say the least, but when Lennon refused to sleep in her bed even after two weeks, I refused to allow her to go on like that. I offered my room in exchange for the couch, but when she saw my feet hanging off the edge, she demanded I take her bed. I'm twice the size of Lennon, but I wanted to be respectful of her space. She's barely walked into the room she and Brandon shared and has kept everything the same inside. If sleeping on the couch was what it took for her to finally get some rest, I'd sleep on it every damn night.

However, Lennon handed me a clean set of sheets and refused any excuse I gave her. I wasn't sure I wanted to, considering the endless amount of sex they've had in there, but I was kinda out of options. Sleep halfway off the couch and wake up sore as fuck every morning or sleep in their bed with clean sheets. After the first week, it wasn't so awkward, and it quickly became our new routine.

Each day, I go into my room to grab clean clothes, and she does the same. Then we leave like it's not weird or anything that we switched spaces. She's not so tired in the mornings, but I still hear her crying sometimes late at night. The urge to comfort her is so strong that I often find myself on the other side of the door, ready to let myself in. But I think better of it and force myself to step away and leave her be.

Now Lennon is on summer break and sleeps in, so I tiptoe into my room, grab my things, and quietly leave. I should move my shit over, but until Lennon's ready, I won't. I don't want to overstep my boundaries. I think she likes coming into this room and seeing his things where he left them, but she's not quite ready to stay for more than a couple of minutes. I can't imagine how painful it is.

"Morning," Lennon greets me while I'm in the kitchen. "Coffee. Now," she mutters. The sleepiness is evident in her tone.

"Why are you up so early?" I ask, filling the coffeepot with water.

"Couldn't fall back asleep after someone's loud ass woke me up," she says, but I know she's teasing me by the way she's grinning. I hit the brew button and wait.

"I beg to differ!" I say as if I'm offended by her accusation. "I was being *very* quiet."

Lennon looks at me, then down at the floor. "You have loud feet, Hunter."

"What does that even mean? Loud feet?" I wrinkle my nose, fetching the bottle of creamer for her from the fridge.

"I don't know, but your feet are massive and clunk against the floor." She waves a hand around as if she's trying to think of the right words. "Clammer? Clank? Whatever. You know what I mean." She gets all flustered, which makes me laugh.

"Okay, sorry. I can grab my clothes before bed from now on.

Unless you want me to move them over to my room? Your room, I mean."

I study her face, hoping I didn't upset her. "It's okay. I was only teasing."

Her face holds no expression as she reaches for two mugs and sets them on the counter. "I think I'm gonna read today."

"Oh yeah?" I ask.

"There's a new book releasing today, so I'm hoping the bookstore has it in stock."

I love hearing her talk about getting out of the house without being told or reminded.

"What's it called?" I ask, genuinely interested.

The coffeemaker beeps, and Lennon fills my mug first. I don't use creamer, so I start blowing on mine right away. When I finally take a sip, Lennon answers, "*Snitches Get Stitches.*"

My mouth isn't fast enough to move away from my coffee before it spews from my lips. She starts laughing as I try to hold the cup away from my body. I wasn't expecting that response *at all*.

"Are you okay?" she asks, though she's still chuckling at my expense.

"Um…besides burning the fuck out of my lips, yeah." I set the mug down and grab a paper towel to wipe my chin and shirt. "That's a weird-ass title I wasn't anticipating." I start laughing.

"I know, but that's what makes it fun. It's an MC romance," she admits.

"MC?" My brows rise as I think about it. Wait. "*Motorcycle?*"

"Motorcycle club," she confirms. She pours herself a cup and adds creamer.

"Lennon."

She looks up at me.

"You sure that's a good idea? I mean, considering…" I'm shocked she'd even have an interest in reading that.

She shrugs as if she's unsure. "I think it'll be a way to face my fears or something. I've read the other books in the series, so at least I know what to expect."

Licking my lips, the tip of my tongue feeling burnt, I stay silent as I watch her expression. She wants my approval, to tell her it's okay to enjoy reading even if she thinks she's supposed to be miserable for the rest of her life.

"I think you should get it." I grin, hesitatingly. The last thing she needs is to spiral down again to where she was weeks ago. After finally making some progress, I'd hate to see her beat herself up again. "Only if it doesn't upset you."

Lennon takes a sip of her coffee like it's nothing, probably because it's more creamer than anything else. "Don't worry. If it's too much, I'll put it in the freezer."

I furrow my brows, wondering if she's serious. "Huh?" I grab my to-go mug and pour the rest of my coffee into it. I have to leave for work soon.

"Have you never watched *Friends*?" Her eyes widen with judgment.

"Of course, who hasn't?" I smirk, although it's been a while since I've seen it.

"The episode where Joey and Rachel trade books. He puts *The Shining* in the freezer because it scares him," she explains, laughing at the idea. "Then he reads Rachel's book, *Little Women*, and when one of them gets sick, he gets sad, and Rachel—"

"Offers to put it in the freezer," I finish for her, now laughing as I remember that episode.

"Yes!" She beams. "Best show ever."

Ten minutes later, I'm grabbing my things and getting ready to leave for work. I leave a little easier knowing Lennon won't be alone and wallowing. Either she saves that for when I'm not home, or she's getting better at dealing with her emotions. I'd hate to think she's hiding her feelings for my sake and hope she's comfortable enough to express herself how she needs to. I still have her sisters check on her when I'm not here, and Liam and Mason have even stopped by a few times.

"Don't worry, I'll be okay," she reassures me before I walk out the door. "I cry in the shower, get it out of the way for the day, and I'm usually good until bedtime."

The sadness is evident on her face, though her tone is light. I give her a look, knowing there's nothing I can say to change any of this.

"We should watch *Friends* later," I simply say. "I'll order dinner, and we can laugh our asses off all night long." I figure it's a safe show for us to watch. Nothing overly sexual or sad. We've been watching—or, rather, she's been insisting—on her trash reality shows, and for the most part, I've been allowing it, but enough is enough. A man can only handle so much female drama caused by self-sabotage.

"Sounds like a plan. But I'm still controlling the remote," she adds with a grin.

I shake my head and chuckle. "What else is new?"

Driving to work, I think about Brandon and our old daily routine. Before Lennon moved in, we'd pass each other in the mornings and hang out all night. He wouldn't see her until the weekends, but as soon as she moved in, she consumed his waking moments anytime she was near. He loved her so damn much, that was obvious.

I only wish Lennon and I could've gotten along under different circumstances. I know the majority of why we didn't was on me, and if I could go back and change things, I would. Dealing with my feelings for her is something I was never able to fully process, but I've been able to hide them, shove them down as best as I can, and continue being the friend she needs right now. The guilt burns inside me, knowing how I've felt about her all this time, but I try to give myself a break, considering I never acted on them or would. Lennon is my best-kept secret.

At almost noon, I get a text message.

MASON

I was gonna stop over and bring Lennon some
lunch. You think she likes Del Taco?

I laugh.

HUNTER

Who doesn't? She likes the beef and bean
burritos.

MASON

Good to know. Thanks!

HUNTER

Wait, she talked about going to the bookstore
today. Let me see if she's home first.

I press her number before waiting for his response. It rings twice before she picks up.

"Hey," she whispers.

"Hi. Are you home? Mason wanted to bring you lunch," I tell her.

"No, I'll be home in about fifteen, though. Walking to the registers now," she whispers again.

"Why are you whispering?"

"Because I'm at the bookstore and don't want to be rude when people are shopping and reading," she says in a condescending tone and laughs.

"Okay, just asking." I chuckle, shaking my head. "Did you find your book?"

"Yep! Grabbed a few others too. A new adult fantasy, a young adult romance, and a self-help book on grieving."

I wasn't expecting that last one, but I can't say I'm surprised either.

"They sound…interesting."

"I guess we'll see." She breathes out. "Tell Mason I'll be back home shortly. Wait. Do you know what he's bringing me? Maybe I'll stay," she asks with a soft laugh.

"Freeloader," I tease. "He said Del Taco."

"Hell yeah. Okay, I'll be home as soon as I check out."

After we hang up, I text Mason and give him the update. He sends back a thumbs-up emoji, and I relax the rest of the day knowing Lennon is slowly but surely becoming herself again.

I don't get home until after six and am anxious to eat and watch TV like we planned. Today was the Monday-est Tuesday ever, and I'm over it.

Seeing Lennon on the couch with a book in her face makes me smile. The other two books she bought are on the coffee table, and by the way she's grinning, I assume she's not reading the grief book.

"I'm gonna shower quickly since I was on the worksite all afternoon. You okay with ordering tonight?" I ask, kicking off my boots.

"Sure, that's fine," she answers without looking away from the page. It makes me chuckle.

"Think about what you want while I'm in there because I'm hungry as fuck," I say, unbuttoning my shirt. "Guessing tacos are out of the question since you had that for lunch."

I pull off my shirt and rub a hand over my jawline. Shit, I need to shave too. The scruff's getting a little thick.

"Anything besides sushi, though. Maybe burgers?" I say aloud, undoing my jeans. I'm too far in my head thinking about food to see Lennon's staring at me over her book with perked up brows. "What?"

"Um…" She clears her throat. "Didn't realize you were providing dinner *and* a show."

"Huh?" I look down and realize I'm down to my boxer briefs. "Fuck." I grab my clothes off the floor and turn to walk down the hallway. "Sorry!"

Laughter echoes from behind me.

I was so distracted and eager to get out of my work clothes, I wasn't even thinking. Now she probably thinks I'm a pervert. I've walked around in my underwear before, usually as I'm escorting a one-night stand out the door, but this was like a private strip show, which was unintentional.

I wash off and think about the past two months and how much has changed. Some days are better than others, but Lennon and I are still taking it one day at a time. The grief hits me at random times and is often unexpected.

Not only do I miss my best friend more than I ever thought possible, but I'm struck with guilt anytime I look at Lennon and wish I could kiss the sadness off her face. It's fucked up, this whole situation is, but what happened didn't automatically erase the deep-rooted feelings I had for her. If anything, they've intensified as we've grown closer, and I feel like a fucking prick for it.

On top of that, I haven't gotten laid in over two months, which means fucking random girls to forget about her is no longer my coping mechanism. At least when I was with another woman, I could hide those feelings and bury them in someone else. Now they're all pent-up and piling up.

My dick grows hard thinking about it, and I know I'm an asshole for considering my own needs at a time like this. It wouldn't be the first time I've jerked off to thoughts of her, but now it feels more wrong than before. Still, the desire hits me, and I palm my length, stroking it hard and fast until I'm cursing and releasing a deep, animalistic grunt. I feel like a fucking bastard afterward, but I can never cross that line with her.

Lennon needs a friend right now, someone familiar who knew

Brandon as well as she did, and that's all I ever plan to be. Eventually, she'll move on, and as I've done since day one, I'll step aside and let her find happiness again.

Because she deserves all the happiness in the world.

That day will be here before I know it. This will be a distant memory, and it'll be as if our temporary friendship never existed. As painful as it is to think about, the only way I can fully prepare myself for the destruction of my heart is to acknowledge it's going to happen and even expect it.

"Hey," Lennon calls out, pulling me from my dark thoughts.

I turn off the water and open the shower curtain at the same time as Lennon opens the bathroom door. Her eyes widen in shock as she stares at my body as if she's unable to look away. I quickly grab a towel and wrap it around my waist, scrubbing a hand over my face as the water drips down my chest.

"I'm so sorry," she stammers, covering her eyes and turning around. "I thought you were still showering and wouldn't hear me, and I clearly shouldn't have barged in."

A smile splits my face at how flustered she is, considering the romance novels she's reading. "Lennon," I say her name, but she refuses to budge. "I'm wearing a towel now."

"I-I didn't see anything. I mean, I saw you, but I didn't *see* anything. Wait, that sounds bad. I mean, I saw, but I wasn't looking. Or rather, I didn't mean to look. Like I said, I didn't think you'd be able to hear me over the water and—"

I'm full-on laughing now. "Lennon, it's okay. I turned off the water because I heard your voice and wanted to be able to respond to whatever you needed."

"It's not funny. Stop laughing."

Placing my hands on her shoulder, I spin her around to face me. I tilt up her chin, but she squeezes her eyes tight, and I'm cracking up all over again. "Are you going to look at me?"

She shakes her head. "I'd rather not."

I smirk. "Okay, what is it you needed then?"

Lennon swallows, still insisting on keeping her eyes shut. "I was going to suggest Chinese food and that I'd order it because now I'm starving and wasn't sure how much longer you'd be, but I guess that's irrelevant now."

Studying her features, I notice the freckles on her nose and how adorable they are. Her long blond hair cascades down her back, and I know she's hiding blue eyes behind her lids. Whether she throws her hair up in a messy ponytail or she styles it with lots of curls, Lennon always looks gorgeous without even trying. And when she smiles, it brightens the entire room.

"Chinese sounds great," I tell her softly. "I'll take the chicken and broccoli with fried rice."

"Great." She pinches her lips tight. "I'll place the order."

She turns around quickly and rushes out, shutting the door behind her.

I blink, wondering if that just happened and if things are going to be weird now. The last thing I want is any awkwardness between us, so I try to think of something funny to say once I'm dressed and back in the living room.

"What season was it where Chandler walked in on Rachel after she took a shower and saw her naked? The whole episode she was embarrassed about him seeing her 'boobies' and tried to get him back but ended up walking in on Joey naked instead," I say with a laugh, hoping to lighten the mood.

"Can we please not talk about it? I'm already embarrassed and unable to look at you now."

Lennon keeps her head low and avoids eye contact.

"Too soon?" I quip, then realize how red her cheeks still are. "*You're* embarrassed?" I ask with amusement. "I had just gotten out of a hot shower, and cold air hit me as soon as you opened the door." I sit on the other side of the couch. "I'm the one who should be embarrassed here."

I'm not at all, but she doesn't need to know that.

But that makes Lennon laugh, and I smile.

"Cold air isn't good for a man's pride, by the way. Especially naked," I add, hoping she stops feeling weird.

"I know you're feeding me bullshit so I'll feel less guilty," Lennon accuses, finally looking up and meeting my gaze. "But thank you. I do feel awful, though. I should've waited, but my stomach was growling. After Mason fed me lunch, I buried myself in a book all afternoon and haven't eaten since then."

"It's fine, Lennon," I tell her honestly. "Did you order?"

"Yep. Should be here in thirty minutes." She grabs the remote from the coffee table and turns on the TV. "I bought a few seasons of *Friends* so we can start from the beginning."

We get through one and a half episodes before the doorbell rings. Pushing myself up, I stand and answer it. Memories of the night Brandon died rush through my mind, and I think about how Lennon reacted to the delivery guy. I look over my shoulder and see her eyes glued to the screen, so I'm not even sure if she remembers it.

"Thanks," I tell the man and bring our food inside. Setting the bag on the coffee table, I go to grab some plates and forks. "You need a drink?" I call out once I'm in the kitchen.

I don't get an answer, and moments later, I hear Lennon rushing down the hallway and a door slamming. "What the hell?" I mutter, following the sound. Standing outside the bathroom door, I hear her dry heaving.

Tapping my knuckles on the wood, I call her name. "Lennon? Are you okay? Can I come in?"

She's emptying her stomach, which wasn't full to begin with, and it worries me even more. I don't wait for a response and walk in to check on her.

"Go away." She sounds defeated as she kneels next to the porcelain.

Rolling my eyes, I ignore her request and grab a towel. After handing it to her, I wrap my hands around her shoulders and fist her hair so it's out of the way.

"I think I'm done," she says softly, sitting back, looking pale. "That hit me out of nowhere. I opened the bag of Chinese, and as soon as I smelled it, nausea hit me."

"Hope you aren't getting a stomach bug." My eyes narrow in worry.

"I don't know. Maybe." She wipes her mouth with the towel, and I hold out my hand to help her to her feet. "I did go out in public today, so my system probably went into shock." She laughs at herself. "I think I'll be okay, but maybe no Chinese."

"Probably a safe bet." I smile in return. "I'll find you something else."

We walk out of the bathroom and back into the living room. I take the bag of food and bring it into the kitchen, then place hers in the fridge. Grabbing the loaf of bread, I make her two pieces of toast with butter. Whether or not she's getting the flu, she needs to eat something.

Once I deliver her food, we sit and watch more *Friends* episodes. I keep my eye on her and ask if she's still feeling sick. I offer to bring in a bowl, but she reassures me the toast is helping.

"Thank you, Hunter," she says once we shut down for the night. I have to be up for work early, but time flies when we're hanging out and not drowning in our sadness.

"For what?" I ask, locking up and flicking off the main lights.

She lowers her eyes for a moment, then brings them back up to mine with a small smile on her face. "For not making me go through this alone. Your company has helped me during this time, and I wanted you to know I appreciate it. I'm sure you have a dozen other things you'd rather be doing."

Studying her face, I wonder if she truly thinks that. Walking toward her, I close the gap between us and wrap my arms around her. "I promise, there's nowhere I'd rather be, Lennon." I pull back, looking at her. "You're not bad to be around when you aren't screaming at me and threatening my balls." I shoot her a wink, which makes her swat at my chest.

"You deserved it," she reminds me before her smile falls. "I hope one day I can wake up without this weight of sadness on my chest. It helps knowing I'm not suffering alone, though. I know you cared about him too."

I hate hearing the pain in her voice. She doesn't openly talk about her feelings, at least not in the past few weeks. She seems content with burying them, but the fact she's talking about it now without bursting into tears is a good sign.

"One day at a time," I remind her. Before I have time to think better of it, I pull her back into my arms again and kiss the top of her head. "It's okay to be sad, Lennon. Just don't let the sadness consume you so much that you stop living."

"I know," she says softly. "I try to remind myself of that daily. Doesn't always win, though."

I step back, distancing myself from her. "And that's okay. *Some* days are better than *every* day."

Lennon flashes a sincere smile and follows me down the hallway where we split into our new rooms. Once I shut my door, I lean against it and squeeze my eyes shut. She has no idea how much restraint I've used these past two years, and the fact that she's leaning on me now as we both grieve our loss makes it even harder to keep my emotions in check. Pulling her close felt right. I won't allow her to go through this alone. Even though it hurts more and more each day, I'll be what she needs as I continue to pretend my feelings for her never existed.

Even if it kills me in the end.

CHAPTER FIFTEEN
LENNON

THE DAYS DON'T SEEM as long, and getting out of bed in the morning isn't as hard. Still, the loss exists and hits me without warning. A few nights ago, after the smell of Chinese food made me sick, Hunter showed a caring side I didn't know existed. Part of me says he's being nice because I was Brandon's girlfriend, but I know he's being genuine now. Hunter wouldn't spend his nights with me if he truly didn't want to, but I have this anxious feeling in my gut that things will eventually change, and he won't want me around anymore.

Perhaps it's because I've lived in an apartment that never truly felt like mine. It's always been a temporary living situation until Brandon and I moved out. Now that I have no reason to be here, I'm waiting for Hunter to be ready to move on with his life that won't include me lingering around in my sadness.

Still, he continues to reassure me he has no problem with me being here. I can't even remember the last time he's brought a date home, which is odd considering Hunter's previous habits. He goes to work, comes home to make or order dinner, then we hang out and flip through channels until bedtime.

"Lennon, have you been cleaning?" Maddie asks, looking

around the spotless apartment. Sophie sits next to me and does the same.

"No." I snort. "What's there to clean?"

"Did you get a housekeeper?" Sophie asks, glancing from the living room to the kitchen.

"No," I say, dragging out the word.

They both look at me with confused expressions on their faces.

"Apparently, Hunter knows how to clean after all," I say, chuckling. "Or he does it to keep his mind busy." I shrug, not really knowing why he's been keeping up with the apartment. I was a mess in those early weeks after Brandon's death and barely moved off the couch. Hunter did everything. Hell, he still does.

"I can't picture it," Maddie says. "He's like this big, beefed-up dude, and now you're telling me he walks around in an apron and feather dusts the place?"

Sophie and I burst out laughing at her exaggerations. "I didn't need that image in my head." Sophie cackles.

"I never said that!" I'm laughing so hard there are tears in my eyes.

But now my mind wanders to the moment when I walked in on him in the bathroom. I could've sworn the water was still on, and the last thing I expected to see was a *very* naked Hunter. I pull my lips into my mouth so I don't blurt out my thoughts. My sisters are the last people who need to know what happened. They'd never let me live it down and would probably want all the details. My cheeks heat thinking about it, and I hope neither notices.

"Well, regardless, he's doing a good job," Maddie praises.

"He definitely is," I admit. "But it's as if he's flipped a switch from mega asshole to mega sweet. It's weird."

"Probably trying to make things easier on you," Sophie suggests.

I shrug again, not knowing why either.

"So aside from going to the bookstore on Tuesday, have you left the apartment?" Sophie asks, changing the subject.

"Yes, thank you very much. I did a load of laundry and grabbed the mail," I say smugly, though I know it's not going to be enough to satisfy her.

"Oh, I should've been more specific," Sophie says dramatically, rolling her eyes. "Have you left the premises?"

"No. What for? I'm on summer break!" I try to defend myself.

"That's it, we're going out tonight!" Maddie announces way too loudly. "Girls' night out. We're gonna get shitfaced, have sex in bar bathrooms, and dance like no one's watching!"

Sophie and I stare before we both start laughing. "You need a leash, woman," I tease. "And we aren't doing any bathroom stuff because that's unhygienic."

"I mean, I'm not opposed to the first two," Sophie quips.

"Okay, I'll settle for the Coliseum since they won't kick my underage ass out. We can play pool, and I'll school you in darts." Maddie's nearly begging, which makes it even harder to say no.

"I don't know…" I hesitate. Brandon and I went there a lot, which will be another reminder he's no longer here. "I don't know if I can go in there yet."

My sisters look at me with sympathy in their eyes and are probably wondering when I'm going to allow myself to live again. It's only been two months, but no matter if I'm ready to merge back into life, the world moves on around me. I know Brandon wouldn't want me to waste away and do nothing, but losing him is still very raw.

"Let me think about it," I tell them.

"Think about what?" Hunter's booming voice makes the three of us jump. I didn't even hear the front door open. He's in his work clothes, which are surprisingly nice. I know he works on construction sites, but he's in his office quite a bit too.

"Hunter, talk some sense into your roommate and tell her it's time to go out and have a little fun tonight," Maddie says before I can respond to him.

He shoots me a look, examining my face, then blinks. "Where at?"

"The Coliseum," Maddie responds. "She's barely left the apartment in weeks." She turns all the way around to face Hunter. "Hell, you should come too! Both of you could use a night of fun."

I bite my lower lip, anxious to hear his response. Maddie's good at being unpredictable and blurting out the first thing that comes to her mind.

"In fact, let's invite Liam and Mason, and we can *all* go out!" She claps her hands as if her idea is pure brilliance. "Whatcha say, Lennon?"

Sophie looks as if she's given up taming our sister. Hunter studies me, wondering if he should put in his two cents. I know I should get out of the house, but I'm not sure if I'm ready to be with the gang without Brandon.

When Hunter steps forward, he must sense my concern. He takes a seat next to me on the couch and faces my sisters, who are sitting on the coffee table. "What if we go to Home Base? I know a guy who works there who'll let you in," he says, turning to Maddie.

She jumps up, then wraps her arms around Hunter. I chuckle at the way he furrows his brows in confusion. "Hell yeah! Let's do it!" Maddie gives Sophie a high five, who shakes her head at our little sister.

Part of me is shocked Hunter would suggest this since I know how he and his friends love the Coliseum, but maybe he's not ready to go back there yet either. I'm sure he could see the uncertainty in my eyes, but I'm glad he's going to be there tonight.

"Great, we'll meet you guys there at nine?" Sophie suggests, standing and grabbing Maddie. "I need to give this one a swig of NyQuil so she calms the hell down."

That has Hunter and me laughing. When they're finally gone, Hunter turns toward me.

"Sure you wanna go out tonight?" He studies my face, concern written all over his. "Because you don't have to if you're not ready."

I nod, lowering my eyes before looking back at him. "Yeah. I was worried about going to the Coliseum, so thanks for suggesting somewhere else. It might be fun to try a new place."

Hunter pats his hand on my knee and nods before pushing himself up. "I'm gonna take a quick shower. Do you wanna eat something before we leave?"

"Sure, I was thinking of cooking."

He raises his brows in shock.

"I know how to cook, remember?" I laugh at his facial expression. "Plus, I kinda owe you."

"Okay, just don't poison me." He winks before turning away and walking down the hallway.

It's nothing glamorous, but I make a pan of baked spaghetti with lots of mozzarella cheese and a side of garlic toast. As soon as Hunter emerges from his shower, all dressed and ready, he compliments how great it smells and dives in.

The anxiety of how this doesn't feel weird when it should hit me. Hunter and I eating together is our new normal, yet I'm waiting for the rug to be pulled out from under me. This was Brandon's and my routine, and without him here, I feel as if I've replaced him. Though I know that isn't the case, I can't shake the feeling. After dinner, I clean up, then go to my room to dress.

It's a quarter to nine when Hunter knocks on the door and asks if I'm ready. I can't decide what to wear since everything reminds me of Brandon. The dresses and shirts I wore during special moments or dates are automatically out. It doesn't feel right wearing them now.

"Hold on," I call out, slamming the hangers as I brush through my closet again. I haven't moved my clothes into my "new" room, so he probably needs to get in here now.

"Lennon, if you changed your mind—" His voice is soft, but when his words stop, I look up and see Hunter in the doorway. "Shit, sorry." He closes his eyes and spins around. "I thought you'd be dressed by now."

I look down and realize I'm standing in only my bra and jeans.

After hating the last shirt I tried on, I took it off and threw it on the floor.

"Considering I walked in on you naked, you were probably waiting to get even with me," I tease, though I know he didn't do it intentionally.

Hunter's shoulders shake as he laughs off my comment. "Not true. I'm not Rachel," he says, mentioning that episode of *Friends* that we joked about last time. "I was checking to see if you had changed your mind. If you don't wanna go anymore, it's okay."

I inhale a deep breath and sigh. "It's not that. I can't figure out what to wear. A lot of the things I like remind me of Brandon," I tell him honestly.

Hunter bows his head and nods, keeping his body turned away from mine. I find it pretty funny and ironic, considering he's probably seen dozens of naked women in his lifetime.

"What about that one dark blue shirt with the three top buttons and your black jeans?" He says it so casually that I'm shooting him confused looks, though he can't see me. "I swear I haven't been creeping in your closet. I remembered how nice they looked on you the last time you wore them." His words are coming out choppy almost as if he's nervous to admit that.

"That's a good combo." I dig around for the shirt and jeans and tell him I'll be out in five minutes. Hunter leaves, and I dress, admiring how it looks in the full-length mirror on the back of the door. They're a little loose on me since I haven't been eating much these past couple of months.

When I meet him in the living room, I notice he's dressed in dark wash jeans and a nice gray shirt. Though when I notice how tight the sleeves are on his arms, I burst out laughing. I can't help but glance at his tattoos when I look at him.

"What?" He shoots me a look.

"Don't bend or move because I'm pretty sure that shirt will rip to shreds." I smile, grabbing my purse. I stuff my phone inside and slide on my shoes.

Hunter looks down at his shirt and flexes his arm. "Damn thing shrank in the wash."

"I'm sure," I quip. "You've worn tight shirts for as long as I've known you."

"Well, how do you think I got all those tips when I was bartending?" He waggles his brows, and it brings me back to the first night we met.

"I think it's time to go up a size." I look him up and down.

He grabs his wallet and stuffs it into his back pocket before taking his keys off the table.

"There's the bossy Lennon I've been missing," he taunts, opening the door for me.

"I was never bossy," I argue.

"And I'm a virgin," Hunter deadpans, shutting and locking the door behind us.

"Oh, look. Rude Hunter returns."

He snorts, shaking his head. "Not true and you know it."

We walk to his truck and get inside. I haven't been here since the day of the funeral, and the whiplash of memories hits me in full force. A tear slips down my cheek, and I'm not quick enough to wipe it away before Hunter notices.

"Lennon." His voice is soft and tender. "We don't have to go."

I keep my eyes locked on my feet, trying to find the willpower to do this. I know I can't stay cooped up in the apartment all summer, but this feels like a big step.

"No, let's go. They're all expecting us."

"Look at me," he demands, and I do. "I don't give a shit if the queen herself is expecting us. If you're not ready, we're not going."

Hunter stares like I'm his to protect and care for, which confuses me more than I'd like to admit. I'm not sure if he's doing it because Brandon was his best friend and he feels obligated for another reason. Although I'm appreciative of how much he's been there for me, I need to remind myself we're still only roommates, who are grieving the same person.

"I'm good." I smile reassuringly. "Let's go."

We drive in silence to Home Base. It has a restaurant inside with a full bar. As soon as we walk in, my mood lifts. The music's loud, and people are everywhere. By the size of the crowd, I know it's definitely a Friday night. The guy at the door knew Hunter just like he said and told him he was waiting for two more. Sophie and Maddie arrive a few minutes later, and as soon as Maddie gets through, she fist pumps the air.

"No alcohol," I warn, pointing at her. "You're here to hang out."

"Soph already gave me the lecture." She rolls her eyes. "Are Mason and Liam here yet?"

Hunter checks the time on his phone. "Should be in about five minutes."

We walk to one of the bar top tables and all take a seat except for Hunter. He's standing next to me with his arm around the back of my chair. "You want me to get you something?"

When I turn, his face is directly in front of mine. Leaning back a little, I tell him to surprise me. He asks my sisters what they want, and he's off to place our order.

"I like this place!" Maddie bounces in her seat. "Lots of fresh meat."

Sophie and I laugh at the way she's eyeing every guy who walks by.

"You're like a cat in heat. Ready to mount the first thing that purrs at you," I quip.

"Worse, she's the one purring for a mate," Sophie adds, and we laugh at Maddie's death stare.

"You two suck. I hate you both."

Sophie snickers. "No, you don't."

A moment later, Liam and Mason arrive, and Hunter returns with our drinks.

"Where's ours, asshole?" Mason asks.

"Get your own shit," Hunter tells him. "I'm not your bar bitch anymore."

I laugh at their banter, knowing it's all harmless fun.

The six of us sit and hang for a while before a song comes on that has Maddie out of her seat, begging for one of us to dance with her.

"Hulk…" She drags his name out to taunt him. She knows damn well Liam ignores her every chance he can. "Come with me?"

He grabs the neck of his beer and brings it to his mouth, shaking his head at her request. He rarely talks to her, yet she tries to get his attention regardless. It's this weird game of how many times can she hit on him before he finally gives in to his attraction. Though he pretends to be annoyed by her, lust lingers in his gaze.

"I'll go with ya," Mason finally breaks the tension and offers. "No backing that ass up on me, though."

"Why you gotta be a mood killer?" I hear her asking him as they walk off.

Liam releases a breath, and the three of us notice.

"What?" he asks as if he's confused by our reactions.

"When're you gonna stop pussyfooting around and admit you like her?" Hunter's words come out rugged as if they've had this conversation before, which takes me by surprise. I thought Sophie and I were the only ones who knew.

"She's way too much for a guy like Liam." Sophie smirks, holding back a laugh.

Liam drops his eyes to her and shoots daggers. "When're you gonna stop looking at Mason like you're a lost puppy and ask him out?"

I nearly spit out my Jack and Coke I sipped.

Sophie's jaw drops, glaring. She smacks him on the chest, which has Hunter and me laughing.

"I do *not* look at him like that, you bastard." Sophie narrows her eyes at Liam, scowling. "He doesn't even acknowledge my existence."

"Yeah, and it drives you insane," he retorts, chuckling, and I feel like I'm missing an inside joke between them.

"Someone wanna catch me up?" I finish the rest of my drink.

"They've been going on double non-dates," Hunter fills me in.

"What?" I gasp. "How come no one told me?"

Sophie tilts her head, and her silence is all I need to know. I haven't been the best company.

"We ran into them a few times," she explains. "Then hung out and whatever. Nothing really."

Liam snorts. "It was mostly Sophie trying to talk to Mason, who then talked to everyone *except* her."

"No, you mean it was mostly you trying to ignore Maddie anytime a guy hit on her. You're such an ass." She pushes his shoulder when he tries to sit closer. "Go away."

"Soph, you don't mean that," he taunts, sticking out his lower lip.

When the hell did they grow so damn close?

Not that I'm remotely mad about it, but I'm sad she felt like she couldn't tell me.

"So…" Hunter lingers, pointing his almost empty beer at the two of them across from us. "Sophie wants to bang Mason, except he put her in the friend zone, and Liam wants to deflower Maddie, but he's afraid he's not man enough for the job."

I burst out laughing when Hunter grins smugly at his own summary.

"Alright, I'm caught up now," I say, laughing in amusement.

"Both of you suck. No, *all* of you do." Sophie frowns, taking her drink and chugging it.

"For the record," Liam begins, looking at me, "I don't think that. I'm plenty confident."

"Trust me, Liam." I pat him on his rock-hard shoulder. "We know."

Mason and Maddie are dancing, and for a moment, I'm brought back to when Brandon and I used to dance together when we'd go out. We'd have so much damn fun. He'd spin me around and rock our hips together to the rhythm of the music, and we'd laugh the night away.

A numb feeling hits my gut knowing the last time we danced together was the *final* time. I always assumed there would be another time we'd go out and have fun. There'd always be more kisses and hugs, ass grabs, and we'd wake up next to each other every morning for the rest of our lives. Though we always exchanged *I love yous* like it was our last time, I knew we'd say it later. Never in my worst nightmares did I think I wouldn't get to tell him again.

"Lennon, you okay?" Hunter's voice has me blinking away the fog and there's concern on his face. With pursed lips and brows pulled together, he studies me.

I swallow, shaking my head lightly. "Yeah, fine. Anyone want a refill? Next round's on me."

"Yeah, I'll go up with you!" Sophie offers. "Hulk, you need another drink?"

Liam groans, handing over his empty beer. "Better watch it, woman."

"Or what? You'll man up?" She chuckles, grabbing his bottle and walking with me to the bar.

I can't deny how much I love hearing my sisters laughing and having a good time. I know they both work so hard, and it puts a small smile on my face when they can let loose.

"Should we cave and get Maddie a drink?" I snicker.

"We could get her a diet cherry Coke and tell her there's alcohol in it, and she'd never know," Sophie says, laughing. "Let's do it and see if she notices or pretends to be tipsy."

"We're going to sister hell," I quip, chuckling with her.

"It's our obligatory duty to tease her." Sophie shrugs, then orders.

While we wait, Sophie looks at me with an odd expression on her face. I give her a confused look in return.

"So…you gonna tell me what's going on with you and Hunter?"

CHAPTER SIXTEEN

HUNTER

Lennon and Sophie walk to the bar and think about how good it was to hear her laugh again. She looks gorgeous, as always, and I'm shocked she went with the outfit I suggested. I thought for sure she'd tell me it was a bad choice, but the moment I saw her walk into the living room, I had to remind myself not to react.

The fact she's letting her guard down gives me hope that someday she'll be able to move on and find happiness again. It's all I've ever wanted for her. It's all Brandon ever wanted.

"You know she'll always be off-limits, right?" Liam's words have me snapping my gaze at him.

"What the fuck are you talking about?" I ask roughly, not appreciating his accusing tone.

"Lennon," he clarifies as if I'm a fucking idiot. "I don't know what's going on between the two of you, but she'll always be Brandon's girl. No matter what."

I swallow hard, not wanting to lose my cool with Liam. Fuck, I wish I had my beer right now.

"Nothing's going on," I reassure him. "I'd never cross those boundaries, and for you to think otherwise is pretty fucking shitty, man."

"Look, I'm only calling it like I see it. You two are getting chummy, and I know how vulnerable she must be right now."

"We lost someone close to us," I harshly remind him. "She lives in my apartment that she barely leaves, so yeah, we've grown closer over the past month or two. Doesn't mean I'm trying to fuck her."

Liam shrugs. "Doesn't mean you don't want to, though."

"What's your deal?" My hands ball into fists.

"Hunter, calm down." He keeps his gaze locked on mine. "You're more transparent than you think."

My jaw clenches, not appreciating what he's implying. "What's that supposed to mean?"

"It means Mason and I knew you had feelings for her before Brandon passed. Whether or not you still do, I'm not sure, but now that you two are getting closer, I'm just reminding you not to act on those feelings."

Liam, the relationship wizard. *Pfft.*

I want to ask him how the hell they knew when I never told a damn soul other than Hayden. Didn't make it obvious as far as I knew, considering I was an asshole every possible chance I got. Doesn't matter that he's right because I'm not going to confirm anything.

"Just like you're not acting on your feelings for Maddie? What's up with that?" I turn the tables, not wanting to talk about this anymore.

He scoffs, then laughs. "Don't change the subject."

"Then stop talking about it."

"Okay, let's talk about how you haven't hooked up with a girl in two months." He gives me a look that dares me to prove him wrong.

"Are we gonna paint each other's nails too? Or maybe I can braid your hair while you text scandalous crotch shots?" I quip, turning toward the bar, wondering where the girls are, when I notice a guy standing next to Lennon. He's too fucking close, and she looks uncomfortable as hell. I wait to see if she or Sophie will tell the guy off or not.

"You still dating that Jenna chick?" he asks.

"We were never dating. And no."

"Hmm." He grins, and I'm ready to smack it off his face.

"Fuck off."

Mason and Maddie finally come back at the same time as Sophie and Lennon return with drinks.

"Which one's mine?" Maddie asks.

"This one. We decided to put a little something in there for you." Sophie hands her a glass.

"What, really?" Maddie takes it and sips it. Her eyes widen, and she lights up. "This is delicious!"

Lennon snorts, holding back laughter. She stands next to me as she continues handing out beers.

When she gives me mine, I lean in and whisper, "What'd you girls do?"

"Nothing." She struggles to contain her smile.

I tilt my head, grinning. "Liar."

Shrugging, Lennon takes a sip of her drink. "She thinks we gave her alcohol."

"And did you?"

"Not unless grenadine is alcoholic." Lennon breaks out into a smile. "It was Sophie's idea."

I shake my head, smiling at how she's finally letting loose. I know it's only temporary, but that's how grieving typically works —with constant ups and downs. But for now, I'm going to soak in these moments.

"Did you forget me?" Mason asks with a pout.

Lennon looks around the table and notices two beers in front of Liam.

"Oh, were one of these for you?" He smirks, taking a swig from both bottles. "My bad."

"You fucker," Mason says.

"Liam!" Lennon laughs. "You're buying the next round now. Hold on, Mason. I'll grab another one."

I give Liam a look. He's being a next level asshole tonight.

"Rough week," he offers.

I ignore him and take a drink of my beer, glancing at Lennon. The same guy moves toward her, and Lennon takes a step away, but the motherfucker gets closer.

My fists clench under the table, and it's taking all my willpower not to get involved. I stand, wanting to go over there so I can hear what he's saying. The others are too busy chatting to notice me leave, so I inch closer to the crowded bar.

"So you here alone tonight, baby?" The guy slurs his words. Asshole's wasted.

"No, my friends are here." Lennon's response is short.

"Ah okay, cool. You wanna come hang with me for a bit?" Fucker has balls of steel.

"I don't wanna ditch my friends." Lennon's being way too damn nice for her own good.

"Oh yeah, cool. Well, are you single? You could give me your number, and we could hang out another night." My jaw tightens, ready to get in this dude's face. Lennon's showing no signs that she's even remotely interested, yet he continues to push for her attention.

Lennon freezes, and I know she's lost in her head right now. She's always been able to say she has a boyfriend, and I bet she's wondering how to answer the question.

When she doesn't, I know she needs an out and say fuck it and walk up to her other side.

"You okay?" I ask her, purposely ignoring the other dude.

She looks up at me with tears in her eyes. Yep, I knew she was thinking about how she's single but not by choice and how much that hurts.

The bartender finally comes up and apologizes for taking so long. I slap down a five-dollar bill, and Lennon grabs the beer.

When we walk away, the guy shouts behind us. "Fuckin' whore."

Without hesitation, I stalk toward him. "The fuck did you call her?"

"I think you heard me loud and clear." He stands taller.

"Better back the hell off," I warn, getting in his face.

"I was asking her out, and you come up and pay for her beer, and now she's willing to go home with you?" He scoffs. "So yeah, she's a *whore*. A cheap one too."

It takes me less than a second to pull my arm back and deck this asshole in the nose. He whips back and hunches over, covering his face with both hands.

"Hunter!" Lennon screeches, grabbing my attention. "He's not worth it! He's drunk," she tells me.

She's never seen me fight before, which is something I don't talk about. I've been fighting since I was a teen, not that my dad left me any other choice.

The guy pushes against my chest, blood dripping from his nose. "What the fuck was that for, you pussy!"

People at the bar fan out. I vaguely hear the bartender telling us to get the hell out, but the moment this fucker calls her that name again, I see red and lose control.

I swing again, my fist connecting with his face even harder this time. That should successfully break his nose. "You're gonna apologize to her, dickwad. Have some fuckin' manners when talking to a lady next time."

Before I get a response, Mason and Liam are pulling me away as the bartender threatens to call the police. They walk me toward the door, and I push them off before we get out.

"I can walk by myself," I scoff.

The crisp air slaps me as I hit the sidewalk and start walking. I'm not leaving without Lennon, but she's probably pissed at me for ruining her evening.

I turn around and wait for her to come out. The guys left me out here to calm down so I don't get arrested, but I need to make sure Lennon's okay.

A bit later, she comes rushing out and looks for me. I say her name, and she hurries toward me. I'm in complete shock when she runs forward and wraps her arms around me. She hugs me so tight, I feel every inch of her body. I wrap an arm around her and hold her closely. She pulls back slightly and inspects me for injuries.

"Are you okay?" Her voice shakes.

"Lennon, I'm fine. The guy barely touched me."

I glance over her head and see Liam and Mason. They're staring in disapproval, but fuck what they think. They have no idea that I've beat myself up every single day for having feelings for Brandon's girlfriend. I tried to fight it, and neither knows the pain this causes me. I know she could never be more than a friend. It's all we can ever be. The fact that I knew Brandon's plan to propose eats at me daily, but there's nothing I can do about it. Telling her would only hurt her, and she's finally allowing herself to have a good time again.

Looking down at Lennon, I see her lips tremble. "Are you alright?" I grab her shoulders and force her eyes on mine.

"I can't believe you did that," she says, studying my face. "Why would you get into a fight because of me?"

The fact she's asking that question means she has no idea how I feel.

Friends. *Just friends.*

"Because that asshole called you a whore. He couldn't deal with your rejection."

"So that merits hitting him in the face…several times?" I'm not sure if she's scolding or ready to high-five me.

I release her and brush a hand through my hair. "Lennon, listen." I pause, trying to get my thoughts straight.

"Thank you," she says before I can speak. Her words take me by surprise, and I'm not sure I even heard her correctly. "No one's ever stood up for me before. When he asked if I was single, I…

froze. It was like I couldn't get the words out. I didn't want to say them."

"I know, Lennon." I give her a sincere look. "Wait. You aren't mad at me?"

"Are you kidding? No. I mean, I don't usually encourage fights, but hell, that guy wouldn't get a clue even if I shoved it up his ass."

Her words have me laughing and pulling her in for another hug, then I kiss the top of her head. Fuck it, I'm going to hell for the dirty thoughts I've had about her.

"Still, I should've controlled my temper," I say, separating us. "Sorry for wrecking your night out."

"You didn't." She shakes her head. "Thanks for having my back."

"Of course. Always, Lennon."

Her face contorts, and I know I'm probably confusing the shit out of her right now. She has no reason to believe those words, considering how I've treated her in the past, but I'm determined to be what she needs—a friend, someone to rely on, and someone she can trust.

We ride to the apartment in silence, and it's not even midnight by the time we make it home. Lennon walks to her bedroom, and for a moment, I think she's going to sleep in there tonight, but she comes out with a change of clothes.

"It's still early. Wanna watch a few episodes of *Friends*? I'm not tired enough to sleep." The hopeful look in her eyes has me nodding in agreement.

Even though I should go to bed and cool off, I can't deny Lennon. She doesn't want to be alone, so I'll do whatever she needs.

"I'm going to wash off this makeup and change in the bathroom if you want to get out of your clothes."

"Yeah, I'll go grab some." I walk to my bedroom and pull out a pair of gray sweatpants. I strip down to my boxer briefs, then slide them on. It's been a while since I've done laundry, and now I can't find my favorite California State University T-shirt.

"Hey, Lennon?" I tap my knuckles on the bathroom door. "Did I leave my black CSU shirt in there by chance?"

She opens the door in her pajamas and stands in front of me with a toothbrush in her mouth. "Huh?" Her eyes widen the second she stares up at me. Her gaze rakes down my chest, and I arch a brow at the way she's gawking.

I clear my throat, leaning against the doorframe and crossing my arms.. "Is my CSU shirt in there?"

"Uh…" She blinks, looking around. "Oh." She holds up a finger, then turns to the sink and rinses out her mouth before facing me again. "I borrowed it. It's in my laundry basket."

I raise my eyebrows, not saying a thing. She wore *my* shirt? I don't know why this seems so sexy, but I quickly shake the thoughts away.

"I got warm in my leggings and sweater the other night and was afraid I'd wake you if I came in to get a pair of shorts, so I grabbed the first thing I found. I'm sorry." Her voice sounds so small when she apologizes, and it causes me to smile and laugh.

"Don't be. I was just looking for it and couldn't find it. No biggie. But don't think we're swapping clothes now." I wink, and she teasingly shoves me.

"Funny. Now go put on a shirt."

"What're you trying to say? Don't like my muscles and tats? That's like every girl's wet dream," I taunt, backing away into the hallway toward my room.

"Trust me, I know. I've met your parade of women." She rolls her eyes but playfully smirks, so I know she's not *that* annoyed.

Ten minutes later, we're on the couch watching the episode where Rachel and Ross get into a fight and take a break. During the whole episode, Lennon grins, and it's hard not to smile right along with her. It's so damn contagious.

"Seriously," she begins. "Who gets into a fight with their girlfriend and then jumps into bed with the first girl he finds?

Ugh. He's my most disliked character on this show." She grumbles about it, which is freaking adorable. She's getting all worked up over a TV show that's almost as old as we are.

"But they were on a break?" I say smugly.

She shoves me and hisses. "So? He couldn't go *one* night without getting a woman's attention? Oh wait, look who I'm asking?" she teases, rewarding me with a playful smile.

"Really?" I smirk at her dig and put a hand over my heart. "I almost got into a fight for you."

"I can tell it was a real hardship." She chuckles, her eyes trailing down my body, knowing I don't have any battle wounds.

"Well, now I can see why Ross went crazy. Girls." I shake my head, that nagging feeling hitting me hard in the gut just like when Liam and Mason looked at me as if they knew my secret. The one I've tried so damn hard to hide.

"Uh, no. He could've kept it in his pants," she states matter-of-factly.

"Hey, he was trying to be sweet and romantic for their anniversary, and she basically told him her job was more important," I try to defend the guy, but it's a lost cause. I already know he's an idiot for cheating on a woman like Rachel.

Oh my God. Now she has me thinking these characters are real people.

"We need something else to watch," I deadpan. "I'm too invested."

Lennon snorts. "There's a series I've been meaning to start. It's based on a book and is about a hot stalker or something."

I face her with both brows perked up. "What's wrong with you?"

"What?"

I laugh. "He's hot, so it's okay he's a stalker?"

She pinches her lips and rolls them from side to side, bobbing her head. She shrugs. "It's called *You.*"

"Never heard of it."

"Let's watch the first episode and see what we think," she suggests.

"The last time you said that, we ended up ten episodes deep into *Friends*."

"And look how into it you are now." Lennon smirks proudly. "Okay, maybe you're right. I should go to bed." When she raises her arms over her head and stretches, the fabric of her shirt rises up slightly.

She doesn't move to get up, so neither do I. Lennon glances at me but doesn't say anything. She fidgets with the hem of her shirt and stays silent.

"What is it?" I ask, grabbing her attention. "I can see something's on your mind."

Lennon nods, then turns to face me. "Earlier, you said you should've controlled your temper."

I nod.

"Has that always been an issue for you, or is it recent?"

Fuck. I hadn't expected her to ask something like that. It's a part of my past I don't talk about much to anyone. Not even Mason and Liam know much about my family. Only Brandon knew the ugly truth.

"I guess, around middle school." I shrug, ashamed to admit it.

"Why's that? Does something trigger it?" she asks, genuinely curious.

"Well, if you wanna know, I'll tell you," I begin and swallow hard.

She nods, keeping her eyes locked on mine.

"I'm not sure how much Brandon told you about me, but my dad's a state senator."

Lennon's eyes widen as the realization hits. "Oh my God. Harris Manning. I never put two and two together."

I'm impressed she knows him by name, considering anyone else I've told had no clue.

"I can't believe that's your dad. How cool."

"Yeah, unfortunately."

"Oh. Sorry. Not a good relationship, huh?"

"Nope. He's been in politics my whole life. Started on the city council, ran and won for mayor of Sacramento, worked his way up to attorney general, then lieutenant governor of California, and now he's a senator. He's always picked his career over his family, yet still had time to pressure my brother, Hayden, and me into playing football all through middle and high school and then college."

"I thought you loved playing football?"

"Didn't have a choice. I grew to like it eventually. Mostly because I was able to channel my anger for him through sacking other people." I half-laugh, but it's true. I put all my rage into the sport.

"So you didn't have a good relationship because of all that?"

"Wasn't just that." I inhale, thinking about how much I want to share. Deciding to say fuck it, I tell her the truth. "He had an affair for years, and the media found out. His money covered it up mostly, then he put on this whole charade about having the perfect happy family. Two sons who played football. A loyal wife. He sold himself as a family man to get reelected over and over, and as ridiculous as it was, it worked. I hated him for it. I hated how people fell for it too."

"Oh God." She sucks in a breath, her gaze never wavering from mine. "That's awful. How could he do that?"

"Because he's corrupted by money and his career. I was so pissed when I found out what he did to my mother, but she didn't leave. I still don't know why she stayed or continues to. I love her, but I wish she'd get out."

"Maybe she feels like she has no choice," she suggests with a half-shrug. "A lot of women feel that way, especially when the man is the breadwinner. Maybe she didn't want you and Hayden to have a broken home. Did you ever ask her?"

"I did after the media released it. She told me it was a misunderstanding. Clearly, she was in denial." I groan, remembering it so clearly. "I knew there was no fucking way. There were pictures."

"Eww." Lennon scrunches her nose. "Did your dad ever talk to you boys about it or anything?"

"Nah. He'd have to man up and admit what he did to talk to us. It was swept under the rug like it never happened. He came downstairs for breakfast, talked to us about football and school, then went about his day. Made me so goddamn pissed. That's when the fights started."

"With who?"

I shrug, thinking back to my middle and high school days. "Anyone and everyone. In middle school, they'd pick on me for being from a wealthy family, though I never felt that way, and called me a rich snob. They thought since my dad was in politics, it would be fun to mess with me. After a while, I had enough of it and started pushing back. When words weren't enough to get them to back off, I used my fists. In high school, other team players who got in my face about my dad's reputation got tackled to the ground even when they weren't my targets. They all thought I'd do nothing and assumed I wouldn't be able to because of my last name, but they were wrong because I didn't care. I didn't want any part of his campaigns or his life. So instead of dealing with it through words, I fought people to get my feelings out."

"Wow…" she says, and I realize I probably rambled off way too much information. "I can understand that."

"Oh yeah?" I laugh. "Well, you'd be the first one then."

"It was your form of rebellion and releasing pent-up anger you didn't know how to express. I mean, I sorta did the same thing."

"You?"

"Yeah! I dated a guy my freshman year in college. He was my first real boyfriend since my parents were too damn strict to allow me to date in high school. It was a toxic relationship, to say the least, but I didn't know any better. He used me as an emotional punching bag, and for a long time, I let him. I thought that's what love felt like. But I saw my friends in these loving relationships, and their boyfriends were so sweet and caring. I started wondering what was wrong with me because mine wasn't like that. It finally hit me that it wasn't *me*, it was him, and I got so mad. One day, I found out he was messing around with three other girls, and I felt so filthy. I'd let him be my first everything, and I stupidly trusted him. Everything he'd done to me in the past on top of his cheating made me want revenge. I didn't want to just break up with him. I wanted him to feel the same kind of pain he'd caused me."

"I'm kinda scared to ask what you did, Lennon." I blow out a laugh.

"Well, we were at a huge party with all our friends one night. When it was nice and packed, I told him to come stand in the middle of the room with me. I stood on a chair, told everyone to be quiet, then said 'Malcolm, you sorry, cheating piece of shit. I'm done with you, with how you treat me, and your three-inch dick. It's *not* average. So you can fuck off because I'm done.' Then I jumped off the chair, grabbed a cup of beer, and—"

"Please tell me you dumped it over his head?" I ask with amusement.

"Hell yeah, I did!" She chuckles. "He deserved it too. But anyway, I'd never done anything like that in my entire life. I'd never done anything to grant me extra attention or make a scene before that. However, it was the realization as to what he'd been doing to me, using me, for all those months that finally struck a nerve. I was ready to fight back."

"Lennon," I say with a proud smile. "Who knew there was a badass under those polyester clothes?"

She laughs so loud it nearly makes me jump. I love the sound so much. I want to bottle it up and store it away so I can hear it anytime I want.

"It was a one-time thing."

"Well, I'm glad you stood up for yourself. Bet that guy didn't get laid for a long time."

She snorts. "Pretty sure he left that party with his tiny dick between his legs. Only saw him a couple of times after that."

"I'd hide from you too after that."

"Ha! I'm not that scary. Just don't piss me off and there's no problem."

"Yeah, I learned that the hard way," I quip but realize it doesn't come out that way.

Her lips form into a frown as she looks down in her lap.

"I should get to bed." She pushes herself off the couch and starts to walk away. I'm quick to follow and grab her shoulder.

"Lennon, wait."

She turns around but keeps her gaze low.

"I didn't mean it."

"Sure, you did," she says, bringing her eyes to mine. "All we did was fight up until the night Brandon died, so don't pretend we didn't. I know you hated me. Maybe you still do." She shrugs, and I can see the tears forming in her eyes.

Fuck. Fuck, fuck, fuck.

"You had every right to get pissed at me then," I tell her. "You had every right to yell, trust me. But I never hated you." Even though I wanted her to think I did. "I'm glad you never took my shit, Lennon. I purposely pushed your buttons, and you pushed back. I'm happy you didn't put up with it."

She looks confused as hell, not that I'm surprised. I'll never tell her why I acted out because my feelings for her don't matter. They can never matter.

"I don't understand, Hunter."

"Just know that I'm sorry, okay? I'm sorry for how I treated you, and I don't want us to ever go back to that. I wish I could explain it, but I can't, so you'll need to trust me on this."

Surprisingly, she doesn't push further. "Okay."

"Well, I'm going to lock up and turn off all the lights," I tell her, needing some space between us before the temptation to push her against the wall and claim her mouth becomes too strong to deny.

"Okay. Good night, Hunter." She walks away but stops right as she reaches the bedroom door. With her hand on the knob, she looks over her shoulder until our gazes meet. "Thanks again for tonight."

"Of course." I flash her a small smile. "Night, Lennon."

I wait until she's safely tucked into the room before making sure the door is locked and the lights are off. I'm still worked up, even more now because of Lennon, and I don't know how much longer I'll be able to control myself before I slip up. Sharing my past with her wasn't something I intended to do, but it was easy to talk to her about it. Lennon doesn't judge me. She tries to understand, and when she shared her own story about her past, I forgot for a moment who we are.

Two people bound by grief.

Two people who can never be together.

Two people who need each other more than ever.

As long as I keep remembering that, I can do this. I can be there for her in the way she needs me. *Friends.*

Before I go to sleep, I take a shower and jerk off until my dick is nearly raw. I can't act on these feelings, but I can allow myself to live in the fantasy for a few minutes. As wrong as it is, for just a moment, I pretend I live in a world where we could be together— if she'd even want me.

CHAPTER SEVENTEEN

LENNON

I WAKE up feeling like absolute shit. Not that it's any different from the past two and a half months, but this isn't the same. After last weekend's bar fight between Hunter and that drunk guy, I've gladly stayed inside the apartment. That was enough socialization for me for a while.

Something about that night brought Hunter and me closer, and I'm genuinely thankful for his friendship. I wouldn't be able to get through this without him. When that guy at the bar asked if I was single, I had no idea how to respond. What would I say: "Technically, yes since he's buried six feet under, and I'm still in love with him."

Talk about emotional baggage.

Thank God Hunter showed up when he did. I probably would've broken down in tears right then and there.

I mean, I could've gone without him having to fight for me. But it was a nice gesture considering the guy called me a cheap whore for no damn reason.

Over the past week, I've buried myself in books and even managed to cook dinner a couple of times. I know I'm going to need to go shopping soon because we're running out of shit again, and it's not fair to make Hunter do everything. He works all day long while I'm off, and I should be chipping in more even if I'm unmotivated.

It's as if Sophie reads my mind from across town and sends me a text.

SOPHIE

Wanna hit the grocery store with Mads and me?
I'm sure you need supplies in your cave.

I huff, laughing at her assumption, but only because she's right.

LENNON

I do, but God invented grocery delivery for a reason.

I'm messing with her, but I like seeing how far I can push her.

SOPHIE

Pretty sure God would say get off the couch and go see your sisters. Oh wait, he's talking to me now. Yep, that's exactly what he said. Picking you up in 20. Gives you enough time to scrub off the couch stench.

I roll my eyes. She definitely plays the older sister role well.

LENNON

Rude AF. But fine. Give me 30.

Once I'm showered and dressed, I patiently wait since I'm ready before she arrives. Doesn't take that long since I only blow-dry my hair and don't worry about styling it. For work, I used to always curl it and make it look nice, but while I'm on summer break, I can't find a reason to.

"You look nice," Sophie says as soon as I plop down in the passenger seat. "Smell fresh and clean too."

"You have a very backward way of saying I was smelling like shit and looking like hell," I deadpan.

Sophie drives out of the parking lot with a smile.

"For the record, I'm not feeling the best, so this isn't me giving up or anything. I feel exhausted. Probably coming down with a summer flu or something." I groan dramatically loud as I lean back in the seat.

"Better buy some Lysol. No one wants to catch whatever weird sickness you have." Sophie laughs.

She thinks I'm making excuses, but I do feel off.

"Anyway…" I clear my throat loudly to emphasize I'm ready for a subject change. "How's the roommate situation going? Did Maria's boyfriend move in, or are they off again?"

"Carter's moving in this weekend. Can't you tell how excited I am for it?" She narrows her eyes, frowning. "Apparently, he wanted to wait for his lease to be up and has been slowly bringing his shit over."

"Did you talk with Maria about making some house rules at least? Figure out stuff like food, cleaning, laundry." I only ask because I know what she's about to go through. I know if Brandon's accident never happened, Hunter and I would still hate each other, and I don't want that for her. It's stressful as hell.

Sophie sighs, turning onto the highway. "I tried, but Maria's too in love to realize this is going to change things. She basically said we'll figure it out as we go and that we'll all be responsible for our own messes and food. Except that asshole always eats my snacks when he's over. Carter doesn't even ask. He takes whatever the hell he wants."

"Maybe you should get a mini fridge for your room? At least that way he won't go in there and take it," I suggest.

"Probably a good idea. Well, anyway, I'm going to need you to keep me company and distracted when I'm not at work. Luckily, things are busy right now, so I won't be home much."

Maddie meets us at the store with Erin, her roommate from school. They live in the dorms, but it's set up more like an apartment. Maddie has her own bedroom and only shares the kitchen and living space. We've met Erin a few times now, and she seems sweet. I'm glad Maddie has someone like her to count on because dancers can be cutthroat and competitive during the audition season.

"You have all junk food in your cart." I snort when I look inside. "What happened to your dietary restrictions?"

"We're going on a beach trip this weekend with a few others, and we're in charge of snacks," Maddie explains. "Plus, it's only a few days. I'll be back to ice cubes and oxygen on Monday." She rolls her eyes even though she really is disciplined. She's always had a slender build, the perfect dancer's body, but we like giving her shit anytime we can.

"Pretty sure I gained ten pounds just looking at all of that," Sophie adds with a mock smile. "Oh, speaking of feeling fat, I need to get tampons too."

Her comment makes me laugh because I always feel super bloated before my cycle begins. My periods were so heavy and painful, I finally went on birth control in college to regulate them and ease the cramps. However, after Brandon died, I basically gave up on everything and stopped my pills. Probably need to get back on them so my periods don't try to kill me next time.

"Lennon, you need some?" Sophie asks as she reaches for the ones she wants.

"So glad I don't have to worry about that every single month," Maddie singsongs. Since she's been a dancer for half her life and trained so much, she developed late. In fact, training takes such a toll on her body that she rarely gets one at all.

"No, I'm still stocked from the last time."

"You didn't buy any last time we went shopping," she replies, tossing a couple of boxes in the cart.

Blinking, I try to remember when I bought them. I've only gone to the store a couple of times since the accident because Hunter's been going. "It must've been before that then." I shrug, taking the cart to the next aisle.

"Are you sure? Should I grab a box in case?" Sophie offers.

"Because there's no way you're stocked up for more than a couple of times. Your bathroom is way too small for that."

That's true. "I have a box in the cabinet under the sink." I know that for a fact because that's where I keep all my shit and see it in there each time I grab my blow-dryer.

"Lennon." Sophie inches closer, lowering her voice. "When's the last time you had your period? Aren't you on the pill? You should have it every twenty-eight days."

"Geez, *Mother*." I huff. "Why do you care so much?"

"Because you've gone through some shit, and it can take a toll on your body just like your emotional and mental states. I'm worried about you, is all." She gives me a genuine look of concern, and now I feel bad for scolding her.

"Stress can affect them too," I remind her. "I can't remember the last time I had it, but I stopped taking my pill after the funeral. Mostly because I forgot." I was too distraught to even eat.

Sophie gets out her phone and taps on the calendar app. "What're you doing?"

"Counting the weeks."

"Why?"

"Because if you stopped taking your pill over two months ago and you still haven't gotten your period, that means something could be off." She starts holding up her fingers to keep track of how long it's been.

"I'll go back on it as soon as I get my period and start a new cycle. I don't know why you're freaking out." I continue walking, looking at the items on the shelves.

"You should get a pregnancy test," she blurts out, which causes me to freeze.

She walks up to me, and I turn to face her. "Have you lost your mind?" I'm getting angry now. "You know I haven't had sex with anyone."

"Lennon, I'm sorry. I'm not saying you have. But you could be pregnant. Brandon passed away less than three months ago. You could've gotten pregnant right before."

I hear the sincerity in her tone and know she's not trying to upset me, but the reality is I don't want to discuss this right now in the middle of the grocery store.

"That'd make me like over two months pregnant, Soph. I think I'd know by now." I scoff at the insane thought.

"Not always. A lot of women don't show the first trimester or even have symptoms. I knew a girl who didn't find out until she was basically giving birth."

I wrinkle my nose at the thought. That seems impossible.

"What's taking you guys so long?" Maddie interrupts, walking up behind us. "Having a sisterly chat without me?" She stalks around the cart and faces us. "What's wrong?"

Turning away from Sophie, I respond, "She thinks I'm pregnant."

"What?" Maddie covers her mouth when she realizes how loud she is. "I mean, how?"

Sophie and I both give her a look.

"No, dummies, I know *how*. I meant, wouldn't you know by now if you were?" She's treading lightly, and I appreciate the fact she doesn't assume I'm sleeping with another guy already.

"Instead of fighting about it, let's get you a test?" Sophie suggests.

"I'm not pregnant," I say dryly.

"Have you had any symptoms? Why does Soph think you're knocked up?" Maddie asks.

"She hasn't had her period since before Brandon died," Sophie replies.

"Gee, why don't we broadcast it over the loudspeaker?"

"Well, isn't it common for your body to change during a traumatic event or something?" Maddie asks.

"See?" I point my finger at her. "Exactly what I'm saying. Sophie thinks I'm whoring around."

"I never said that!" She scowls. "But let's think about this. Aside from no period, you're fatigued, you haven't had any appetite, and your hormones are all jacked up." She holds a hand up to stop me when I try to defend all those things. "Those could be symptoms from grieving, I'm not saying it couldn't be, but it could also possibly be due to pregnancy. Those are all signs, and if you weren't grieving, you'd know one hundred percent that something was different. So take a test and know for sure. For my sanity, please?"

I hate that she has a point even though I'm certain she's wrong and making this a much bigger deal than it is.

They stare at me, waiting.

"Fine. I'll take a test if that'll shut you both up!"

"Okay, I was on your side until that last comment, so now I'm Team Pregnancy," Maddie says with a smug grin.

I can't be pregnant. There has to be another explanation for missing it.

I stopped taking my pills.

My cycles are all jacked up because of how much stress I've been feeling between losing Brandon and working. Except now I'm not due back to work for a couple more months. So my period will probably show up, and this whole thing will be a total waste of time.

I haven't had the appetite to eat because I've been too damn sad to even care about food.

Ugh, but fuck it. If it'll shut them up, I'll pee on a damn stick.

I march over to the aisle and look at all the options. Why do there have to be so many? When I don't return, Sophie and Maddie hunt me down.

"What's wrong?" Sophie asks.

"I don't know which one I'm supposed to get. Early response? Pink lines? Blue lines?"

"Have you never had to buy a prego test before?" Erin chimes in, and I didn't even realize she was behind us.

"No," Sophie, Maddie, and I all respond at once. Having a baby before being married was always out of the question. Our parents would lose their damn minds and disown us. It's why I could never tell them Brandon and I lived together 'in sin.' I love them and want their approval so bad that lying was the better option.

"The digital ones have more clear readings," Erin confirms. "But the pink line ones are cheaper."

"Fine." I grab a box that says 99.99% accurate and has two tests inside. "Happy now?" I ask my sisters, making a show of tossing it into the cart and walking away.

That's gonna be a waste of fifteen bucks.

Less than an hour later, we're back at the apartment, and I only got enough food for the week. I didn't have time to ask Hunter what he wanted, so I got the essentials for now.

"Want help?" Sophie asks when I take the two plastic bags and a gallon of milk from the trunk.

"Nah. They aren't that heavy."

"You want help to unpack everything inside?" she asks, nearly hanging out the window.

"No…" I give her a weird look. "You just want to come up and make me pee on that stupid test."

"Duh! I'm curious. Plus, you're my sister, and I'm worried." She gives me a pouty face so I can't be mad at her overbearing behavior.

"When I drink enough to gain the courage to take the test, I'll let you know."

"You can't have alcohol!" She nearly jumps out of the car.

"Oh my God, I'm messing with you!" I laugh. "Calm down. I'm not that dense. I know the basic pregnancy dos and don'ts."

"Please call me when you take it, okay? I wanna be there for you."

"I know. Thank you."

We say our goodbyes, and I go inside the apartment and start unloading everything. I always organize things beforehand so when the checker bags my items, the freezer, pantry, and nonfood items are together. They're all laid out on the counter when the door opens.

"Lennon?" Hunter calls.

"In the kitchen," I respond, putting the milk in the fridge and moving some things around to fit the meat and yogurts. "You're home early. Unless you came to bring me lunch."

Hunter doesn't always have the time to pick something up like he used to, and that's fine because I hate being a burden. Though I can't deny I appreciated it when he did because I had no desire or energy to think about making anything for myself.

"I have a meeting in an hour across town and forgot some shit."

I turn and admire him. His slacks and button-up shirt are so snug they look painted on. I'm sure his female coworkers don't mind, though. "But I did bring you a fish sandwich from—"

As soon as the smell hits me, I step back and cover my mouth with the back of my hand. "That has to go. It smells." I'm across the kitchen by the time Hunter understands.

"Oh, sorry. I'll take it with me." He's out of the kitchen, and I finally release a breath.

My eyes snap to the counter where the pregnancy test box sits. Hoping he didn't notice it, I push it behind the coffeemaker to hide it. Then it hits me.

Oh my God.

The smells.

The nausea.

The throwing up.

No. No, no, no.

This has to be a weird coincidence. I can't be pregnant.

"Want me to get you something else?" Hunter walks in and asks. He takes one look at my face and steps closer. "Lennon. Are you okay? You look really pale." Hunter closes the gap between us and cups my face and studies me. "Are you sick?"

I don't know what to say. He's had to put up with me being here all this time, so there's no way he's going to want a baby living here.

Hell, I can't process this right now. I don't want to tell him anything until I know for sure.

"I'm just tired. Sophie and Maddie dragged me to the grocery store with them. Hopefully, I'll feel better after a nap."

Hunter narrows his eyes as if he doesn't believe me, but he doesn't push it. Releasing me, he tells me to call if I need anything. He grabs his work stuff and is out the door.

I grab the pink box and head to the bathroom. I've never taken a pregnancy test and try to quickly read over the instructions.

"Okay, well, seems pretty basic. Pee on the stick, wait two minutes, life changes forever," I mutter to myself, my hands shaking as I take off the cap. Since there are two tests, I decide to pee on both of them.

Once I'm done, I set them down on the counter and pace the tiny bathroom floor. It's then that I think about what this could mean if I am.

The last time Brandon and I had sex was the night before he died. That was two months ago. If I remember from learning about this in school, a pregnancy gets calculated from the first day of your last period, so it's like two weeks before conception. That means if I am, I'd be ten weeks pregnant already.

The realization hits me hard and fast. I could be having Brandon's baby, and he's not even here to experience this with me. He won't get to meet his child. I won't have a husband to rely on and be joyful with. Leaning against the bathroom door, I fall to the floor. I can't raise this baby alone. My parents will never approve. So not only will my baby not have a father, but it won't have grandparents either.

My phone goes off, telling me the two minutes have passed, and it's time to know for sure. My palms are sweaty, and my heart is beating so hard, I can feel it all over my body. Part of me already knows what I'm going to see when I look at those tests.

Crawling over to the counter, I grab the two sticks from the sink and lower them. I clench my eyes tight, trying to steady my breathing before I open them and look at the two lines in front of me.

Positive. Both of them.

Two bright-ass pink lines.

The tears fall as I come face-to-face with reality and what this means for my future.

A future without Brandon. The grief hits me all over again.

I curl up into a ball on the floor, unable to find the strength to move as I cry myself to sleep.

A loud knock on the bathroom door startles me awake, and as I peel my eyes open, I realize I'm still on the floor and have no idea how much time has passed. I can't believe I fell asleep, and now my body is sore from lying on the tile. As I pick myself up, I see the two tests next to me and tear up all over again.

"Lennon, you okay?" Hunter knocks again. "I got home about twenty minutes ago and am starting to get worried about you."

"I'm fine," I croak out. "Be right out."

Shit.

He just got home from work, which means I've been in here for hours.

Standing, I stuff the two tests in my back pocket and look at myself in the mirror. I'm a hot fucking mess. My face is blotchy, my hair is still pulled up from this morning, and you can tell I've been crying. You'd think all my tears would've dried up after Brandon's death.

After washing my face and adjusting my hair, I leave the bathroom and walk into the living room. Hunter's digging around in his bag, and when I take a seat on the couch, he lifts his head and studies me.

"Shit, Lennon. Are you sure you're okay?"

I shake my head, my gaze staring into nothingness. "No. I don't think I am."

Hunter moves around the coffee table and comes into my view, and though my eyes don't focus on him, I can feel his movements.

But a part of me feels numb.

How could this be happening now?

Being pregnant should be a positive and happy experience, but all it does is finalize the fact that Brandon's never coming back.

And I'm alone. I have my sisters, but I can't expect them to rearrange their lives for me. They each have dreams they're chasing too. I nearly gasp for air when I think about my parents and what their reaction will be.

"You're starting to scare me," Hunter says. "Did something happen?"

My heart races as I blurt the words, "I'm pregnant."

Hunter stares for a long moment, and I know he's just as shocked as I am. When I'm certain he's not going to say anything, I open my mouth, but he speaks first.

"Wow…uh. You're sure?" He brushes his hand through his hair as if he's trying to process all of this.

Leaning over to one side, I grab the tests from my pocket and hand them to him.

"Well, I'm 99.99% sure."

He blinks, trying to read them.

"Two lines means positive…"

"Uh, yeah. I figured that out. I'm just—"

"Don't worry. It's not your responsibility," I blurt, worried he's thinking about the worst-case scenario. I didn't tell him because I expected him to do anything, but more so because of our newfound friendship. "Just because Brandon was your best friend doesn't mean you now have to take care of me or our baby. So I'll start looking for another place as soon as I can." I shift to stand, but Hunter grabs my knees and gently pushes me back down.

"Why the hell would you think that's what I was thinking or going to say?" His tone is harsh, and my heart beats rapidly, my breath increasing at how hurt he looks. "Have I not proven to you over the last two months that I want you here? That this place is as much mine as it is yours? Have I not shown you that I have your back no matter what?" His volume increases with each question as if he's upset, which confuses the hell out of me.

"Hunter, I assumed—"

"I've apologized to you over and over for the way I treated you. I know I was a dick, okay? I've been trying to make it up to you because I didn't want either of us to grieve alone." His tone holds so much sincerity that it makes my heart hurt seeing how regretful he feels about the past.

"Hunter, it's not that," I try to reassure him. "But this is more than leaning on each other through a hard time. This is a *baby*. I don't even know how to process this, much less expect you to. It's easy for you to say that you want to be here for me, but what happens when you're ready to move on with your life? How are you going to bring a girl home when your roommate's baby cries all night long? Why would you even want that? You're used to going out all the time. I know you're going to eventually want that again. You can't know how this will change everything, but it will. This changes *everything*."

Instead of firing back like I expect him to, he stands and walks off. Hunter's done nothing wrong, but here I am, pushing him away. I know it's for the best. He wants to think we can still go on like this as two roommates, but eventually, he'll want his old life back. And when he does, I'll be left to pick up the pieces of what's left of mine.

When he doesn't return to the living room, I decide to go find him instead. I hate that he thinks I don't appreciate everything he's done because I have so much. This is more than feeding me and making sure I get a good night's sleep. This is a life-changing moment, and he doesn't have to take responsibility for it. I don't expect him to.

His bedroom door is half open, so I assume he's in there. Probably to pack up my shit and give me a head start out the door. Hell, I wouldn't blame him if he did.

"Hunter, I'm—" I push it open to check if he's inside, and my jaw drops when I see him standing in only his boxer briefs. His back is ridiculously cut, like the rest of him, and tattoos wrap around his side. Part of me has always wondered what they represent.

He doesn't turn around at the sound of my voice but continues to dig through his dresser. He grabs sweatpants and a T-shirt and spins to face me. "I'm moving my clothes over to the other room, and you should do the same. This room is bigger and will fit a crib and whatever else you'll need. This is your room now."

I release a gasp, shocked. "Hunter," I start, but he cuts me off and closes the space between us. He's only a couple of inches from me, and I'm pretty sure he can hear the rapid beating of my racing heart.

"Nothing you can say or do will make me want you out of my life, Lennon. You got that? You aren't leaving. I'm not leaving. This is our home, and we're going to make it work. I don't give a fuck about my old lifestyle. Trust me. It wasn't what you thought anyway, and I have no desire to return to it. You can yell, make your assumptions about me, and call me an asshole all damn day, but I'll still be here for you. Nothing's going to change that, so you better get used to it."

I suck in my lips at his blunt honesty. It's the last thing I expected from him, but if I've learned anything these past several weeks, it's that Hunter isn't anything like I thought. He's more unpredictable and has proven that to me over and over.

"I'm sorry." I swallow hard. "I hope you know how much I appreciate everything you've done for me. This has nothing to do with our rocky past, Hunter. It's ancient history now."

He nods, keeping his gaze tight on mine. "Good. So you're staying?"

I can't help but laugh. "Yes. I'm staying."

Hunter wraps his large arms around me and kisses the top of my head. "You're going to get through this, Lennon. You always do."

CHAPTER EIGHTEEN

HUNTER

AFTER FINDING out about Lennon's pregnancy last night, I experienced a whirlwind of emotions—happiness, anger, excitement, and even bitterness. The truth is, I don't know what or how to feel because I'm in complete shock. Part of me is happy Brandon left a piece of himself behind, but it also breaks my fucking heart that he'll never know he and Lennon created a little miracle. He would've been overjoyed about the news, so damn happy and proud. I have no doubt he would've been a great dad. When I close my eyes, I can almost imagine his exact reaction, and I try to find peace in that, though it's another reminder that Lennon will always be Brandon's girl.

My thoughts are all over the place as I get ready for work. I meant every word I said to her. She's staying, and I'll help her any way I can during her pregnancy and once the baby arrives. I have no clue what I'm doing, like a new dad wouldn't, but I'm going to try to prepare the best that I can.

The apartment is dark, and since Lennon is still sleeping, I try my best to keep quiet. As I pour coffee into my to-go mug, I think about the news. Her being pregnant makes so much sense—the mood swings, loss of appetite, nausea. Combined with the stress and sadness of losing Brandon, though, no wonder she didn't notice. But it explains so much. I'm surprised I didn't think of the possibility sooner.

Before heading to work, I crack open the door to check on her. She's sleeping soundly, and she's snoring lightly. On the bedside table, there's a stack of her books, and it makes me smile knowing she's still invested in them. I quietly close the door and leave for the day.

I spend most of the morning going back and forth between the jobsite and the office. We're finally pouring the foundation for the condos and seeing the footprint of the buildings blows my mind. Sure, we mapped it out, and I've studied several schematics, but standing in front of it is almost unbelievable. We have four more months to go on the build and this project will be over. As long as no disasters happen, I'll be moved to another one. The hours pass quickly, and as I'm loading shit into my bag, I get a text from Lennon.

LENNON

Do you have plans tonight? 😢

The smiley face is perfectly placed at the end because she knows damn well my world revolves around her right now.

HUNTER

Just hanging out with my wang out.

LENNON

OMG! Could you keep your wang in? I invited my sisters over for dinner. I need to tell them the big news. It's not something I want to text or do over the phone. Would you be here with me, please?

A smile touches my lips, one that she causes because she wants me there with her. If someone had told me six months ago this would be my life, I'd have called them a fucking liar to their face.

HUNTER

I'd be honored.

LENNON

Thank you. I just can't do it alone, you know?

HUNTER

I'll always be there for you, Lennon. No matter what.

And I mean every single word I text her.

LENNON

I'm so thankful for you. I know Brandon would be too.

Another punch straight to the gut.

There's so much I want to say to her, but instead, I keep it short. It's better this way.

HUNTER

I'll be home soon 

I stand in my office and run my fingers through my hair. It's so easy for me to live in this make-believe world where Lennon secretly feels the same way about me, but I know that's not the case. I'm not trying to swoop in and steal her. Boundaries—I've got to make them and not break them.

On the way home, I try to imagine how Sophie and Maddie are going to react. Considering they're the ones who forced Lennon to buy a pregnancy test, I doubt it'll be a complete shock. I bet there are a few told you sos thrown in because that's how Sophie is, being the oldest sister and all.

When I make it to the apartment, music blares throughout, and it smells so damn good. I drop my bag by the door and walk to the kitchen where Lennon dances around in those damn tiny jean shorts and a tank top, mixing something in a bowl. I lean against the doorframe and watch her, soaking this all in and wishing things were different for us.

"Holy shit!" she screams, pointing the mixing spoon at me with a death grip.

I burst into laughter. "Sorry! I didn't want to interrupt your solo."

She places a hand on her hip. "You almost made me pee myself, which apparently is another delightful symptom I get to experience."

I shake my head and snort, walking farther into the kitchen. "Whatcha cookin' for me?"

"Homemade chicken pot pies," she answers with a smile. "For *everyone*. I was watching the Food Network earlier today, and it looked good." She shows me her phone where the recipe is. "So I thought I'd try it."

"So you find out you're pregnant and become Betty Crocker?" I quip.

She's always cooked with the exception of the past couple of months.

That earns me a smirk.

"When the cravings call, you follow them." She shrugs unapologetically.

Lennon pulls the crust off the cookie sheet and stuffs it in a baking dish. After she pours in the filling, she carefully places the second dough on top and puts it in the oven.

"I'm gonna take a shower. How much time do I have?" I ask.

"My sisters will be here in twenty minutes."

I nod. "It'll take me ten."

I rush to the shower and turn on the water. I told her it'd take me ten minutes, but I finish and get dressed in eight. There's just enough time for me to walk into the living room and sit on the couch before a knock echoes on the door.

"I got it," I call out as she comes rushing out of the kitchen. She makes it just past the couch when the timer goes off on the oven.

"I didn't change clothes!" She looks down at herself. "Shit!" She goes back to the kitchen, the timer stops, and I hear the oven door pop open.

Laughing, I open the door. As soon as I do, Maddie and Sophie rush inside.

"Oooh, you smell good," Maddie says, making a show of inhaling my chest. Sophie smacks her shoulder.

"Don't start."

Maddie plops down at the kitchen table with a huge smile on her face. "Lennon, why'd you insist Buzz Killington come over too?"

Sophie rolls her eyes and sits at the table as Lennon comes out carrying the masterpiece she made.

Maddie's eyes widen. "Holy shit. You made this?"

Lennon beams proudly and passes out the plates and forks. "Why's everyone so shocked? I know my way around the kitchen!"

"Because growing up, cooking meant Pop-Tarts and a can of tuna," Sophie adds to the blow.

When I burst out into laughter, all three of them turn and look at me, then go back to giving each other shit. I can only imagine how they were all under one roof.

Lennon's soft gaze meets mine, and she lets out a ragged breath. Her sisters aren't paying attention as they scoop food onto their plates, but I notice every little thing about her, even if she thinks I don't.

Once we all have food and start eating, Lennon clears her throat, and I can tell she's nervous. I look over, encouraging her with one simple glance.

"I'm sure you two are wondering why I invited you over," she begins. I can see her pulse throbbing in her neck. I almost reach over to hold her hand, to calm her, but I don't.

"To tell us you and Hunter are finally a couple?" Maddie says with a huge grin.

Lennon's face contorts. "What?"

"No," I add at almost the same time, seeing how Lennon's face reddens at Maddie's words. Sophie gives Maddie the death stare, and she shrugs like it's no big deal. I'd find it humorous that Maddie constantly gets scolded by them, but I'm too terrified to react because I don't want Lennon to see my true feelings.

"I'm not sorry for saying that. So I'm not gonna apologize." Maddie playfully smirks. "I mean, come on!" She flails her arms in the air, and it takes all the willpower in the world not to look at Lennon for a reaction.

"We're just friends, Maddie. Stop it. You're embarrassing me," Lennon sternly tells her, glancing at me with apologetic eyes.

Sophie clears her throat, then places her hand on Lennon's. "You took the test without calling me first. You're pregnant, aren't you?"

Lennon swallows hard and nods.

"You owe me twenty bucks." Sophie turns to Maddie with a chuckle.

Both of them stand and rush to Lennon, wrap their arms around her, and I lean back and watch the three of them, seeing the love they have for each other.

Sophie starts crying. "I'm so happy for you. I know how much you've wanted this, wanted a family."

My heart feels like it's being torn into a million pieces. At any moment, I could throw it up in the air as celebratory confetti. It's official. I'm a bastard for being jealous that I wasn't the man to give her this. It wasn't in the cards for me, *can't* ever be.

"Great, now I'm crying too," Maddie says.

"Stop!" Lennon sniffles with a half-laugh. "You're making me so emotional."

I stand and grab one of the boxes of tissues from the living room and pass it around. It's a happy moment, one that should be cherished. After they've exchanged hugs and cried tears of joy, we sit and finish eating. The room gets quiet, other than the sounds of our silverware scraping against plates.

"So," Sophie begins, "when are you going to tell Mom and Dad?"

Lennon stills. "I haven't thought that far ahead yet, but as soon as I do, you all will be the first to know because I'm going to get disowned."

"They'll get over it," Maddie says with certainty, glancing

down at the tattoo on her wrist, one of many, I've heard. "And we'll be here for you, no matter what."

Lennon smiles, but I can tell she's getting lost in her head. I wish I could say what I want, but I keep quiet. My mind's still hung up on what Maddie said, and I realize the only person who doesn't see how I feel about Lennon is Lennon.

Once everyone's finished eating, I take everyone's plates to the kitchen. Once they're rinsed and in the dishwasher, I work on the rest of the kitchen. When everything is spotless how she likes it, I peek my head out and tell them I'm going to bed.

"Already?" Lennon says, shooting me a smile.

"Yeah, I'm tired. Long day," I tell her with a grin and leave them to sister time.

A week has passed since the big news. Lennon doesn't want to tell anyone else besides her sisters and me until she sees her doctor. As we're sitting on the couch watching another episode of *Friends*, she bursts into tears.

"Lennon?" I ask, confused at her sudden breakdown. "Everything okay?"

She sniffles. "Sorry. I'm scared about tomorrow and having to go to my OB alone. Sophie and Maddie can't break away from work and—"

"I'll go with you," I blurt without thinking.

She wipes tears from her cheeks. "You'd do that for me?"

When I move closer, she leans into me. I wrap my arm around her small frame, and she hugs me, melting into me fully. It takes everything I have to keep my emotions at bay and not pull her onto my lap.

I place my hand on the back of her head. "I'd do anything for you, Lennon. What time?"

She sucks in a deep breath. "Ten." She pulls away and looks up at me. "Are you sure? What about your job?"

"Absolutely. Let me worry about work," I tell her. "Plus, I don't know anyone who's cried during one of the funniest episodes of *Friends*." I wipe away a rogue tear that's struggling to spill from her face, and she watches me.

If I weren't keeping the biggest secret of my life from her, I'd be kissing those tears away.

Letting out a stifled laugh, she sighs. "Thank you. I feel like all I'm doing is thanking you lately. And it doesn't feel like enough."

"It's more than enough," I tell her, forcing myself to move away. "Want to watch the next one? We're almost done with season three."

Lennon nods and leans back on the couch. I feel her eyes on me, but I keep mine facing forward. *Boundaries*, I remind myself.

The next morning comes quickly. It feels like my alarm was screaming for me to wake up as soon as I closed my eyes. I go to the office and take care of some paperwork before I leave and pick up Lennon for her appointment. She meets me in the parking lot to save time.

"I'm so damn nervous," Lennon says, her leg shaking in anticipation as we drive to the clinic.

"It's going to be fine. I'm sure you're a little excited." I'm trying to be as supportive as I can because right now, more than ever, she needs it.

"Yes, I'm excited," she says, flashing a half-smile before she adds, "Sad, though, too."

I wondered when she'd mention it.

Reaching over, I grab her hand and squeeze it. She doesn't flinch or pull away, but I do before it gets awkward. I put my fingers back on the steering wheel, not knowing what came over me. It felt right and natural, and it must've for her as well.

As I turn into the parking lot, we both stare at the building. Lennon lets out a deep breath and a nervous laugh.

"We've got this." I unbuckle and open the door. She follows my lead, and we head inside. We sit in the waiting room as she fills out the necessary paperwork, and a long twenty minutes later, they finally call her name.

For some reason, I'm as nervous as she is. I have no idea what to expect with a visit like this, so I can only imagine the anxiety she's feeling. I don't want there to be any issues with her or the baby for obvious reasons but also because she can't handle any more bad news.

We follow the nurse to an exam room where they take her weight and height. The nurse asks her a thousand questions based on her paperwork, gets her blood pressure reading, and then asks about her last period. Lennon can't give her the exact date, but she gives an estimated timeframe. If talking about this in front of me is awkward as hell for her, she doesn't show it. Lennon answers all the questions effortlessly, describing how she's been feeling and talking about her diet. Once the nurse has everything she needs, we're informed that Dr. Potter will be in shortly.

Fifteen minutes later, the doctor enters with a file in her hand. "There's the happy couple! Congratulations on your pregnancy," she says with a big smile, looking back and forth between us before taking her seat at the tiny desk.

"Oh, um," I begin but quickly stop when Lennon speaks up.

"No, he's not the father," she explains, her bottom lip trembling.

I reach over and grab her hand, squeezing it again, just as I did in the truck. "It's okay, Lennon."

"I'm so sorry," Dr. Potter immediately apologizes. "I know better than to assume."

Lennon nods, and I lean back into my chair so the two can talk.

"The father died in a motorcycle accident a couple of months ago. This is Hunter, his best friend." She pauses. "My best friend."

My heart falls into my stomach at her declaration. I know I shouldn't allow those words to affect me, but they do. If being her best friend is all I can ever be, I'd still die a happy man by just getting to be in Lennon's life at all.

The doctor's eyes soften, and she apologizes profusely for her loss. Dr. Potter basically repeats everything the nurse asked, which is annoying that Lennon has to go through it twice. Talks about taking her daily prenatal vitamins and discusses how far along she could be. Since the first day of her last period was over two months ago, the doctor recommends getting an ultrasound. She explains they'll be able to get the baby's measurements and better estimate her due date.

Once she's finished with the office visit, we're sent to another floor for the ultrasound. A tech brings us into a darkened room and explains the whole process to Lennon, which has my mind spinning. Since she's apparently at the end of her first trimester, they can do a traditional ultrasound, whatever the hell that means.

As soon as Lennon lifts her shirt, I glance away to give her some privacy. Moments later, the ultrasound tech stands closer to her, so I take that as my sign it's okay to look. Lennon's jeans are lowered a bit where the wand is sliding over her belly. The screen grabs my attention as we watch weird movements play out. I have no idea what I'm looking at, but it doesn't matter because soon, the tech explains everything in detail.

"See that little flutter there?" She points at the screen, and Lennon and I both look up. "That's the baby's heartbeat." She grins, and I shift my gaze to Lennon, whose eyes are watering. She's smiling, and I know how much this means to her. "Looks like you have an active little baby in there."

I gasp when I see a seahorse shape swimming from one side to the other.

"Isn't that cool?" Lennon asks me, bringing my attention back to her.

"You have a creature inside you," I tease.

Lennon wrinkles her nose, and we both laugh.

The tech continues to take the measurements, making lines from one side to the other. I can't help staring at the screen and flicking my gaze to watch Lennon. It feels so surreal to be experiencing this with her. I can't help the sadness that takes over, knowing Brandon will never get this opportunity. I'd take his place in a heartbeat so he could have his happy family.

"Alright…you ready for some pictures?" the tech asks, and Lennon lights up. "Let's see if we can get some good ones. He or she is pretty excited in there."

Lennon giggles as she watches the tech freeze the screen and take screenshots. "According to the measurements, you're eleven weeks along, which makes your estimated due date December twenty-third." The tech's entire face lights up. "Ooh, maybe you'll have a Christmas baby."

"A baby for Christmas. Sounds like a Hallmark movie." Lennon snorts and grins.

The tech finishes up, hands Lennon a towel to clean up, then gives her half a dozen photos. Once she's ready to go, we walk to the truck and ride in silence. I don't know what to say and don't want to put her on the spot either, so I don't push it.

Lennon holds the photographs as if they're her lifeline, almost as if they'll disappear if she lets go. We pick up some food and bring it back to the apartment and eat. Instead of going back to work, I call my boss and tell him I'm taking the rest of the day off. I don't want to leave Lennon right now. It's been a big, emotional day for her. Hell, and for me. I'm in way over my head if that doctor appointment taught me anything.

"I can't believe this," she finally speaks as we sit at the table to eat.

I give her a small smile. "Well, you better because it's happening."

She stares at the wall, transfixed. "I'm having a baby. This is unreal. I mean, I always wanted kids. I knew I wanted a big family. But why right now?" She ponders, but it's almost as if she's thinking aloud to herself and doesn't expect an answer. I wish I had answers for her, but I don't. "It's like Brandon left a piece of himself behind for me so I wouldn't be alone forever," she says.

My eyes soften, and my heart beats faster. "You won't be alone forever, Lennon."

"Well, not as long as you're with me," she says. "At least I'll have you."

Her words nearly have me gasping for air and choking on it. When she says things like that, I know she doesn't mean it the way it sounds, but it still affects me. I wish with everything I am that she meant them the way I mean them.

"And I'm not going anywhere," I confirm.

She rewards me with one of her sweet Lennon smiles that always turns me to mush. I'm a fucking love-sick puppy, a whipped one at that, but I don't even care. She's not mine to claim, but she's mine to protect now.

Once we're finished eating, Lennon stands and cleans up the mess, then we go to our spot on the couch to watch our show. She yawns over and over before she eventually drifts off, and I fan a blanket out on top of her. Since I'm not anywhere near tired, I try to get some work done from home.

I catch up on emails and reply to as many people as I can, and by the time I look up, it's nearly dark outside. Instead of ordering food, I throw a pizza in the oven, and the delicious cheesy scent eventually wakes Lennon.

"What's that smell?" she asks with a raspy, sleepy voice.

"Pizza," I tell her.

Five minutes later, it's done, and I'm putting pieces on plates and delivering drinks to the coffee table for us. As we sit and eat, I realize how fucking envious I am of Brandon for everything he had. I try not to allow the dark thoughts to take over, but I can't help it. I try to push them away, not wanting to have them at all.

"What is it?" Lennon asks with concern in her voice. Maybe she notices me as much as I do her.

"Nothing," I say around a mouthful of the saddest pizza I've ever eaten.

She gives me a weak smile. "You can tell me. It won't upset me. I know it was about Brandon."

I swallow hard, wondering how the hell she knew that. Shrugging, I decide to tell her some. "Just hate that he can't be here for you. That he doesn't know he's having a kid. That he can't eat this shitty pizza with you."

The last part has her chuckling. "I wasn't going to say anything. But yeah, I'm never buying this brand again. It was a total fail on my part."

She doesn't say anything about my other admissions, though, and I'm happy she doesn't because I know she feels the same way. It's the elephant in the room. Once we're full, Lennon gets up and lets me know she's going to take a shower.

She typically showers in the mornings, but after Brandon's death, she's used the bathroom as an escape to cry, so I don't question her about it.

I pick up our mess, and just as I throw the rest of the pizza in the trash, the water comes on. Then I hear her singing.

Slowly, I walk down the hallway and stand outside the bathroom door to make sure I'm not imagining things. My eyes flutter closed, and I rest my head against the door, wishing I could tell her all my secrets and put my heart out on the line. Her soft and sweet voice sings so beautifully, I nearly give her a round of applause when the water turns off.

I go into my room and shut the door. Sitting on the edge of the bed, I rub my hand over my face. It's the first time she's sung since Brandon's death, and it has me crumpling, falling, so damn happy that I can barely compose myself.

The bathroom door creaks open, and I hear her walk to her

room and shut the door, then moments later, she knocks on mine. After a second, she turns the knob.

"Hunter?"

I straighten my stance, and she grins. "Just checking on you."

"I heard you singing..."

Heat hits her cheeks. "I'm sorry—"

"I've missed it," I cut her off. I never want her to apologize for singing again. "It sounded perfect."

"I thought you hated my singing." She crosses her arms over her chest as she scowls, but I notice the pulse point in her neck throbbing.

"If I told you I liked it, do you think you would've kept it up?" I chuckle, reminding her of our antics.

A smirk spreads across her face. "Fair point."

She walks into the room and looks around the space that once belonged to her and Brandon, then sits on the bed next to me. "It was a lullaby my mother used to sing to us when we were kids. It's a song called 'Baby Mine.'"

She carefully rests her hand on her stomach, and it fucking breaks me. I can see the tiniest bit of a bump there.

"Growing up, music was such an integral part of my childhood, and I want to share that with my baby. Music connects people in a special way, and it's a way for us to bond."

"Wow," I whisper. The revelation as to why she's singing again hits me. "Love like that...it's powerful."

She looks down at her hands and fidgets with the hem of her shirt. If I didn't know any better, I'd say being vulnerable around me made her nervous. Not wanting it to grow awkward or for my last shred of willpower to snap, I stand and notice her yawning again.

"You should probably get some sleep."

"You're right. This baby wears me out, and I don't even do anything." She laughs at herself. "I can't seem to catch up regardless of how many naps I take." Lennon stands and walks past me, and the smell of her shampoo and soap takes over my inhibitions. I almost reach for her hand, pull her back, and kiss the fuck out of her, but instead, I ball my hand into a fist. Instead of following her, I give her space because I need it as well. Just long enough to get a grip on reality.

After an hour of messing around in my room, I try to sleep. I stare into the darkness for at least an hour when I hear Lennon's quiet sobs in the other room. I thank the paper-thin walls for that.

I close my eyes tight, knowing I should let her be, but I can't. I throw the blanket off and walk into the hallway, then stand outside her door and listen. I shouldn't knock on the door. I should give her privacy. I need to go back into my room and leave her be. Instead of doing those things, though, I go against all my senses and slowly open the door.

"You okay?" I ask softly.

"No," she whispers, curled up into a ball, facing away from the door. "I need to be held," she answers truthfully.

Fuck me.

Regardless of what my head says, I follow my heart and go to her. To hell with it. I can't let her cry in here all alone. I push the sheet back and slide under it. Feeling how cold her skin is, I wrap my arm over her petite frame and pull her body to mine.

I squeeze my eyes tight, trying to hide my truths from her. Even though I want to say so many words at this moment, I allow the silence to speak. Regardless of how much this fucking hurts, how much I'm beating myself up inside, I'll do anything to comfort her and to help her heal, even if it means I'm destroyed in the process. Lennon's quiet sobs diminish, and I know she's finally asleep by how her breathing changes.

I should slip out of here now that she's asleep, but I'm a selfish bastard who can't give up the opportunity to hold her like this while imagining we're two different people than who we truly are.

In another life, she and the baby are mine. As my eyes grow heavy, the truth of our situation smothers me, but I force myself to fall asleep.

CHAPTER NINETEEN

LENNON

Soft lips trace my jawline, and I pant as he memorizes every inch of my body. At this moment, I need him like I need air, and I beg for him to take me, to fuck me, to make me his, because I am. Always have been. My breathing increases as lips slide down to my nipple, then feather kisses across my swollen stomach. As he hovers above me, I spread my legs apart, wanting him to claim me. He stops for a moment, leans back, and removes his shirt. When I look up to meet his gaze, my eyes widen in shock when I don't see Brandon.

I see Hunter.

"Hunter?" The sound of my own voice wakes me. I sit up in bed and freak the fuck out when I realize he's lying next to me. I squeeze my legs together, feeling the need and want take over. My body practically begs for him, and I'm so damn confused that I don't know what to do. I'm blaming it all on hormones, all of it, because it's the only explanation for what I'm feeling.

"Huh?" he mutters, blinking awake and leaning up on his elbow. He finally looks around with wide eyes, realizing he's in my bed. "Oh fuck."

I swallow, studying his face, the same face that ripped me from sleep as he rushes out of the room. I'm so damn flustered and worked up and, more than anything, *sexually* frustrated. Why the hell would I be having dreams like this about Hunter?

Guilt courses through me as I think about Brandon, and it feels like I cheated on him. I'd never do that. Hunter and I have grown close, so I know it's my subconscious playing tricks on me. I close my eyes tight, pushing every single thought in my head away, and blame it all on the pregnancy. That's what's causing this, right?

My bladder is about to burst, so I hurry to the bathroom. Once I've taken care of business and brushed my teeth, I head to the kitchen where Hunter moves around quickly as he makes breakfast, shirtless. I look at the tattoos on his arm and can't stop staring at his biceps and how they flex as he cracks eggs into a pan.

"Hungry?" he asks, glancing over his shoulder with a shit-eating smirk.

He has no idea what I'm hungry for, but I keep it to myself. Bastard knows exactly what he looks like half-naked, which is fucking ridiculous. I've seen him without a shirt before, and each time, it takes my breath away, though I've never admitted that before.

"Starving," I say, leaning against the doorframe to watch him. Randomly, he peeks over and shoots me a grin. As soon as the coffee maker beeps, he pours himself a cup. When I found out I was pregnant, I stopped drinking caffeine, and it might end up being the death of me.

"I've got about fifteen minutes before I have to leave," he tells me as he slides some sausage and eggs on two plates. "You okay?"

Dammit, I'm gawking. "Uh, yeah. Just wish I could drink some of that delicious coffee."

"Why? You mostly have creamer in yours," he teases, and I'm tempted to smack that grin off his face.

I force myself to walk away and go to the table to eat.

"I read in a pregnancy article that women are allowed to have up to twelve ounces of coffee a day without it affecting the baby."

The hand that's holding my fork freezes midair, shocked at his words. "What?" I ask as Hunter practically inhales his food. "You're reading pregnancy articles now?" I can't hide the amusement in my tone and smile wide at his admission.

He shrugs it off as if it's no big deal. "Well, I came across one or two. But anyway, it said it was perfectly safe for the baby as long as you limit your intake."

"Hmm…" I chew on my lower lip. "Sounds like torture, though. Coffee is like a can of Pringles. I can't stop at one."

Hunter laughs and continues filling his mouth with forkfuls of food. Even though he's always been like this, it still makes me chuckle.

Awkward silence lingers between us while I slowly eat my plateful. Memories of last night unfold, and embarrassment seeps in.

I told him I needed to be held. I was so fucking lonely that I needed to feel the warmth of someone else, even if we're just friends. I was too lost in my head missing Brandon, which usually happens while I'm in bed. In the darkness, my thoughts speak loudly, and nothing stops my emotions from boiling over. Sometimes I'm able to cry myself to sleep, but it wasn't working because my emotions about the baby took over. Hunter, being as caring as he has been since the accident, checked on me. I'm sure it was the last thing he thought I'd say, and though he probably didn't want to hold me like that, he did. Once again, I owe him so much.

Being alone and being lonely are two different things, I've quickly learned.

Hunter finally looks up from his plate and gazes at me. "I'm sorry about last night. I was so tired when I came in and ended up falling asleep. Good thing you woke up because I didn't set the alarm," he admits with a nervous chuckle. It explains his reaction this morning at least. The corners of his mouth turn up into a boyish grin, and I can't stop looking at him.

"It's okay," I say. He doesn't have anything to apologize for, but I can't find the right words. Thank you? Sorry I'm such an emotional disaster? Hope I didn't fart in my sleep? *Oh God.*

He must notice how awkward I'm being right now because he furrows his brows and studies me. The sex dream replays in my head, and thinking about it has my heart racing and my face flushing.

"Are you sure you're feeling okay?" he asks, cleaning his plate. "You're being weird. Your cheeks look all hot." He probably thinks I'm about to throw up everything he made me, but no worries, I'm just confused as hell about my own body's reactions. I want to roll my eyes at myself for being so stupid.

Instead, I let out a forced laugh. "I'm fine. Just pregnancy hormones getting to me. That's all it is."

At least that's what I tell myself. Yep.

Hunter shoots me a weary grin and stands, taking his plate to the kitchen before heading down the hallway.

Exhaling a relieved breath, I finish my sausage and eggs, and as I'm walking to the kitchen, he steps out wearing nice slacks and a polo that hugs his body in all the right places. My eyes meet his, and I quickly look away as heat rushes through me. I place my plate in the sink and lean on the counter, trying to get ahold of my emotions.

Hunter steps inside the kitchen, slowly walking past me to grab his to-go mug and fill it with coffee. The smell of it has me shooting daggers at him. Hunter laughs to himself, and I groan.

"You're scary as fuck without caffeine." He holds back a grin, but I notice it anyway as he snaps the top on his cup. "This is me walking on thin ice," he taunts, tiptoeing out of the kitchen. "If you need anything, lemme know."

"You know I will," I call out loud enough for him to hear.

His laughter echoes through the apartment before the front door clicks closed, and I let out a deep breath.

What the hell? I was gawking like a love-sick teenager all because of that stupid dream.

The clock on the microwave shows it's past eight. Though I

slept like heaven last night with Hunter curled next to me, I'm still exhausted, so I catch up on more sleep, hoping to stay far away from fantasyland.

Hours pass, and I'm woken when my phone rings. I grab it off the nightstand and Sophie's name flashes across the screen.

"Hungry?" she asks as soon as I mutter hello and hear the smile in her voice.

"What time is it?" My internal clock is off, and I already know I'm gonna have a hell of a time getting back on schedule when school starts again.

"It's almost noon. Did you already eat?"

"I haven't eaten since breakfast." My eyes fly open, and I can't believe I slept half the day away.

"I'm coming to pick you up. I'll be there in ten minutes." She hangs up without allowing me to say another word.

Shit. I need to get up and make myself presentable. After my feet are on the ground, I look around the room and think about what needs to be done before the baby's arrival, but it's all so overwhelming. I throw on a sundress and slip on my sandals. Once I'm in the bathroom, I put my hair in some sort of messy topknot and decide to go with it. Right on time, I hear a knock and rush to the door to open it.

Stepping aside to allow her in, she shakes her head. "Go grab your purse. I'm seriously hangry right now."

I laugh at her, knowing how she gets when she doesn't eat, so I grab my things and follow her outside.

"I seriously couldn't get out of my apartment quick enough. Carter's a fucking terror, Lennon. I feel like I'm losing my goddamn mind," she says, driving through traffic.

I sympathize with her, knowing what she's going through.

"All you can do is ignore him or move out. There aren't many options. But I understand and feel for you." I offer her a smile and notice how tight she's gripping the steering wheel as we pull into the parking lot of the sandwich shop.

She lets out an angry huff before we get out of the car and

walk inside. We place our orders, grab our drinks, and sit at a table by the windows while we wait for our food.

Sophie is fuming, and as soon as we settle into our spot, she starts going off. "Carter is so oblivious. I went into the bathroom this morning, saw a giant-ass turd in the toilet, and I nearly threw up. Who the hell takes a shit and doesn't flush? We're adults!"

I try to hold back my laughter, but it escapes me before I can stop it. "Seriously? Oh my God, that's disgusting!"

"I know! I'll spare you the nasty details. Not to mention, I also caught him wearing my black dress socks the other day. They barely fit over his huge man ankles, and it nearly ate me alive seeing them on his feet. On top of the fact that he didn't ask, they're going to be all stretched out and smell. They can burn in hell right with him now." She pauses, releasing a tense breath. "Oh, and the other day, an empty Coke can was left on my practice keyboard in the corner of the apartment, like it was a fucking drink coaster! Can Maria be so blinded by love that she doesn't see how annoying her boyfriend is? He's a damn slob and not at all like Hunter, who did it on purpose to piss you off. No… Carter is the real deal. He lives like a raccoon who sleeps in a dumpster."

She's pissed and frustrated, and I hate that I can't snap my fingers and change her situation. I reach across the table and take her hand, trying to calm her down. "I'm gonna help you find another place. Just stay there until you can't take it any longer, and we can figure something out. I'd offer for you to come live with Hunter and me, but I doubt you'd want to share a bed with me every night, and the couch sucks. Trust me, my back still hurts from sleeping on it."

She forces a grin through the sadness on her face. "Thanks. And I know there's nothing anyone can do. I'm half-tempted to go live with Maddie in the dorms." She chuckles, but I know she feels defeated. "It sucks because what Maria and I had going was working out so well."

Shrugging, I offer her a weak smile. "Things change. Nothing ever stays the same. I learned that the hard way."

Sophie nods just as our food comes. My mouth waters in anticipation of the chicken wrap and soup I ordered. We dig in, and she practically moans as she takes a bite of her club sandwich.

"So how's the roommate situation since finding out about the baby?" she asks nonchalantly, but I see a sparkle in her eye.

I give her a pointed look, wondering if this is a setup. "Good, I guess. Not much has changed." Oh, except I fantasized about him. No biggie.

"You guess?"

I blow out a breath, knowing I can't lie to her. "Last night…" I start. Sophie leans forward, waiting in anticipation for my next words, and I playfully roll my eyes. "I might've asked him to sleep in my bed with me."

"Uh…*might* have?"

"Shut up. Not like that," I tell her. "I was missing Brandon so much. I needed a warm body next to me."

Her eyes soften as she gives me a pity look. The one I absolutely *hate*.

"And so he did." I shrug casually.

"Of course he did," she says as if she's not even a bit surprised. "Hunter's a good guy. He'd do anything you ask."

My heart flutters at her words, but I push it away. "So I fell asleep, and when I woke up, I was completely flustered because I was in the middle of a sex dream."

"Yeah? Was it good?" She waggles her brows.

"It was *Hunter* in the dream," I confess, and she sucks in her lips, but I know she has a snarky comment. "I'm losing my mind, Soph. Why would I dream about him like that? I couldn't stop staring this morning while he made us breakfast. Shirtless." I release a frustrated breath, needing to knock those images out of my brain. "It seemed so damn real. And now things are awkward because it's all I can think about."

Sophie leans forward and speaks barely over a whisper.

"Maybe you should think about getting a vibrator? Girl, your hormones are going crazy, and you're getting zero relief. You went from consistent sex to becoming a nun," she states, then hurriedly adds, "Obviously not by choice, but still."

I know my face tells all my secrets as heat rushes through my body. I look around the room, but no one is paying any attention to us.

"It's nothing to be embarrassed about."

"Oh my God." Realization hits me. "How many of them do you have?" I ask, imagining her nightstand full of sex toys.

She twists her lips. "I can count them on two hands."

My eyes go wide in shock. "That means more than five but less than ten. You sex kitten!"

"Hey, a single girl's gotta do what she's gotta do. And you know I'm not about those fuck boys." She gives me a pointed look, which has me bursting into laughter. Sophie's so damn modest, I never would've thought she'd be all about self-pleasure. Part of me wants to bring up Mason, but I know she's already on edge with her new roommate situation. "Honestly, though, you've been around Hunter so much lately, I'm surprised *I'm* not having sex dreams about him. He's hot. Big muscles, tall, looks at you as if he can see inside your soul…" She's basically salivating at the mouth now, which makes me chuckle at her ridiculousness.

"Shut it." I snort. "Okay, fine, maybe you're right. I probably do need some sort of…*release*. Maybe then the dreams won't return, and I can go back to looking at him like my friend instead of…" I trail off, thinking about him hovering above me, ready to claim my mouth and body.

Sophie clears her throat. "It must've been *really* good." Pure amusement fills her tone, but this is way out of my comfort zone.

I frown. "I'd never, Soph. I couldn't. I feel like I've cheated on Brandon by having that dream about Hunter. I wish it hadn't happened, honestly. I don't want things to change between us, but eventually, it has too, right? He'll move on and find someone who doesn't have baggage. And when he does, I'm sure his girlfriend wouldn't want me hanging around him the way I am right now, or at least I wouldn't want that if the positions were reversed. But we've become good friends, and I think my subconscious is playing tricks on me because I genuinely care about him."

She finishes eating and slides her plate away. "I don't think he's going anywhere, Lennon."

"Why does everyone keep making jabs like that? We're just friends. That's all we'll ever be. That's all we *can* be." I let out a ragged breath, wondering why that thought brings me sadness.

These fucking hormones.

Sophie drops it and doesn't say another word about it. We talk about one of her students as she takes me back to my apartment. Before I get out, we exchange a hug, and I promise to call her if I need anything.

After she reverses from the parking spot, she stops and rolls down the window. "I'm ordering you a present. It'll be on your doorstep in two days." She shoots me a wink before driving away, and I stand there with my jaw on the ground.

It's been a little over a month since I found out I was pregnant, and each time my parents FaceTime me, I keep it short, worried my mother will notice I've gained ten pounds. The thought of telling them gives me anxiety because I know what their reaction will be. Before we get off the phone, I make sure to stress how much I love them. Mainly because I've learned you never know when it'll be the last time, and because I want them to know they mean a lot to me, regardless if I'm lying to them. If they decide they don't want anything to do with me or the baby, I may never be able to say those words to them again, and that thought makes me so fucking sad.

Their last call was to confirm I'm still going for the Fourth of July holiday weekend in less than two weeks. They know I've been a mess since Brandon's death and are eager to see me. I haven't said much or confirmed if I'm going or not, but now that I'm pregnant, I need to be truthful.

I still have the plane tickets. Though I thought about canceling the trip several times, I haven't. I've been thinking about how to break the news about the baby and them being grandparents. Telling them in person is the only logical, respectful choice. One ticket is still in Brandon's name, and I kept hoping Sophie or Maddie could come with me so I didn't have to do this alone, but their schedules won't allow it. I'll probably have to cancel it soon and go alone.

Checking the clock, it's almost time for Hunter to get home, and the thought excites me. I've grown to miss him when he's working because it gets lonely here.

However, Sophie and Maddie are coming over tonight, and we're going to look through baby name books. We try to get together at least once a week, and though it can be hard with everyone's schedule, we've somehow been able to make it work.

I grab the stack of books and sit on the couch. As I flip through one of them, I start thinking about my parents again and what their reaction will be. A tear slides down my cheek when the front door opens. Hunter notices, and his face contorts.

"Everything okay?" he asks, setting down his work bag that's stuffed full. He comes over and sits beside me on the couch.

I shrug, wiping my cheeks. "I'm thinking about my parents and taking that trip to Utah during the Fourth of July. I'm so fucking scared about what they're going to say or do." My voice cracks. "But I know it has to be done."

He stills as he studies me.

"I'll go with you, Lennon."

Wait, *what?* "Hunter..."

"I don't want you to have to tell them alone. Plus, I have a few vacation days I can take." He shrugs as if this is no big deal, but to me, it's huge.

I shake my head. "You can't always be there for me, Hunter."

"Yes, I can, and I will."

We sit in silence for a moment, both of us in our heads, until he notices the books stacked high. "Still searching for baby names tonight with your sisters?"

I burst into laughter. "They'll be here in thirty minutes."

"If Sophie's driving, it'll be fifteen." He stands, shooting me a smirk. "Gonna take a shower. It's hot as fuck outside, and I'm sweaty."

"Well, I wasn't gonna say anything but…" I tease even though he smells as good as always to me.

"Hilarious." He walks backward, giving me a pointed look. "Just think about it, Lennon."

"Okay," I tell him, then he walks toward the bathroom.

I think about how he'd give me the confidence I need to face my parents. He's supported me so much that when he's around, I feel as if I can do scary things—like telling my parents I'm pregnant out of wedlock.

Leaning my head back on the couch, I hear the water turn on and remember seeing him naked, which is the absolute last thing I should be thinking about right now. I squeeze my legs together, trying to get a hold of my thoughts, and am so thankful for Sophie and her knowledge of adult toys. She got me this clit vibrator thingy, and it basically has me singing to the heavens. Luckily for me, it's also waterproof.

A knock on the door pulls me back. When I open it, I find Maddie, who's still wearing her dance clothes. Past her, Sophie climbs up the stairs, who obviously couldn't keep up, and it makes me laugh a little.

"There's my favorite sister," Sophie says, and Maddie lights up, both of them walking inside and making themselves at home.

"I love being your favorite!" I gloat to purposely fuck with Maddie, who playfully narrows her eyes.

"Tell her," Maddie demands. "Soph, you know I've always been your number one."

Sophie snickers as they funnel into the living room. "You both are."

The bathroom door swings open, and Hunter walks out with a towel wrapped around his waist before going to his room. Our eyes meet, and the only thing that pulls me away is Maddie's gasp.

"Oh. My. Damn." She releases a breath as if she's affected and glares at me. "How are you not aroused by that man?"

I roll my eyes and look at Sophie, who, not surprisingly, agrees.

"You two better stop it," I warn, pointing at them to emphasize my point. "And neither one of you is allowed to gawk at him."

"Because he's only yours to drool over?" Maddie taunts, and I'm half-tempted to slap that silly grin off her face.

Sophie, knowing I'm getting annoyed, leads Maddie to the couch. "Don't start with her. She's hormonal and may gouge your eyes out."

"Exactly," I agree with a fake glare. I sit between them, and they both attack me, rubbing their hands over my belly and trying to feel the baby.

"C'mon, baby, kick!" Maddie orders.

"It's too soon, you weirdo." I snicker. "She's the size of a lime."

"She?" Sophie squeals.

I look down at my bloated stomach and rub a palm over it. "I think it is, but I don't know for sure yet. Just feels like a girl."

"So that's why you're doubly hormonal?" Maddie cracks.

I nudge my shoulder with hers and scoff.

"Don't worry, baby," Sophie coos, patting one side of my belly. "I'll be your favorite auntie who will love you no matter what."

"Hey, no way!" Maddie flicks Sophie's hand, and soon they're fighting over my unborn child.

"You two are insane." I laugh, pushing them both away. "Neither of you will be the favorite if you don't help me name her!"

We pick up the books off the coffee table and start flipping through them. Hunter walks into the living room and tells us he's ordering pizza, which only makes my stomach growl in anticipation. Grabbing his bag, he brings it to the kitchen table and pulls out his laptop for a makeshift desk. He's been working so damn hard lately with his project, which I find admirable considering how much he's already doing for me.

"How about you make a list of boy names and girl names you like and then you can start narrowing from there?" Maddie suggests.

"That's a good idea," Sophie adds. "We've got a lot of books to go through." She glances at the stack I ordered. I might've gone a tad overboard. I won't find out the gender until my August ultrasound appointment, which is exciting, but I won't care either way. This baby is a miracle.

"If it's a boy, I'm leaning toward Brandon Jude Locke, Jr," I say, a smile touching my lips.

"That's perfect," Hunter says from the kitchen table, and Sophie and Maddie agree in unison.

I've been thinking about it for a while, and each time it crosses my mind, my heart lurches forward. Though Brandon's not here, I'll make sure he continues to live through our memories together. The baby will know how great of a man their daddy was. Before I get too sucked into my head and emotional, I continue.

"So maybe we should look at girl names? Hell, that cut our job in half." I hand Sophie a book as thick as a dictionary. I flip open the one in my lap and see an overwhelming number of names listed in alphabetical order. Most I've never heard of like Athwenna and Aoife.

"I, at least, want people to be able to say and spell her name correctly," I say aloud after reading words I don't even know how to pronounce.

Maddie and Sophie throw out different cute names, and I write a few down in my phone app, but others I pass on. The pizza eventually arrives, and we set the books aside while we move to the kitchen table. As we eat, making small talk, Maddie eventually brings up our parents.

"Do you know when you're going to tell them?" She looks at me just as Sophie did last week when she asked. Time will eventually run out, we all know it, and I have to decide soon.

"Well, I've been thinking about it a lot. Every time I get in the shower, I notice my growing belly, and I won't be able to cover it up much longer." Even though we live in different states, they won't be happy I hid it from them and didn't tell them right away. The longer I wait, the more disappointed they'll be.

Hunter gives me a sympathetic smile but doesn't interrupt.

"I've decided to keep my Fourth of July trip and tell them in person and get it over with. I hope they're not heartless enough to throw me out on my pregnant ass, not after everything I've been through this year, but it wouldn't surprise me." It hurts my hormonal heart to think about it, but I know it's something that has to be done. "Plus, it's too easy to hang up on someone if it's done over the phone. At least then they'll have to dismiss me and the baby to my face."

Once I tell my parents, the entire congregation of the church will know my business in less than a day. I can only imagine the prayer lists I'll be added to.

"This isn't going to be good, Lennon. Are you crazy?" Maddie says.

"I know they'll be highly disappointed and won't hold back what they think about any of this, but I'm their daughter. They're supposed to love me unconditionally. They taught us compassion all of our lives." I pause, collecting my thoughts. "Honestly, I'm fucking scared of their reaction because I don't want to lose them."

"I'm going with you," Hunter speaks up, his eyes not leaving mine. "I'm not going to let you go through that alone. I know I've already offered, but I'm not giving you a choice anymore. I want to be there for you." He crosses his arms over his broad chest and holds his stance as if he's not giving me any room to argue this.

"You're insane. You have no idea how stressful and awkward this will be." I shake my head, turning my body toward him. "I'm already preparing for the worst, and if you're serious about this, you'll need to as well. The moment they see my belly and no wedding ring, I'll be the black sheep of the family. What hurts the most is knowing how disappointed they'll be when all I've ever wanted is to make them proud. They might literally tell me to leave and never come back."

I've been stressed and worried enough about this pregnancy, and while this is a giant hurdle to cross, they deserve to know they'll be grandparents. Plus, I can't lie forever. They'd eventually find out. My emotions take hold when I think about what could happen. Sophie and Maddie look back and forth between us.

"I wish I could go with you." Maddie takes my hand. "I can't because of my show. I'm so sorry."

I wipe a rogue tear that spills over. I hate that I'm crying right now, but the more I think about it, the more upset I become. Telling them they're going to be grandparents shouldn't cause me this much stress.

"I'll try to get out of rehearsal, Lennon. If you want me to—" Sophie starts but is cut off.

"We'll tell them we're married and having a baby," Hunter blurts out, pulling our attention to him. "We got hitched, and you got pregnant on the honeymoon." Hunter shrugs, pursing his lips as if the idea he came up with isn't completely insane. "There, problem solved."

He picks up a piece of pizza and takes a bite of it as I swallow down my heart that's lodged deep in my throat.

My eyes widen at his idea and so do Sophie and Maddie's. The three of us stare at him, wondering if we heard him correctly at his offer to be my fake husband and baby daddy.

By the smirk on his lips, I know I did.

We *all* did.

CHAPTER TWENTY

HUNTER

I COULD LITERALLY KICK my own ass for blurting that out in front of her sisters because I feel like they see right through me. Sometimes I don't think about the repercussions before I speak or how it will make Lennon feel. As the three of them stare at me, I smile because that's all I can do after putting myself in this situation.

I won't allow her to go through this without some support, and if she doesn't want her parents to completely write her off, then what's the problem with a teeny white lie? For a moment, I try to think about why I said it as the guilt floods through me. I'm doing this for Brandon, right? Well, I am, but also for Lennon. She needs me.

However, lately, the lines have blurred, but regardless, I meant what I offered.

"I-I'm sorry. What did you say?" Lennon asks barely above a whisper, and as I look into her eyes, it feels as if her sisters disappear, and it's just her and me.

I play it off like it's no big deal even though it is to me. I'd do anything to keep her safe and happy, even if it means pretending to be her husband, pretending the baby in her belly is mine, and lying to her parents. If it means she'll be able to get through this pregnancy easier, sign me up for all of it. The only person I'm concerned about is Lennon because she's already in a vulnerable state.

"I was thinking that if they'll disown you for this when you're so happy about it and desperately want them in the baby's and your life, why not tell another white lie? You've been telling them for a year that you live in an apartment alone when you obviously don't. The part of me who's selfish for you and the baby thinks lying to protect you would be the best plan. If we went to Vegas and got married, then having a child is the next step in the relationship, right?" I take my focus from her and glance at a smiling Sophie and Maddie, who are nodding in agreement.

"It's the perfect plan," Sophie adds. "And we grew up in Utah, Lennon. It's almost normal for people to get married and pregnant within the same month."

Lennon opens her mouth, but Sophie continues before she can argue. "Before you try to dismantle this idea the way you always do, we all know our parents are going to be upset that you didn't get married in the church and eloped instead. But with that being said, they wouldn't write you off, kick you out, and pretend you never existed. They'd probably be thrilled they're going to be grandparents too, as long as you're married." Sophie turns to face Lennon. "You know what happened to Shelby Greer."

There's a long pause, but I'm dying to hear this. "What happened?"

Maddie giggles, and Lennon gives me a pointed look.

"Her parents refused to talk to her. The whispers around our small town essentially broke her to the point that she moved away. The rumors spread like wildfire, and her mother told her story like it was a lesson for everyone," Lennon explains. "She was a disgrace to her parents and lost everything. And I'd be lying if I said I wasn't worried the same thing will happen to me."

"What the hell did she do to deserve that?" I scoff, appalled.

"Adultery," Sophie answers. "Except the guy never told her he was married, but it didn't matter to them. She'd committed the ultimate sin."

"And she ended up pregnant with his baby. It was a double whammy," Maddie adds.

My eyes widen at the reality of this. My family wasn't overly religious, but we pretended to be. Or rather, my parents did, and I had to follow along, so I guess in a way I get it. You don't want to let your family down because they're all you have. Even with my strained relationship with my father, I'd be devastated to lose my mother or brother.

What happened to forgiveness and understanding? I want to ask her more questions, but with her sisters here, I hold back.

"Well?" I lift a brow.

"Hunter has a good idea," Sophie concludes.

"I agree," Maddie says. "Plus, what is it we always say? What they don't know won't hurt them?" Maddie arches her brows, the known rebel of the three.

"Am I living in a freaking twilight zone right now?" Lennon's eyes search my face and then turns to her sisters. "We're talking about a big lie here. I was just with Brandon, and now I'm supposed to be married? You think they'll even buy it?"

I can see she's freaking out, overanalyzing it all before we sit and talk through this, and I can't blame her. This is a crazy idea, but I wouldn't have suggested it if I wasn't sure we could pull it off.

"Lennon." I pull back from the table and go to kneel in front of her. I want her to see how much I care for her and that this would ease some of her worries so she can enjoy the rest of her pregnancy while staying healthy. "Just hear me out, okay? I know this sounds off-the-wall insane, but I want to protect you. I know a little bit about messy families. I don't want you or the baby to go through any extra stress, and I know it's taking a toll on you. I know how much it means for you to have their support. You've already lost so much, and this is all avoidable," I tell her softly.

Though I'm trying to act as calm as can be, my heart hammers in my chest.

Lennon looks down at her hands for a second, contemplating my idea. I can almost see and hear the wheels turning in her head. I'm hoping she doesn't have a meltdown with the way her hormones have been lately. She's eerily quiet, which starts to concern me, so I keep talking about it as I think of more ideas to make this work.

"I don't have all of this figured out, but when they'd ask us questions about the relationship, all we have to say is we became friends through Brandon, but I always had unrequited feelings for you. We started leaning on each other and grieved him together, which made us grow even closer and eventually my feelings were reciprocated. His death put into perspective that life's too short not to be together, and once we set aside the guilt, we ultimately didn't want to be apart." I have to pause because there's too much truth in my words for me to continue. Brandon comes to mind and all the conversations we had about Lennon and how much he loved her and was planning to ask her to marry him. Now here I am on my knees, begging her to fake a marriage with me.

I think about how Brandon wanted to meet her parents this summer and propose on their trip. A trip he never got to take. The thought of it all nearly chokes me, and I feel like I need to gasp for air as the guilt consumes me.

He should be going with her, not me. His timing would've been almost perfect with the pregnancy. I think about the ring he bought her and how I can never tell her about it—that secret will have to die with me. If she ever found out the real reason for this trip, it could potentially destroy her and the trust she had in me. All I want to do is keep her happy after all the tragedy she's endured. That's all Brandon would want me to do.

I suck in a ragged breath. When she meets my eyes, waiting for me to continue, her gaze pierces straight through me.

"I—" Lennon starts, then stops. She's conflicted, which I'm not at all surprised by. I'm offering a lot here.

Instead of waiting for her, I continue to sell her my idea. "So we say we drove to Vegas and got hitched. I know it sounds crazy, but people do it all the time since there's no waiting period. We'll say you got pregnant right after the wedding before we even told anyone we eloped. They don't know how far along you are and won't know the difference if you move it back a few weeks. You can hide your belly, and when the baby arrives, we'll say he or she came early. I'm sure it's nothing new for due dates to be off," I tell her confidently while trying to keep my voice even and calm.

"Aww." Maddie interrupts our moment, looking back and forth between us as if I confessed my undying love to Lennon, and considering my words, I somewhat have. I want Lennon to say something, but she doesn't. Meanwhile, Sophie grins wide, eating up every word.

"This could work," Sophie confirms with a nod, looking at Lennon and me. "It's smart and nearly foolproof. If you told me this, I'd believe it one hundred percent. Plus, you're not showing, at least nothing you couldn't hide with some leggings and a baggy T-shirt, so you could play it off like you're still in your first trimester instead of entering your second."

As I look at Lennon, I know she's in her head, and I want to talk her off the ledge and tell her I'm here, that I've always been here and always will be, but she knows. I can't allow her to go through this by herself, she's already lost so much. Losing her parents would nearly kill her, and I know it's not healthy for the baby for her to be this stressed out. Though she talks about how strict they were, she loves them with everything she is, that much is certain.

"Lennon," I plead, barely above a whisper. "Talk to me, *please*."

By the way she's looking at me, I wish I hadn't said anything with Sophie and Maddie around, but it was a random thought that popped into my head, one that will solve all her problems. Her sisters would've found out eventually if this plan goes through because they'll have to be in on it too. As I beg with my eyes for her to speak, Lennon's demeanor changes, and she shakes her head.

"Hunter, have you seriously lost your mind?" She rests her hand over her belly as if she needs to protect the baby, which is exactly what I'm trying to do.

That was *not* the response I was expecting.

Maddie's mouth falls open in shock.

"Have you *all* lost your minds?" Lennon fires back at us. "I'll have to pretend to be *married* until the end of time. They don't allow divorce either, so then what? Anytime I have to go for a visit or they come here, we're gonna continue pretending? What if I meet someone who actually *wants* to marry me? Or what if you meet someone?" Her eyes flash to mine. "Think she'll let me borrow you for the weekend when it's time to visit my parents?" She raises her brows in a mocking question.

The thought of her ever being with someone else rips a dagger through me. I don't want to find anyone—that's the problem. I'm not sure when either of us will be ready for that.

"I do understand, Lennon," I say, treading carefully. "When that happens"—the word *when* is a knife to my heart—"we'll cross that bridge then. If you need a divorce or a way out, you can blame it all on me, say I was unfaithful and walked out or something." The words taste like poison as they leave my mouth. I know this is all fake and the worst-case scenario, but I hate thinking of there being a time when Lennon isn't in my life. "All I'm suggesting is an option that'll make you stress-free and keep your parents happy," I simply say.

"You make it sound so easy." She sounds defeated. "Lying to my parents to cover up another lie. It's not gonna be as easy as you think."

I nod, understanding her concerns. I know it won't be, considering my true feelings for her, but I know she needs an out, and I'm offering her an option.

"Just think about it. We still have time. I'll do whatever you need or want, Lennon. You know that, but you'll need to decide soon so we can prepare and get our stories straight." I stand, knowing she probably needs some space. "Either way, I'm going with you to Utah because you're not going by yourself," I tell her matter-of-factly.

Before it gets awkward and more tense, I excuse myself and go to my room, leaving the ball in her court. This is ultimately her decision, one that she's going to have to make on her own. I sit on the edge of the bed and scrub my hands over my face, blowing out deep breaths. I feel as if I've betrayed my best friend for even suggesting this. Though my intentions are pure, my feelings aren't. It'll be torture for me to experience a glimpse of something I can't have and will never have—Lennon as my wife.

Brandon would want me to take care of her, protect her from harm, and that's what I'm trying to do, regardless of how it'll affect me personally. Luckily, her parents are miles away, so keeping up the façade will be easy. At least then she won't have to lie about not living with someone anymore.

I can still hear them chatting but can't make out what they're saying, and a part of me doesn't want to know. I lie back on the bed and stare at the ceiling until my vision blurs. Everything I said in there was the truth, even if the feelings I've felt for her all this time are one-sided. I won't have to do much pretending, so it'd be easy for me to play the fake husband, though showing affection might be awkward at first since I've coached myself to keep my distance for so long.

Releasing a deep, conflicted breath, I try to push it all away. Maybe it was a stupid idea after all.

I close my eyes, exhausted from my day at work, and fall asleep with the light on. I'm dreaming about nothing when I think I hear Lennon calling my name. My eyes flutter open, and I'm surprised she's standing in my room, watching me sleep.

"Hey," I say, clearing my throat and sitting up on the edge of the bed.

She walks toward me and sits next to me as she bows her head and slumps her shoulders. "My sisters left."

I study her, trying to gauge her next words.

"I'm sorry for the way I acted," she starts.

Before she can continue, I stop her. "Don't be."

"I was just shocked." She nods as if she's confirming it to herself, then shifts her body slightly so we're face-to-face. "But the more I talked it over with them, the more I realized how right you were. It's a brilliant idea, considering how I'm limited on options, and I'm kinda upset with myself that I didn't think of it first," she says with a laugh and shoots me a playful grin. "Seriously, though, I think it'll work."

"Ahh, it feels good to be right," I tease, needing to relieve some of the tension in the air.

Lennon giggles and smacks my arm.

"I know I talked about a fake divorce and all that, but honestly, I think I might be alone for the rest of my life. I don't see myself ever moving on."

When I shift my body, our faces are close enough for me to feel her warm breath on my cheek. But I need some distance because the way she's looking at me makes me want to kiss all her worries away. It's almost as if she wants me to, but I resituate myself, finding the space I desperately need before I cross a line I know I shouldn't. I know I'm reading into her body language and expressions way more than I should, but at times, it's hard to remind myself of that when her expression is filled with so much sadness and longing.

"You'll move on when you're ready, but I promise you won't be alone forever. You're a beautiful woman, Lennon. I've always thought that. You're caring, thoughtful, and compassionate. I know one day you're going to find someone who'll love you and your baby. It might not be soon, or even five years from now, but eventually. That I know for certain." I swallow hard, meaning every word, but also realizing how much they hurt me to say.

Her eyes meet mine, and for a second, I'm lost in them, lost in the sound of her ragged breaths as her lips slightly part. So much emotion and electricity streams between us that I force myself to look away to break the silent conversation we were having.

"You'll find someone too, Hunter," she assures, and I'm not sure why there's a tinge of sadness in her voice when she says that. I want to tell her that I've never wanted anyone else other than her—explain that she's always been the one for me, the woman I think about when I close my eyes—but confessing my truths will only make things tense between us, so I keep it to myself just as I have for the past two years.

"Thank you," I tell her without saying what I want to say.

"Well," she says, her tone changing. "I guess it's settled. We'll have to come up with a plan, transfer the plane ticket to your name, then start learning all the nitty-gritty about each other, so our fake relationship is believable at least, because, trust me, with my family, you'll get the interrogation of your life." She stands, seeming happy that we have a plan.

"Yep, I guess so. Now you'll have to tell me all your secrets," I quip, but as I glance in the top drawer where the engagement ring Brandon bought her is tucked away, I know that not everything can be discussed. Some things have to stay buried deep inside.

"I'm an open book, but tomorrow, it all starts. You might not want to be my friend after you learn some things about me," she teases.

I chuckle, shaking my head. "Impossible."

"When I was a kid, I loved to eat sugar and butter sandwiches."

"Okay, that's a deal breaker," I tease.

She doesn't respond, only smiles as she walks out the door, and she's gone for the night.

The word *friend* lingers around my head and brings me back to reality. I have to remind myself that we're just friends, regardless of how close we've grown. If it's the only way we can ever be, then I will selfishly take it, even if it shatters me in the end.

CHAPTER TWENTY-ONE

"Take a selfie with me," I say, plopping on the couch next to him, so close that our shoulders touch.

"Another one?" he asks with a laugh, side-glancing at the way my body presses to his.

I hold out my phone until our faces are in the frame. "Can you at least look like you're happily married?" I tease, scooting even closer. "Put your arm around me or something. We're supposed to convince them we're newlyweds and all."

Hunter clears his throat, rubs his hands over his jeans, and wraps his arm around me. It falls to my hip so I can lean into him, my shoulder resting against his chest as my forehead presses against his cheek. "Say cheese!"

I hold my phone up again, and we look into the camera. Hunter's forced smile makes me laugh. "Can you at least pretend you don't hate pictures? I need to load my Instagram with a variety of photos of us. My parents and their nosy friends will no doubt ask to see some."

Considering my parents always wanted me to get married in the church, they'll definitely be suspicious. So I made a fake Instagram account, started loading pictures with overly sappy posts, and followed all kinds of random accounts so they'd follow me back. I have to make it as believable as possible.

"Let's try a few more," I say, scanning through our other pictures. It's been over a week since Hunter suggested this plan, and we still have a lot to do before we leave in two days.

When I tuck my legs under my butt and wrap my arm over his shoulder, he tenses. "What? Is this not okay?" I ask, feeling self-conscious.

"Oh no, it's fine." He clears his throat again as if he needs a second. "I just don't like taking pictures."

I furrow my brows. "Really?" Brandon and I took hundreds. "Too much of a manly man?" I tease, and he cracks the tiniest of smiles.

"Nah, it's fine. We'll take all the ones you need," he says, leaning in close to me when I put my phone up again.

I snap three in a row, resting our cheeks together like the super cheesy couple we're pretending to be. Part of me wants to laugh at the irony, the fact that I haven't ever seen Hunter with anyone serious and now here he is taking selfies with me.

"Do you mind if I kiss your cheek?" I ask, looking over the photos.

"What?"

I snap my eyes up to his when the word comes out hoarse.

"For a picture," I confirm, noticing his nervousness. "This was your idea, remember?" I snicker, and his shoulders relax.

"Yes, I know…for *you*," he reiterates with a grin.

"Hunter," I say softly. "I know you want to help me out, but if this is going to be too uncomfortable and awkward, I won't be upset if you want to back out. I know you probably don't have a lot of experience with relationships and maybe didn't realize everything we'd have to do to make this look real, so—"

"Lennon, stop," he growls, turning to face me. "I'm not backing out. I said I'd do whatever you needed, so don't be afraid to ask, okay? I can handle it." His words come out confidently, and though a tinge of guilt surfaces at what we're doing, I know it's the only way. Once I confirmed my visit with my mother, she was so excited. I told her I had a surprise guest coming as well but never said who. She'll be getting a son-in-law and a grandchild all at once.

The corner of my lips tilts up, and I nod. "Okay. Thank you, Hunter."

I reposition myself on the couch until I'm practically on his lap. We've been quizzing each other all week long, sharing as many details about our childhood and pasts as possible. It's definitely made us closer, knowing more about him and what his family life entailed. So even if all of this goes wrong and my parents don't buy it, at least one good thing came out of it, and that'd be the growth and strength of our friendship.

I raise my phone once again, then bring my lips to his cheek and click the button. As I pull back, Hunter laughs. "I think I blinked."

That makes me chuckle. "It shouldn't be this hard to get a picture." I press my photos app and look. "Oh my God, Hunter!" I nudge him with my shoulder.

He's full-on sticking out his tongue and crossing his eyes, sabotaging the shot on purpose. I can't stop laughing, though, because it's Hunter in true fashion. Always messing with me.

"That'll have to do for now. Actually, I kinda like it." I shrug, putting a filter on it, and upload it to my fake account. But first I need a super cheesy caption.

Speaking out loud as I type, I say, "Every day is filled with love and laughs with this guy! Two red hearts. Hashtag newlyweds, hashtag love of my life, hashtag married life." Then I click post.

Once it's on the feed, I turn my phone toward Hunter and show him. "Whatcha think? Are we the cutest fake couple ever or what?" I snicker, thinking about the ridiculousness of this all. He has no idea how intense things will get when we arrive. Considering my sisters won't be there, all the attention will be on me. Fucking joy.

Hunter narrows his eyes at it and scrolls through the dozens of pictures I've posted. Everything from our morning coffees to "breakfast in bed" and movie nights. Some are just pictures of our legs as we lounge on the couch, but I know we're gonna have to keep it up even after we're back home. My mom will probably have the entire congregation follow me for updates on us and the baby.

"The Mrs. Manning," he reads my handle aloud. My profile picture is of the two of us with my 'married' name beneath as "Lennon Manning."

"Yeah." I shrug. "I thought it was cute. And cheesy." Chuckling, I study him and watch as his breath hitches and his jaw tightens. I'm not sure what kind of response I was expecting, but he looks affected. Maybe the reality of what we're doing is settling in. Maybe he thinks he's betraying Brandon, or hell, maybe he realizes his life will never be the same once we do this.

I know those thoughts have crossed my mind. But I'm the one with no options. He can still back out.

"Yeah, it looks nice. I'm sure they'll buy it." He nods, handing my phone back.

I grab my notebook from the coffee table and check off where I wrote "Daily Instagram post" under the Friday column. Ever since we decided to do this, I started making a daily to-do list so I don't forget anything. Getting our stories straight, learning everything we can about each other, and taking pictures and posting them on social media are a few tasks I have listed. If we're going to pull this off, we have to do whatever it takes.

Speaking of which…

"I have a weird request." I pull in my bottom lip and wait for his response.

Hunter went to grab a beer for himself and a bottle of water for me. He thinks I need to be hydrated twenty-four seven and forgets as soon as I drink it, I have to rush to the bathroom so I don't pee myself. I've been getting up at least three times at night, which is annoying when I'm warm and comfortable in bed for once.

"Any weirder than faking a marriage?" he mocks, taking a sip of his beer and setting my water down on the coffee table. Hunter plops down on the couch, leaving space between us.

I decide to let it go, figuring Hunter's in a weird mood tonight. Since we've been sharing more details about each other, I think it's made him more vulnerable than usual, and I don't want to push it.

Getting up, I ignore his comment and walk to the kitchen table where I had set out a few items that I still need to pack. There's a stack of notecards with random things about ourselves written on them as well as some with our "couple" information. I know the name of his first pet was Reagan, after the president. His first kiss was with a girl named Brittany in second grade. His brother's name is Hayden, and he lives in New York with his girlfriend, Savannah. Hunter's middle name is John after his great-grandfather on his mother's side. His birthday is November 23rd and lands on Thanksgiving every six years. His favorite holiday is Christmas because growing up, it was the one day of the year his family was "normal," and his dad didn't make work a priority. He told me funny stories of his uncle dressing up as Santa and how he found out the truth one year when he discovered a bag of presents in the laundry room.

We've talked so much and dug into some deep shit, it almost feels like it's been over a week since we started sharing details about one another. I like knowing more about him. It makes me feel confident that we'll look like a legit couple to my family.

"Lennon." Hunter's voice has me jumping out of my skin.

I turn around with my hand over my racing heart. "Shit, you scared me."

I didn't even hear his footsteps behind me. He's holding his beer in one hand and brings over my bottle of water I left in the living room.

"Sorry. I said your name a few times, but you must've been in your head again." He smirks, then hands me the water. "Wasn't sure if you wanted this or not."

My shoulders fall, and I grin. "I'm fine, but thank you. Baby's already using my bladder as a trampoline."

His brows shoot up to his hairline, making me burst out into laughter. "You can feel that already?"

I shrug, uncertain. "I don't know, but lately, I have to pee once an hour."

"That's gonna be a fun plane ride for you." He snickers. "Good thing it's not a long flight."

"Right." I sigh. The anxiety about telling my parents hits me. Hopefully, after the initial surprise, they'll be supportive and won't ask a million questions even though we're preparing for it.

"My nerves are gonna be shot anyway," I admit, lowering my eyes, then turn back around to my lists and notecards.

"Well, you won't be alone, so try not to stress too much," he tells me, and I feel him behind me. The guilt of what he's agreed to eats at me, though I try to push it away. Hunter wouldn't be doing this if he didn't want to, but because he's so willing has me wishing I could repay him someday for what he's subjecting himself to.

"I'll try," I say softly.

Hunter walks back into the kitchen, the fridge door opens and shuts, and he's by my side again.

"Lennon."

"Huh?"

"You said you had a weird request before," he reminds me. "What was it?"

"Oh, um…" A blush rises to my cheeks. "It's nothing. Never mind."

"C'mon," he urges. "You know I won't say no."

That has my lips tilting up a bit. "It's too much right now. Forget it."

Hunter sets down his beer, grabs my shoulders, and makes me

face him. He gazes into my eyes and gives me a pointed look that tells me he's not going to drop it. "Ask me."

My breathing picks up, and nervous butterflies form in my stomach as I look at the man who's going to be my fake husband for who the hell knows how long.

Sucking in a deep breath, I release it slowly. "Okay, but you *can* say no if you want."

Hunter drops his arms and crosses them over his chest. "Sure." His tone lets me know that won't be the case.

"I don't know how to ask this, so I'm just going to come out with it," I tell him, though I'm trying to convince myself to do it.

"Please do," he encourages.

"We're gonna need to kiss," I finally blurt and swallow hard as I wait for his reaction. He stands firmly, not moving or speaking. "If we want to convince my parents we're newlyweds, ones who are pregnant, they're going to expect us to be…touchy-feely. In love. So instead of it being weird around my parents, maybe we should…practice first." My voice cracks at the end, and I feel like I'm an inexperienced teenager all over again.

"Okay, I was not expecting that," Hunter finally replies, brushing a hand through his hair, then over his chin with a couple of days' worth of stubble. I've learned it's a nervous tell, which makes me feel better knowing I won't be the only one who feels awkward.

"I understand if you say no. It's a lot to ask. I shouldn't have mentioned it. It's odd, right? Sorry, forget it. I don't know what I was—"

"Lennon," Hunter interrupts my rambling. "I didn't say no. I just wasn't anticipating it, but you're right. We'll need to act like we've done it a time or two." He cracks the smallest of smiles, which eases my mind a bit. "Probably a good thing, so we don't act like two virgins on prom night."

I laugh, the tension fading. "Well, considering they demanded I wait until my wedding night to lose my virginity, it's not uncommon for couples in my church to get pregnant right away.

Most get married only after dating for a short time and announce they're having a baby a month later. Couples like that, who wait until their wedding night, are noticeably all over each other because they refrained so much beforehand."

"So pouncing on you in front of your parents is a must," he teases, taking a step back when I attempt to smack his chest.

"They're pretty modest, so while they won't mind touching and kissing, we need to be respectful in their home." I shrug, thankful for that specific rule.

"Sounds good." He stands in front of me with an unreadable expression. As he studies me, I know he's probably waiting for me to make the first move, but shit. I can't.

"I'm nervous," I admit with a half-smile.

"Don't be. I don't bite." He winks. "Well, unless you like that sorta thing."

"Oh my God, Hunter!" I blush hard. "You aren't helping!"

"Okay, sorry," he says with a chuckle. "Don't be scared. We'll start slow."

My chest rises and falls. Heavy breaths release from my nostrils as I try to gain some control. I don't know why I'm so anxious, but kissing Hunter like this feels so…calculated. Weird. Forbidden.

"Okay," I finally say, not moving.

After a few silent moments, he cracks a smile. "Are you gonna kiss me?"

I cover my face, hunching over in embarrassment. "Ugh. I can't stop the nerves."

"Lennon." His deep voice pulls me from my thoughts. "Just relax, okay?" He takes my hands and places them on his waist, bringing us closer together. "Breathe."

I release a deep, steady breath as his palms cup my face.

"Do you trust me?" When his eyes bore into mine, I feel as though I'm looking into the depths of his soul. I know without a doubt this man would do anything for me.

"Of course I do," I whisper, tightening my grip on his hips.

"Good." He gives me the sweetest smile. "Now close your eyes."

I do, and a beat later, I feel his mouth on me.

Slow and soft, he presses his lips against mine as he moves us together in perfect harmony. He pulls back slightly and his tongue traces my bottom lip before bringing us even closer together. My heart pounds so hard, I'm sure he can feel my pulse throbbing in my neck.

Hunter cradles my face as if I'm the most precious thing in the world. Gently, he rubs his thumb against my cheek, and when he slides his tongue between our lips, the kiss deepens, and I unwillingly release a moan. Hunter pulls back slightly, and my eyes pop open, looking right at him. By the expression on his face, he's asking for permission to keep going, and when I don't push away, he brings our mouths back together.

His hand slides down my throat, neck, and down my side, sending electricity everywhere he touches. I squeeze my fingers in his shirt and arch my back, forcing us closer together as he cups my ass. Reaching up, I wrap my arms around his neck, removing the remaining space between us. Hunter's other hand falls from my face, and he snakes his arm around my waist, holding me tight. The kiss grows eager, faster, *desperate.*

I feel his kiss down to my core. I feel it *everywhere.*

Mixed feelings surface as his tongue dances with mine, sending butterflies to my stomach as my heart races with eagerness. Each touch feels hot against my skin, and I'm powerless to stop it.

A deep groan releases from his throat, and when I feel his hardness against my stomach, I realize this is escalating too far. Quickly, I push him, stepping back to create distance. That kiss was way too heated and intense to be fake. My breathing quickens, and when his chest heaves, I know it affected him just as much as it did me. My gaze lowers to the noticeable bulge in his jeans. A rather *big* bulge.

Wrong, wrong, wrong.

"I'm sorry, I shouldn't have—"

"No, I—"

"I didn't mean—"

We can't get our words out and now it's awkward.

Why did that feel so damn good?

I'm blaming my hormones.

"That was…" I pause, watching him lick his lips and looking as conflicted as I feel. "Nice."

Hunter releases a short breath and snorts. "Uh, thanks?"

I study him as he wipes his hands down his jeans, a nervous tick I've not seen him do before.

"Guess we won't have any problems convincing them," I say, not knowing what else to say. My heart races, torn in two as I think about Brandon—the man I'll always love—and the man in front of me, who cares for me deeply.

"Guess not," Hunter replies casually.

We stare at each other, neither speaking nor knowing what to do. The silence lingers until his phone rings, pulling us both away.

Hunter reaches into his pocket, grabs his phone, but declines the call.

"You can get that if you need to." I pick up my water and walk toward the kitchen before he can respond.

Shit, I could use a shot of tequila right now. If not to erase the inappropriate thoughts from my brain, then at least to give me the courage to face him again. I blow out a breath, needing to calm my racing heart.

Squeezing my eyes tight, I will the images of him hard and aroused out of my mind. It doesn't work. As I'm sucking down my bottle of water, I feel Hunter behind me.

"Lennon, I'm sorry." His pained voice crushes me. I know this can't be easy for him, considering he hasn't been with a woman since the accident. He probably has the same amount of pent-up sexual frustration as I do and didn't mean to take it that far.

When I face him, his expression makes me frown. "You have nothing to be sorry for," I reassure him. "It was my idea, remember? I know it didn't mean anything, and we got lost in the moment."

His jaw locks as if he's holding back, but I don't give him a chance to reply before trying to lighten the mood. "On the plus side, I'm starting to see the appeal other girls had over the years."

Hunter rolls his eyes with a small smirk. "Would you just let me apologize, please? It'd make me feel like less of an asshole."

I shrug, giving in. "Fine, but you have nothing to—"

"Lennon." He grits through his teeth.

"Fine!" I raise my arms and drop them to my sides.

He inhales deeply, then steps back slightly. "I'm sorry I kissed you that way. I shouldn't have let myself go that far. It'll never happen again, I promise." He sincerely rests a hand on his chest over his heart as if he needs to stop it from bursting out of his chest.

Never?

I swallow at his words, hating that he feels the need to say them in the first place. I'm the one who brought it up, after all.

"Alright, apology accepted." I tell him what he wants to hear. "But we might want to practice again tomorrow."

Hunter raises his brows.

"Practice *normal* kissing," I reiterate. "Without the possibility of giving my parents a show. Or a heart attack." I shrug, all dignity going out the fucking window at this point.

Slowly nodding, he grins and moves away from the counter toward me. "Like this?"

He doesn't give me a second to answer before his lips are back on mine.

CHAPTER TWENTY-TWO

HUNTER

ALL THE OXYGEN escapes my lungs as I push off the counter and lunge for Lennon like an animal. She gasps in my mouth as I bring our lips together, colliding in a desperate battle of wanting more but not letting myself get carried away again.

I'm pretty certain my heart stopped beating the moment she asked me to kiss her. Hell, I think I blacked out for a second. My head knows this is fake—it's all show, an act, *not* real—but fuck, my heart doesn't care. Tasting her, a desire I've craved for over two years, brings back the memories of the night we first met.

Her flirtatious smile, seductive voice, and lingering eyes were on me as I moved behind the bar to mix her drink. Goddamn, it makes me hard.

Then the reality of what I'm doing—what we're doing—hits me like a ton of bricks, and I beat myself up all over again. I saw her first. But it didn't matter because she chose him, and Brandon was my best friend. I'd never take what wasn't mine, and she clearly made her decision that night. However, that didn't stop the way I've felt about her, and when our mouths press together in a soft, sensual kiss, it takes all the fucking self-control in the world not to go any further.

My lips brush against hers, light and sweet with just enough pressure to nearly steal her breath away. We have to make it believable that we're in love. Then as quickly as I grabbed her, I pull back.

"Was that better?" I ask above a whisper.

"No." She pops her eyes open. "I mean, yes. Yes. Sorry."

My brows arch. "You're sure?"

Lennon chuckles, which has become my favorite sound in the world, and swats at my chest. "You know what I mean. That was…perfect."

A blush on her cheeks indicates she liked it way more than she wants to admit. I felt every fiber of her body press into mine when I kissed her the first time. She was begging for and needing more, taking everything I'd given her.

But I know she got lost in the make-believe of it all. She probably wishes it were Brandon and not me, and the fact that I'm jealous of my dead best friend rips me away from her.

"Okay, well, I'm gonna head to bed. Or take a shower. Probably a cold one." I walk backward, and she laughs at my expense. "We have a busy day tomorrow, so you should probably get some sleep."

"I'll get right on that," she mocks.

Lennon pretends to hate how much I take care of her, making sure she's eating enough for two, drinking water, and not stressing, but I think deep down she appreciates it. She nearly gave me a stroke when I saw her doing yoga last week with her body bent in half. After the panic subsided, she reassured me it was perfectly safe for the baby.

Doesn't mean I didn't have to drink a beer after that to calm down.

If I thought Lennon was gorgeous before, seeing her swollen belly grow is beyond anything I ever imagined. She's glowing, completely stunning, and beautiful. I can't stop looking at her, watching her, appreciating every inch of her tempting body. Her shirts have grown a tad snug, showing off her breasts. Since her body is changing, she'll need bigger clothes soon, but she's being stubborn about it.

There will be more doctor appointments too, which I've already reassured her I'd go to. I don't want her to be alone through this, and even though I say it's for Brandon, I'm not too selfish to admit I want to be there for me too. This kid is going to be in my life, and I want to support Lennon every step of the way. Knowing my best friend is missing one of the greatest moments of his life has my emotions in overdrive.

As I step into the cool shower, I speak to him. Tell him how amazing Lennon has handled everything so far. Tell him how much we both miss him. Lastly, I tell him how sorry I am for kissing his girlfriend. For being in *love* with his girlfriend.

I can't say with certainty if Brandon would ever approve of a relationship between Lennon and me, but I'd like to think he'd trust me enough to care for her and their child. I'd never hurt her. Keeping his memory alive is something I vow to always do. I miss him so much, sometimes it chokes me alive.

Once I'm in bed, I stare at the ceiling and think about that kiss. Fake or not, it felt every bit real to me. Her breasts pushed into my chest, back arched to deepen it, and then she moaned.

Fucking hell, that moan.

My cock gets hard just thinking about it.

Because I'm a glutton for punishment, I lower my hand into my shorts and stroke my dick. The cold shower did nothing to subside my hard-on, and I relive the way she responded to me. I think about how things have shifted between us, how close we've gotten, and how comfortable we are together. Lennon makes me feel safe talking to her about things I keep inside. She's managed to do something no one else ever has, and I doubt I'll ever feel this way about anyone else again.

My cock grows harder, my fist squeezing tighter as I increase the pace. Lennon is all I can focus on—her sweet face, luscious tits, contagious laugh. Fuck, she's the full package. Always has been.

Grunting, I slide my fist over the tip, again and again until I'm coming, hard and fast. I release a harsh breath between gritted teeth, hoping she can't hear me in the next room, but shit that was intense. I use my shirt to clean myself off and grab a new one, feeling temporary relief.

Over the past few months, I've jerked off as much as I did when I was a teenager, but having Lennon this close to me every single day makes me edgy. I have no desire to go out on the weekends or find someone else. The mere thought of it has me laughing at myself. All those times I teased Brandon for being pussy whipped, and here I am, whipped without the pussy.

Lennon invades every part of me, more than ever before, and after tasting her lips, I'm worried I'll lose my self-control. Though I can't. Things can't escalate, no matter how badly I want it. Lennon needs a friend, someone she can trust and rely on.

Not to mention, I'd forever live with the remorse of betraying my best friend. Though there's one secret of his I plan to take to the grave. I can't lie to Lennon, not if I want to stay in her life, but it's one thing I promised Brandon. He's no longer here to propose, and I don't know if knowing would hurt her worse or give her closure. She's in better spirits from a few weeks ago even though I know she's still grieving. With that, we're now going to pretend to be married, so how in the hell do I mention Brandon bought her an engagement ring and was ready to ask her to be his wife on this very trip?

Hell, if I knew, I'd know what to do with the damn ring that burns a hole in my nightstand.

Ever since I found the ring in their bedroom, I've gone back and forth on what to do with it. Give it to his mother? Let her decide? Keep it for when Lennon's ready to know, if she'll ever be ready to know. I hate that I'm left to make this decision when either one could hurt her, or worse—have her running from me.

Each night over the past week, I've dreamed of Lennon and our fake marriage. It feels so fucking real, I forget it's not. She looks at me as if I'm the only man in the room, and as soon as I touch her, Brandon's face appears. Every damn time, I wake up gasping, ready to take a beating from him because that's what I deserve.

I'm so fucked.

Battling my emotions has been the hardest part of this arrangement. I didn't even take a second to think about how this plan would affect me before blurting it out, but I don't regret it. I'd do it over and over again if it meant keeping her happy and stress-free.

"Hey, sleepyhead," I greet as soon as I hear Lennon's feet pad into the kitchen. I love being able to sleep in a little on Saturdays, but it's never much. After I start a pot of coffee, I make breakfast, knowing Lennon needs food to fully wake up.

"Ugh." She leans against the counter, her blond hair a mess on top of her head. She looks freaking adorable.

"Rough night?" I arch a brow, glancing over my shoulder as I cook an omelet on the stove. "Looks like you got into a fight with a toaster in the shower." I smirk when she glares.

"It's not fair that you literally wake up like that…" She waves her arm up and down, motioning to my body.

I chuckle. "It's a curse."

Lennon snorts, moving around me to reach the fridge. "I had a hard time falling asleep. My nerves are shot, not to mention it's getting uncomfortable to sleep. My boobs are annoying and sensitive, and I feel like a beached whale."

I shoot her a look, linger over her breasts, and move my gaze down to her belly. "You have the tiniest bump."

She takes the jug of orange juice and slams the door shut. "Well, it doesn't feel tiny when I'm trying to sleep."

Her death cracks me up.

"I heard a body pillow can help during pregnancy. Want me to find you one?" I ask casually, expecting to catch heat for reading up on this kind of shit.

"I was thinking about getting one." She pours juice into a cup and takes a long sip. "Wait. How do you know about those?" She pauses but continues before I can respond. "Never mind. I should know the answer to that one." Lennon laughs and gives me an appreciative smile.

"I like reading up on stuff so I have more knowledge about what you're going through. You know I'm not going anywhere, so I want to educate myself." I flip the omelet once more.

"Well, it is your apartment, so it's not like you'd leave." Lennon takes a seat at the table, and I shoot her a glare before turning off the stove.

"Yours too since your name's on the lease," I mutter softly, grabbing two plates from the cabinet.

"What?" she asks loudly.

"I put your name on the lease," I repeat, emphasizing each word. "So it's not just *my* apartment. It's yours too."

She gives me a quizzical look, glancing up from her glass. "When did you do that?"

I place an omelet on each of the plates, grab two forks, then bring them to the table where I set one in front of her and take the other. "About a month ago."

Lennon stares at me. "Were you ever going to tell me?"

I shrug, not seeing why she's so rattled about this. "I guess it hasn't come up till now."

Digging into my food, I take a huge bite so I have an excuse not to speak. Lennon's eyes burn into my skin, and after a minute, I can't take it any longer and stand to get myself a glass of juice.

By the time I sit back down, I'm happy to see Lennon's eaten half of her omelet.

"Hunter." Her scolding tone has me bringing my eyes to hers. "You added my name to the lease?"

I set down my fork and give her my undivided attention. "Yes. Why wouldn't I?"

She looks around and blinks. "Well, I don't know. It seems kinda significant."

"I said it before, and I'll say it again in case you're experiencing pregnancy brain," I begin, which makes her chuckle. "You aren't going anywhere, and neither am I. This place is just as much mine as it is yours. You and the baby and me…as weird as that is, I don't give a shit. This works."

Lennon frowns, which is the opposite of what I was expecting. "That's a big commitment from someone who can't commit to the same pizza place."

"That's different," I tell her. "Not to mention, I like a variety of pizza."

"And what happens when you're ready for a change?"

"I order Chinese food instead."

"Hunter!" She bursts out laughing. "You know what I mean."

"Don't you trust me?" I ask her.

She nods, sucking in her lips.

"If we're pulling off a fake marriage, don't you think my wife should be on the rental lease?"

"Who the hell is going to check that?"

"I don't know, you tell me," I mock.

"Pfft. It's my apartment, remember? So I added *you* to my lease when we got *married*." She snickers. "Except you didn't think of this plan until a week ago."

"Lennon," I warn. "Drop it."

Thankfully, she does, and we go back to eating in silence. Once I'm done, I rinse my plate and load the dishwasher. Then I make a cup of coffee, and Lennon glares at it.

"You can't hate me for drinking caffeine," I quip.

"No, but I can still scowl about it."

"You can have one cup, Lennon," I remind her, smiling as I take another sip. "If you want."

"Of course I want to, but I'd rather be safe than sorry. The last thing I need is a hyperactive toddler running circles around me." She places a hand on her little bump.

"I don't think it works that way, but suit yourself." I wink. "Let me know when you're ready to finish those notecards."

She takes her last bite and slides her plate next to mine. "Thanks for breakfast. I'm gonna shower, then I'll be ready to play wifey." She rolls her eyes, frowning.

"You sure know how to make your husband feel good," I mock as she saunters off.

Lennon stops before leaving the kitchen. "Oh sorry, did I bruise your inflated ego? Figured that was impossible." She makes a face and walks down the hallway.

"Pretty sassy for a pregnant woman!" I holler so she can hear me, but I can't stop smiling as I finish my coffee.

Deciding I better take this opportunity to call Hayden since we've only randomly texted over the past few months, I grab my phone. I haven't filled him in on the details of what's been going on since Brandon's death. Honestly, I don't even know where to begin. He texted me a few days ago, and it slipped my mind to call him when I got off work. I wait until I hear the water running and Lennon singing before I dial his number.

"Hey, bro," he answers. "I was wondering when I was gonna hear from you again."

"Shit, I know. I'm sorry. Lots going on," I tell him, walking into the living room.

"I bet," he says with insinuation in his tone. I ignore it and decide not to call him out on it. "Well, I'm glad you called either way. I have some news."

I pause and wait. "Well, you gonna say it, or do I have to guess?"

Hayden laughs. "Sav and I are officially getting hitched! I

popped the question, and she said yes!" he announces, loud and proud.

"I told you she would!" I'm smiling so wide, my cheeks hurt. "About goddamn time! I was wondering when you were gonna do it, considering you picked that ring out two months ago."

He laughs, and I can hear how happy he is. "I wanted the proposal and everything to be perfect and special for her. Donny helped me plan it. It's still soon, but I think we're gonna get married in California next summer so everyone can make arrangements and be there."

"Wow, that fast?"

"It's been over ten years, Hunter." He chuckles.

I roll my eyes at his exaggeration. They haven't been together for ten years, but them finally getting engaged has been a decade in the making.

"I'd get married tomorrow, but she wants her parents there and the whole big fancy white wedding, which is understandable. So I'm going to do whatever she wants because her happiness is all that matters to me."

"Well, I'm excited as fuck for you guys. Seriously."

"Thanks, man. If you had texted my ass back, you would've known the day it happened…" He doesn't finish his sentence, but he doesn't have to for me to know what he was going to say.

"I know. I've been preoccupied. I'm sorry. Congrats to you both, though! I'm glad you two are finally gonna tie the knot."

"I get it. I do," he sympathizes. "And thanks. Sav's pretty fucking thrilled."

Since we're chatting about our lives, I decide to spill my own truths. "Well, there's something I need to tell you, but you can't judge me."

"Hunter, what'd you do?"

I roll my eyes at his accusing tone.

"Nothing. But—"

"So, *hubby*…you ready to do this?" Lennon comes into the living room at the worst fucking time possible.

Son of a bitch.

I pinch the bridge of my nose, knowing Hayden heard her.

"Oh sorry, you're on the phone. I'll finish packing for our honeymoon while you're chatting." She laughs to herself and walks back to her room.

"You've got to be fucking kidding me, Hunter! What the hell?"

Hayden chews my ass like I figured he would. He fucking roars.

"Are you done?" I deadpan.

"Don't make me jump on a plane to come kick your ass," he threatens.

Guess not.

"It's not what you think. Fucking relax." I lean forward on the couch, grabbing my mug and chugging the rest of my coffee.

"I heard 'hubby' and 'honeymoon.' Not sure how that can be interpreted any other way."

"We're faking it," I explain.

"Just when I thought you couldn't possibly say anything stupider, you do. Christ, Hunter. What the hell does that even mean?"

Inhaling a deep breath, I begin to tell him. From Lennon finding out she's pregnant, to the story of her parents and their religious background, to the plan that has us flying to Utah to fake our marriage. I tell him everything. He's the only person I trust with my life, so I know he won't rat me out, but there's no doubt he's judging me pretty hard.

"Well?" I ask after he doesn't say anything.

"Hmm. Part of me wants to pat you on the back for helping her out and doing what you think is best, while the other part wants to shake some sense into your puny brain for even suggesting it. You know this isn't going to end well."

"It wouldn't end well either way, Hayden," I tell him honestly. "At least this way her parents won't disown her, and she'll have support for the baby."

"Yeah, and what does that mean for you?"

"I'm not worried about me right now."

"Clearly." He scoffs. "You're in love with her, Hunter. How the hell do you plan to pretend? I mean…"

"I know," I grit, not wanting to say anything Lennon can overhear. "I owe her. I owe Brandon. This isn't about me, I promise."

After a beat of silence, he sighs. "Okay, well, I wish you the best. I'm just worried about you, but you're a big boy, so I trust you know what you're doing."

Do I know what I'm doing? Christ, I hope so.

We chat for another couple of minutes before ending the call. I'm excited for him and Sav, but part of me is so envious he gets to be with the love of his life. He deserves it all, and I can't wait for the wedding. When I was a teenager, I watched him self-destruct after their breakup, and it was a wake-up call.

Don't trust women.

Mostly, I didn't. It was proven to me time and again that they'd chew you up and spit you out without a second thought. Then Lennon entered the picture, and everything changed.

"Hey, if you're done, I wanna show you something," Lennon calls from the bedroom.

"Yeah, sure," I shout.

She steps into the living room wearing a knee-length sundress that fits her perfectly. I can't even see her bump from this angle. It's not until she turns to the side that I notice there's one.

"What do you think? I want to look nice so they don't ask me a hundred questions about how I feel about Brandon or the pregnancy. So if I look decent, they'll assume everything is great." She shrugs, but there's sadness in her eyes.

Pushing myself up, I stand and walk toward her. I smile and nod. "You look amazing. Really good."

"Yeah? Okay, well, thanks. I need to dress the part. Now that I'm a *wife* and future homemaker." She snorts.

"I don't even wanna know what that means." I shake my head, the nerves setting in about meeting her parents tomorrow evening. Tonight's our last night of normalcy—well, normal for us —and then everything's gonna change.

"No, you don't, but don't forget to pack some dressy clothes. You'll need them for dinner and whatever else they drag us to."

"I won't."

"Well, I'm going to change back into some comfy clothes so we can continue looking over those notecards and finish packing."

She goes to walk away, stops and turns back to me. "I know I've said it a million times, but thank you." Lennon closes the space between us and wraps her arms around me. I wrap one around her, pulling her to my chest, and kiss the top of her head.

"Whatever you need, Lennon," I promise.

"Oh, that does remind me of one more favor…" She pulls back so our eyes lock, and she bites her bottom lip.

I raise my brows, wanting her to say it. At this point, nothing she could say will shock me.

"We're gonna need to sleep together tonight."

Okay, except that.

CHAPTER TWENTY-THREE

LENNON

Hunter looks as though he's seen a ghost. He takes a step back, wrapping a hand around the back of his neck and squeezing.

"Come again?"

I know he heard me.

"I need you to sleep with me. In bed. Together."

His throat moves as he swallows hard. "Why?"

I chew the inside of my cheek, twisting my lips from side to side. I hate how I'm constantly asking him for shit.

"Quick version: we're going to be expected to sleep in the same bed at my parents' house."

Hunter narrows his eyes. "And they're going to be watching to make sure of that?" he asks, his voice edgy.

"Pfft. Seriously wouldn't doubt it, but no. And the bed is only a full size."

His eyes widen, finally understanding.

"So we might want a practice night." I suck in for air. He held me that one night shortly after Brandon died, but that was different.

"How the hell are we going to fit in a full size?" Hunter raises his brows. He's well over six feet tall and twice my build, so that's a damn good question.

"Uh, well…being very, very close?" I grimace. "I'd say one of us can sleep on the floor and pack an extra pillow, but the doors don't lock, so they could walk in at any minute."

He tilts his head, studying me. "The doors don't have locks? What the hell kinda environment did you grow up in?"

I throw my arms up. "I told you! They're crazy! They wanted to control everything, which meant a lack of privacy."

"That's fucking nuts, Lennon," he says. "Are there cameras in the bathroom I should know about too?"

"No!" I playfully push him. "But I did warn you! I told you we were really gonna have to sell it because they'll pry into *everything*."

He blinks, taking a step back. "Alright, it's fine. I'll do whatever it takes. But if I squish you and the baby in the middle of the night, that's on you," he teases.

"Ha-ha. I won't think twice about shoving your ass off the bed," I warn playfully.

"Fair enough." His tone is weak, almost as if he's in pain. I've been asking a lot of him, but as soon as we return from this trip, things will go back to normal, and we can both forget this ever happened. Or try to.

My phone rings from the bedroom, so I tell Hunter to hold on and rush to answer it. As soon as I see Sophie's name on the screen, I pick it up with a pleasant *hello*.

"You holding up okay?"

"I think so. Nerves are setting in. I think once we're there and the news is out, I'll be able to relax a teeny bit. Even better when we get it over with." I sigh, my shoulders slumping as I sit on the bed.

"How's Hunter doing? You two get all the details figured out?" She wants more info, which doesn't surprise me at this point.

"Uh, well. Yes," I hesitate on how much to tell her, but she's my sister, and I tell her almost everything. "We practiced kissing."

"I'm sorry, what did you say?" Sophie nearly chokes out the words.

I roll my eyes, knowing damn well she heard me. "We had to! We have to be convincing, which means acting and looking like a real couple."

She's silent for a beat, then speaks up in a too perky tone. "With tongue?"

Laughter escapes me as my cheeks heat. "You're ridiculous."

"That means yes," she says matter-of-factly. "I bet he's a good kisser too." She sighs as if she's imagining it, which has me chuckling. Hunter *is* a fantastic kisser. *Fuck my life.* "So are you hot for Hunter? Because I wouldn't blame you in the least."

"Hot for Hunter?" I repeat, blushing. "Are we back in middle school?" I ask defensively.

"That's not an answer."

I groan, not wanting to have this conversation. Things are getting complicated even though I don't want to admit it. Last night after we went to bed, I'm pretty sure I heard Hunter jerking off. Part of me wanted to press my ear to the wall and listen, but I knew that'd be wrong. Still, it didn't mean I wasn't intrigued, wondering if he was thinking about me or not.

And as soon as that thought crossed my mind, I pushed it away.

"No, of course not. This is all pretend, Soph."

"Hmm…but is it?" she asks in a condescending tone. "I see the way he looks at you. The way he's *always* looked at you. It's okay to admit you're attracted to him. I know you feel guilty because of Brandon, but Hunter's a hot piece of single man meat."

"Eww," I say, laughing. "Please don't ever say man meat ever again."

"Stop dodging the question, sis." I hear the smile in her snarky tone, but I don't allow myself to think about those things. I can't.

"Hot for Hunter sounds like an ad campaign for a new men's cologne." I snort, hoping she drops it.

"Hell, it should be!" She chuckles. "The man always smells so damn good."

So much for dropping it.

"Well, we were going to go through our notecards again, and I need to finish packing." My stomach growls. "And apparently the baby's hungry again."

"Okay, fine. Go feed my niece or nephew and please text me when you can. I'm going to be a nervous wreck waiting to hear from you," she pleads.

"I will, promise! Everything okay over there?" I quickly ask. "Are you avoiding Hurricane Carter?"

"Yes and no." She groans. "I'm ready to dick punch him, cut it off, then serve it on a platter to Maria."

"That's…graphic." I snicker. "Well, good luck. If you want to stay here while we're gone, I can leave you a key."

"Ooh, maybe. I'll let you know."

Minutes later, we end the call, but I need a moment to get myself together before going back to Hunter. Sophie's words linger in my head, my heart races, and I'm nervous about facing him after what she said.

This is all just pretend, I remind myself.

Once I'm good, I walk into the living room with a smile plastered on my face. I grab the notecards from the kitchen table and sit on the couch next to him, hoping he doesn't notice my awkwardness.

"Where did I grow up?" I ask, keeping my eyes down.

He answers right.

"What school did I graduate from?"

Right again.

"What's the name of the church where my father preaches?"

Right once again.

I ask him at least twenty more—a mix of childhood questions to more recent stuff—and he answers all correctly without pause.

"What's my favorite color?" I ask randomly, though it wasn't written down in the cards. He's so on top of his game, I want to throw a wrench his way.

"Yellow," he answers, not as confident as before.

"Why do you say that?" It's a trick question since I don't have one.

Hunter shrugs one shoulder. "You remind me of sunshine, so I thought yellow suited you best."

"I do? How so?" I ask, genuinely interested.

He shakes his head just the slightest, twisting his lips almost as if he wished he hadn't said anything, but I'm too curious to let him off the hook, so I anxiously wait.

"Well, when you weren't scowling, you were always laughing and smiling, singing and dancing around. You were the epitome of a ray of sunshine, lighting up every room you walked into. It wasn't hard to notice, I guess." I hear the vulnerability in his tone as our eyes stay locked.

"Wow…" I say, blinking. "I think that's the nicest thing you've ever said to me." I think yellow just became my favorite.

Before he can respond, my stomach growls…loudly.

His brows pinch together as he laughs. "Was that you?"

"Yeah. Apparently, breakfast wasn't enough." I blush.

"Good time to take a break. I think I have your notecards memorized." Hunter wipes his palms down his jeans and stands. "Want me to make you an early lunch?"

"How about you let me make you something for a change?" I grab his arm and pull him back to face me. "Seriously, I can."

"Sure. I was just trying to help." He thrusts his hands into his front pockets. "Actually, I'm not super hungry, so I'll pass this time. I'm gonna hit the gym for a couple of hours since I'm all packed." Hunter's tense, and I wish I knew what he was thinking.

"Oh, um, okay. I'm about done too, so maybe I'll take a nap after I eat."

We stare awkwardly at each other before he breaks away and walks to his room.

As I make a sandwich, I think about everything I need to do once we're back from the trip. I haven't told Brandon's parents yet, and I'm not sure how the hell to do that. Mrs. Locke has texted me some, checking on me, which I appreciate. I hope she'll be ecstatic with the news, but honestly, I don't know. Either she'll be excited to have a part of Brandon with us or she'll be too grief-stricken and not want anything to do with me and the baby.

As I'm sitting at the kitchen table, looking over the stack of notes I need to memorize, Hunter saunters in wearing his workout clothes. He grabs his keys and wallet, then says he'll be back in a couple of hours. We say goodbye, and he's out the door.

Looks like we've reached the awkward stage of faking a marriage and things being weird between us. Asking him to practice kissing and sleeping with me was probably too much. I'm starting to worry all my requests are taking a toll on him.

The conversation with Sophie lingers in my mind as I clean the apartment. Guilt consumes me as I think about how close Hunter and I have become over the past few months, but a part of me believes Brandon would be happy we're leaning on each other. He always wanted us to get along, but I'm afraid we've crossed those lines now. If Hunter and I had met under other circumstances—if he had only been the roommate and we didn't share a moment at the bar before I met Brandon—the entire course of our friendship would've been different.

Was Hunter an asshole to me because he thought I stole his best friend? Was he angry all this time because I ended up with Brandon and not him?

Shit. Why hadn't I thought of this before?

Hunter taking care of me, nearly begging me to stay here, suggesting this insane plan of being my fake husband…

And then kissing me like that.

Oh my God.

Realization hits me in full force as I tidy up the bathroom. Every time he heard me singing, he screamed at me to shut up, and now he loves it. He says Brandon would've wanted us to get along, which I know is true, but he has gone above and beyond to make sure I'm okay. He hasn't brought a girl home in months or even gone out to the bars without me.

Have I been that dense this entire fucking time?

After Hunter gets home from the gym three hours later, he takes a shower, and we hang out for the rest of the night. He seems a lot less tense, which eases the awkwardness between us. He makes us dinner, and we talk about the plans once we arrive in Utah. I told my parents I'd be renting a car so they didn't have to make the hour-long drive to pick us up, but that was mostly because I didn't want to do introductions in the middle of a busy airport.

"So, uh, if we're going to be sleeping in the same bed, you're gonna have to wear like eight layers of clothes," Hunter says.

"I'm three and a half months pregnant, so yeah, that's not happening," I tease. "I'm an oven as it is."

"Well, I can't sleep in clothes, so I figured one of us should."

I look at him on the couch, enough space between us to fit two other people. "If it's a problem, we can skip it. Once we're at my folks, we'll wing it." I stand to walk away so I can wash my face and get ready for bed, but Hunter follows behind me and grabs my hand before I can get too far.

"Lennon, wait." He spins me around so we're facing each other. "Sorry I'm being weird about this. It's just…" He pauses and looks away for a split second. "You're still Brandon's girlfriend to me, and I'm trying not to cross any lines."

I nod, wanting him to know I understand. "I think we're at that point where we can admit the lines have blurred."

His eyes drop to my lips, and he blinks as if he can't let himself go there. Hunter, the asshole roommate, is long gone, and I know that. I trust *this* Hunter with my life, and I can see he's fighting with himself the same way I am.

Before he responds, I continue. "Things are about to get messy with having to be close and showing emotions for each other, so what if we put our past on the back burner, pretend it doesn't exist, and start over as if it's only ever been me and you?" I know that sounds awful, and I feel terrible even suggesting it because I still love Brandon—will always love him—but this is my new reality. I wish more than anything he were here to experience this with me, but he's not, and I have to do whatever it takes to get through it.

"You really want that?" His eyes pierce through me, showing me how hard this is for him, though he's been insistent on helping me.

"I think it's the only way you and I can get through this without feeling like it's wrong."

His throat moves as he swallows hard. "Alright."

Once I'm ready for bed, I let Hunter know so he can join me. He's in sweatpants and a T-shirt, which has me cracking a smile. I know with certainty he does not wear that to sleep.

"You're gonna burn up in those," I tell him.

Considering it's early July, we're both going to roast wearing any layers in bed.

"I'll be fine." He walks to the other side and moves the sheets. I feel him moving around as I stay on my side, nearly hugging the edge of the bed, and stare at the wall like this isn't the strangest sleepover ever.

Hunter shifts around, fluffing the pillow, then stills. "Uh…" His voice lingers. "Lennon."

"What?"

He starts cracking up, and when I turn to face him, my eyes widen, and my heart drops.

"Oh my God." My cheeks heat, and I take the vibrator from his hand. "That's, uh, not what you think."

Dammit, Sophie.

I spin around and shove the toy into my nightstand, hoping like hell he'll drop this. I bury myself back in bed, closing my eyes tight.

"That's a nice back massager you've got." He chuckles. "Might want to find a new hiding spot, though, now that I know where it is."

"Ugh!" I slam my arms down over the covers and turn toward him. "Can sweet and caring Hunter return now, please? This is embarrassing, and I'm already nervous you're in here."

His face drops as he looks at me. "Okay, I'm sorry." The tiniest smile flashes across his face, making me roll my eyes. He knows damn well that it was a vibrator, one I've been using regularly to relieve stress and tension.

I lean over to the nightstand and click off the lamp. "Good night, Hunter."

Sometime in the middle of the night, I hear Hunter shed his clothing. I snicker, knowing I was right. He climbs back in, and minutes later, his arm snakes around my waist. I should push him away, but when he closes the gap between us, and the warmth of his skin hits me, I can't deny how good it feels to be held again.

I fall back asleep, and when my eyes pop open at the sounds of a deep, agonizing groan, I notice sunlight peeking through the curtains.

When I roll over, Hunter's curled into a ball, hissing through his teeth.

What the hell?

"Are you okay?" I ask, sitting up. Strangely, I feel rejuvenated. Hunter held me most of the night, and at some point, we shifted, and I rested my head on his chest. I could hear his heart beating and felt protected all night long.

"No." He groans. "Your knee…" He pants, blinking. "In my junk."

"I did?" I gasp, bringing a hand to his shoulder. "Oh my God. I'm so sorry."

"Just…give me a second." His head falls as he cups his groin.

Sliding out of bed, I walk to his side and watch the agony take over. Shit, I feel awful. I've never kicked Brandon in the nuts before, so I don't know how I managed to kick his.

After five minutes, he finally relaxes and releases a relieved breath. "I thought I was gonna die."

"Hunter, I'm—"

"Gonna kill me?" He raises his brows, pretending to be amused, though I know he's not.

"I'm sorry! I don't know how that happened. I guess I twitch in my sleep a little."

"Well, I was trying to slide out from under your legs, and your knee went straight for my dick."

My eyes widen, realizing why my aim was so good. We snuggled all night. Then it dawns on me—*morning wood*. I wince, knowing that had to hurt like a bitch.

Hunter stands, and I stare, willing my eyes to stay focused on his face and not the fact that he's down to his boxer briefs. "Well, I better go pack a cup for my junk so you don't bruise me in Utah."

"Okay, now you're purposely trying to make me feel bad." I chuckle, following him out the door.

"We have to leave in two hours," he reminds me. "I'm gonna make breakfast and shower unless you wanna go first?"

I want to comment on the fact that he did last night after his workout but decide against it. I hope sleeping with me wasn't torture for him, but that doesn't mean I'm not contemplating bringing my vibrator in there with me to release all the tension building inside me.

The thought makes me feel guilty as hell.

No, I remind myself. I can't let it consume me right now. Hunter's friendship and finding out I was pregnant with Brandon's baby have been the only things keeping me afloat. I'm certain I would've drowned with grief by now if the baby didn't exist. In a way, our child saved me from falling into a deep depression.

Aside from harming Hunter, sleeping with him felt more natural than I anticipated. Maybe it's because I was so used to having Brandon next to me that it felt right or that I've been so lonely without him here. Either way, sharing a bed might not be as bad as I thought.

"You have everything?" Hunter asks after we've both showered and finished getting ready, pulling a suitcase behind him. "I'm going to make a trip to the truck and put everything in the back. Then we can get going."

"Yep. Let me grab my bags."

"Bags?" he asks, his brows arching. "You know we're only staying for three nights, right?"

"Yes," I say. "I had to bring shoes and a few different outfits."

Shaking his head, he chuckles. "Women."

Once he's loaded everything, I look around to make sure I don't forget anything, though I know a part of me is stalling. Once we leave this apartment, we're really doing this. We're going to Utah as a married couple.

"You ready?" He stands in front of me, smirking.

"Ready as I'll ever be, I guess." I shrug, the nerves hitting me hard.

Hunter brings his hand up, rubs my cheek, and tucks strands of hair behind my ear. "I'll be here for you no matter what. You know that, right?"

My eyes start to water because I do know. Nodding, I lean into his touch and exhale. I wrap my arms around his waist and pull him into a hug. It takes him by surprise, but he relaxes and hugs me back.

"Thank you. I don't know how I'll ever repay you for this. Even if it goes to shit, I can't thank you enough for…just being here. Holding me up. Being my best friend."

I try to express what I'm feeling, knowing things are about to get intense, but I need him to know I appreciate him more than words can describe. So much has changed in the past three months, and admitting he's been one of the best friends I've ever had has my heart racing.

"Anything, Lennon." He squeezes before pulling back. "I'll do anything for you. I'm not going anywhere. You, the baby, me. We're gonna be a makeshift family, and I don't care what anyone says about it."

I smile at him calling us a family. "You know I'm overly emotional right now?" I laugh with tears in my eyes as my gaze drops to his mouth.

He laughs at my admission and presses a sweet kiss on my forehead as if to seal his promise.

A knock on the door interrupts our moment. With minutes to spare before we have to leave, Hunter goes to answer it. Sophie and Maddie know we're flying out today, so I doubt it's them. It's probably Liam or Mason. I'm still not sure if he's told them or not.

Following him, Hunter opens the door, and my heart stops when I see it's the girl who spent the weekend with him before Brandon died. The one who wore my damn shirt. Ugh.

"Jenna." Hunter's uneasy tone implies he's just as surprised to see her as I am. "What're you doing here?"

The girl has the nerve to scowl.

"You left me no choice, Hunter. I've been calling and texting you for weeks with no answer," she says accusingly, and my mind goes back to those few times I saw him declining her calls. "We need to talk. *Privately.*" Her eyes flick to mine for a second before going back to Hunter.

He crosses his arms over his chest, not budging. "I don't have time for this. We're about to leave."

"It'll take two minutes," she persists. "Alone."

"She's not going anywhere," he snaps. "Whatever you need to say, just say it because we have to go."

"Alright, suit yourself." She shrugs, shifting her body to just the right angle where I notice how tight her shirt fits.

Oh my God.

My breakfast threatens to come up when I see her swollen stomach.

"I'm pregnant."

All the blood drains from my face as I stare at her bump that looks to be as big as mine. Hunter called us a family, and now… he's having a baby. With *her*.

CHAPTER TWENTY-FOUR

HUNTER

THE WALLS in the airport feel as if they're closing in as Lennon and I enter. Though we're only visiting Utah for a few days, we have enough luggage between the two of us to check bags as well as bring a carry-on. Hordes of people crowd around, and the line to the service counter is long as hell, but that's typical on a Sunday before a holiday. It's why we had to leave immediately after Jenna unexpectedly showed up at our door.

After Jenna announced she's pregnant, which was obvious once I saw her stomach, she expected me to fall to my knees, excited and happy, but I refused to give her the attention she's wanted from the very beginning.

Once Jenna left, Lennon closed up so tight, I couldn't get through to her. I'd told her we were a family, that I'd be there for her and the baby no matter what, and then this clusterfuck happened. Last night, sleeping with Lennon in her bed was everything, and it felt so damn right. While I hate the circumstances that led us to this point, I'm happy I get to be the man to keep her safe and protect her.

We didn't have time to talk about it, though I wanted to spill all my truths and explain how I knew Jenna's baby wasn't mine. It's not an easy conversation to have, so I can't just spit it out and expect things to go back to normal. The thought reminds me of Brandon and the insecurities my father instilled. I never felt good enough for him and definitely knew I wasn't good enough for a woman like Lennon, which was why I never got between her and Brandon. I knew he was the better man for Lennon. He could give her everything she needed, give her a family, and now he's not even here to be a part of it. I wish I could give her that family she craves, but I can't give one to anyone, even if I wanted to.

On the drive to the airport, Lennon's responses were short and to the point, so I got the hint and stopped talking. After the first time Jenna and I hooked up, I knew better than to continue seeing her, and it came back to bite me straight in the ass.

Stupid, stupid, stupid.

Once we make it through security, we walk toward our gate. Lennon stops for a quick bathroom break, and when she returns, I let out a huff.

"Are we going to talk about this?" I ask, her silence eating me alive.

When Lennon glances over, her blue eyes burn straight through me. "Talk about what?"

We're standing in the middle of the airport as people pass us by. "About Jenna. About what happened at the apartment. You're obviously upset." Heat rushes through me when she clenches her jaw. I can almost see the wheels turning in her head as she contemplates what to say. She's transparent, and I see every inch of her and hear the words she refuses to say. Part of me wants to pull her into my arms and tell her it's not what she thinks, but now is not the time or place.

Eventually, she speaks. "I'm not upset. I have no right to be, Hunter. You're a single guy. I'm just shocked, that's all. You keep saying you'll be there for me, but I feel like my fucked-up situation will hold you back from your own life and from being there for your baby. Hearing that news was a wake-up call for me." Lennon shrugs. "I should be used to things drastically changing when I get too comfortable." The sadness in her tone isn't lost on me, and my heart lurches forward as I think of her and Brandon. They were living their happily ever after, and it was ripped away in a snap. I swallow hard, pushing down the thoughts of it, wishing things were different.

Turning my body to face her, I take her hand in mine and rest it against my chest. I'm sure she can feel my heart beating rapidly. "Trust me when I say that baby isn't mine, Lennon. It's not."

"It doesn't matter if it is. *You* aren't mine, Hunter, and I'm not yours to worry about." Her words pierce straight through my heart like a dagger. If she only knew how much I wish that were my reality, she wouldn't have said that. It has me questioning everything, though. Does she want me to be hers? All she'd have to do is say the word.

I'm yours, and you don't even realize it, I want to say, but I keep it to myself.

With the conversation clearly over, I refuse to push it any further. Lennon's under enough stress, and the last thing she needs is more drama, so I drop it. We continue toward our gate, with the carry-on suitcase in tow, but I stop when a jewelry store catches my eye.

"We forgot something," I tell Lennon, my heart pounding with the realization.

"What? Is it important? Is it something we can buy in Utah?" she asks, perplexed at my reaction.

I nod at the jewelry store in front of us. "Wedding rings."

Her mouth falls open. "Shit. I thought of everything but that." Lennon shakes her head and inhales a deep breath. "Well, I'm blaming pregnancy brain. What's your excuse, *hubby*?"

I give her a small smile and laugh at the change in her tone. Shrugging, I say, "Guess we need to go shopping."

"Do you think they have cubic zirconia? I don't need anything fancy, just something presentable."

"Hmm. Not sure. Let's go look, though, because we can't show up ringless if we want to pull this off."

Lennon nods and follows me into a store with a sizable

selection of jewelry—rings, earrings, bracelets, and necklaces. Glancing around the spacious room, especially for being in an airport, I know we don't have a lot of time before our boarding begins, so I quickly scan the display cases. The diamonds sparkle against the light, and I overhear Lennon asking for the location of the clearance rings. As one jeweler walks her across to a small case in the corner, I spot the one she's meant to have. Another woman comes to help me, removes it, and allows me to study it. A few minutes pass before Lennon notices and comes over.

"That's too much, Hunter," she tells me in a hushed tone. I search her face and shake my head as the woman hands me the other band that goes with the set. Lennon's mouth practically hits the floor when I hand it to her with a grin.

"It's meant for you, though. You like a princess cut, right?" I shoot her a wink, then want to kick my own ass for my slipup.

Lennon furrows her brows and tilts her head. Blood rushes from my face, but I somehow keep my composure.

"How'd you know?" she asks with a curious smile.

There's no way I could tell her the truth. I think about the ring tucked inside my nightstand that she doesn't know is hers—the one I have to keep secret. It's official, I'm a fucking idiot.

I quickly shrug, looking back at the sparkling diamond. "Lucky guess, I suppose. Don't all girls like princess cuts?" I hurry and shoot her a smirk, trying to cover my stupid misstep.

The woman behind the counter lets out a fake laugh because I'm sure she wants the sale. "You're so right," she says. "It's a beautiful set, though. Two carats total."

Lennon glances at her, then back at me. "It's too much, Hunter. I can't ask you to do this. It's way too expensive."

I grin. "If I'm going to impress my in-laws, I need to buy you the ring you deserve. Plus, you didn't ask me. I'm insisting."

She stubbornly shakes her head, and I understand her resistance, considering we're pretending, but I have the money for it. I've been saving since my first real check, and if I'm being honest with myself, I want to make her happy, even if only temporarily.

I grab Lennon's left hand and slide the set onto her finger. It fits like it's meant to be, and her breath hitches as she looks down at it. When her eyes finally meet mine, I see the fire behind them as if her thoughts are going wild.

The jeweler interrupts our moment, beaming with anticipation. "So is this the one?"

Lennon glances back down at the diamonds gleaming under the lights. "Are you sure about this, Hunter?" She circles it around her finger with her other hand, and it feels right, so I don't hesitate.

"I've never been more sure about anything, Lennon. This has to be done. I want your parents to know I can take care of you," I tell her confidently, though there's nothing pretend about my words.

The woman happily leads us to the register after taking the rings from Lennon to clean them. Lennon reaches for me and grabs my arm.

"You need a ring too," she reminds me.

After quickly sizing my finger, a salesperson gives me a few choices, and Lennon picks out a white gold band. By the time we have what we need, and thousands of dollars later, there's apprehension written on Lennon's face. After I pay, we slip our rings on and walk out of the store wearing them.

"Hunter…" Her voice is soft. "What're you gonna do with these rings after this is over? I feel guilty you're doing this as it is."

"We'll need them for a while, Lennon. And after this is over, I'll sell them online or something. People buy secondhand jewelry all the time," I explain as we arrive at our gate and find a seat. I wrap my arm around her shoulders and pull her in close, hoping to calm her. "I'm not worried about how much it'll cost, so you shouldn't either. We'll cross that bridge when we get there, okay?"

She relaxes. "Alright. I'm nervous about this and stressed to the max. I'll be better once we get back and return to normal."

We sit in silence for a while, people watching as they walk by us. Lennon eventually pulls out her phone and sends her sisters a picture of the rings. I can only imagine what they're saying right now, considering I'm so fucking transparent to them. They've made way too many side comments over the past month not to see right through me. Shit, they'll probably show Mason and Liam too. I'm so fucked.

As she laughs and texts, I get lost in my head, thinking about Brandon. I shouldn't be the one going to Utah with Lennon. I think back to when he mentioned proposing over the summer. We were sitting at the kitchen table eating breakfast, and I remember how fucking excited and nervous he was about it. It seems like yesterday when the jealousy took over, and I regret ever feeling that way, especially now. Guilt consumes me as I stare out at the sea of strangers waiting to board their planes.

Lennon notices me withdrawing. "Are you okay?"

"I'm fine."

She doesn't ask me what's on my mind, and the awkward tension between us returns. I'm sure she assumes I'm thinking about Jenna and the baby.

A man comes over the intercom and lets us know we'll begin boarding in ten minutes. Lennon and I move to stand in line, and as I look over her shoulder, I catch a glimpse of one of the text messages from Sophie about Jenna—about me becoming a father. Lennon lets out a long breath and tucks her phone into her purse as we walk down the passenger boarding bridge.

After I put the carry-on suitcase in the overhead storage, we sit and wait for everyone to board. The awkward silence returns, and she's lost in her thoughts again. Lennon glances down at the sparkling diamonds as the plane takes off, and I look at her.

"I know this whole Jenna thing is on your mind, but I don't want you to worry about it. This doesn't change anything, especially what I said before she showed up." I lower my voice and move closer so I'm practically whispering in her ear. "It's not mine. I can promise you that."

Her eyes meet mine, and our mouths are so damn close. *Too close.* "How can you be so sure? Even if you double wrapped it and she was on birth control, a pregnancy can happen." She points her chin down to her swollen stomach as if to imply she and Brandon were careful too.

I swallow hard, pinching the back of my neck. "I just know. I'm one hundred percent positive, okay? Please…just trust me."

Lennon inhales a deep breath. I need her trust more than ever right now.

"Okay," she tells me with a tight nod. "I trust you."

CHAPTER TWENTY-FIVE

LENNON

My words come out ragged. I want to trust him more than anything, but I know his past. I saw the countless nameless women he brought home before and after I moved in. He was a classic fuckboy. Honestly, this shouldn't surprise me as much as it has. I'm shocked he hasn't knocked up some random girl before this, but hell, why did it have to be *her*? When I think about it, what bothers me the most is the jealousy that courses through me. I have no right to feel that way, no claim on him, and that only irritates me more. Between this and the stress of seeing my parents, those are the only constants I have.

Nothing has been easy or worked in my favor. Each time I think I might be okay, a curveball comes my way, and something else happens. First, Brandon's unexpected death, then finding out I'm pregnant with his baby, and now Hunter's situation. At this point, I'm wondering what else could possibly occur.

As soon as Hunter told me we'd be a makeshift family, Jenna came barreling in like a freight train. Knocking me off my axis, she forced me back to my sad reality. I'd been so caught up in preparing for Utah that it was almost easy to believe Hunter's promises, believe every word he said to me. For a moment, in my heart, I knew I'd be all right. The worry and stress had temporarily vanished as I got caught up in the fantasy of Hunter always being there for me and the baby.

Jenna was the wake-up call I needed. It snapped me out of my fairy tale so fast, I might have a concussion from the whiplash.

Hunter and I have nothing more than a solid friendship. Eventually, he'll find someone who makes him happy, fall in love, and want to start a family. How could he not? Hunter deserves it all.

Even though he swears Jenna's baby isn't his, I don't understand how he can be so sure. Sometimes the best birth control and protection fail because nothing is one hundred percent. I'm a perfect example of that. But if Hunter wants me to trust him, I'll try my damnedest to. It's the least I can do after everything he's selflessly done for me.

We sit in silence as I try to get ahold of my emotions. Being with Hunter and spending most of our free time together has been different. Months ago, if someone had told me we'd be so close, I would've laughed in their face, but he's quickly become my best friend. I've learned things about him I never knew and understand him on a much deeper level. We've shared so much of our raw selves with each other, and I can't help but trust him. He knows every detail about me—the way I feel about certain topics and my insecurities, down to the names of the pets I had as a kid. I keep having to remind myself we're just friends and that's all this is. It's all it can ever be.

As I think about Jenna, another wave of jealousy hits me in full force, and a bolt of guilt follows. Something unspoken has been simmering between me and Hunter, and neither of us wants to admit it. I sure as hell don't. I *can't*.

I didn't expect to feel anything when we practiced kissing, but I felt *everything*. I couldn't make any sense of it. As soon as he poured himself into me, I was left gasping, my body buzzing with something I couldn't explain. That wasn't supposed to happen. I shouldn't feel that way. I can't give those thoughts attention, so I push them away and bury them deep.

My mind wanders back to seeing Jenna at the door with desperation on her face and in her voice. I'm sure she's scared, and I can only imagine how much strength it took to confront Hunter. I know he's rejected her calls for weeks, and part of me wonders if that was due to me and how much I needed him. While I don't like her, I admire her fearlessness. What if the baby truly is his? All the scenarios and unknowns almost make me panic. Will he move out? Will she move in? The selfish part of me doesn't want to lose him. I've already lost so much, and this is another reminder of how alone I am.

"Everything okay?" Hunter asks as I wipe a rogue tear from my cheek.

I push the thoughts aside and give him a small smile. "Yeah, just nervous about seeing my parents."

He nods, though I'm not sure he buys it. "I'm getting nervous too. Meeting the parents…it's a big deal." He waggles his brows, making me laugh.

"You're supposed to be the strong one," I quip, sighing. "But yeah. It's a big deal, at least in my family."

They hadn't even met Brandon.

I twist the metal around on my finger. Once again, he was right. Having rings like this will help make our story more believable. I can't get over the amount he spent, knowing he'll never get the price he paid for it when it's sold later. I was shocked he knew what type of ring I'd like, but then again, after sharing so much with him, it shouldn't surprise me. Sometimes, I think he knows me better than I know myself. All this makes me feel like a burden, and I know he'd argue that I'm not, but I can't help it. He's done so much for me, and I feel like I'll never be able to repay or thank him enough.

The rings feel foreign on my finger, but I can't stop looking at them. If the circumstances were different, I'd be over the damn moon about having something so gorgeous, but I have to remind myself it's pretend. All of this—the rings, the kissing and touching —is nothing more than a façade for the outsiders looking in.

Eventually, the plane lands in Salt Lake City, and we deplane without delay. After we get our luggage, we wait in line for the rental car, which doesn't take nearly as long as I thought it would. I give Hunter the address to my parents' house so he can plug it into his phone because it's much easier than directing him. Soon, we're pulling out of the airport parking lot and heading toward my hometown of Park City. As I glance at the mountains surrounding the city, I realize we're actually doing this. My nerves kick into overdrive, causing my leg to shake as Hunter drives.

As my anxiety gets the best of me, I can't stop imagining the worst-case scenario after telling my parents I'm pregnant. At least Hunter is here with me, so it won't be as scary. When we're twenty minutes away from my parents' house, Hunter's cell phone vibrates, and Jenna's name appears on the screen.

"Are you going to answer it?" I ask, a tinge of jealousy returning.

"No," he deadpans, rejecting the call.

I look out the window, trying to keep my voice level and calm. "You can't keep ignoring her. What if something happened? Being stressed while pregnant isn't healthy for her or the baby."

A chuckle releases from Hunter. "I'm sure she's fine. This whole situation isn't anything to worry about. Take your own advice and stop stressing." He grabs my hand. "It's not healthy for you or the baby." He repeats my words in a mocking tone. "Lennon, I'm here for you. Always. We're gonna get through this."

I know he's trying to comfort me, but it's easier said than done. "Hunter, I don't want you to make promises you can't keep. Jenna showing up today was proof that things always change. I know you said the baby isn't yours, and I'm putting my trust in you when you say that. But it's a reminder that you'll meet the woman of your dreams one day and want to start your own family. I know you said you'll always be around for me and the baby, and while that might be true right now, there'll come a time when you can't, and I'm trying to accept that." I suck in a deep breath. "I don't want you to feel obligated to me, Hunter. When you're ready to date and forget about this fake marriage, let me know. It's tearing me apart to know that my fucked-up situation holds you back. I can't be that person. I won't be."

He tenses, grabbing the steering wheel tight before glancing at me. "You have nothing to worry about. I know we're just friends, Lennon, so stop believing you're going to ruin some relationship of mine that doesn't even exist because you're not. I don't know if you've noticed or not, but I haven't been with anyone in a while. And before you even start, it's not because of you. I don't want to be with anyone, especially not right now." His words linger, filling the car.

I open my mouth to say something, realizing how confused I am about this. Instead of speaking, nothing comes out. I want to ask him how he can feel that way, how he can be so content with this plan or how it could mess things up with his potential dating life. But I don't. My hormones are completely out of whack, and I'm overly emotional. I need to gain control because, in ten minutes, we'll be face-to-face with my parents. I can't show up upset or crying with a man I'm claiming to be my husband. It would be the worst first impression ever. My mother will notice, and it'll be a conversation I don't want to have before I drop the pregnancy bomb on them.

"Listen. We're almost there, and I think it might be best to put this on hold and wait to talk about it when we're back home. Right now, we have a fake marriage to pull off. We have to get into character and play the part of the madly in love newlyweds for my unsuspecting parents." I look at him, and he nods in agreement.

"That's probably for the best," he says, turning down my parents' street.

I swallow down the knot in my throat as the house comes into view. We pull into the driveway, and I try to gain an ounce of strength, though I feel like I'm crumpling from the inside out. Hunter grabs my hand and squeezes.

"Do I look pregnant?" I ask him with a smirk, gesturing to my baggy shirt. Although I'm only fifteen weeks pregnant, my small bump is noticeable in tight shirts. They can't know how far along I am because it would ruin our entire lie.

"You look great," he reassures me with a wink, which should calm me down, but I'm hit with a rush of nerves. "Let's do this, wifey."

"What if this is a disaster? What if my parents freak the hell out? What if they figure out we're lying, and this was all for nothing? What if—"

"Lennon." Hunter's deep voice snaps my gaze up to his eyes. He wraps a hand around the nape of my neck and pulls me close until our lips collide. I instantly relax, letting his mouth erase all my fears. He pushes back, and I frown. My breathing is erratic as I replay what just happened in my mind. "Better?" he croaks out as if the kiss affected him too.

"Uh-huh," I manage to say, thoughts of my parents vanished. Why does he have this effect on me? I blink, wishing I had time to figure it out but knowing I don't.

A chuckle escapes him. "Good. We've got this."

"Right." I nod in agreement. "Did you just kiss me to shut me up?"

"I'd never." His light tone has me thinking otherwise. "Let me say this, I've not met a woman's parents who haven't loved me."

I scoff with a chuckle. "Oh, overconfident, are we? Well, my parents aren't like most," I remind him.

Hunter lifts my hand and presses a soft kiss to my knuckles. Electricity streams through me when my eyes meet his. "It's going to be so damn believable, *we* might end up believing we're married by the end of the trip."

His encouraging words have me laughing, and I feel a lot better. Hunter knows what he's doing, and we've prepared for this.

Hunter gives me a reassuring smile and opens the door to get out. Rounding the car, he comes over to open mine. He helps me out, being the sweet gentleman I've seen these past few months. As we walk around to the trunk, I glance down at my left ring finger and wonder what the fuck I'm doing. There's no time to break it down, though, because my mother's voice causes me to still. When I look up, I plaster a smile on my face. She closes the space between us and pulls me into a big hug, with my father behind her.

"Lennon! I'm so happy you're finally here," she squeals. "How was the flight?"

Hunter pops his head up from the trunk and gives her his infamous boyish grin. My mother's eyes meet mine right before her jaw falls to the ground. He does seem to have that effect on people. My mother included.

"Mom. Dad. This is Hunter," I introduce.

He gives my father a friendly handshake, and my mother hugs him. I think I even catch her squeezing his muscles.

"So is this my surprise, honey?" she asks, grinning wide.

Hunter lets out a hearty laugh.

"So now you know where Sophie and Maddie get it from," I tell him, my cheeks heating.

Mom's eyes light up. "So you've met all my girls?"

"I have," he tells her, but before the conversation can go any further, my father suggests we head inside, which I'm grateful for. Hunter swings his duffel bag over his shoulder and grabs my carry-on as Dad takes my giant suitcase. As we're walking to the door, Hunter places his hand on the small of my back, making my entire body light up. I'm trying so damn hard to find my confidence as we step inside.

I keep my left hand hidden and so does Hunter, not wanting my parents to notice the rings until we're ready. Dad suggests we go into the sitting room and catch up.

"Do you guys want some coffee? I'll get a pot ready," Mom asks, and we both nod, though my heart races because she'll definitely notice that I'm not drinking caffeine.

"That'd be great, Mrs. Corrigan," Hunter says.

Dad takes a seat as Mom heads into the kitchen. Hunter and I sit on the sofa across from him. We chat about the flight, my job at the school, and he asks how Sophie and Maddie are doing. Hunter's as calm as can be, keeping eye contact and loosely resting his arm around my waist, but I feel as if I'm unraveling one thread at a time.

It's easy to lie to them over FaceTime, but I'm not sure I can do it to their faces. So much rides on this week, though, so I try to swallow down my insecurities.

Mom comes back and sits next to Dad. I know the real grilling will begin now.

"So…are you the Hunter I spoke to on the phone a few months ago when Lennon was avoiding me?" She's being direct, almost *too* direct.

Hunter's smile doesn't falter a bit. "Yes, ma'am, I was. I didn't want you to worry."

Mom nods. "I appreciate that because I was, especially after everything that had happened with Brandon."

I was hoping she wouldn't bring him up so quickly. The color drains from my face as I think about this trip and how I was supposed to be here with him. The guilt of what we're doing stabs me in the gut, knowing how different it'd be with Brandon by my side, but it's too late. It's now or never. Mom continues, but I'm lost in my head until I hear her next words.

"Are you Lennon's new boyfriend?" She looks accusingly between us, her brows furrowed as if she's trying to solve a mystery.

I open my mouth, but I can't seem to get the words to come out. I choke, knowing I need to say something, but I'm at a loss.

"Actually," Hunter speaks up when he notices I'm freezing. Moving a few inches closer, he tightens his grip on me and grins. "I'm her husband."

CHAPTER TWENTY-SIX

HUNTER

WHEN I ADMIT to being Lennon's husband, her parents become eerily quiet. Lennon's mentioned her strict and traditional upbringing, and their stunned reactions are the first hint of that. They sit like statues, in complete shock. I pull Lennon closer, and she lets out a nervous laugh before looking at me. For a second, panic flashes in her eyes, so I lean over and place a sweet lingering peck on her lips, hoping to once again pull her out of her head and back to me. Kissing her feels so damn natural that I have to remind myself it's all pretend even though I feel her shiver against me.

She's clearly freaking out, and the hard news—telling them about the pregnancy—hasn't even come out yet. Their response will determine if she talks about the baby now or later when things have calmed down. We never discussed when we'd tell them the news, but it's why we're here after all. If my head is slightly spinning, I know theirs are too.

"Surprise!" Lennon finally speaks with a sheepish grin and turns toward her parents. I quickly grab her hand, and her mom notices our rings.

When I meet her father's gaze, he looks as if he's chewing rocks, and his jaw clenches. I'm almost scared he might kick us out on our asses, considering it's one of Lennon's biggest fears. The air in the room seems to evaporate, and I'm not sure what else I should say or if I should speak at all. Lennon's parents care deeply about her, that much was obvious the moment we arrived. However, right now, they're completely unreadable. Her mom and dad look at each other, holding a silent conversation. Lennon sits quietly, waiting patiently for them to say something, so I follow her lead and stay still.

Mrs. Corrigan smiles and shakes her head. "I'm sorry. I'm just a little surprised. It seems so…quick. How did this all come about?" I can't tell if there's judgment in her tone or just curiosity. It might be a combination of both. I try to be understanding and put myself in their shoes. If my daughter brought a random man home and told me they were married, I'd be shocked as well.

Lennon squeezes my hand so tight she might break my fingers off. I rub my thumb across her knuckles to remind her I'm here and that we're in this together, and I feel her slightly relax.

Starting from the beginning, Lennon tells them what we rehearsed verbatim, but it sounds so natural coming from her. When she explains how we fell in love and couldn't be without one another, Lennon smiles so damn sweetly. For a moment, I almost believe it—want to believe it. I swallow down those emotions because she has no idea how I wished it were all true, and she was my wife—*mine*.

Mr. Corrigan watches Lennon closely as she speaks about the details of our relationship and marriage. I wonder if he senses our lies, but she's speaking so effortlessly that I highly doubt it because even I'm buying the story she's selling.

"When you find the person you're meant to be with, you just know," she tells them, squeezing my hand as her blue eyes meet mine. For a moment, we're the only two people in the room, and her breath hitches when her eyes meet mine. Did she feel an electric current too? I'm brought back to the first night we met at the bar and how I knew how special and amazing she was then.

As she continues to talk about us, I study her with a smile

playing on my lips. Lennon's so goddamn beautiful without even trying, and the urge to kiss the fuck out of her takes over, but I hold it back. Chuckling, Lennon grins wide as she talks about how she feels like she's known me forever and how we've been friends for years.

She even mentions how much I love her singing, comfortably improvising and sharing parts of our real story.

"Right, Hunter?" She glances at me, shaking me out of my thoughts as I listen to her talk about us.

I nod, pulling her closer, wishing I could scoop her up onto my lap. "Absolutely. The best way to start my day."

"You both seem very much in love," her father states robotically, looking back and forth between us.

"You do," Mrs. Corrigan agrees, grinning. "If you're happy, that's all that matters, Lennon. While we wish you'd told us sooner, I understand why you didn't, considering the past few months. I'm glad you were able to find someone after losing Brandon. I know how much you loved him, and I can't even begin to imagine how hard that must've been for you, for both of you."

"Even so, you should've gotten married in the church," Mr. Corrigan says.

I can't tell if he's disappointed or upset, but it's obvious he doesn't agree with us eloping to Vegas.

Lennon's prepared for this response and explains without waiting for a beat. "I know, Dad. It wasn't a decision I made lightly. But planning a wedding, flying back to Utah, doing everything from afar with school starting soon and having to get ready for all of that, on top of grieving would be too overwhelming. Especially after everything I have—*we* have— already been through." When she looks at me, I notice tears welling in her eyes, but she doesn't let them fall.

"I kept thinking how something bad could happen before we could tie the knot because tomorrow isn't promised to any of us. I'm sure you can understand why I didn't want to wait…even a month was too long." Lennon sighs dreamily. "Hunter was okay with having the wedding next year, but I refused. I wanted to start my life with him immediately," she explains, and I bring her hand to my lips and kiss her knuckles in full agreement.

If I could give her a standing ovation for her speech, for standing up to her father in a roundabout way, I would. His face softens, and he gives her a small smile, not pushing it any further.

"I can't believe you've been married for a while and gave no hints or anything," her mother says in a pained tone.

Lennon explains how we wanted it to be a big surprise since the trip was already planned. I can't help but think about Brandon but push the thoughts away. I can't get into my own head right now because I already feel like shit for the boundaries I've crossed.

"So…Sophie and Madelyn know, I take it?" her mother asks.

"Of course they do, Mom, but they only found out after the fact. The only person at the ceremony besides us was the one random witness they provided. It was private and super small, but that's what made it so special to us."

Her parents give Lennon and me a hug. She shows off her rings, and I think they're more than impressed when they see the size of the diamond. That wedding set is everything she's ever deserved.

"Welcome to the family," Mr. Corrigan says, giving me a firm handshake.

We stand, laughing and chatting, and Mrs. Corrigan excuses herself to the kitchen to grab the coffee, and Lennon follows. The scent fills the room, and I'm looking forward to having a cup.

I'm left alone with Mr. Corrigan, and he's exactly how Lennon's always described—firm and reserved. I sit on the couch, watching him study me, and I try to tuck my nerves away. All I know is I don't want to be on this man's bad side.

He's tall and built for an older guy with salt-and-pepper hair. Lennon's a combination of her mother and father, but she definitely has his eyes. Though his are a tad more fierce and threatening as he regards me.

Mr. Corrigan speaks, breaking the silence. "I have high expectations for the men who marry my daughters, Hunter. Call me old-fashioned, but I expect my future sons-in-law to ask for my daughter's hand before proposing, so I can make sure they're worthy of my girls. It's a sign of respect. But since you disregarded that…there's nothing I can do about it now."

"I apologize, sir, I really do," I say, patiently waiting for him to continue. Lennon warned me he'd probably bring this up, so I expected it.

"Part of your responsibility as her husband is to be the man of the household and provide for her. I assume you have a decent job, at least?" He pauses, waiting for my response.

"I'm a construction project manager. It pays very well, with great benefits," I respond. "I'm not afraid to get my hands dirty or work hard."

"Good." He nods his approval and even flashes a small grin, allowing me to relax a bit. "You both should be attending church each week as well, but most importantly, divorce isn't something I support, Hunter, so—"

"Mr. Corrigan," I cautiously interrupt, our easy conversation obviously over. "With all due respect, I love your daughter more than words can describe. I'll provide for her and make sure she's taken care of for the rest of our lives. That's one promise I'll always keep. Eventually, I want to buy a house for us to grow old in with the white picket fence and wraparound porch. Anything she wants. Lennon means everything to me, sir," I tell him with confidence.

I don't even have to lie about my feelings. I'd give her everything if she'd let me. Everything I said is the truth, and I'll do whatever it takes to make sure Lennon is okay, even if all we can ever be is friends.

Her dad smiles. "That's what I like to hear, son. Though we just met, I can see you two love each other, and I believe everything you're telling me. But don't interrupt me again."

I'm not sure whether to laugh or cry, but I nod in understanding. "Of course."

Mrs. Corrigan disrupts our man-to-man talk when she enters with four cups of coffee on a tray with sides of cream and sugar. Lennon looks at her dad, then back at me, and I know she's wondering what he said.

I wink, easing her mind that everything went smoothly, and pat the spot next to me on the sofa, so she relaxes and sits. We're each handed a mug, and I blow on it before taking a sip. Caffeine is exactly what I need right now. Too bad it doesn't come with a side of whiskey to numb the pain for the almost beating I took.

Lennon adds sugar and cream to hers but holds it tightly in her palms. Since the day she found out she was pregnant, she's refused to take even the smallest of sips of coffee, regardless of how many times I've told her one cup a day is perfectly fine for the baby. She's stubborn but protective, which I can't blame her for considering what she's been through.

Lennon's mom sits and does the same to her coffee, then takes a drink. Mr. Corrigan chats about the church and what they've been doing this summer for their congregation.

"The big Fourth of July celebration is tomorrow. Did Lennon tell you? We're so glad you'll be coming with us. Are you two excited?" Mrs. Corrigan asks, but before either of us can answer, she continues. "Why aren't you drinking your coffee, Lennon? Is it too bitter? I tried some new beans this time, and now I'm not sure I care for them."

I grab Lennon's hand and intertwine our fingers together, knowing she's about to deliver the news she's been nervous about since the moment she found out. Letting out a deep breath, she smiles. *It's go time.* I look at her, and when she rewards me with a sweet grin, I know she's going to make the announcement.

"Actually…" She slowly enunciates the word as she sets her mug down on the table.

Her mother watches intently, waiting for a response, but I'm willing to bet it won't be the one she's anticipating because it has nothing to do with coffee.

Lennon looks at them and releases a nervous breath. It feels as if time stands still until she says her next words.

"I'm pregnant," she announces with a shaky voice, the confidence in her tone slipping. I'm here for her and refuse to let her do this alone, so I get ready to play the happy husband, soon-to-be father role.

"Oh my gosh," her mother squeals, sliding to the edge of the chair, and I'm worried she's going to fall right off.

"We found out a couple of weeks after the wedding," I tell them. "It's a blessing getting pregnant so soon, and we couldn't be more excited to start a family right away."

"Some women have a hard time and struggle, but we were so fortunate." Lennon grins, and my stomach turns at her words.

I know she's thinking about Jenna and the conversation we had right before we got here, but it's the last thing I want her thinking about right now. We have so much to talk about, but it'll have to wait until we're back home.

"We're going to be grandparents," Mrs. Corrigan cries with joy. Her dad is just as elated about the news. Relief flashes through Lennon as her parents congratulate us.

"I didn't expect to find out we're going to be grandparents today," Lennon's dad says, grinning proudly. He stands and pulls me into a side hug. "Congrats, son. It's going to be a lot of responsibility and—"

"Dad," Lennon interrupts with a laugh. "He's reading all the baby books to prepare, so he doesn't need your speech right now."

I silently thank her with my eyes for interrupting. Though her dad obviously loves her, he's intimidating as hell.

"Okay, fine. Sorry." He grins. "I just remember when I first found out I was going to be a father…" He places a hand on his wife's shoulder, and she turns and smiles. "It was one of the happiest times of my life. I'm sure you feel the same way, Hunter."

With a relieved chuckle, I agree with him, though it hurts like hell—more than they'll ever know—that she's not actually carrying my baby.

Lennon wraps an arm around my waist, pulls me close to her, and kisses me so damn sweetly she nearly steals my breath. I cup her cheek, wanting to deepen the kiss, but I remember this isn't real.

Her happiness is contagious, and I smile as we break apart. We did it. We really did it. And they bought it.

Lennon sits and gives them information about her health and how she's been feeling. "I stopped drinking caffeine and am following everything by the book. Before you start with more questions, I didn't want to say anything until I was out of the first trimester but wanted to tell you in person because I love you both so much."

"I think this calls for a celebration," Mrs. Corrigan announces. "A big one!"

"No, no, Mom. I don't mind if people know, but I don't want a special party or anything," Lennon insists. "I want to spend time with you, Dad, and Hunter."

Her mother frowns, then flashes a toothy grin. "Okay, sweetie. But the ladies at church are going to be so excited for you, for *us*. How far along are you? Do you have a good doctor in California? Are you showing? Let me see!" Her mother asks fifty questions, and Lennon's shoulders relax with a relieved laugh.

"Kay, don't bombard her," Mr. Corrigan states, placing his hand on the small of her back. They're so thrilled about the news, and it seriously couldn't have gone any smoother. A heavy weight lifts from my shoulders, and by Lennon's actions, I know she's relieved too.

When Lennon yawns, her parents tell us to take her old bedroom upstairs and rest before dinner. Before I carry our luggage up, her parents stop me.

"Welcome to the family, Hunter," Mrs. Corrigan tells me as Lennon watches us.

"Thank you. I truly appreciate that. I'm excited to be a part of it and am thrilled to be starting one of my own with Lennon. Can't wait to give her and our baby the world."

So damn happy, her parents are buying our story, though I'm not lying when I talk about the life I want to give her. As I walk toward Lennon, she locks her fingers with mine, then I dip down and place a kiss on her lips while her parents watch.

"You're really impressing them," she whispers just loud enough for me to hear. As we pull apart, her eyes flutter open.

I smile, her lips so close I could kiss them again, but remind myself we have an audience and pull away. "I meant every word."

CHAPTER TWENTY-SEVEN

I'm on a complete high from the past two hours. Finally telling my parents the news has lifted a huge weight off my chest. I never should've doubted Hunter for a second because he freaking nailed his part. He was almost too convincing. I had to remind myself several times we were acting.

"My parents adore you," I tell him once we're in my old room with our luggage.

"I told you," he singsongs. "Parents love me."

I snort and roll my eyes. "My sisters were right. You sure know how to charm people." I rummage through my suitcase and look for some comfy clothes. I can't wait to change into them after dinner and sleep for twelve hours. With Hunter lying next to me, I probably could.

"Only when I need to," he corrects.

"Actually, I don't think I'm going to nap. Do you want a tour of the house? We can take a walk around the neighborhood, and I'll show you all the ways we tried and failed to sneak out," I say with a laugh.

Hunter leans against my old desk with his arms crossed over his chest, looking at me so intently. "Sure, I'd love that."

Once I've organized my clothes and unpacked my toiletries, I lead Hunter around the house and relive childhood memories. My mom busies herself in the kitchen while my dad works in his office. Though he gave a sermon this morning, he's already working on the next one. He cares about his members, and his devotion to their needs often means staying late at church. Considering tomorrow is the Fourth of July, and the volunteers at the celebration will include members of the congregation, I know my parents have a jam-packed day for us.

Hunter and I go on a walk so I can show him where I grew up. I point out the elementary school my sisters and I attended, the park we used to hang out at, and the walking trails we'd meander along with our friends on the weekends. Going down memory lane brings feelings of nostalgia. Even though I somewhat wish I could raise my child here too, I'm happy with my life in Sacramento even after all the heartbreak I've endured.

By the time we return, I'm beyond exhausted and ready for food and sleep. Mom makes a fuss, so we sit in the formal dining room as she serves roast and potatoes. While we eat, we talk more about our "relationship" and how excited we are to become parents. I stand to show off my belly, then make a joke about how bloated and big I am for only being a few months along. Mom reassures me it's normal since she started showing early with each of her pregnancies and was always asked if she was carrying twins.

Crisis averted.

For now, at least.

Hunter answers questions about his job, and I can't help but notice how he lights up when he talks about it. He's definitely passionate about his work, and my parents eat it up. They love how he's driven and has a career, and considering the rings he bought, it's safe to say I didn't realize how good of a living he makes.

When Mom passes out slices of homemade apple pie, my father asks Hunter about his family. Reaching under the table, I take Hunter's hand and pull it on my lap for support as he tenses.

"He isn't close with his parents," I tell them so he doesn't have to explain.

"It's okay, Lennon. I figured they'd be interested." Hunter shrugs nervously, but his confidence quickly returns when his gaze falls to our interlocked fingers.

He tells them about Hayden and how close they are. Then he directly dives into his childhood and how he grew up in a political household but had nothing to do with that once he left home. He speaks so effortlessly, opening up to my parents without a second thought. It's amazing to watch him be so candid.

"Well, you're a part of ours now, Hunter," my father says after, and my heart pounds with a mixture of pride and guilt. We're deceiving my parents, and for a minute, I think about revealing our hoax and telling them the truth, hoping they'll accept what is, but my father continues, reminding me why I can't. "We know your lives are in California, but we hope you've found a place of worship that follows our beliefs. Teaching you and your sisters the right way—God's way—was important, and my grandchild's life will be easier if the written word is taught and followed."

My stomach drops. He's being entirely too preachy, and it almost makes my skin crawl. I've heard it my entire life—go to church, get an education, date with the purpose of finding a husband, get married, then have children.

Having a job was never forced, and being a stay-at-home mom was considered the norm. My sisters and I wanted careers we were passionate about and left to pursue them in California. None of us dreamed of being a homemaker like my mother. She was "the wife of the pastor" and in charge of bake sales and getting us to our extracurricular activities. Mom loved it, and I know plenty of other mothers in the church who did, but that life wasn't for me.

"I can assure you we'll raise the baby together and make those decisions as we go," Hunter answers, saying enough to make my father happy.

Yawning, I get my mother's attention, who luckily changes the subject. "You kids should get to bed after such a long day. Tomorrow's going to be a blast!" She claps excitedly. "Did Lennon tell you all about it? Oh my gosh! All the church ladies are going to die over your handsome husband."

Hunter clears his throat, sitting straighter. "Yes, ma'am, she's told me some. Though I have a feeling I'm going to be in for quite the surprise." He smirks, making my mother melt.

"It's tradition. Trust me, there's no getting out of it." I snicker, giving him an apologetic smirk.

Hunter wraps his arm around my shoulders and leans in closer. "Can't wait."

After we say good night to my folks and head upstairs, I use the bathroom, brush my teeth, and change clothes. By the time I'm done and go back to the room, Hunter's already under the covers, halfway off the bed.

Chuckling, I bite my lip. "Gonna be snug, huh?"

As if he could be any sexier, he puts his arms behind his head and stretches out. "Yeah, I don't know where you're gonna sleep."

"Ha-ha, funny. I warned you."

"Yeah, but we *practiced* in a big bed, and now I'm realizing how ridiculous this is gonna be."

I stop at the edge of the bed and frown. "I'm sorry. I know this isn't ideal."

"Lennon." His face drops as he pulls back the covers. "Get in."

My feet stay frozen to the floor, unable to move as I take in Hunter's large frame and notice he's only in his boxer briefs. It's hot as hell up here, and my parents never turn the central air below seventy degrees. It's why I'm only wearing a pair of mesh shorts and a tank top.

Swallowing, I nod and finally snap out of it.

I will *not* stare at him.

Hell, who am I kidding? I'm gawking so hard I'm surprised my eyes haven't popped out by now. I turn off the light and suck in a breath.

I can do this.

We're snuggling because we have to. If we don't, one of us will literally fall off the bed. Hunter's huge, which means he can't help but take over two-thirds of the small mattress.

Climbing in, I pull the sheet over us and melt into his body. He brings one arm down and wraps it around me, holding me closer. I rest my hand on his chest, and we try to fall asleep glued together.

"Hunter," I whisper after a while. His heartbeat has been steady and his breaths even, so I'm shocked when he answers.

"Yes?"

Looking up at him, I smile when he gazes at me. "Thank you again for today. I'm pretty sure my parents fell in love with you."

He tenses. "It's obvious they want the best for you, so I'm happy to play the part."

I blink, the moon giving just enough light for me to see his face. Hunter's features are relaxed, which sends warmth down my body. Being this close should feel uncomfortable and awkward, but it makes that lonely feeling evaporate, even if only temporarily.

"Are you comfortable?" I ask, realizing he's shifted over to give me room.

"I'm fine."

Sitting up, I look at my side and compare it to his. "If we spoon, we'll both have more space."

Hunter's throat moves as he swallows hard. "Sure, whatever you want."

I roll my eyes, knowing he's trying hard to keep boundaries between us. I understand the guilt he feels, but we need to set that aside while we're here.

"It's just me and you, Hunter. Remember? No history or past," I remind him, repeating my words from the night before. The guilt feels heavy on my chest, but it's the only way we're going to get through this without it consuming us. He says I'll always be Brandon's girlfriend, and even if that's how he sees me, it's no longer the reality.

I don't wait for him to respond before turning to my other side. A moment passes before he finally shifts his weight, and his body curls around mine. Wiggling closer to him, I grab his hand and wrap it around my belly. Our legs mold together, and we both finally have enough room to breathe.

"You okay?" I ask after a few minutes.

"I'm regretting not bringing that cup with me," he teases.

"Hey! I can't even kick you in this position." I laugh.

Then I hear him growl. Against my ear.

Holy hell. It sends shivers down my spine as I wait for his response.

"That's not what I'm gonna need it for."

"Huh?" It takes me a good five seconds to put the pieces together. "Oh."

"Good night, Lennon," he says, tightening his hand around my belly as if he's protecting both of us.

"Night, Hunter."

Sleep comes quick and easy, but when my alarm goes off, I curse at my phone. *Motherfucker*. Seven in the morning came too soon, but if we don't want to be late, it's rise 'n' shine time.

"Ugh." I hit snooze and slowly start shifting.

"For the love of God, stop moving."

My eyes pop open at Hunter's words, his breath brushing against my cheek. It's then I notice our compromising position. My butt fits directly against his groin, and one of my legs is between both of his.

"What's wrong?" I ask, swallowing hard.

"You were wiggling your ass against my dick."

The blood drains from my face, and heat rushes between my legs.

Oh God.

"Sorry. I didn't mean to."

Hunter moves his hand to my hip and slides his other arm out from under me. I adjust my leg so he can free himself.

Once his weight shifts, I sit up on the edge of the bed.

"Did you sleep okay?" I glance over my shoulder but can only see his back and messy bedhead.

"Mmhmm," is all the response I get before he stands and walks to his suitcase. He grabs his clothes and goes to the door. "I'm gonna shower first. Is that okay?"

When he finally looks at me, I notice the pained expression on his face. We were definitely too close last night, but I'd be lying if I said it didn't feel good. *Too good.*

Guilt hits me hard and fast. I hate how I can't get a hold of my emotions when it comes to Hunter, but I need to. There's no denying I miss having someone close to me, someone to hold me, to touch and kiss. Brandon and I were together for two years and losing that has been worse than a painful breakup because there's no chance of closure.

Hunter makes me feel things, and I don't know if it's because I miss Brandon and I'm projecting them onto him or if it's something else completely.

I shake my head, clearing it. There's no time to think about that now. I'll suppress my feelings until I'm forced to deal with them.

"Sure, go ahead. I'll go see if my mom needs help with breakfast or anything." I flash him a smile, hoping he relaxes.

"Okay." He opens the door and walks out.

Do guys always wake up with morning wood? Brandon did occasionally, but now I'm wondering if it's a regular occurrence for some men. My experience in that department is minimal, and I'm pretty sure Googling that question would lead me to some scary websites.

Grabbing my phone, I open my messages and text Sophie.

LENNON

Forgot to tell you we made it here safe and sound. Mom and Dad love Hunter (shocker, right?) and today is when the REAL fun begins.

SOPHIE

About damn time, woman! I wasn't sure if they kicked your asses out or not. I mean, based on the situation, it was kind of a toss-up.

LENNON

Funny. Well, for future reference, they'd much prefer a daughter who secretly got married and knocked up versus one who gets pregnant out of wedlock.

SOPHIE

Duly noted.

LENNON

Anyway. Do all guys get morning wood?

SOPHIE

Why would you assume I'd know the answer to that? Also, does Hunter?

Sighing, I should've figured she'd ask that.

LENNON

Why do you think I'm asking! Brandon did sometimes, but Hunter has all three times we've slept in the same bed together. Is that normal?

SOPHIE

Probably when there's a body pressed against it. Especially YOUR body.

I groan, wondering why I even asked her in the first place.

LENNON

I bet that's uncomfortable for men. Kinda explains why he's always so moody in the morning.

SOPHIE

Where is he right now?

LENNON

In the shower.

SOPHIE

And I rest my case.

LENNON

What case?

SOPHIE

You gave him morning wood, and now he needs
to go "relieve" himself.

Rolling my eyes, I quickly type out my response.

LENNON

Oh yeah, I'm sure my pregnant ass is such an
aphrodisiac. He probably had a sex dream about
someone else.

SOPHIE

Keep lying to yourself, sis, but it doesn't refute
the fact that he's the one who came up with this
idea in the first place and has been all too eager
to play the role of your husband.

LENNON

He's doing it as a friend, Soph. For Brandon.

SOPHIE

Mmhmm.

LENNON

Ugh! I'm going to text my FAVORITE sister from
now on.

SOPHIE

Nice try. It's you two who are always fighting
over that title, not me. Either way, I love you, and
I'm glad the plan is working.

My shoulders slump as I reread her last few messages. Even if
she was right about Hunter, it doesn't change the fact that Jenna

could be carrying his baby or change the dynamic of our friendship. We agreed to push it all aside for now so we could focus on our fake relationship, so that's what I need to do even if it hurts.

LENNON

I love you too. I'll tell you all the details when we get back!

SOPHIE

BTW. Can I tell you how much I HATE CARTER? I'm beginning to hate Maria for allowing him to act this way. After the shit he pulled this morning (I'll tell you about it later), I'm over this stupid living situation.

LENNON

I'm sorry. It gets better. I promise.

I know she won't believe that, but it's all I can do to offer her some peace.

SOPHIE

Gotta go. Chat soon. Tell your hubby I said hello. Hehe.

I finally make it down to the kitchen, where I find my parents sitting with their cups of coffee. Groaning about the delicious smell, I wrap my arms around my mom and give her a hug.

"Morning, sweetie. How'd you two sleep?" she asks.

"Good. Hunter's in the shower now."

"There are scrambled eggs on the stovetop for you and juice in the fridge. Want some toast?" She loves taking care of her kids, something I missed when I first left.

"Thanks, Mom. I'll get it."

As I'm stuffing my face, Hunter comes strolling in wearing nice shorts and a tight-fitting T-shirt. I nearly choke on my food when I look at him, remembering how all that hard muscle felt wrapped around me last night, and I force back the mixed feelings that surface.

"Morning," he greets my parents sweetly, reaching for the coffee after my mother tells him to help himself. He grabs a plate of food and sits at the table.

Hunter flashes me a wink, and all my nerves wash away. "Morning, sweetheart." He leans down, cups my face, then presses a soft kiss on my lips. "Feeling okay?"

"Uh, yeah," I mutter, swallowing down the lump of food in my throat. "Baby's hungry."

"Have you had a lot of morning sickness?" my mom asks after Hunter takes a seat.

"No, not really," I respond. "Certain smells make me sick, but other than that, I've been blessed with an easy first trimester."

I quickly finish my food and excuse myself to get ready. Oddly enough, I'm not even worried about leaving Hunter with them, knowing he has this husband thing down.

Once I'm showered and look presentable in a sundress and flats, I make my way down and announce I'm ready to go. It's already eight thirty, and my parents wanted to be there before nine. The 5k run has already started, so we're supposed to meet up with their church friends at the park.

"You look beautiful," Hunter whispers when he's standing in front of me.

Smiling, I reply, "Thank you. I like this getup you have going on." I run my eyes down his body before looking back at his face.

Hunter chuckles. "Thanks. Figured casual wear was best for outside activities." He shrugs as if he's insecure about it, but he has no reason to be.

"It's perfect," I reassure him.

My parents meet us at the door, and we follow them outside. We ride in the back of the car, and Hunter grabs my hand as if we've done it a hundred times and he doesn't even have to think about it anymore.

"This city is so impressive. It's gorgeous," Hunter says, looking out the window.

"You should see it in the winter. It's a huge tourist attraction," my father chimes in.

"Maybe you could come back for a visit?" My mom looks over her shoulder at us. "Maybe after the baby's born?" she asks, hopeful.

Hunter squeezes my hand and responds before I can. "We'd love that."

Clearing my throat, I grab my mom's attention as she's easily gawking over my fake husband. "The baby's due in the middle of January, so I'm not sure we'll be able to swing it."

Lying to her about the baby's due date makes me feel guilty, but it's inevitable at this point.

"We'll play it by ear, sweetheart," Hunter says, looking at me with a wide smile. I know he wants them to like him, so I nod in agreement so the subject can be dropped.

Finally, we arrive at the crowded park. Hunter gets out of the car and leaves the door open for me. After he slides out, he takes my hand and helps me up.

"Relax," he whispers, closing the door behind me. He rubs a palm over my shoulder, then down my arm before he grabs my hand. "We've got this, remember?" The wink he flashes sends a shiver down my spine. Hunter's charm puts every other man to shame.

With a deep breath, I nod and smile. "You're right. It's just… we're about to get bombarded."

Hunter shrugs. "I've had these unrequited feelings for you since the moment I met you, but I've always kept my distance out of respect for your relationship with my best friend. After his death, we leaned on each other and grieved our loss together. We grew closer and could no longer deny what was brewing between us."

My heart races as his words come out so confidently, and I almost lose my breath.

"Wh-hat?" I blink, looking at him with confusion, my chest squeezing.

His smirk deepens. "That's the story we're going with, right? About how we got together?"

My stupid heart. It nearly stopped beating with how casually he said those words. A part of me wonders how he plays this role so easily while the other part knows he's doing this for Brandon, but I can't help thinking there's so much more to it.

I finally snap out of my thoughts. "Oh duh, yes."

"And after the circumstances that brought us together, we decided that life was too short and wanted to be together for good. Got hitched in Vegas and knocked you right up." He winks, sending butterflies straight to my pregnant belly.

Ugh. These damn hormones. They need to be locked up because I can't take how they're confusing me.

I snort at our story recap. "Sounds about right."

Hunter takes my hand, pulls me against his chest and dips his head. "Showtime, Mrs. Manning."

And then he slants his mouth over mine for a breathtaking, heart-stopping kiss.

CHAPTER TWENTY-EIGHT

HUNTER

Park City is unlike any place I've ever visited before. It has a mountain town vibe, and I can see the appeal for those who live here. The views alone have me wanting to stay longer than a few days, and I love seeing where Lennon grew up. It's so different from Sacramento.

Lennon's parents lead us to a spot at the park filled with picnic tables and lots of people. As we walk across the green grass, I notice she has her mother's features but know she gets her fierceness from her dad. Mrs. Corrigan begins introducing me to members of their church, and many are shocked to hear the news of our marriage and pregnancy. We socialize, playing our roles, and Lennon seems to enjoy catching up with people she hasn't seen in quite some time. Our hands stay interlocked, and I make sure to show affection like a typical newlywed, with soft cheek touches and lingering kisses.

A weight on my chest reminds me I need to distance my heart, not get attached, and remember this is not real life. I *know* this. But playing this part comes way too naturally, causing tension to course through me. If I'm not careful, Lennon's going to see right through me.

"You okay?" Lennon asks when we're finally alone again.

"Absolutely. You?"

She releases a breath, her shoulders relaxing. "Yeah, surprisingly. This is going well, almost too well."

"You look like you're waiting for the other shoe to drop," I say, studying her.

"Kind of. Maybe. I don't know."

I grab her shoulders and tilt her chin up to look at me. "Stop thinking that way. Do I need to remind you that stress isn't good for the baby?" I smirk and get a smile from her in return. "I was thinking I should join one of these sports activities."

Lennon's brows snap up. "You wanna play?"

Shrugging, I say, "Why not? Gotta impress my in-laws and all their friends. And not to mention, my hot, pregnant wife." I wink.

When she reacts to my words and blushes, I let myself believe that maybe, just *maybe* she feels what I feel. Part of me knows it's selfish to keep pining for her after what she's been through while the other part feels like the worst fucking human ever, considering she was my best friend's girlfriend. Either way, I know it's not right to get excited about it.

Doesn't mean my heart listens.

"Trust me, everyone's plenty impressed. But if you want to, I say go for it. Just don't get yourself hurt."

I give her a pointed look as she lowers her eyes down my body.

"On second thought, don't *you* hurt anyone else." She laughs, and I catch her biting her lower lip, which I love.

"I'm gonna sign up for the rugby game." I grab her hand to take her with me. "Can't be much different than football."

"Are you crazy?"

"Yes." *Most definitely.* Crazy because I'm in love with her, and she doesn't even know it.

Once I've signed up, we walk back to her parents where we're introduced to another handful of people.

"Do you have any pictures of the wedding?" one woman asks.

"Oh my gosh! Do you?" Lennon's mom looks back and forth between us.

"No, it was just the two of us," she reminds her mother. "But I do have an Instagram with a bunch of pictures if you want to follow for bump updates and stuff." Lennon easily gets their mind off wedding photos and clicks on her Instagram app to show them all the fake posts.

"You two are seriously so adorable," the woman squeals. "I've known Lennon for most of her life…" She directs her comment toward me with a wide smile. "And I've never seen her happier."

A knife in my gut twists at her words, the ones I wish were true, *could* be true if Lennon and I were together.

"I'm the one who's never been happier in my entire life. She's made all my dreams come true," I tell the woman as I wrap my arm around Lennon's waist, holding her tighter.

"And now grandbabies?" The woman turns toward Mrs. Corrigan. "You must be so excited."

"I am! In fact, Lennon…" Her mother turns toward her. "We should do a shopping trip tomorrow before you guys leave. Buy some baby stuff!"

"You don't have to do that, Mom—" Lennon starts to argue, but her mother cuts her off.

"I want to!" It's hard not to smile right along with Mrs. Corrigan's excitement.

"I think it's a great idea, baby." I squeeze Lennon's hip. "You two should have some quality time together."

Once that's settled, the group walks to the field for the first rugby game. Mr. Corrigan goes back to the car to grab the folding chairs and blankets so they can watch.

I meet up with the guys on my team, and we decide on positions. Having no idea who these men are, I introduce myself as Lennon's husband, and a few of them give me disapproving looks. They're about my age, so if I had to guess, I'd say they're sizing me up. Part of me wonders if it's jealousy, making me smirk at the thought. I'm not against showing off how lucky I am.

Right after the team has a game plan, I walk to Lennon and wrap my arm around her body. I know a dozen pairs of eyes are on us, so I don't hesitate to cup her face and crash our mouths together.

"Wish me luck." I smirk, reluctantly moving away.

"Uh, good luck. No showing off."

I reach around my neck to grab my shirt, then pull it off. Handing it to her, I wink. "I'd never."

Lennon smiles and rolls her eyes as I walk backward with a grin. As soon as I'm on the field, I spin around and join the team.

An hour later, sweat drips down my chest, and I realize not working out religiously in the past couple of months has caught up to me. Though I'm in shape, I haven't played sports in over two years, and running back and forth tired me out.

"Looking good, hubby," Lennon catcalls as I pass.

I waggle my brows, and she giggles.

"So Lennon Corrigan, huh? She's always been a little dick tease. How'd you score that?" Matt, a guy from my team, asks. I don't like his salty tone.

"That's my pregnant wife you're talking about, so unless you want my fist in your nose, you'll shut your damn mouth," I tell him harshly. His condescending question has me seeing red.

"Whatever," he mutters and walks away like he should.

The game finally ends, and, luckily, my team won. We'll have another one in an hour, though I'm not sure I'll be up for it.

I run toward Lennon and scoop her up in my arms, nuzzling my face in her neck. "Oh my God, you're drenched!" She giggles, throwing her head back.

She slides her body down, but I notice she keeps her hands on my chest a moment longer than needed. I see the side-glances from people who are most likely judging my tattoos. I don't have a ton, but I have a sleeve of ink on one arm and some wrapped around my waist and back.

Since we already have an audience, I grab Lennon and crash my mouth to hers. I should stop kissing her so damn much, but now that I've had a taste, I can't seem to help myself. *It's for the role*, I lie to myself, but I don't even care anymore.

My heart be damned.

I slide my tongue between her lips and her breath hitches as I bring her closer. Lennon moves her tongue against mine, and she's goddamn lucky we aren't alone right now because it's the only thing that has me pulling back.

She presses her fingers to her lips, staring at me in question or perhaps longing, but I can't allow myself to think that.

Her mother appears, smiling wide and proud. "You did so good out there, Hunter!" she squeals.

"Well, he did play football in high school and college," Lennon adds like a proud wife, making me smile.

I'm introduced to so many people, I lose track of who is who, but Lennon whispers it to me anytime they return for another conversation. This is nothing like I've ever seen or experienced, but I'm seriously loving every minute of it. It's the alternate life if Lennon had picked me, if Brandon hadn't died, and if she and I had had our very own happily ever after. I force the thoughts out as soon as they come, wishing things were different but knowing they can't be.

Lots of food, the Fourth of July parade, and a ton of children's activities fill the rest of the afternoon. Lennon stays glued to my side, and when the sun begins to set, the live music becomes the main attraction as we wait for the fireworks.

"Dance with me," I whisper to Lennon so only she hears me. We've been sitting at a table snacking on food with her parents for the past hour, and I'm ready to get her alone.

She grins. "Okay. Show me whatcha got."

Standing, I hold my hand out for her, and she hesitantly takes it. I lead her to the dance floor and wrap my arms around her. The band sings a slow song and our bodies are so close, I can smell her shampoo. The lyrics nearly make me choke up as I hold Lennon tight.

"Kinda impressed you're such a good dancer." She looks up at me with a devilish grin. "Then again, you've been surprising me for weeks."

I smirk, knowing she's right. After the way I treated her, she would have no reason to trust me. "It's our first dance as husband and wife."

Lennon chuckles, stepping closer. "Good thing it's a good song."

"It's perfect."

"You know…" She pauses, biting her lower lip. "You're better at this relationship stuff than you let on."

I raise my brows, shocked at her honesty. "Is that so?"

"Yeah, you're a natural."

Kill me. Kill me now.

She tilts her head and furrows her brows. "How come you've never had a serious relationship?" she asks hesitantly. "I mean, it seems to come pretty naturally to you. Most guys who run away from commitment tend to have a fear of failing."

I let her question sink in, unsure of how to respond. There's no way to answer it without confessing my feelings, so I say what I've always told everyone else who's asked.

"Didn't have a lot of time in college for something serious. With football and work, it wouldn't have been fair to balance a relationship between that." I shrug as if that's a plausible reason.

Except Lennon sees right through it and narrows her eyes. "But you've been out of college for over two years. You didn't want something serious with Jenna? She seemed like she wanted more."

As soon as the words come out of her mouth, her body tenses as if she hadn't meant to say them. Part of me is convinced she's jealous while the other part knows better.

"Jenna should've never happened," I tell her truthfully. "Her feelings were always stronger than mine, and it wasn't fair to lead her on, so I cut it off after—" Deciding not to finish that sentence with our *last time together*, I pause. Lennon's grip on me softens, and I tighten my hold on her back, bringing her even closer.

"Anyway, I've never had feelings for someone who made me want…more, I guess." *Lies.* I keep my gaze on her, watching her reaction. Either she believes the bullshit I'm feeding her, or she's good at keeping up a front.

"I hope you do someday," she says softly. "You're pretty great at it when you want to be."

Not sure how to respond to that, I nod, then rest my chin on top of her head as the song fades away. People start clapping around us as the guitarist does a solo, and when we slightly pull away, I see Lennon tense.

"What is it?" I study her, but she doesn't respond as she looks around me. "Lennon."

Her eyes snap back to mine, and she plasters on a fake smile. "It's nothing."

I know she's lying, and when I look over and see three women around our age watching us, I glance back at Lennon.

"Gonna tell me what's going on?" I arch a brow.

She inhales a deep breath as the band starts a new song, my arm still wrapped around her. Lennon chews on her bottom lip, looking down at our feet.

I look at the girls again, whispering to each other and staring at Lennon. "Do you know them?"

"Yes, unfortunately." She releases a short breath.

I don't get a chance to ask her to elaborate before the three of them walk toward us. They look straight out of a Stepford Wives magazine. Stank expressions and all.

"Lennon, hi," one of them singsongs in the fakest tone I've ever heard. "It's been so long since we've seen you. Surprised you're even here."

"Hi, Gretchen," Lennon clips. "Yes, it's been since graduation."

I can tell she's less than thrilled, and the dirty looks they're giving her make my blood boil. Lennon's the sweetest person I know, and this girl is throwing attitude around like fucking glitter.

"And who is *this*?" Gretchen asks in a sultry voice. "Surely, he didn't come with you."

Oh fuck no.

They look at me like meat on a stick, which pisses me off, considering Lennon and I were dancing together. It's more than fucking obvious we're together.

"I'm Hunter," I harshly introduce, then grin wide before continuing, "her husband."

"What?" One gasps and turns her attention to Lennon for clarification. "You're married?"

"Yep!" Lennon finally finds her voice and proudly shows off the big-ass ring on her finger. Her eyes are filled with pure lust, and I have to mentally remind myself she's just pretending.

"Really?" another asks, narrowing her eyes as if she doesn't buy it. "Your mother never announced it."

"She must not approve," Gretchen adds.

"Actually, she very much approves," I growl, stepping closer to Lennon, feeling the need to shield her from these mean girl wannabes. The vein in my forehead is about to pop. "We're newlyweds."

And without waiting for their reactions, I place my hand around Lennon's neck and pull her in for an earth-shattering kiss, sliding my tongue between her lips and catching her gasps with my mouth. Since these girls want to be catty bitches, I'm gonna give them the show of their lives.

Hesitantly, I pull back and give Lennon a reassuring wink.

"We're also expecting," I announce like a proud dad-to-be and turn toward them as all three of their jaws hit the ground. I rest a hand on Lennon's belly and rub it. "It was *very* nice meeting you."

I give them a fuck-you smile, then grab Lennon's hand and lead her to another part of the dance floor, swinging her around until she's plastered against my chest again.

"You sure gave them something to gossip about for the next month." Lennon cackles, glancing past me before tightening her arm around me. "Ugh. I hate them."

"Didn't realize girls acted like that after high school. Geez." I groan and my jaw clenches at the way they treated Lennon. "Wanna tell me the story?"

Lennon sighs. "They made my life hell without really doing anything."

"Huh?" We move from side to side, my hand firm on her lower back, feeling so right.

"Their little snide comments about being a pastor's daughter, little Miss Goody Two-shoes, forever virgin, Little Miss Perfect—just anything condescending and rude. I couldn't ever do anything about it, so I ignored them." She shrugs as if she's embarrassed about it, which I fucking hate.

"Lennon." I tilt her chin up so she'll look at me. "Fuck them. Seriously. They're clearly envious of you, and they fucking should be. You're amazing."

She releases a small laugh. "I don't even know why I still care."

"You're human, but don't waste another thought on them. In fact…" I look over my shoulder and see they're standing by the picnic tables, still eyeing us. "Wanna give them something to talk about?"

Lennon furrows her brows, tilting her head. "How?"

I smirk, knowing what I'm about to do is half-selfish, half for her benefit. "You trust me?"

"You know I do," she states matter-of-factly.

Without warning, I spin her body out and move her back into my chest. Switching hands, I dip her in my arm, and when she chuckles, I lean in and bring my lips centimeters from hers. "You're so beautiful when you laugh, Lennon."

She stares into my soul and before she can speak, I bring us back up and cup her face. Our mouths collide, and this time, it's one hundred percent selfish.

Fuck it.

My thumb arches over her cheek as I deepen our kiss, sliding my tongue against hers. Her hands are on me, in my hair, fisting my shirt. There's no way she can't feel this, can't see what's been brewing between us for weeks.

I'm a bastard for even wanting her to feel it.

When her breath hitches, I slow our kiss and reluctantly pull apart. This is a family function, after all. Luckily, no one seems to notice in the jam-packed park.

Except for the three girls.

Gretchen's arms are crossed over her chest as she shoots daggers, and just as Lennon peeks at them, she huffs, and the three of them stomp away.

"Told you," I say, breaking the silence.

"What?" Lennon asks, her chest rising and falling rapidly as if she still hasn't caught her breath.

I smirk. "They're jealous."

She chuckles, a wide smile splitting her cheeks. "Well, they can shove that up their asses and pout all they want."

"Agreed."

Lennon wraps her arms around me in a hug. "Thank you, Hunter. Even if it was on false pretenses, it feels good to finally get under their skin for once."

"Are you thanking me for kissing you?" I arch a brow. "It wasn't exactly a hardship."

That makes her laugh harder. And if I'm not mistaken, blush too.

"C'mon, let's get ready to watch the fireworks." She grabs my hand this time and leads me off the dance floor, purposely walking right past our audience.

CHAPTER TWENTY-NINE

LENNON

I DON'T KNOW why kissing Hunter sends butterflies to my stomach every damn time, but I've decided it's the hormones, and it doesn't mean anything.

It can't.

Abort. Abort. Abort.

Sometime over the past three months, he's become my best friend. More than my best friend, he's someone I trust wholeheartedly, someone I can't wait to spend time with and ask about his day.

And every day as we grow closer, I fear the memory of Brandon will fade more and more. We only got two amazing years together, but I know his legacy will live on in our child, and I'll never forget that.

"Where are you taking me?" Hunter asks after we grab blankets from my parents' stash.

"To the best spot to see the fireworks," I tell him, looking over my shoulder with a mischievous grin.

It's still an hour till dusk, but the crowded park will only continue to fill with more people as it gets closer to showtime. There's a spot on top of the hill that's blocked off, and as teens, my sisters and I would sneak up there every year for the best view.

"Pretty sure that sign back there said—"

"Yes, I can read," I tease. "You trust me or not, Manning?"

"Sassy," he taunts. "I like it."

Chuckling, I continue leading him to the perfect location. "The fireworks will literally be above us."

Hunter looks around, realizing how close we are, then scratches his hand over his scruffy jawline like he's worried. "This seems like a hazard."

"Are you pussying out on me?" I raise my brows, fanning out one of the blankets.

He cocks his head. "I'm still here, aren't I?"

"Good." I smile, feeling like a rebellious teenager. "Take a seat."

I use the other blanket and roll it up into a makeshift pillow. We both lean back and look up at the sky.

"This is stunning," he comments, and when I look over, I see his arms resting behind his head. I don't know why, but it's sexy when he does that.

Ugh, hormones. Go. Away.

I mentally slap myself. Then the guilt of Brandon missing this seeps in.

Sharing the news of our pregnancy and celebrating would've been so romantic with him. He'd hold me under the stars, and we'd kiss till our lips bruised.

Before Hunter notices my internal freak-out, I lie down next to him.

"I always love that you can see mountains from almost anywhere in town, but they look a little better this time of year," I explain, looking up at the sky. "I have so many memories here."

"Do you miss it?" Hunter turns and faces me. "Living here?"

I shrug, feeling indifferent. "Sometimes, I guess. The town mostly, not always the people."

"Yeah, I can understand that. No offense, but they're judgy as fuck."

His words make me laugh because it's the truth. "Told ya." I snicker.

We chat and laugh for the next hour until the first *boom* echoes in the air, and the fireworks begin. When Hunter notices me shivering from the chill in the air, he tells me to move closer. Without a beat of hesitation, I do, and soon, we're snuggling on the blanket just like we did last night. With my head on his shoulder, we watch the show.

After the grand finale, neither of us moves. I'm so comfortable and content, I don't want to.

"Lennon," Hunter whispers, tilting his head toward me. "Did you fall asleep?"

"No." I laugh. "But you're so warm and cozy."

His chest vibrates as he chuckles. "Remember that when we're squeezing onto a twin-sized bed later tonight."

My heart rapidly pounds just thinking about it. The things he's had to go through to make this plan work are nothing short of amazing.

We meet my parents at the car, and my mom's smile is so wide, it hits her eyes. "Did you kids have fun and enjoy the fireworks?"

She's so happy. And by the way she looks at Hunter and me, I know it's because of us.

Gah, fuck me.

"It was amazing," Hunter replies when I don't. He opens the door for me, and before I slide in, he grabs my arms and places a soft kiss on my cheek. "A day I'll never forget." He gives me a wink even though his words are meant for my mother.

"Everyone is so smitten with you," Mom says as we settle in the back seat. Then she looks over her shoulder and continues, "Can't say I blame them." She smirks and buckles.

I can't stop the smile that covers my face as I look down and try to hide it. Hunter is definitely a parent-charmer. Leaning over, I grab his hand and let it settle on his lap as if it's been our routine for years.

The next morning and day seem to pass by in a blink. We eat breakfast with my parents, and Mom and I go shopping for the baby. It takes us nearly all day because she wanted to drive to Salt Lake so we could hit up more shops. By the time we head home, I'm buzzing with happiness even though I'm exhausted. Regardless of the less than ideal circumstances, this trip has gone exactly the way I wished it would—full of acceptance and love.

When we walk through the front door carrying several bags in our hands, I can hear my father's laughter, followed by Hunter's. The sound of their chatter echoes throughout the house, causing me to suck in a ragged breath.

"Honey, I don't know if you're gonna have room to pack all this in your suitcases. Maybe I'll ship everything to you instead." She gestures at all the stuff she bought. Considering I'm already packed to the max, it's a great idea.

I laugh in agreement. "Yeah, maybe we went slightly overboard, especially since we don't know if I'm having a boy or a girl," I tell her.

"I'm almost positive it's going to be a girl. You seem to be carrying the same way I did." Mom shoots me a sweet smile.

I walk into the kitchen where Hunter and my father are. Even though they stop talking when I enter, the wide grins on their faces remain. Dad sips a cup of coffee, and it smells so good, I'm half-tempted to steal it from him.

"Your dad was telling me about the time you thought you could do tricks on your bike," Hunter says as he walks toward me, then places a chaste kiss on my lips.

"Dad! You're not supposed to tell anyone about that," I playfully scold.

He chuckles. "You thought you could jump over a puddle, but you fell in it instead. Just giving Hunter a warning because I'm sure your kid is going to be as adventurous or clumsy as you were."

Hunter rests his arm around me, and I can't help but soak in his touch. I look at him, smiling. "No telling what else he said."

With a laugh, Dad shakes his head and pretends to zip his lips.

"Did you have fun today?" Hunter asks.

"Tons, but now I'm tired," I admit with a sheepish grin.

Mom enters and pours herself a cup of coffee. As she's stirring in the sugar and cream, she looks over her shoulder. "Don't forget we have dinner with the Andersons tonight. We'll need to leave in two hours."

Dammit, I forgot, but I smile and nod. "Of course."

"You'll need to dress up a bit. We're going to Sebastian's Steakhouse," Dad tells me, then glances at Hunter.

"Great. Sweetheart, do you want to take a nap before going? I know you've had a long day," Hunter quietly asks, and I nod, thankful he can read my mind. We make our way out of the kitchen, and as soon as we're in the bedroom, Hunter takes a few steps toward me and tucks loose strands of hair behind my ear.

"Was today okay?" he asks, searching my face.

"It was. My mother and I bonded on a completely different level. It was as if I got an invisible adult card as soon as I told them I was married and pregnant. She didn't treat me like a child but more of an equal." I keep my voice low. "They're so happy. Does this make me a horrible daughter?"

"No," he says matter-of-factly. His warm breath brushes against my cheek, and when I look up into his brown eyes, I feel as if I'm falling… The urge to kiss him nearly overtakes me, and I bite my bottom lip to hold myself back, but I'm pretty sure he notices. His tongue swipes across his bottom lip, and I force myself away because, behind closed doors, there's no one to pretend for. At that point, what we're doing is real.

And this can't be real because my heart can't take another heartbreak.

I walk to the bed and take off my shoes, trying to get ahold of my emotions. Hunter turns and watches me, and I laugh. "I wasn't kidding about a nap."

"Oh, I didn't think you were," he says. "Shopping wears me the fuck out. So I can only imagine how it made you feel, considering all the bags I saw in the living room."

"She wouldn't stop buying stuff." I slide under the blankets, set the alarm on my phone and sigh.

Hunter sits on the bed, and I roll from side to side, unable to get comfortable, though exhaustion is settling in. Noticing, because he notices everything, Hunter lies down and wraps his arm around me. With his body warmth blanketing me, I fall asleep almost instantly.

The sound of the alarm on my phone forces me awake. Opening my eyes, I look around and see I'm still in my old bedroom, but I'm alone. I slept so damn hard, I wasn't sure where I was. Knowing we're going to eat dinner with the associate pastor and his wife tonight makes me nervous. Mrs. Anderson isn't one to keep her comments to herself and talks in a condescending tone when she's trying to hide what she truly wants to say. My mother only tolerates her because of her husband's position at the church.

I slip on the dress I packed along with some flats. When I walk down the stairs, Hunter is in the living room with my parents. I stop before making my presence known and listen to their conversation.

"I've never felt this way about anyone before. Lennon is my everything, and I can't imagine my life without her," he tells them.

My chest aches at his words.

"You two are adorably in love." My mother practically swoons.

"Madly in love," Hunter adds. Trying to save him from my parents' interrogation, I walk down the stairs and enter the living room, hoping they can't see how hard my heart is beating.

When Hunter sees me, he stands and walks over. "Sleep okay?"

I can't help but study him from top to bottom with a smile on my face. Damn, he's even wearing a tie. "Like a baby," I tell him. He dips down and kisses my cheek, and when he pulls away, I feel guilty for desperately wanting more of him.

My parents stand, and Dad grabs his keys. "Guess we should get going. Don't want to be late."

"I need to go upstairs and grab my wallet real quick," Hunter says, and my parents tell us they'll meet us in the car.

Before I walk out the front door, Hunter grabs my elbow and swings me around to face him. Without a word, he cups my face, then presses his mouth to mine, and our tongues twist and dance together. Warmth rushes through me as he pours himself into me, and I'm so fucking greedy, I don't want him to stop. I don't know what it is about his kisses, but they're more addictive than caffeine or chocolate. When he pulls away, I'm breathless and confused. *Shocked*.

"What the hell was that for?" Blinking, I search his face. That wasn't for the sake of my parents, considering they're not even in the house. That was *real*.

Do I want it to be real?

"It was a good luck kiss." He reveals a boyish smirk.

I narrow my eyes as he walks toward the door. "Wait. Don't you have to get your wallet?"

He pulls it from his back pocket and flashes it, popping an eyebrow up. "Nah, I had it after all."

My mouth falls open, and he grabs me by the hand to pull me outside, not giving me time to question him or my racing heart. The smile on my face as we slide into the back seat is genuine. We buckle, then Hunter interlocks his fingers with mine and kisses my knuckles—something that's become my new favorite gesture of his—as the car travels down the street.

Mom and Dad sing gospel music during the ride to the steakhouse. By the time we pull into the parking lot, I'm even singing along with them as Hunter taps his leg. He's such a good sport about all of this.

We're laughing as we enter the restaurant, but my smile fades as soon as I see Mr. and Mrs. Anderson. She's already judging everything about me, and my nerves teeter on edge. As Hunter introduces himself, he keeps me close by, and I plaster a fake smile on my face. Soon we're seated, and it doesn't take long before we give our drink and food orders.

It feels awkward as hell as my mother tries to make small talk about the Fourth of July celebration. Eventually, the conversation moves on, and I feel like I'm under Mrs. Anderson's microscope as she begins hounding me with questions.

"So, Lennon. What was the rush to get married so early? I didn't get the full story yesterday." Her gaze pierces through me over her glass as she sips her water.

"Well…" I hesitate before continuing and repeating our rehearsed story.

Hunter naturally picks up the conversation as I grow quiet, adding all of his charm. "—and we knew then, that we wanted to spend the rest of our lives together."

After he eloquently finishes, Hunter leans over and places a chaste kiss on my lips. Mom and Dad watch us, eating up the whole thing.

Mr. Anderson couldn't care less, but his wife, she's not giving up. "So how far along did you say you were?"

"Twelve weeks," I tell her, and she lets out a sarcastic laugh. "Honey, you seem way farther along than that. You're pretty big for only three months," she says, causing my mother to butt in. My cheeks heat, and I'm sure the entire restaurant can hear my rapidly beating heart.

"You know, Theresa, everyone said the same thing to me when I was carrying Sophie. Many assumed I was carrying twins." Mom throws her a forced grin, but I notice how tense she is. The last thing Mrs. Anderson wants to do is bring out Mama Bear because that side of her is scary.

Hunter leans back and chuckles at something my father mutters, interrupting our conversation, and I'm so damn thankful he's the buffer. "Did you hear what your dad said?"

I shake my head.

Hunter leans over and whispers in my ear, "He said he prayed his water would turn into wine."

Dad must be annoyed with Mrs. Anderson like the rest of us are.

Our food arrives, and though Mom keeps the small talk going while we're eating, the attention shifts from my pregnancy to our relationship.

"It's so cute how they met," my mother continues. "You have to share it again."

I don't remember discussing this previously. Hunter glances at me and winks.

"Most people think Lennon and I met through Brandon, but that's not true…"

Blood pumps harder through my system, and I feel like the pulse in my neck is throbbing in overdrive.

"I was at work, and Lennon ordered a drink from me. I knew how amazing Lennon was after one sentence. Sometimes, when you meet someone—and you share a special moment—it's like you just know. When she dated my best friend, I sat on the sidelines, happy for them. But after the accident, no one understood the loss and pain I was feeling better than Lennon. We were there for each other when we both needed someone the most. She was my saving grace. She's my everything." He turns to me with a sincere look on his face before going back to the story. "The day we met, I had no idea Lennon would be my wife, or we'd be starting a family, but I'm so grateful. I can't imagine a day without her now." He gives me his infamous smile, and I practically melt. The only thing that pulls me away from staring at Hunter in awe is my father's voice.

"It was almost as if God brought you together to heal and grieve," my father says.

I give him a grin, but I officially feel like an asshole for lying. Though Hunter edited some of the details, it isn't a completely fabricated story.

"It's almost as if your guardian angels were looking out for you guys, knowing you two needed each other in desperate times. I'd like to think adding you to that prayer list after the accident helped," Mom says.

I grab Hunter's hand and squeeze because he has protected me and made sure I was safe. I was supposed to be on the back of that bike that night, and it hits me like a freight train that I was pregnant at that point. I sink into a black hole as I think about Brandon and that night. Hunter leans over and kisses my forehead, causing my eyes to flutter closed and bring me back to our temporary reality.

Eventually, the server comes to the table and picks up our empty plates, and Dad pays the bill. The Andersons give us all hugs and congratulations before saying goodbye, believing every word of our story. When we walk to the car, I let out a relieved sigh. Hunter pulls me to his body and whispers in my ear, "Everything went fine. Stop overanalyzing it all."

"How do you always know what to say?"

His fingers graze across my arm. "Because I know you, Lennon."

We climb into the back seat and make our way to my parents' house with soft music playing in the background. I'm lost in my head, staying silent, replaying every question that was asked and every answer Hunter gave. The lines are so damn blurred I'm not sure what's pretend and what isn't. When we get back to California, hopefully, we'll be able to figure it out because what I feel is so damn wrong that it almost paralyzes me.

Once we're back at the house, Hunter tells my parents good night, and before I can follow, I turn around. I move toward my mom and dad, fighting back my emotions.

"Good night. I love you both so much." I smile, happy tears streaming down my cheeks.

Mom opens her arms, and I fall into them. "We love you too." She pulls back to study my face. "What's wrong, honey?"

"I'm just so happy, that's all," I tell her, and it's the truth.

"Love does that to a person," Dad says with a smile. "We're thrilled, Lennon. I can't imagine a better man for you."

My heart sinks.

"I can feel the love you two share, and it's beautiful," Mom tells me, and my mind goes into overdrive.

I wipe the rogue tears determined to fall. "Thank you."

"We love you. Good night," my father says.

"Good night." I walk away, wishing my parents had had the opportunity to meet Brandon. I like to think they would've liked him just as much. With a heavy heart, I climb the stairs.

It took all of forty-eight hours for my parents to fall in love with Hunter. They officially believe our relationship is real, and after these past two days, I almost believe it too.

CHAPTER THIRTY

HUNTER

I WAKE up with Lennon in my arms. The curve of her body presses against me, and I want to stay here all day and hold her because once we get on that plane and head back to California, everything will go back to normal. Or at least that's what I keep telling myself. I'm not sure we can go back to normal after this, but I'll try my damnedest, for her sake.

Lennon shifts, and she lets out a hum.

"You awake?" I whisper, and she shakes her head, which makes me chuckle. "Better get up, so we don't miss our flight."

She lets out a sigh. I slide out of bed and go to the bathroom. When I come back, she's sprawled out, looking beautiful as always. Her shirt slides up her body and reveals her belly, and I can't help but smile. That baby has no idea how lucky it is.

"Lennon…"

"I know, I know," she tells me in her cute sleepy voice as she pushes herself up. After tucking her messy hair behind her ears, she stretches before standing. She walks out, and by the time she comes back into the room, I'm dressed and ready for breakfast. When she passes me by, her eyes slide up and down my body. She doesn't say a word, though I have an inkling of what she's thinking.

Lennon may be able to suppress her feelings, but she can't hide her physical reactions from me—never has—even when she hated me.

She swallows hard and forces her eyes away. "I'll meet you downstairs," she says, digging through her suitcase.

I give her a side grin and a nod, wishing I could read her mind. As I walk out of the bedroom, I hear her parents' laughter in the distance. The house smells like bacon, and my stomach growls thinking about it. Lennon's parents greet me with a cheery good morning when I enter the kitchen.

"I'm finishing up breakfast. Will Lennon be down soon?" Mrs. Corrigan asks as she begins plating the food.

"Yes, ma'am," I tell her as she sets a large spread in front of me. She even made homemade waffles. "Wow, Mrs. Corrigan. This looks amazing. You're spoiling me."

She smiles and pours me a cup of coffee. "I'm going to miss you two being here."

"I am too," her dad adds. "It's been great having kids in the house again."

This causes me to laugh just as Lennon enters. She's thrown her hair into a sloppy ponytail, and when our eyes meet, the electricity streaming between us seems to pull her closer. She places a sweet kiss on my lips and sits down next to me where her mother put a plate piled full. I don't miss the fact that she initiated a kiss this time. Fake or not, but the way she looks at me is genuine.

"Ready to go back to California?" her dad asks.

A smile barely touches Lennon's lips. Her eyes meet mine before shifting them to him. "Yeah, but it's been a perfect visit."

I couldn't agree more, but I don't admit that aloud. Leaving means our fake relationship is over, and everything we pushed aside these past three days will need to be dealt with head-on.

"Honey, you two can come back anytime you want." Mrs. Corrigan beams. I notice the twinkle in her eyes when she looks at Lennon and me. It's easy to pretend this is real when everyone believes it so easily. If only our innocent lie were the truth.

"I'm sure we'll be back," I offer.

"We'd like that," Mr. Corrigan tells me.

We make small talk for the rest of the time, and when we've finished breakfast, Lennon and I go upstairs to pack. As soon as we step inside the bedroom, I notice a rogue tear spill from her cheek. Carefully, I study her, holding back the temptation to kiss away her tears.

But fuck, I want to.

"Pregnancy hormones, I think. And I'm not looking forward to the flight," she explains.

I pull her into a hug, and I swear she breathes me in as she rests her head on my chest. We stand there until my vision blurs, and I know we have to get going. The less stress Lennon is under, the better.

After we pack, I swing my bag over my shoulder and grab her heavy suitcase. As I go to walk out of the room, Lennon reaches for me and pulls me close. I turn to her, feeling her breath brush against my skin. Instead of ruining the moment with words, I stare into her crystal blue eyes and wait.

"Hunter…" she says. Letting out a ragged breath, she pulls her bottom lip into her mouth, almost begging for me.

Considering this might be the last time I kiss her, I place my palms on her cheeks and pull her mouth closer. When our lips finally touch, the fireworks we watched on the Fourth of July cannot compare to what I feel. We're lost in each other, falling then floating, in a reality where nothing else matters. It almost hurts to stop kissing her, and I allow every emotion I have to release because our façade ends here. As soon as we're in the car, I'll go back to wearing a mask and pretending we're only friends.

When we break apart and Lennon places her fingertips over her lips, I think I might've kissed away her ability to speak. By the way she greedily twisted her tongue with mine behind closed doors confirms something more simmers between us, even if she doesn't want to admit it. I hold on to the dream of her being mine, as wrong as it is. For a second, she looks as if she's lost in her head, and it causes the guilt to drip over me.

"I'm sorry. I—"

"No," she firmly stops me. "Don't be."

Maybe I've overstepped the boundary or pushed her too far, which causes my mind to rush a million miles per hour, but she did too.

"Ready to go home?" I ask, changing the subject, escaping the silence that lingers between us.

"I'm ready to walk around braless, eat junk food, and sleep late," she admits with a smirk.

I laugh, the sound bouncing off the walls as we exit her old bedroom. Lennon insists on grabbing the smaller suitcase, and when we go downstairs, her parents are waiting in the sitting room. I hurry and load our bags into the car, then come back inside and tell them goodbye. Hugs and kisses are exchanged between Lennon and her parents.

"We followed your Instagram account so we can see all your updates. Let us know as soon as the baby's born, and we'll come to visit right away," Mrs. Corrigan says. Her happiness radiates like sunshine.

"It was nice to finally meet you," I say honestly.

Her dad gives me a hard handshake and a grin. "Glad to have a son now. Happy you're a part of the family."

The smile on my face doesn't fade, and I can't help but feel like a piece of shit for deceiving them.

Lennon doesn't wait for a beat before speaking up. "Well, we gotta go. I love you both so much. See you soon!"

They follow us outside and wave goodbye when we get in the car and back out of the driveway. I beep the horn a few times as Lennon waves, and soon, the two-story house fades in the distance. As we enter the highway, Lennon lets out a long sigh, which makes me laugh.

"I'm kinda sad we're leaving," she finally says.

"Me too." I don't reach for her hand even though I want to. Instead, I keep both hands tightly wrapped around the steering wheel.

"They liked you a lot. Thank you again for…*everything*." She grins and looks out the window.

"Lennon, you know you don't have to keep thanking me, but you're welcome." I meant every word, every touch, every kiss. The guilt I pushed aside for the sake of getting through this slowly returns to haunt me as we drive away from our personal haven. A place where we didn't allow ourselves to feel remorse for what we were doing—what we had to do—and what I'd do ten times over again if I had to. Instead of pouring my soul out to her, I turn on the radio and try not to ignore the way I feel. A piece of my heart will remain in Utah, a sliver of what's always been reserved for Lennon.

Once we reach the airport, we return the rental car and get through security in hyperspeed, but a delay in our flight means we won't get home until after dark. I wish we had known beforehand and could've spent time in Salt Lake City. But instead, we sit and wait. With every passing hour, Lennon grows more anxious, and so do I. By the time we have lunch, we find out we've been delayed even longer, so the entire day has been spent sitting and waiting. Lennon falls asleep on my shoulder, but I remain wide awake as I process the past three days.

Eventually, we board the plane, and I'm sure every passenger who steps on is pissed. I shove Lennon's suitcase in the storage compartment and almost worry it won't fit because it's stuffed to the max. Lennon packed as much as she could of her mother's gifts, though she'll still be shipping packages to us.

As the plane lifts into the air, Lennon takes my hands in hers, and we interlock fingers. Though it's a small gesture, touching her feels like home. Whether she does it out of habit or comfort, I brush my thumb across the top of hers, and she leans her head against my shoulder, falling asleep. My mind is in marathon mode as I think about how holding Lennon under the booming fireworks will forever be etched into my heart. And brain.

So many people commented on how in love we were, and it's something I can't seem to shake.

Was it all pretend for her? Was she acting the entire time?

Regardless, it can't turn into anything real, though a part of me knows or rather hopes it were.

Not once did our act falter, and we performed together so well, we both deserve Oscars. But the reality is, I didn't have to pretend. For the first time ever, the walls I've been so adamant about building have crumbled to rubble. Being able to kiss and touch her and openly love her came naturally and too easy.

Before we came to Utah, I already had it bad for her—but now I've completely fallen.

I'm so fucking doomed.

Once we land, we deplane and grab our bags from the carousel. On the way back to the apartment, we're both yawning. The past few days were nothing short of exhausting. Between meeting new people, waking up early, and trying to impress Lennon's parents, I'm ready to pass out. We pull into the apartment complex, and I manage to carry all the bags up the stairs in one trip.

"I could've helped, you know." Lennon unlocks the door, and we step inside. Our sighs happen in unison, and it causes her to smirk.

"Home sweet home!" she says, removing her bra and dropping it on the floor. "That feels so much better."

"Just let it all out." I chuckle, and she shrugs, going to the bathroom.

I bring her suitcases to her room and throw my bag on the floor. I'm pissed I didn't take off work tomorrow. The reality that our rendezvous is over hits me in full force. The line in the sand reappears, reminding me of where we were before Utah, before Brandon's death, before it all. Lennon needs to be kept at arm's length, but the thought causes my heart to skip a beat. The sound of her voice startles me.

"Now that we're home, can we discuss the Jenna thing tomorrow?"

Fuck, she's jumping straight into that.

"Yes," I say. Giving her a small smile, I know we're back to the real world already.

"Perfect. I'm gonna take a shower if that's okay."

I nod and watch her walk away.

When the water comes on and I hear her singing, a smile hits my lips. She takes the shortest shower ever, and I decide to take one too. I'm sure she was saving hot water for me, which has me holding back a laugh because we've come so damn far from the days of fighting over it.

After I finish washing my body and get dressed, all the lights in the apartment are turned off other than the lamp in the living room. I turn it off, and when I walk past Lennon's room, I crack the door open.

"Good night, Lennon."

"Night," she says sleepily, but I hear the smile in her voice.

When I lie in my bed, my room feels like an empty box. Tossing and turning, I search for sleep, but it doesn't find me even though I'm tired as hell. Maybe the small-ass bed we shared wasn't so bad after all. I find myself missing the way her warm body feels, the smell of her hair, and how she fit so perfectly against me as I held her all night.

Rolling over, I force my eyes closed and try to steady my breathing when my phone vibrates on my nightstand. I'm half-tempted not to grab it, but I do. When I see a text message from Lennon, I'm confused.

LENNON

My bed is way too big.

My laughter bounces off the walls of my room, and I know she heard me.

HUNTER

> I'm sure we can get you a smaller one if you want.

I know what she wants, and I want it just as much as she does, but I refuse to offer. She's going to have to ask me to lie with her. I can't always be the one to reach out. My heart races at the prospect of it, of being close to her again, because right now, I want nothing more.

LENNON

> You're going to make me beg, aren't you?

I grin, playing dumb.

HUNTER

> What are you talking about?

LENNON

> Okay, never mind.

A light chuckle escapes me as I imagine the expression on her face.

LENNON

> I just heard you laugh!

She giggles, and I love that I'm the reason for it.

LENNON

> Fine. I'll play your game.

HUNTER

> What game?

I'm smiling from ear to ear.

LENNON

> Please come sleep with me.

HUNTER

> I'm not sure I got your text. What did you say?

She groans loudly, then shouts, "Hunter Manning!"

I change into a shirt and jogging pants, then grab my phone and go into her room. She rolls over and looks at me, the glow of her phone illuminating her gorgeous face. Sitting up on her elbows, she gives me a playful eye roll. "I knew you'd come."

"How'd you know?"

"Because friends don't leave friends in need."

Though the word is like a knife digging into my heart, I force a smile. "You're right."

Lennon pats the bed and lies down, and I crawl under the sheet next to her.

"Thank you," she says sweetly, placing her head on my chest. Pulling her into my body, I hold her tight as though if I close my eyes and wake up, she'll be gone. Her breathing quickly steadies, and I know she's already asleep. It takes no time before I'm drifting off and dreaming of a life where we can be together without worry, care, or guilt.

CHAPTER THIRTY-ONE

LENNON

I FEEL Hunter's lips on my forehead as he softly whispers, "I'm heading to work. See you tonight."

I was so exhausted from traveling these past few days that I slept in and skipped breakfast. Eating with him each morning is a tradition I've come to love, but fatigue is kicking my ass after our trip.

"Mmkay, bye," I mumble in a sleepy haze, squeezing my eyes tight and rolling over.

A rumble of laughter escapes him as he brushes my hair off my face. "Get some rest. Baby needs it." The door clicks shut.

Shifting around, I take the pillow Hunter used and bring it to my chest, inhaling his scent. I settle it around my belly and drift back to sleep.

When I wake up a couple of hours later, I see a group text from Sophie and Maddie asking if we can meet for lunch. I know they're dying to know if the plan worked. I shoot a text back, telling them I can meet them in an hour, then I slowly roll out of bed and get into the shower to wake myself up.

As I wash my body, lathering soap around my swollen breasts and belly, I sing lullabies. At four months pregnant, I know the baby can hear me and not only do I want him or her to recognize my voice, but I also hope the music will comfort them the way it's always comforted me.

My favorite "Baby Mine" cover by Alison Krauss makes me think of my mother. I vividly remember her singing it to me while I was throwing a tantrum in the middle of the shopping center. Instead of yelling, she started singing, and it immediately grabbed my attention. Her voice was so soothing and calming, it snapped me out of my meltdown. I was four or five years old then. Even as a teen, she'd hum the melody whenever I had a bad day at school or was upset about something. There are dozens of other songs I love too, but this one was always my favorite and still is.

I can't wait to share it with my baby.

"You okay?" Sophie asks me an hour later when we meet at a little café down the block.

"Just a little tired, I guess," I lie, looking at the menu, unsure what to share about this weekend. Some details I want to keep to myself—hidden in my heart.

After we order, they look at me.

"Well?" Maddie finally asks. "Give us the scoop. You haven't told us anything except that you arrived and weren't kicked out on your asses."

I shrug"They bought it and really love Hunter." It's the understatement of the year.

Sophie exhales a relieved breath, placing a hand over her heart. "Thank God. I was dying."

"Of course they did," Maddie says, playing with the straw in her drink. "What's not to love, amirite?"

Sophie gives her a side-eye of disapproval.

"Because of his charming personality," Maddie tries to deflect. "Plus, he's a project manager, right? So he's a people person and used to captivating them with his good looks and piercing eyes. Hell, I get pregnant every time I see him."

I glare. "Anyway..."

Sophie chuckles. "So Mom and Dad *really* liked him, huh?"

"Yep," I confirm. "Said they were happy for me—*us*—and could see how much we loved each other."

They both go silent.

"We were *acting*," I emphasize before they get any ideas. Before *my* heart gets any ideas.

Sophie and Maddie glance at each other, and I roll my eyes.

I tell them about the Fourth of July events, how Hunter blended in with everyone, made them believe we were a real couple, and how smoothly it all went. It not only looked real, it felt real too, but I don't disclose that part.

"Was the kissing an act?" Sophie asks me, concern written all over her face.

"You kissed? Like a lot?" Maddie leans closer.

"Well, we had to look convincing as newlyweds," I remind them. "We practiced a couple of times beforehand, so it wasn't awkward or anything."

"So like sweet pecks or full-on make-out sessions?" Maddie taunts me by waggling her eyebrows suggestively.

Rolling my eyes, I lower my face to hide the blush on my cheeks. Hunter's kisses are what wet dreams are made of. Thankfully, our lunch arrives, interrupting our conversation. I dig in, needing to fill my stomach before the guilt eats me alive.

"So why don't you two tell me what you did while I was gone?" I ask. "Fill me in."

"I nearly murdered my roommates over drinking all the milk and not buying more," Sophie says with a groan. "I need to get the hell out of there."

Maddie and I both give her a look of sadness. "We'll come up with a game plan," I tell her. "Have you tried looking in the roommates wanted ads?"

"I can't afford to move right now, but as soon as I get the chance, I'm out of there," Sophie admits, and I understand that more than she knows. I know she has student loans, her car payment, rent, and other bills to pay, which doesn't leave her a lot of extra to save for situations like this.

Maddie changes the subject. "Oh, so Mason, Liam, and I went to watch Sophie play in the park before the fireworks."

"Oh right! That was nice they went." I look at Sophie, wondering if there's more to the story.

"Mason was intrigued by your strings, that's for sure," Maddie taunts around a mouthful of food, then swallows.

"Shut up, Mads," Sophie hisses, her cheeks turning pink.

"He was. You're a badass with that violin. Looking all serious up there, and then you start playing, and your whole face lights up. Mason was…entranced, to say the least." She slowly enunciates her last word, smirking at Sophie, teasing her. What cracks me up the most is they're so busy giving each other shit about Mason and Liam, they nearly forget about me and Hunter.

"He couldn't take his eyes off you," Maddie continues.

"Must've been too entranced to hold a conversation with me." Sophie's tone makes me snort, and I shake my head.

"Well, the only time he looked away was to dodge all the girls parading around him," Maddie explains. "I had to shoo them off more than once. Now that I think about it, he used me as a buffer to ignore them. He put his arm around my shoulders, and I wrapped my arm around his waist as we walked around. No wonder he was being so…friendly. Asshole was using me."

That causes me to laugh. "Sounds like he was killing two birds with one stone." I take a large bite of my sandwich. They both look at me with curious expressions. "To make himself seem unavailable and to make Liam jealous."

Sophie smirks. "That's why Liam's jaw was about to snap in half."

Maddie slams her palms down on the table. "I gave him every opportunity to… basically do anything to me! One minute, he lets his guard down, and then it's as if he suddenly remembers I'm a virgin and puts a wall back up. Ugh! Being a virgin sucks!"

Her voice goes up an octave, and the people sitting next to us look over, giving us death glares at her outburst.

"Might wanna say that louder next time, Mads. Don't think the church down the street heard you," I quip.

"I'm this close to selling it off to the highest bidder," she says, pinching her fingers together.

"Maddie, stop it!" Sophie tries to cover her mouth with her hand, and I snicker at them. It's like we're kids all over again.

"I doubt that's the reason Liam is acting this way. It has to be something else. Maybe he's preoccupied with his job. Isn't it something serious?" I ask, hoping it comforts her. I haven't known Liam that long, but I'm sure he wouldn't write her off because she's not experienced in the bedroom.

"Maybe. He's a bounty hunter or something, and chasing down bad guys sounds intense. Maybe that's his problem," Sophie chimes in. "He travels for it too sometimes."

I hold my hand out toward her. "Yes, see? Or he has small dick syndrome. Or he's covered in warts or something. Definitely *not* you."

"Eww." Maddie scrunches her nose. "Well, I doubt that's the case. His phone was blowing up with messages from Serena all day long." She rolls her eyes to emphasize her disapproval. "Whoever the hell that is."

"Hmm…I'll ask Hunter. Maybe he knows." I shrug and continue eating until my food's gone. "Are you going to finish those chips?" I ask Sophie when my plate is clean.

"Nope, all yours." Sophie pushes them toward me.

"Hey, did you know Liam and Mason have another roommate?" Maddie asks, stealing Sophie's pickle.

I furrow my brows, thinking back if I remember hearing anything about it, but nothing comes to mind. "No, I don't think so. I thought it was just the two of them."

"Apparently not. Mason casually mentioned her," Maddie adds.

"*Her*?" I nearly choke. "They live with a woman?"

"Well, not for long," Sophie chimes in. "Guess she's moving out soon."

"Who is she? An ex? A friend? A seventy-year-old grandma?"

Maddie snorts. "Nope, but I'm pretty sure she's a little older than them from what I overheard."

"That's odd. Brandon never told me that." Blinking, I think back to all the times he'd go over there to hang out. "Brandon and Hunter partied there a lot before I moved in. I wonder why it was kept a secret."

"Well, now that you and Hunter are…*friendly*," Maddie says, smirking, "perhaps you can bring it up and ask. Then give us all the details."

I scoff. "I'm not gonna go all Nancy Drew on him." Though I am curious.

"Oh, come on! You wanna know just as badly as we do."

"If there's a casual way to bring it up, I'll try," I concur.

I've finished the rest of Sophie's food, and the waiter has cleared the table, but we don't leave. Hanging out has become more rare with their rehearsal schedules, so I want to spend as much time with them as I can.

"How are you feeling? Any morning sickness?" Sophie asks as we settle back into our seats after getting drink refills.

"Any kicking yet?" Maddie perks up, trying to reach for my belly.

"I'm good, just tired. I think I feel a little something, which the pregnancy book says is common around four months, but I'm not exactly sure. It feels like a little flutter."

"It could also be gas," Sophie interjects. I scowl. "Well, it could! That's what I heard anyway."

"Well, baby kicks can't be felt for a while from the outside, but the mother should be able to," I say, repeating what I read.

"I can't wait until you're so big that when the baby moves around it looks like an alien inside your stomach," Maddie states in a giddy tone.

I furrow my brows, giving her a weird look. "That sounds painful."

"I've seen videos on YouTube and Instagram. There was this

one woman whose baby's foot pushed the skin so far you could see its tiny toes! Looked freaky as hell!"

"Stop scaring her," Sophie scolds.

"If I have nightmares about giving birth to an alien baby, I'm blaming you!" I point my finger at her.

"Wait!" Sophie interjects. "You haven't given us an update about…" She draws it out, unsure if she should say it aloud or not. I've only told her, so now Maddie will freak out when I explain the Jenna situation.

"I asked if we could talk more about it tonight," I say after sharing the news with Maddie who, in fact, lost her shit. "I don't know how he's so sure, but he asked me to trust him so…"

"If they were casually hooking up, maybe he thinks she was sleeping with other guys too?" Sophie looks at me with a pitiful expression.

"I might be a virgin and all, but even I know you can get pregnant after one time," Maddie chimes in, and her confused tone makes me laugh. "I mean, right?"

I purse my lips and nod. "There's always a chance, even if using protection, unless they did it while…" The thought is so gross, I can't continue.

"While what?" Maddie pushes.

Sophie catches on to what I was about to say and grimaces. "Ew." She laughs. "Though I'm sure it happens."

"Can you two fill me in, please? I'm clueless." Maddie pouts.

I lean in toward her and lower my voice. "Unless they had sex while she was…you know…*on* her period."

We pull apart from each other, and she twists her lips. "People do that?"

"You can't normally get pregnant during that time of the month, but hell, stranger things have happened," I tell her.

"That's…interesting." Her eyes widen in disbelief.

"To each their own, but now imagine how our talk is gonna go tonight." I sigh. "Not that I'm going to press him on specifics because it's not my business, but we decided to wait until after the trip to discuss it so we could focus on being *newlyweds*."

"It is too your business," Sophie disagrees. "You two are in a weird 'non-relationship' relationship."

"No," I argue. "We're just friends, Soph."

"A friend you want to see naked." Maddie snorts, and I'm seconds away from slapping it off her smug face.

"Joke's on you because I've already seen him naked," I blurt, then cover my mouth. *Shit.*

"What?" they exclaim.

I look at the imaginary watch on my wrist and start shuffling out of the booth. "Oh look, it's getting late. I still have to unpack and do laundry."

"Not so fast." Maddie grabs my arm, pulling me back. "Spill the tea."

I slouch back in the seat and they stare at me. "It was an accident. I walked in on him just as he was getting out of the shower."

"And you didn't faint?" Maddie snickers.

"I was so embarrassed!" I hiss, my cheeks heating at the memory. "I turned around immediately."

They both chuckle, and I mutter at them to shut up. "Can we drop it now? I need to be able to look at him tonight."

"Were things weird when you got home last night?" Sophie asks.

"No, but…" I stop myself, realizing it's too late, and they're going to press me on it anyway. "We slept in my old bed at Mom and Dad's, and when we were in our own rooms last night, I missed him." I shrug, knowing they're going to give me so much shit. "Well, I missed having a body next to me."

"And?" Sophie raises a brow.

"I asked him to lie with me. So he did, and we fell asleep snuggling."

"Aww…" Maddie singsongs. "So now you're what? Sleeping buddies?"

My head drops, and I groan. "I don't know. It sucks sleeping alone when you're so used to having someone next to you." Though if I'm being honest with myself, it was much more than that. I didn't just miss that feeling—I missed *him*—and the realization makes my head spin and my heart sink.

"What happened to boundaries, Lennon?" Sophie gives me a pointed look.

"Pretty sure they're nonexistent at this point." I chew my bottom lip, thinking about how quickly things have escalated. We won't be able to fall back into watching *Friends* and eating dinner together every night. Not after our trip.

They both give me wary looks.

"Do you want me to be truthful about all this?" I ask them. My heart flutters, knowing I can't keep this from my sisters. I trust them with my life and hate keeping secrets from them. The only thing I have to lose is my heart, though I'm convinced I already have.

They nod and smile as they lean forward, waiting for me to speak.

"I'm scared of falling for Hunter and opening myself and my heart to him. I'm also afraid of losing him and everything we have right now. Hunter has been my rock, my best friend, and I'm not sure I could handle him not being in my life if we didn't work out."

My heart beats erratically at the thought.

Sophie's sad eyes meet mine, and Maddie frowns.

"I can't imagine how difficult this is for you. It's okay not to make any decisions right now. Time will tell all, Lennon. You're not over Brandon, you're concerned about our parents, and you're hormonal *and horny* as hell." Sophie smirks, grabbing my hand. "Add in your feelings, and it's a lot for anyone to deal with. He's your biggest cheerleader and might understand you on a different level than Maddie or I do at this point. I think he'll give you time if you ask, but you can't lead him on."

"I know. I don't want to be that person at all. The feelings are there, but I have to stop acting on them. I have an overwhelming amount of guilt for wanting more or thinking about him in that way. While we were in Utah, I could no longer tell what was real and what wasn't. I know I said we were acting, but at times, I wondered if he was…" I trail off, then shake my head because I can't allow myself to think of the possibilities. "I would never, ever intentionally hurt him," I add, though I'm afraid it's too late for that.

"We know," Maddie says. "Hunter knows that too. You're in a vulnerable place at the moment."

As the conversation comes to an end, the three of us get up and make our way to the parking lot. Maddie hitched a ride with Sophie so she didn't have to Uber or take the bus. I give Maddie a hug and tell her to keep me updated on her shows and rehearsals. I love hearing about them and can't wait to watch her perform soon.

Sophie pulls me in for a hug next and then pushes us apart slightly. "Be careful, Lennon. I know you're in a sensitive situation right now, and you two went through some shit together in Utah, but I don't want you getting hurt again."

"Trust me, I don't either," I tell her honestly. "Hunter will always be Brandon's best friend, and even though Mom and Dad bought the story doesn't mean it could ever be real life. But this side of Hunter…it's hard not to like him."

"I'm glad he's there for you as a friend, Lennon. But I hope he's being sincere and won't suddenly change his mind about wanting a roommate with a baby or something."

"It's my biggest fear, Soph. Especially after Jenna. One day, he's going to move on with his life, and when that time comes, I won't stand in the way. He deserves to be happy."

A tear escapes, and I quickly brush it away, but not before Sophie sees it. She tilts her head and looks at me. "You can text or call me anytime. You know that, right?"

I wrap my arms around her again. "Of course I do. And the same goes for you."

After I go to my car, I crank it and wait until Sophie and Maddie drive away. I lose track of time as my eyes fill with water and tears stream down my cheeks. Admitting my feelings and saying them aloud have my emotions tightly twisted together, and I'm in knots over it. I blink up at the blue sky and watch the fluffy clouds float across as I suck in a deep breath, then back out of the parking lot.

Needing to clear my head before I head home, I drive around town. Soon, I'm close to the church where Brandon's funeral was held, and I blame my subconscious for guiding me here. I let out a ragged breath and turn onto the road that leads straight to the cemetery.

My head is in a fog as I think back to that day. It all happened so fast, then too damn slow. Over the past three months, I've avoided visiting the burial site because the wound is still too raw. It hurts each time I think about Brandon no longer being here and not getting to meet his baby. Being in the cemetery makes it more than real, but I can't put it off any longer. I enter the wrought-iron gates and park close to where he's buried.

My muscles grow tight, and my heart pounds hard in my chest. The guilt from Utah, from how things happened with Hunter, all of it comes to the forefront, taking complete control of my thoughts. I suck in a deep breath to clear my mind and even try thinking about something else.

Knowing it's not good for the baby, I calm down first and find a bit of courage to walk across the grass and search for his headstone. At first, I'm not exactly sure where it is and begin to frantically look around. Just as I start to panic, I see it.

The grass has barely begun to grow over the dirt, but I move closer. As I read his name and birthday and death date carved into the black stone, I nearly fall to my knees.

Walking forward, I steady myself and kneel, knowing my legs will give out at any moment. The memories of the funeral are still hard to think about. Bending down, I support myself and wrap a hand around my belly, then run my fingers across the photograph his parents had forever encased.

"I'm so sorry," I croak out, the sobs quickly taking over. Betrayal nearly chokes me while the guilt strangles me. Memories of Brandon and me together come in quick flashes, but they're followed by Hunter and me in Utah.

"I'm so confused, but I do know one thing for certain, and that's how much I miss you," I say aloud. Staring at his picture, I wish he could hear me and comfort me the way he always did when I was upset.

"I'll never stop loving you, Brandon. No matter what. You'll always be the man who has a piece of my heart. Always. And you left me with the best gift I could ever ask for. We're having a baby. At first, it was hard to come to terms with that, but now I couldn't be more excited. He or she is going to know all about you, about us, about their kind-hearted, selfless daddy who loved me until his dying day." I swallow, wiping my face. The light breeze brushes across my skin, causing goose bumps to form. It's almost as if he heard me and he's happy about the pregnancy. "I'm trying to learn to be myself again, to be happy, because I know that's what you'd ultimately want. I'm going to make it through this pain, aren't I?"

I sit on the ground, cross my legs, and listen to the wind travel through the trees as I pour it all out into the open, needing him to know it all. "I've asked myself why I wasn't on the back of that bike with you. If you hadn't dropped me off at Sophie's and if any of this would've happened. The survivor's guilt consumes me, but I like to think it's because I was pregnant. That our little angel was the reason I'm still here." I place my hand on my belly, allowing it to rest there, wanting to protect him or her from it all. It's the first time I've allowed myself to even admit that. I give myself permission to process my admissions as I close my eyes and take in slow, deep breaths as my thoughts travel.

I let out a stifled chuckle. "Hunter and I are getting along like you always wanted. The irony, right? I'm scared of the feelings starting to form. It feels way too soon, and I wonder if my heart is confused because it's trying to replace the ones I had for you. I don't ever want to forget you, and I can't even begin to think about being with someone else, but you'll be glad to know Hunter has been here for me and the baby. He's as protective as I know you'd be. Our friendship developed through dealing with the heartache of losing you, and it confuses me. I worry these mixed feelings are because I'm so damn lonely, and I haven't had enough time to fully process you being gone. They say you can't love someone if you don't love yourself, but what if you're still in love with someone who is no longer here? Will I ever be able to love again after losing you? It feels wrong."

My heart beats in my ears. He's always known all my secrets, and now he knows these too. "I know I need more time to heal. I'm so fucking broken and lost, but I know the baby needs me to be strong, and I want to be for him or her. They're gonna need me more than ever since I'll be alone." The reality of those words hit me like a ton of bricks. Just as I wipe the tears from my cheeks, I look up and see a songbird land on the black stone. It looks at me, and a small smile hits my lips. It's as if Brandon sent a sign, letting me know he still hears me and everything will work out.

"I will always love you, Brandon." My breath hitches. "God, I miss you more than you could ever know." The tears hit my cheeks, and the bird flies away. It disappears into a nearby tree, and I sigh. By the time I stand, my head has cleared slightly, and I know what I have to do going forward.

I have to give myself time.

After letting my emotions out at the cemetery, I come home, unpack, and do two loads of laundry. Then I grab Hunter's dirty clothes and do his too. While waiting for the washer to finish, I clean the kitchen, scrub the floors, clean out the fridge, then straighten up and vacuum the living room and hallway. We weren't gone that long, but I need something to keep my mind busy because we're supposed to talk about the Jenna situation tonight.

Once five o'clock hits, I start dinner, and an hour later, Hunter comes through the door. My heart races, and I hate that after all this time, I'm nervous around him again. Knowing what we need to discuss tonight and my admissions has my nerves in overdrive.

"Hey, wifey," Hunter singsongs as he walks into the kitchen. I keep my eyes locked on the stovetop as I stir the chicken and Alfredo sauce. "Something smells good." He opens the fridge and grabs a beer. "Whoa…did you clean in here?"

I swallow, turning to look at him with a forced smile. "Yeah, I was on a roll after I did our laundry and cleaned the apartment."

"Lennon." He keeps his gaze locked on mine as he takes a sip of his beer. "You didn't have to do that." Hunter leans against the door, his eyes boring into me as if something is on his mind.

"I knew you'd be busy with work and probably wanted to relax tonight." I shrug, bringing my attention back to the pan. "It wasn't a big deal. I folded and hung everything up too."

"Oh, well, thank you."

I smile briefly. "No problem. Dinner will be ready in about ten minutes."

"Great, I'm starving."

Laughing, I turn the burner down. "You always are."

Hunter gulps his beer, then tosses it into the recycling.

"I'm gonna change quickly. Be right back."

"Sounds good."

Shamelessly, I watch as he walks out, but he looks over his shoulder and catches me. He gives me a quick wink before he makes it into the hallway and is out of sight.

Ugh. I squeeze my eyes tight, trying to gain control of my emotions, but I feel as though they're slipping through my fingers.

CHAPTER THIRTY-TWO

HUNTER

Waking up with Lennon in my arms was heaven, and I hated having to get up and leave. My only motivation was knowing I'd see her after work because even though our fake relationship is over, I still enjoy spending time with her in the evenings.

Nothing monumental happened at the office while I was gone, and after reviewing the current progress, I left the jobsite pleased. We'll be finished in two to three months, and we're on target to meet our planned budget as long as nothing terrible happens. Before lunch, just as I'm sitting at my desk to turn on my computer, my phone vibrates. I unlock it and see a text from Jenna. Considering I rushed her out of the apartment on Sunday, then rejected her call, I'm surprised it took her this long.

JENNA

Can we talk?

The dread sets in, but I know this conversation can't be avoided—not this time and not with what she's claiming. Her showing up at the apartment again can't happen, and we have unfinished business to resolve. I think about what to say to her and know it's a conversation we should have face-to-face. Sure, I'm an asshole at times, but this is a serious accusation. I ask her to lunch, and we decide to meet in thirty minutes a few blocks away at a small burger place.

Her being pregnant weighs heavily on my mind as I contemplate what I'm going to say. I check the time, grab my keys and drive over. When I arrive, she's already sitting at a booth by the window in the corner. Jenna waves, and I force out a grin and take a seat in front of her. It's awkward as hell, and I'm grateful the waiter quickly walks up and takes our drink and food order. Moments later, he's setting down our waters.

"How was your trip?" She casually takes a sip of her drink.

"Great. Weather was nice." I'm not sure how to start the conversation, so I let her talk while I find my words.

"Listen. I know this entire situation is awkward for you. It is for me too, but we need to discuss the options of what's going to happen next," she states.

"Were you with other people when we were hanging out?" I come right out and ask. Raising my eyebrows, I watch her carefully and notice she's more tense than I am.

She opens her mouth, then closes it before exhaling. Jenna's always been a bad liar, and her hesitation gives her away.

"You were," I say.

"We never agreed to be exclusive, Hunter," she finally tells me.

I shake my head. "I didn't expect you to be. But you can't be sure I'm the father of your baby if you were with someone else. A few days ago, you were determined that I was, but how can you be, considering?"

"Based on my expected due date, I figured out when I would've ovulated, and you're the only person I was with during that time," she tells me confidently.

"Jenna…" Lowering my voice, I look her straight in her eyes, hoping she'll see I'm not playing her games. I'm not sure how to word my next sentence because I don't want it to come out harsh. She's trying to trap me, and it pisses me off beyond belief.

"I know you're the father, Hunter. You have to be."

I can tell she's getting upset, and it's the last thing I need right now.

"I'm certain I'm not. We used protection every single time. I'm encouraging you to tell whoever else you were with that he could possibly be a father because it's not fair for him not to know." There's more to the story on why I'm so confident I'm not, but it's honestly none of her business. Only Hayden knows.

Our food arrives, pulling us both away from the discussion. Though it's the middle of the lunch rush and the restaurant is full, I know this conversation has to happen right here, right now.

Tears begin rolling down her cheeks. I'm not sure if she's crying because I refuse to accept this or because deep down she knows someone else could be the father.

"This is all gonna work out," I say, trying to comfort her.

She shakes her head. "No, it's not going to be okay. One drunken night, in a moment of weakness, I hooked up with Craig."

Jenna covers her face in embarrassment, and I feel for her since that's her ex who cheated on her before we got together. I understand why she'd be so upset with him being the father. It all makes perfect sense now.

"He deserves to know, Jenna." I pick up my burger and take a bite. She eats too, and we stay silent while we eat.

"You could still be the father, Hunter. I haven't been on birth control since I broke up with Craig months before, and while I know you and I used protection, it's not foolproof. You can't know for sure."

I grow more frustrated with her, but I try to push it away. Her ex was a piece of shit, and knowing I'm not the dad means he's back in her life again. It's not a healthy situation for her or the baby.

"I *do* know for sure," I tell her confidently.

"So what do you want me to do? Forget about us? Forget we ever happened? Take your word for it because you don't *want* to be the father of my baby?" She snarls, her voice rising and drawing attention to us.

"That's exactly what I want you to do. Look, it tears me to fucking shreds to know I hurt you and that you wanted more out of the relationship than I could offer. I told you time and time again that I couldn't give you anything more. Now you're pulling this and—"

"It's because of *her*, isn't it?" She searches my face, and I swallow down the food that feels like it's lodged in my throat.

I can't even find it inside me to argue, so I don't say anything at all.

"You can deny it all you want, but I could tell by the way you two looked at each other when I showed up. The way you've always looked at her. I knew the moment I met her that you had a thing for her. It's more than obvious." Jenna lets out an annoyed huff, wiping away her tears before they fall.

My blood pumps faster, my pulse pounding in my neck. For years, I believed everyone was fooled by the way I treated Lennon, but apparently, I've been transparent, even to Jenna. "What do you want me to say? What do you want from me?"

Jenna glares, and if looks could kill, I'd be dead. She's hurting, that much I can see, but I can't be the man to fix it for her. She digs in her purse and pulls out a twenty-dollar bill and tosses it on the table. "We're done here."

"Wait," I say, and she stops for a second. "You have to tell Craig. You need to tell him today so he can be a part of the pregnancy," I nearly beg, knowing how much she'll need someone during this time. But it can't be me.

"You'll be hearing from my lawyer, Hunter," she hisses my name like it's poison.

"Looking forward to it." Picking up my burger, I take a bite and continue eating without a worry in the world.

She groans and storms out of the restaurant. Though I know this isn't over, I let out a relieved breath and finish my fries.

"You need a to-go box for that?" The waiter looks at the plate of food she barely touched and hands me the bill.

"Nah, man. She ain't coming back," I tell him, and he shrugs as if he can't be bothered by it either. I pay and head back to work.

When I arrive back at my office, I go straight to my computer to answer emails. Being gone even a few days has put me behind, but I don't complain. I reply to people for hours, then update my status reports and send them out to the other project managers who helped cover my job.

When I finally break away from the screen, I realize it's time to go. As I'm packing my laptop in my bag, my boss stops and compliments me on the project. Considering he rarely gives positive feedback, it makes me walk out to my truck with a smile on my face. Even though lunch was a disaster, it's been a good day otherwise. I'm convinced it started on the right foot because I woke up with Lennon in my arms this morning.

Yesterday, I told myself that what we shared in Utah had to stay there. We accomplished what we wanted and convinced her parents, which meant my job of playing husband was done except for the Instagram photos. When we walked into the apartment, I'd accepted it was over until she texted me to lie with her. Thinking about how she instantly falls asleep when I'm close has me grinning like an idiot. I wanted it as much as she did. My bed is too damn sad and empty. The thought of her consumes me the rest of the drive home.

I walk into the apartment that's squeaky fucking clean and find Lennon in the kitchen making dinner. Grabbing a beer, I notice her trying to avoid eye contact. She mentions dinner will be ready, and I excuse myself to compose my thoughts. When I walk away, I glance over my shoulder and catch her staring, then wink. Blush meets her cheeks, and I hold back a chuckle. Lennon is as transparent as me, apparently.

I change into some workout shorts and a T-shirt, then walk back into the kitchen where Lennon is scooping chicken fettuccine Alfredo onto some plates. I grab forks and napkins, and she follows me to the kitchen table. As we eat, I can tell something's on her mind.

"What is it?" I ask, shooting her a smirk.

She shakes her head and continues to focus on her pasta.

"Come on. I know something's up. I know you, Lennon. Plus, I haven't seen the apartment this clean in years," I tell her and her face softens.

"Fine," she huffs. "I've been thinking about the Jenna situation all day. Let me first say that I trust you. I do. I trust you as much as I trust my sisters, so it's not that. But I feel guilty about you helping me with the baby when Jenna is all alone, doing it on her own, and the father of her baby is alive and well. As much as I don't like her, it's not right." Her eyes don't meet mine. She goes back to her pasta, studying it like it's a Picasso painting.

"I get it. I hear you. But it's one hundred percent not mine," I say, recalling the conversation I had earlier with Jenna.

"How do you know? I need to know how you know." Lennon finally looks at me, and all I want to do is swim in the depths of her baby blues.

I suck in a deep breath and release it. Regardless of how hard it is to admit, I know I have to tell her. The silence draws on, but she gives me the time I need to find my words.

"Okay." I nod. This is embarrassing as hell, which is why I didn't tell Jenna. She's the last person who needs to know my personal business. "When I was in college, I was short on money and decided to donate my…sperm. After some initial testing, they noticed my counts were low," I explain, watching her.

"You're sterile?" she asks, searching my face.

"No, but my sperm count is abnormal. Hold on," I say, getting up and leaving her shocked at the table.

I search through the top drawer of my desk and find the envelope. After I find a pinch of courage, I walk back and hand it to her.

She pulls the papers out and reads them.

"I got a second opinion shortly after and got the same results.

It's been my reality ever since I found out," I tell her, resting both hands on my hips. "Not exactly a conversation starter, though."

The sadness on her face cuts straight to the bone.

"I'm sorry. I'm—" She chokes up.

"It's okay." I see a few tears escape, and it practically destroys me that she's crying for me.

"You may never have a family," she says, covering her mouth.

I suck in a deep breath. "I have you, Lennon. You're all I need." My stance softens as I watch her emotions bleed for me.

She folds the documentation and places it back in the envelope, then pushes it away like it's poison. "Wait. Is this why you've been so willing to be here for me and the baby? I've been asking myself why after all this time you'd do this and…" Lennon trails off.

I know she doesn't mean it the way it came out or maybe she does. I tense up, not sure how to respond, but I'm offended. Her words make it seem as if I'm using her or something to have a baby, which is so fucking far from the truth. I already feel like less of a man because of it, but for her to think I've only been nice to her to have one is absurd.

"Are you serious? How could you think that?" My questions come out harsher than I intended, but my emotions and adrenaline are high.

Lennon pulls her bottom lip into her mouth. "Hunter, no. I don't think that." She pulls her chair back and stands in front of me. "I've been trying to figure out why you'd do all this for me, considering our past and how much you hated me. I know we've grown close, and we're friends now, but why come up with the fake marriage, say you're the father, and all of it? Why would you pretend for me unless you had an ulterior motive?"

I didn't expect to have this conversation today, but fuck it. I'm tired of holding it all in. She doesn't realize the avalanche she started.

"*Pretend*?" I ask, my tone harsh and growing louder. "The time we spent in Utah was more real to me than anything, Lennon. If you haven't figured it out by now, the way I feel about you, the way I've *always* felt about you has been real since the moment I met you. Sorry to disappoint you, but I wasn't faking shit."

"Wait, what?" She steps back as if I've slapped her. She's confused as hell, but after all this time, how can she not see it? "What do you mean?"

My heart is pounding, and I'm no longer calm. Waving my hand in frustration, I continue, "Why do you think everyone made so many comments about how in love we looked? About how they could see the love between us? It's because I don't have to act when I'm with you. It was all real for me. Maybe you were going along with the script, but I wasn't pretending, Lennon." I need to settle my nerves and slow my breaths, but now that I've opened my emotional baggage, there's no stopping. "And I know it's fucked up. I know it is. But I'm selfish, especially when it comes to you."

"You weren't pretending?" She slowly repeats the words as if she needs to hear them again. "What do you mean since the moment you met me?" She blinks, then looks up at me, her expression hardening. "What the hell does that even mean?"

I don't think, I just speak, waving my hand in the air as I make my points.

"You didn't notice I took every opportunity to kiss you, be near you, hold you? Even when no one was around, I couldn't help it. I told myself we were pretending for your family, but that wasn't the truth. I couldn't stop kissing you even though I knew better. I fucking knew I was crossing a line, but you were too. You kissed me like you'd been waiting for it, like you couldn't hold back either. You can lie to yourself all you want, Lennon, but I know you reacted to every single touch. It wasn't just me."

She opens her mouth to say something but clamps it shut. She looks like she wants to slap the truths right off my face. Whether or not she wants to admit I'm right, I know I am. She could've pushed me away or told me to stop anytime we were alone. If she was uncomfortable with the situation, she never made it known.

She moaned against me, arched her body, and even held on tighter each time we were close. I know it's not one-sided, but until she admits it, I'm not going to keep acting like it was no big deal. It was a big fucking deal to me.

This is not how I expected her to react or how I wanted shit to go down, but I deserve it because of how wrong this situation is. She directs her attention to the table, nostrils flaring, and grabs her half-eaten plate of pasta and takes it to the kitchen, where she sets it in the sink.

"You need to eat, Lennon," I say, following her and not allowing her to escape this discussion.

She looks at me, then within a few steps, she points her finger into my chest. "You need to stop telling me what to do." Her breasts rise and fall as I look into her eyes. "And I'm still waiting for a goddamn explanation as to why you treated me like shit for two years."

I gently grab her wrist and move her finger to place her palm against my racing heart. "You feel that?"

Lennon sucks in a deep breath, looking back and forth between our hands and my eyes. Swallowing, she nods.

"The moment I met you, I knew you were so damn special. In here." I tap my finger against my chest. "I knew." I shrug, keeping her close. "I wanted you that night and missed my chance to ask you out. But—" Just as I'm about to say that Brandon was the better guy for her, knowing he could give her everything she wanted, she pulls her hand back and walks around me, seething.

"You were awful to me!" she shouts, and I turn around to follow her. "You treated me like an inconvenience and purposely got under my skin every chance possible. You were the worst, Hunter, the biggest dickhead I'd ever met in my life, and I hated you for it!" She's pissed, but I don't blame her. I know I was all those things.

"Lennon, I know. I regret all of it, trust me. I've lived with the guilt of how I treated you for months," I tell her, stepping closer, but she maintains her distance.

She snorts, exaggerating her disbelief. "And now you expect me to believe you always had a thing for me? After you brought home random girls and the way you acted toward me? What do you want me to say? Yeah, we kissed. We had to share a bed. We were close and had to pretend to be married. It was all an act, and that's all it ever can be."

Her words are a slap in the face, considering there was no acting on my part, and I know she's only lying to herself and me if she claims she was only acting too.

"I can't help the way my body reacts to you when we kiss, Hunter. My body may say yes, but my head says no."

Another slap.

"And what about your heart? What does your heart say, Lennon?"

She looks at me, her bottom lip quivering. Maybe I've pushed her too far, but she's not going down without a fight.

Lennon opens her mouth and closes it once again, then refuses to meet my eyes. "All of this is so fucking wrong, I can't even see straight. Telling me that you always had feelings for me is *too* much. I can barely understand it because you made me so damn miserable!" She's screaming, her eyes wide with anger. I can only focus on the fact she's avoiding what her heart is saying because she feels guilty about it. Her actions always speak louder than words.

I know this is confusing to hear because of the way I treated her in the past, how I wanted to rescue her after Brandon passed away, and especially now that I'm telling her how I truly feel.

Holding up my hands, I need her to calm down so I can get out what I need to say. "Lennon, I know!" I'm as heated as she is. "But can you think about my situation for two fucking seconds? For all these years, all I ever wanted was to forget about you. I didn't want to have feelings for you once I knew you were with Brandon. I wanted you out of my goddamn head because it was poison to feel that way about my best friend's girlfriend. But nothing I did helped. Not fucking random women. Not treating you like trash. Nothing. Me being an asshole, me pushing you away? That was me pretending, Lennon. I constantly lied to myself, hoping I'd get over whatever it was I felt, but nothing fucking worked," I shout. "But these past few days with you"—I wave a finger back and forth between us—"were one hundred percent real for me. I know it's fucked up, trust me, and I hate that I could never get over you. But think about this for a moment. Brandon was my best friend, and I loved him like a brother. No matter how I felt, I never wanted to do or say anything to jeopardize what you two had because I knew it was special. I could see how much you meant to him, so I sat on the sidelines, but it didn't mean my feelings weren't there. It meant I had to choke on them every time I saw you with him."

I expose my soul to her, letting the past two years of pent-up emotions release without thinking about the consequences. But that's what happens when feelings are covered—they boil over, and someone gets burned.

Lennon paces in front of me, looking at the floor, and she's sealed up so tight, it's almost scary.

The tension and quietness scream at me. "Lennon. Can you say something? *Please*?" I plead. I dropped a huge confession bomb on her, but I'm desperate for a response. Time slows down, and the silence kills me, but I'm not walking away from this or her. I'll wait.

She finally meets my gaze with tears in her eyes and shrugs. "What do you want me to say right now? I-I don't know how to process this, Hunter. I've got a lot of things to work out in my head. I don't have any words. You've left me speechless." She throws her arms up before slapping them down to her sides.

I can tell she's upset with me, but this isn't over yet. I've opened the door to this conversation, and now I'm walking through. There's no turning back now that it's all out there.

"I don't know…anything! Admit that I'm not alone in feeling this way, tell me to fuck off, tell me it's all one-sided. Just say something!" I'm no longer being rational, my feelings completely on the line as I beg for her to admit what I know is in her heart.

"I don't know what to think! You changed overnight the day Brandon died, and now I'm supposed to believe you had feelings for me all along? That our fake relationship was real to you? What am I supposed to say? That maybe I did feel something too, but —" Lennon stops herself as tears surface in her eyes.

"You don't have to say it, Lennon," I tell her when I see how hard she's struggling with this realization. I know the guilt she feels because of Brandon. I feel it too. "But can you answer one question for me at least?" I ask, then continue when her eyes meet mine. "That night we met at the bar, I asked you to come back. Why didn't you? I had planned to ask for your number and always wondered what scared you off. I could never figure out why you didn't choose me because I would've bet my life that you felt the connection between us. You can't tell me it was all in my head." Laying it all out there—my soul, my heart, my feelings— I've wondered for two years and need to know. Even if I don't like her answer, at least I'll know and can put it to rest.

With her head slightly tilted, her eyes finally meet mine. She looks confused as hell as if she's staring at a stranger, but I see a flicker of something behind her eyes. Want? Need? Maybe I'm imagining it, but I don't think I am.

"Hunter…" she says softly, her chest rising and falling rapidly.

"I wanna know, Lennon," I demand, holding my stance. I'm in too deep to back out now.

"Okay, fine," she responds and swallows hard. "I watched you that night and contemplated going back to talk to you, but you were surrounded by beautiful women all fighting for your attention. I overheard one talking about how she had slept with you the weekend before. It was clear to me that you were a player, and I wasn't looking for that. I figured I'd never see you again. I—"

"Lennon," I cut her off, her words a dagger to my pounding heart. I'm a fucking idiot. "That was my lifestyle back then, there's no denying that, but you were the only woman I saw that night," I admit, my throat threatening to close up. "I felt it from the moment I met you."

She sucks in a breath, and her shoulders rise and fall. "I wanted more than a weekend fling, and I knew you'd be a heartbreaker. You know my past, Hunter. You know how my ex hurt me. I felt like I could never satisfy someone like you, that I would never be enough. I didn't want to compete for your attention. After listening to those women talk, I realized you were nothing more than a fuckboy with good looks to back it up. I couldn't risk getting hurt again."

Frowning, I step toward her, needing to close the gap between us. I brush my thumb over her cheek, feeling the softness against my skin and craving more. "I was, but trust me when I say things would've been different with you. I would've done anything to make you happy and treated you right. Since that night, you've been the only woman I've ever truly wanted even when it was wrong."

My words linger in the air as she pulls her bottom lip between her teeth. She has no reason to believe me after what I put her through, but everything I've said is one hundred percent honest and genuine. Whether or not she'll believe me after everything we've been through is what has me holding my breath, anxiously waiting.

Lennon squeezes her eyes shut and shakes her head. "I'm sorry, Hunter."

CHAPTER THIRTY-THREE

LENNON

WHEN I LOOK AT HUNTER, I feel as if my body's on fire. He drops his hand, and as soon as I lose his touch, I miss it.

He's felt like this since the beginning? All that time, he treated me like shit because he had *feelings* for me? My head spins from his confession and the way I haven't allowed myself to admit my own feelings—the ones I've been avoiding.

You've been the only woman I've ever truly wanted.

"I'm sorry, Hunter." I close my eyes for a moment, and when I open them again, his head falls. "I'm still in love with Brandon, and I don't know if I'll ever be over him. This is a lot to take in right now."

"I know," he replies softly. "I shouldn't have done that or pushed this conversation."

Am I that surprised? Should I have seen the signs earlier? He took care of me right after Brandon died, refused to leave my side, and pretended to be my husband so my parents would accept the baby. How much of that was his loyalty to his best friend and how much of it was because of his unrequited feelings for me this whole time?

"You've never been in a serious relationship and say that you would've tried to make me happy and all that, but you have no idea what would've happened between us," I tell him. "How could you flip a switch just like that and leave your bachelor days behind for me?" My heart is lodged in my throat, and I'm not sure it's even beating anymore. I'm currently living in the twilight zone, and I'm almost tempted to pinch myself to make sure I'm not dreaming. My thoughts are all over the place, and I can't think clearly as his words repeat in my ears.

"I might not be able to predict the future, but I would've done everything in my power to do things right with you. I wouldn't have fucked up that chance. Things have always been different with you, and I can promise I'd never hurt you. But the moment I saw you with Brandon, that was it. I wasn't going to interfere, but I never understood why you didn't give me a chance, Lennon. Guess I shouldn't be that surprised." He wraps both hands around his head and squeezes the tension in his neck as if he's blaming himself for why I didn't return.

"I did feel something that night, Hunter," I admit. "We shared a moment and had a connection. It was evident as soon as I saw you." I feel guilty even saying this aloud, but he deserves to know. "And if I'm being honest, my insecurities got the best of me. Seeing those other women flirting with you—hearing what they were saying about you—I knew I didn't want anything to do with that. Then I met Brandon…"

"You don't have to go on," he tells me as if it's painful to hear. "Brandon was the best guy I knew, and you two were perfect for each other. I wasn't blind. I saw it."

I swallow, holding back tears. God, why is this so hard? How is it possible to be torn between two men when one isn't even here anymore?

Feeling like my legs might give out on me, I walk to the couch and sit.

Of course Hunter follows, but he sits on the opposite end, leaving space between us. He doesn't take his eyes off me as I try to work through all of this. It's almost too much to process on top of everything else that's happened. I replay Utah in vivid detail—

the things he said and the way he kissed me and continually swept me off my feet. I can almost hear my parents talk about how in love we looked and how it made them happy.

It all makes sense now because Hunter wasn't pretending.

But was I? It was way too easy to fall into our roles.

In the past, I'd thought maybe he was upset because I stole his best friend. I had an inkling once when we ran into each other in the kitchen that first night that he was annoyed I went home with Brandon instead of him, but I'd convinced myself he hated me for ruining his bachelor pad. Considering he's had numerous women in his bed, I never thought he was still hung up on that night, or that the one moment we shared in the pitch-black bar mattered to him.

The bottom of my emotions is ready to fall out at any moment, but somehow, I keep it together as I stare at the blank television. Guilt bubbles inside me, and I feel like I might throw up, but I push it away. I rub my hands over my face, needing to be alone for a few minutes to gain my composure.

"I'll be right back." I stand and head to the bathroom, swallowing down my dinner that's begging to make a comeback. I turn on the faucet, suck in deep breaths, and splash cool water on my burning cheeks and neck. Each time he's said he'd be there for me, there wasn't a doubtful bone in my body. Deep down, I knew his words were sincere, and this is why. As my sisters said, we're in a weird non-relationship relationship.

Just as Hunter asked, I force myself into his position and imagine having to watch the person I like not only be with someone else, but my best friend, every single day. And damn. It's hard as hell. Avoiding Brandon's and my relationship was impossible. I finally understand why he was such an asshole, especially when Brandon and I'd kiss or hug. Jealousy drove his actions, and it was easier to openly hate it because it must've hurt and affected him every time.

Living in this apartment with me had to be his own personal hell. Like a drug addict, Hunter couldn't walk away, regardless of how bad being around us was for him. I shake my head, turn off the water, and wipe my face with a clean towel. Sucking in a deep breath and letting it out, I finally understand the past two years in a way I never have.

Between Jenna, lying to my parents, finding out Hunter can't have kids, and learning how he truly feels—this week has been strange and confusing as hell. I'm not sure I can take anything else on top of what I've already been through this year before I finally break.

I think about Sophie and Maddie, who made comments about us all along. I can already imagine the looks on their faces when I mention it and am not looking forward to all the "told you sos" they're going to throw my way. Though I'm stalling, I know I can't stay camped out in the bathroom all night. It's time to put on my big girl panties and face him and the feelings I can't bring myself to accept.

I walk into the living room and find Hunter sitting on the couch watching *Friends*. It's one of my favorite episodes when Ross walks in on Joey and Rachel passionately kissing. Immediately, I'm drawn in and sit too. Each time Ross says he's fine in a high-pitched tone, when he's obviously not fine, I find myself laughing. Hunter's chuckling along with me, and it's almost easy to pretend we're the people we were before Utah, before his confessions, before any of it. I'm not sure we can ever go back to being just two friends.

Not anymore. Not after tonight.

The awkward tension presses on, and I know I'm being weird. Hunter ignores the way I'm acting and sits there as if he didn't just admit the way he's always felt about me.

As we start the next episode of *Friends*, I'm lost in my thoughts, and a sense of sadness washes over me when I glance at Hunter. Knowing he can't have kids hurts my heart because I know without a doubt he'd be a damn good father, especially after how much he's helped me. How many men want to read pregnancy books? Hunter learns every detail eagerly to make sure the baby and I are okay and taken care of.

Knowing this makes sense as to why he was so adamant about me trusting him, and while I did, I had doubts. I understand why he was so confident about Jenna's baby not being his. Because it's not. I saw the results of his test.

He's already had to live a life where he was forced to sit on the sidelines and had to watch me and Brandon. Will the baby be a reminder that he can't have kids? Will it be painful for him? My emotions lurch forward, taking over, and I try not to allow them to get the best of me, but I'm so sad for him.

"What's wrong?" he asks when I wipe my cheek.

Damn tears, always slipping out of my eyes, especially when I don't want them to.

"Nothing."

He tilts his head, smirking. "Really?"

Hiding anything from him is impossible, considering he sees everything. The man knows me better than I know myself most days. "I'm upset for you."

His eyebrows squish together, and his smirk fades. "Why?"

"Because," I whisper, turning my head away from him. Grabbing the remote, he pauses the TV and waits. There's no getting out of this, so I just spill it. "Because you want kids of your own. And it makes me sad for you. You'd make such a great dad."

A small smile touches his lips, but his brown eyes pierce through me. "See, that's the thing about you, Lennon. You care so much about other people and their situations, even while you're going through your own shit. I came to terms with my reality of not being able to have children a long time ago. I was upset at first, considering my chances were slim to nothing. It destroyed me for a while, and Hayden had to talk me off the ledge several times. But I've accepted it."

My heart thumps harder and faster. "Is it reversible?"

He swallows hard, words forming on the tip of his tongue, but he closes his mouth and doesn't speak. For a moment, I think he's getting choked up about it.

"From what I read, yes, but not always. After the second test came back the same, I lost faith and didn't want to get my hopes up again." He shrugs.

Reaching for his hand, I take it and squeeze lightly. "Thanks for telling me."

"I'll tell you anything you want to know, Lennon. At this point, you already know everything about me." He chuckles, and I like how genuine it sounds.

"You know everything about me. There aren't any secrets that I haven't told you."

Hunter's smirk deepens. "How 'bout we finish this episode, then call it a night?"

I nod, grateful he changes the subject.

I'm hardly paying attention, but when Hunter yawns, I stretch my arms above my head. Before the next episode starts, he turns off the TV and stands.

"I have to ask." His expression softens. "Did any of it feel real to you in Utah, Lennon? Any of it at all?"

When I get to my feet, he closes the gap between us, and his scent consumes me. I lose myself in the brown of his irises as he waits for my answer. Closing my eyes tight, I think back to the moment he kissed me as we danced on the Fourth of July. It sure as hell didn't feel fake or wrong to me. Every touch, stolen glance, and sweet thing he said is at the forefront of my mind. When I look into his eyes, I know there's no way I could lie.

"Yes," I desperately whisper. "It felt real for me too. So real, I almost let myself believe it could be right."

Without saying a word, Hunter takes my cheeks in his palms, and a contemplative smile plays on his lips before his mouth covers mine. We're greedy as our tongues twist together in a rhythmic movement. I fist his shirt, pulling him closer, and moan against him. We shouldn't do this, but I can't seem to pull away. With every passing moment, we become more desperate and breathless until we're losing ourselves. It's easy to pretend we don't have a past when his tongue tangles with mine.

"Lennon," Hunter moans my name, but it's impossible for me to stop. My heart doesn't want to, though my head says I should. When I'm with him like this, I lose control, and nothing else matters. There's no sadness or grief—just us.

I finally force myself to break away, unsteady on my feet, and feel as if I'm floating when our foreheads touch.

Then it all hits me like a brick wall.

"We shouldn't have done that," I whisper against his lips, my breathing erratic. If I don't stop now, this could lead somewhere it shouldn't. Somewhere it can't.

Hunter releases a deep breath, holding me so tightly I don't ever want him to let me go. But my head and heart battle, fighting against the guilt and desire. I squeeze my eyes shut, holding in the tears that threaten to pour out. Our heavy breathing is all that can be heard in the entire apartment.

"I'm so sorry," I murmur, choking up.

"I know." Hunter cups my face before kissing my forehead, a farewell peace offering.

Somehow, I find the strength to walk away from him without looking over my shoulder. I can't bear to see the look on his face after that.

I shut my bedroom door and lean against the cool wood as I try to catch the breath Hunter stole. My lips are swollen, and I run my fingertips across them, knowing we can never do that again. There are too many emotions behind it, considering Hunter's confessions. Admitting to how he makes me feel isn't something I can do, and I refuse to lead him on, knowing my heart is still cracked and barely glued back together. I'm a broken mess, and I'm not sure he can repair me, especially now. Maybe never.

What's happened between us is so damn wrong.

I can't stop thinking about Brandon. What the hell would he think about this? Would he be pissed? Or would he rather I have feelings for his best friend than someone else?

I don't know how I can ever move on without the shame following me.

I think about what my life would be like if Brandon were here with me right now. If the accident hadn't happened, we'd probably be a happy family. He would've loved meeting my parents, and I know my parents would've felt the same way about him. The remorse I'm harboring is almost too much, but I deserve it. Did I plug Hunter in where Brandon should be because I'm so sad and lonely?

I'm living in a fucked-up fairy tale, and I'm not sure if I'll get a happy ending or even deserve to. The selfish part of me wants to ask him to sleep with me and hold me close to his strong body, but logic wins this time. It's not a good idea, considering the way he feels—*we* feel.

CHAPTER THIRTY-FOUR

HUNTER

ONE MONTH LATER

I GENTLY PUSH open Lennon's door and see her swollen belly sticking out from her rolled up shirt as she shifts in her sleep. I ache to touch her, to feel her soft skin against mine, and to prove to her how real my feelings are for her. It's painful keeping them in, especially after confessing them, but I do. As I've done for the past two years, I push them down and pretend they don't exist, especially since she walked away.

With summer break officially over, today is her first day of school, and I know she's nervous. She didn't tell her co-workers she was pregnant, but at five months pregnant, she won't be able to hide it anymore.

Things have slowly gone back to our normal after the night I blurted my true feelings and we shared one last kiss. We thought it was best not to sleep in the same bed, and honestly, I'm not sure I could handle it now that she knows how I've always felt. Kissing her—for real—was the most intense thing I've ever experienced, and then it was gone. I knew the second she pulled away she was going to say those words.

I'd been fooling myself to think she'd be able to see me as

anything more than a friend. Even if she claims she felt the chemistry that first night we met, too much has happened, and it doesn't matter now. She's carrying Brandon's baby, and now that she knows I can't have kids, why the hell would she even consider being with someone who can't give her the family she wants? My dad's words about being a failure repeat in my head, and it brings me right back to the dark place I've tried so hard to stay away from.

Guilt. Anger. Insecurity.

Lennon's truly the only reason I've been sane these past four months since Brandon's death. Even if I wish things had happened differently between us, I can't let her go. I'll take her in my life in any way she'll allow.

"Lennon," I whisper, brushing her hair off her face.

"Mmm?" she mutters, stirring lightly.

"I made you breakfast," I tell her softly.

"Sleep," she mumbles, pulling the covers to her chest. "More sleep."

Chuckling, I look at her sleepy face and smile. "Not today, sweetheart. Back to work," I remind her.

Her eyes pop open, scaring the shit out of me. Lennon looks around, and it's as if she's just now remembering it's the day.

"I forgot what getting up early felt like." She groans, finally sitting up. "Though I have a feeling I'm about to be reminded very soon," she says, looking at her stomach, then pulling her shirt down. "No way to hide it."

Furrowing my brows, I hold out my hand and help her to her feet. "Shouldn't hide it anyway. You're not the first teacher to get pregnant," I reassure her.

"It's not that." She shrugs. "It's the pity looks that'll return."

Grabbing her hands, I envelop them between my palms and hold them against my chest. Lennon looks up at me, waiting.

"Ignore the comments and the looks and remember how far you've come. Brandon is so proud of you," I tell her sincerely. "So am I."

A tear slips down her cheek, but she doesn't move to catch it. It falls to her mouth, and she licks it from her lips. I study her, watching her, wanting her to know how amazing she is.

How special she is to me.

"Thanks, Hunter. I appreciate that." I release her hands, and she snakes her arms around my waist. "You always know what to say to make me feel better."

I wrap an arm around her, then kiss her forehead. "Haven't you figured out by now that I'm a very philosophical person?" I tease with a smile.

Lennon laughs and leans back, putting space between us. "You're something else, Manning. That I know for a fact."

Before I can ask her what that means, she grabs her phone and walks toward the kitchen. "Is that bacon I smell?"

"Sure is," I confirm, and my smirk deepens when her face lights up.

We each make a plate of eggs, toast, and, of course, bacon. My favorite morning routine includes us having breakfast together, so now that she's back to work for the school year, I'm glad we'll get to do it again.

Just as I'm about to get up and rinse my plate, Lennon stands and comes toward me. "I need to post on Instagram today for the first day back!"

She sits on my lap and wraps an arm around my shoulders, bringing our faces together. "We need to look sad."

I snort, furrowing my brows. "What? Why?"

Her shoulders slouch. "Because I'm going back to work, and we won't get to spend as much time together."

Fuck, that is sad and sucks if she's being real.

Lennon holds out her phone, clicks on the camera, and gives me a two-second warning. She pouts with her lower lip sticking out, and I do the same before she takes the shot.

"Okay, one more," she says after checking the photo.

We get back into position, and right before she clicks, she

presses her soft lips to my cheek, surprising the shit out of me. But as quickly as it happens, it's over.

"Super cute." She looks at the photo and shuffles off me.

And now I need to sit here for a second.

I don't know how long she plans to update her Instagram or pretend we're married, but I continue to go along with it for her sake even though she knows my true feelings. At this point, I'm a pro at pushing them to the side to protect my own heart.

"First day back to work and going to miss my honey pie," she speaks as she types, then looks up at me and winks at the nickname she always hated. "Hashtag newlyweds, hashtag wifey, hashtag bae."

I raise my brows at her ludicrous hashtags. Even though it's all an act and she's doing it for her parents' benefit, she's been posting pregnancy shots and anything baby and married life related. All the clothes her mother bought, our rings, dinners she's cooked, basically anything and everything. Part of me wonders if it's overkill with all the posting because she wishes those things were for real—but with Brandon.

"Adorable, right?" She sticks her phone in my face and swipes her finger to show me she posted both pictures.

Fuck me. Doesn't she know this is torture?

For the past month, we've acted as if that night never happened, so I plaster on a smile and reply, "Definitely."

I clean up the kitchen while she hops into the shower. Once the dishes are cleared, and I wipe the counters, I walk down the hallway and hear Lennon singing. Pausing, I stand outside the door and listen.

It's a new one today. Straining to hear the lyrics, I eventually recognize the song. Lennon flawlessly belts out the words to "I Hope You Dance." As always, her voice captivates me in every way. She sounds so passionate and sweet, and I've come to love getting this front row seat every morning.

As Lennon sings about giving faith a fighting chance, I lean my forehead against the wood door and inhale a deep breath. I wish I could say how I want to fight for her, how I wish she'd fight for me, how it should've always been her and me—even though it feels wrong. I push all those feelings aside and ignore them, not allowing them to bring me to the dark side.

Willing myself to walk away, I go to my room and dress for work, hoping to get to the office early. I have plans to meet Mason and Liam during my lunch break and have a feeling it's going to take the full hour. It's been a while since we've hung out, and I haven't told them the whole story on going to Utah with Lennon. I could only imagine what they'd say about it, and I didn't need their bullshit attitudes while preparing for the trip, so I know it's only a matter of time before it comes up in conversation.

"Hunter?" Lennon knocks on my door.

"Yeah?"

I'm buttoning up my shirt when she enters. The sight of her nearly takes my breath away. She's wearing a black pencil skirt, stockings, and a maternity tank. She bought it last week when I finally forced her to admit she needed new clothes, especially for work. Luckily, Sophie and Maddie dragged her to the mall, and she reluctantly showed me everything once they got back. It was adorable the way she pouted about it, but honestly, she looks amazing. Maybe it makes me a sick son of a bitch, but she's only gotten more gorgeous with her pregnancy.

Yeah, I'm going to hell.

Pregnant with my dead best friend's baby.

Straight to hell.

"Which top?" Lennon asks, breaking me out of my trance. She holds up two shirts on hangers and puts each one over her body. "They both suck, so which one sucks less?"

Chuckling, I examine the almost identical patterned blouses and point at the one on the right.

"Really?" She narrows her eyes at it and frowns.

"No?" I stare pointedly at her and the way she's looking at it. "I meant *your* right."

Lennon drops her shoulders and scowls. "Liar."

"Stop worrying so much," I tell her, closing the gap between us and grabbing the shirt in question. "It's pretty. Let me see it on."

Sighing, she takes it, then slips it over her head. Her breasts rise, and I quickly avert my gaze until she's dressed.

"Well?" She raises her arms, then lets them fall to her sides with a slap. "I look fat."

"No," I say slowly, knowing I need to tread lightly. She's sensitive to her body's changes, and while I'd love to be able to tell her she's so fucking beautiful, I know I have to restrain myself. "You look pregnant."

Lennon rolls her eyes, then marches to her room, and I follow. She stands in front of the full-length mirror, turning from side to side. Her bump is only visible in that shirt when she rests a hand over it.

"I may be biased, but I think you look cute," I tell her honestly, my voice hoarse at the truth of my words. "I can't even tell you're pregnant from the back."

"Oh great. I'll walk backward from now on."

Her serious expression has me laughing. Walking up behind her, I rest my hands on her shoulders and squeeze. "Lennon. Relax. Maybe you aren't giving your coworkers enough credit. I bet once they find out, they'll want to be there for you and support you in any way they can."

"Yeah, maybe." She shrugs, making my hands move up, and I quickly drop them. The longer I touch her, the harder it is to walk away.

"Lennon." I look at her through the mirror, and she meets my eyes. "What's this about?"

She drops her gaze and swallows hard. "I'm not sure. I should be glad for the change of pace and going back to my students. I know it'll keep my mind busy, but it brings me right back to the week Brandon died and how everyone looked at me. Hell, how they treated me."

"How?"

Lennon turns around and faces me. "Like I was damaged goods."

Before I can think better of it, I pull her into my arms and hug her. She wraps hers around me, and we stay like that for longer than we should. Her heart is racing, and I wouldn't be surprised if she can feel mine thumping hard. Anytime she's close, it goes out of control.

"You're not, Lennon. What happened to you is tragic, and oftentimes people don't know how to react to that kind of news. It makes them feel uncomfortable, so it comes out in weird ways."

I pull back slightly when I hear her sniffle. "You want me to be your fake husband at school too?" I ask, then wait and see if she'll crack a smile at my pathetic attempt to make a joke out of this situation.

"Hmm…maybe, but it'd also come with even more questions." She chuckles, which puts a wide grin on my face.

"Well, if you change your mind, you know where to find me." I wink, and I swear her cheeks redden.

"I know. Always ready to save the day, Hunter."

"Fake husband to the rescue," I say, pretending a dagger isn't shooting straight into my heart.

She smiles sweetly, and I take the awkward silence as an opportunity to leave. "Well, I'm gonna finish getting ready and head to work. Hope you have a great first day." I kiss her forehead and slowly release my arm from her waist. "Text me if you need me, okay?"

"You know I will."

Fifteen minutes later, I'm on the road and almost to the office. Now that it's getting closer to fall, projects are wrapping up, and new contracts are being signed. I'm up to my elbows in paperwork, so I spend the entire morning at my desk until it's time to meet with the guys.

Mason and Liam are both in a booth with drinks by the time I arrive at Rob's Burgers.

"Couldn't wait for me, huh?" I sit next to Mason and grab the menu.

"We were thirsty," Liam taunts, holding up his beer, then takes a swig. "Your bitch ass was late anyway."

I look at my watch. "Three minutes, asshole."

"You're lucky I was able to hold him back from ordering," Mason says.

"Hey, I'm starving, okay? I have a busy week with work, so today is my only downtime," Liam explains.

"I kinda lost my appetite after the shitstorm I've been dealing with today, but I have to eat," Mason tells us. He's interning to be a forensic investigator and works part-time for his dad, who's the district attorney. I can only imagine the shit he's seen and heard working so closely to crime scenes. He's told us about a few cases, but I've purposely blocked them from my memory. I don't know how he does it, but shortly after he graduated from college, he took up boxing. Now he continues to do it because he needs an outlet from the shit he has to see and deal with on a regular basis. You wouldn't know it by looking at him, but he's strong as fuck, and even I wouldn't want to get in a ring with him.

Liam makes a face, and I chuckle and shake my head as I look over the burger options. After the waitress comes over and takes my drink and food order, Liam gives me a pointed look.

"What?" I ask, grabbing my phone from my pocket. I sent Lennon a text before I arrived to see how her first day is going so far, but she hasn't responded yet. I hope that's a good sign.

Before Liam can respond, the waitress arrives with my water, and just as I take a sip, he speaks up. "Where's your wedding ring?"

Choking on my drink, I clear my throat and blink. "What?"

Mason shakes his head and slides his phone toward me. On the screen is Lennon's fake Instagram feed of The Mrs. Manning.

I study it, looking over this morning's pictures and the rest of the photos she's posted this summer. "So I guess you know." I slide the phone back to him. "So what?"

"*So what?*" Liam's voice goes louder as his tone deepens.

"It means nothing. It was a favor to her." I shrug, taking another drink of my water.

"Except it's not nothing," Mason chimes in. "We all know how you feel about her even if you don't want to admit it, and—"

Slamming down my glass, I narrow my eyes. "I know it's fucked up, but when the situation arose, I did what I had to do for *her*. It wasn't for me. Trust me, it's killed me every single day."

"So why didn't you say anything?" Liam asks.

"Because I knew what you fuckers would say, and I didn't need to hear it. Brandon was my best friend too, and I have to think of what he would've wanted me to do to protect her, and that's all it was."

They study me as if they're waiting for me to crack some secret. I debate whether I should tell them that I opened my heart to her, told her how I truly felt and that she ultimately walked away. Regardless of knowing why she did, it doesn't hurt any less. We act like that moment never happened, and if that's what we have to do in order to keep things platonic for the sake of the baby and her emotional health, then I'll suffer through it. The last thing I need is for Liam and Mason to be on my ass about it even more, so I keep it buried away.

"How'd you find out?" I ask.

Mason gives me a side-glance and smirks. "How do you think?"

"Maddie slipped up," Liam confirms.

I notice the way his throat tightens when he says her name.

"The four of you still going on double non-dates?" I chuckle in amusement. Their whole awkward situation cracks me up.

"No, Little Romeo." Liam snickers. "We were hanging out, and they happened to show up."

I snort, knowing that was no coincidence. "Right."

"Sophie confirmed it after Maddie's word vomit," Mason adds, the vein in his forehead about to pop as he talks about her.

These four give me a headache.

Something about the way he acts when Sophie's around or even when he talks about her makes me wonder if something's already happened between them. There's way too much tension in the air when they're in the same room.

What is it about these Corrigan sisters that keeps us all tied up in knots?

Our food finally arrives, and I hope it'll change the subject, but after two minutes, Liam continues. "So you bought her a pretty expensive ring."

"It had to be convincing to her parents," I say. I haven't told them about Brandon's plan to propose or the engagement ring burning a hole in my nightstand. As I promised him, I'm taking that to the grave.

"And you couldn't do that with a smaller diamond? Damn."

I glare at Liam, knowing his mind is running with ideas. Setting my burger on my plate, I look him in the eyes. "Why don't you come out and say whatever you wanna say?"

"Alright." He takes a quick sip of his beer and holds my gaze. "I think you two are treading a fine line that's become too blurred to realize the *friendship* you two have is inappropriate. If the roles were reversed and Lennon was your girl first, how would that feel knowing your best friend is swooping in?"

My jaw clenches, frustration building inside me as I resist the urge to deck his pretty boy face.

"For starters, if the roles were reversed, it wouldn't matter because I'd be dead. However, I'd trust my best friend with my life, so whether he was being there for her during a fucking rough time or if he was swooping in because he'd always had feelings for her, it wouldn't matter. All that would matter is her happiness. If he made her happy, that's all I'd ever want. Why the fuck do you think I stood on the sidelines this whole goddamn time? If I were the asshole you're trying to paint me to be, I would've stepped in a long time ago when Brandon was still alive. So instead of running your mouth, maybe try to realize that we've leaned on each other during this shit time, and even if she only wants me as a friend, that'll be enough for me. And I don't need your blessing for that."

Mason's tense as a board next to me while Liam's stance doesn't waver. I know he's tough as nails and always has a point to prove, but I've had enough of defending what Lennon and I have. Whether it's a friendship or it becomes more, I shouldn't have to always be armed.

"You're right." Mason breaks the awkward silence with a pat on my shoulder. "She needs someone like you in her life through this, and only you understand what's happening between you two."

"Then why all the secrets, man?" Liam finally speaks.

"Because I knew how you'd react. You think I have an ulterior motive in all of this because you know how I've always felt about her, but that was never the case. Since the moment Brandon died, I've only ever wanted to be a shoulder for her to cry on. I didn't expect things to escalate the way they did."

"Sophie and Maddie told us about their parents," Liam says.

"Are they as evil as they sound?" Mason asks.

"They were nice, which was a surprise. However, their expectations and old-fashioned values were crystal clear. Lennon's worries were merited once I heard the way they talked about doing things in order. Even though, deep down, I think Lennon always planned to get married and then have kids because she knew they'd never accept anything else. Especially not living with Brandon and getting pregnant before marriage. This little white lie keeps them in her life and the baby's."

"For how long?" Liam asks.

Shrugging, I look down at my food that's getting cold. "That's the million-dollar question."

CHAPTER THIRTY-FIVE

LENNON

THE FIRST WEEK back to work is all meetings, getting my classroom set up, and reorganizing. Students arrive next Monday, and I'm still not sure where my head is at being back here. I know it's only been a few months, but it brings back so many memories of how things were before the summer break. Luckily, I'll have these next five days to transition back to what was once my happy place.

"Lennon?" I turn around at the sound of my name and see Brenna, the art teacher. "So glad to see you!" She walks in and hugs me. When she pulls back, I smile.

"Great to see you too. How was your summer?" I ask politely.

"Wonderful. Too short as usual," she says with a chuckle. "How about you?" Her expression softens. "I mean, I hope you were able to have some much-needed time to deal with everything."

And there it is.

"I did, thanks. Doesn't make it any easier, of course, but due to some great friends, I made it through." I purposely rest a hand on my stomach, knowing the word will eventually get out. The blouse is flowy, so unless I bring attention to it, you can't see it.

Her eyes follow, and it takes her a second to realize I have a bump. "Are you…*pregnant*?" She whispers the last word as if it's a curse word.

"I am," I say with a smile. "Found out only a few months ago."

"Oh my gosh, Lennon," she squeals, then pulls me in for another hug. "Congratulations."

"Thank you," I say appreciatively. "It was hard at first to come to terms with it all, but I'm happy to be carrying his baby."

"We have to throw you a shower when it gets closer!" Her eyes widen in excitement, her hands on my shoulders as she waits for my approval.

"Oh, um…"

"Lennon, please. You know we like any excuse to eat cake and sweets, so let us do this for you."

I can't argue with that.

Nodding, I smile. "Okay. I'm due in December, though, so…"

"We'll figure out a day, so don't even worry."

By noon, the entire staff knows, including the principal. She poked her head in just before I left for the day to congratulate me. She asked how I was doing and inquired about my maternity plans. I hadn't thought too much about it, considering I'd been living mostly day-to-day, but now that I have a baby on the way, I have to think ahead and plan accordingly. I told her my due date and that I'd hopefully be able to make it until Christmas break. That means I can take a full twelve weeks off for maternity leave and not return until sometime in March.

Hunter texted me to see how I was holding up, and I was so happy to see his message, knowing how hard today was going to be for me. I texted him a *Friends* GIF of Ross in the episode where he says "I'm fine" in a high-pitched voice. He came back with another *Friends* one, which started the GIF battle of the past six hours.

We've certainly come a long way.

The next day of conferences is boring, but knowing I have an ultrasound appointment later keeps me motivated throughout the day. I get to see my baby again, some new pictures, and will finally find out the gender. I'm beyond excited.

Sophie and Maddie are meeting me there. I mentioned it to Hunter and told him he wasn't obligated to go with me since my sisters were coming.

He insisted he'd be there.

I don't argue it, of course. I appreciate that he wants to be here for me, but after the doctor assumed he was the father the first time, I wasn't sure he'd want to join me again.

SOPHIE

We're five minutes away. SOMEONE made us
late.

I snicker when I see a group text with my sisters.

MADDIE

I couldn't find my shoes, sorry! Want me to show
up barefoot?

SOPHIE

She had three other pairs to pick from. Don't let
her fool you.

LENNON

I just got here and am about to check in. Meet
me on the third floor.

MADDIE

Don't find out what that baby is without us!

I snort-laugh.

"Did Soph tell you she's online dating now?" Maddie says a second after they arrive. "Should see some of these creeps she's meeting."

They both give me a hug and rub my belly before sitting on either side of me. I haven't seen Maddie since her dance recital two weeks ago. Things have been crazy getting ready for the baby and going back to work.

"Online dating, huh? Finally gave up on Mason?" I ask, chuckling.

Sophie rolls her eyes. "If I wait for that man to make up his mind or make a move, my ovaries will be dried up, and I'll be wearing bifocals."

"By your driving, I'd say you need them now," Maddie teases.

Sophie glares. "What was that? You wanna ride the bus home?"

"Is this what sex deprivation does?" Maddie asks me. "Once you have it, then no longer have access to it, does it turn you into a hormonal psycho?"

"Look who you're asking," I mock. "I'm both sex-deprived and hormonal."

"Fair point." She slouches back into her chair. "You should see some of these messages, though. Their pick-up lines are cringe-worthy."

"Yes, please tell," I say to Sophie with a shit-eating grin. "Amuse me."

"Ugh, thanks, Mads." Sophie groans and grabs her phone, clicking open the app.

"I bet those braids are useful in the bedroom. Wanna bend over and find out?" she reads aloud, then gives me the side-eye.

I burst out laughing. "What the hell?"

"Oh, it gets way worse. I learned the hard way not to post a picture with braids now."

"Who knew?" I snicker. "Okay, more."

"Violinist, huh? Guess that means you're good with your fingers. How about you come over and play my instrument?"

I crack up all over again. "That's kinda creative."

She reads another one. "Are you a vegan because I wanna nut all over you."

"Ew!" I laugh. "Are they all sexual innuendos?"

"Ninety-nine percent, yes."

"Tell her about Cale," Maddie says with a smirk. "He's my *favorite*."

"Cale got blocked," she says matter-of-factly.

"Oh c'mon! I was having fun with him." Maddie cackles.

I look back and forth between them. "Oh God. You let Maddie talk to him?"

"She couldn't handle Cale, so I handled him for her. Turns out Cale didn't have as big of balls as he said."

"What did you do, Maddie?" I ask pointedly.

"He asked to see a picture of my tits and ass."

I cringe. "And?"

"I sent him a picture of a chicken's breast and a donkey. He wasn't amused."

Shaking my head, I laugh. "Then what?"

"I told him if he could name the US state capitals in alphabetical order, he would earn the right to see one nipple," Maddie explains.

Furrowing my brows, I can't even imagine where this is leading. "And?"

"He asked how many capitals there are," she deadpans.

"Ha!" I laugh, about to pee myself.

"I told him sixty-nine, and he started listing off random ones, and when I told him he failed, he started calling me all kinds of names. Then I said I liked being called those things in the bedroom, but too bad he'd never get to do that since he probably couldn't find my clit even with a map."

"What're they teaching you at dance school?"

"I was born in the social media era, Lennon. I'm not a dummy."

Sophie snickers, and I pray for the guy who ends up with Maddie. She'll make them fight hard and test them at every corner. Part of me is proud that she won't give herself up to just anyone, but I'm also protective of her. I want her to stay as innocent as possible.

A minute later, Hunter walks in wearing his work clothes, and I swear everything inside me comes alive. Ever since he told me how he feels—how he's *always* felt—a month ago, it's been hard not to react around him. I've actively had to stop myself from imagining him next to me in bed, touching me, cuddling like we did in Utah. I won't even admit how many times I've had to resort to my vibrator when fantasies of him take over.

The day after Hunter confessed his feelings, things were awkward between us. I didn't know how to act around him without creating tension. I feel guilty as hell because I can't return his feelings right now. The baby's and my well-being have to come first right now. Above anything, I don't want to hurt him. I wasn't sure we could move on from this even though I wanted to more than anything. We need each other, but I wasn't sure how to go forward after that confession—our confessions.

Hunter, being the resilient and amazing man he is, sat me down and told me there was no reason for things to be weird. We promised each other our friendship could go back to how it was before Utah happened. In an effort to do that, I've tucked them away for when I'm brave enough to relive them.

But as soon as those thoughts hit me, guilt floods in, and I feel sad all over again.

"Hunter," I say almost breathlessly. "You came."

"Of course." He stands in front of us and shoves his hands into his pockets as Sophie and Maddie openly eye him. "Sorry, I'm a few minutes late. I had to go by the apartment quick."

"No worries. They should be calling me back anytime now," I

tell him. "But since you're here…" I stop myself, knowing it's a bad idea to bring it up.

Hunter doesn't let it go, though.

"What?" He pulls on his black slacks before kneeling in front of me. "What do you need, Lennon?"

The way he focuses all of his attention on me has me sucking in a deep breath. Hunter's gaze is so intense, I have to remember to breathe and act normal. He reaches a hand out and rests it on my knee.

"Um, well…I was thinking since you're here we might wanna take a picture," I finally tell him. "To update the 'Gram. My parents will be expecting to see a new baby bump picture."

"Oh." His expression deepens. "Sure, we can do that. You wanna do it right now?"

"Yes!" Maddie answers for me, clapping in excitement. "I'll take it." She holds out her hand, and I drop my phone in her palm.

"Probably a couple and maybe another one once we're in the ultrasound room," I tell her. Ever since I told them about Hunter confessing his feelings for me, they've found any opportunity to bring us closer together. Not that it matters. After walking away from him, I notice the way he looks at me.

Half heartbroken. Half understanding.

I hate thinking about how this tortures him, but he'll never admit it aloud to me. I try to keep space between us, but since we need to keep up the act for my parents' sake and update the Instagram account, I don't argue the idea.

Hunter stands, and I follow him. Almost without a second thought, Hunter reaches for my hand and grabs it. We stand in front of one of the hospital windows with a fake plant in front of it.

As he wraps his arm around my waist, I move closer and fit perfectly into his side, molding together. I barely reach his shoulder because he's so much bigger and taller than I am.

Maddie snaps a couple of pictures with a huge smile on her

face. "So cute!" She takes another handful. "Okay, now…Hunter should put his hand on your belly."

"Maddie—" I start, but he cuts me off.

"No, it's fine." Hunter looks down. "If it's okay with you, I mean?"

My throat tightens, knowing this isn't easy for him. Pretending to be my husband is one thing, but pretending to be the father of my baby has to be fucking torture.

"Sure," I croak, sucking in a sharp breath. Instead of resting his hand over my bump like I expect him to, he kneels and wraps both arms around me with his head on my belly.

"Oh my God!" Maddie gushes, and I know she's losing her cool. "Freakin' adorbs." She takes a million more pictures. Some with Hunter kissing my stomach, with us looking at each other, and others with us laughing at Maddie's lack of a filter, saying whatever comes to her mind.

Then Hunter reaches for my face.

"For the 'gram," he whispers with a wink. Then he cups my cheeks and kisses me.

I melt into him, forgetting we're in public and that this kiss isn't supposed to be real. So softly, his mouth brushes against mine, and his tongue slides in just enough to part my lips. I fight the urge to moan as I hear the camera clicking. I know Maddie is getting all the pictures—ones I probably won't be able to look at.

We're startled apart when a tech calls out my name. Quickly clearing my throat, I blink and look around Hunter.

"Right here," I say, grabbing her attention, then glance up at Hunter. "Thanks."

He licks his lips, his gaze intense as it burns into me. "You're welcome."

"I think I just got pregnant," Maddie mutters to Sophie, and I scowl at her to shut her mouth before Hunter overhears.

He follows me and my sisters down the hallway. The tech introduces herself and makes small talk with me as we walk into an ultrasound room. After her instructions, I lie down on the exam table with a cloth tucked into my pants. My shirt is folded all the way up to my chest, and when the tech puts the gel on the wand, I know we're close to seeing my baby again.

"Do you want to find out the gender today?" she finally asks ten minutes later after taking all kinds of measurements. When she says the heartbeat is strong and everything looks healthy, I smile so wide.

"Yes!" a resounding wave of voices echoes. Sophie and Maddie are just as excited as I am.

Hunter stands next to my head, but when I look up, his eyes aren't glued to the screen like my sister's. Rather, they're laser focused on me. He shoots me a wink and a classic Hunter smirk.

And it sends shivers down my spine.

"Alright, time to find out, Mama…"

My eyes snap back to the screen as she lowers the wand. "Any guesses before the big reveal?" she taunts.

"Girl!" Maddie blurts.

"I think it's a boy," Sophie says.

"What about you, Hunter?" Maddie asks, drawing our attention to him. I want to interrupt and protect him from having to answer. I can't even imagine how hard this is for him now knowing his secret, which is why I was surprised he came today.

"Oh, um…I have no idea." He shrugs. "I'm excited for you either way."

"I have a feeling it's a girl," I say.

"Well, let's find out."

An image appears, and I see the cute little butt on the screen and then…

"There's no penis!"

"Maddie!" Sophie and I both scold.

"How would she even know what one looks like?" Sophie snorts, making Hunter and me laugh.

Maddie scoffs, rolling her eyes.

"Well, she's right," the tech announces. "It's a girl!"

Hunter arrives at the apartment a few minutes before me. I lug my bag and purse in and am ready to sit on my ass after today.

"Hey, wait…" Hunter says as I walk toward my room. "I have a surprise for you in there."

Tilting my head, I narrow my eyes. "You do? What kind of surprise?"

"C'mon, you know I'm not gonna tell you." He comes up behind me and wraps a hand over my eyes. "Okay, you can walk now."

"Oh, okay, sure," I reply dramatically. "I can't see a damn thing."

"I'll lead you."

I hear a door open and the click of the light switch flicking on. "Okay." He removes his hand, and I blink a few times before my vision clears.

"What's that?" I walk toward it. "Oh my God. You got me a rocking chair?"

"Yep, figured you'd need one."

I look over my shoulder, and he's grinning.

"I can't believe you did this." I close the gap between us and wrap my arms around him. "Thank you, Hunter."

"You're welcome." He kisses my forehead, making those damn goose bumps appear again. "Go take it out for a test drive."

I sit and rock, the chair soft and comfortable. "It's perfect."

Hunter crosses his arms over his chest, standing tall and proud. His smile is genuine and sweet, and I wish I could express how much this means.

"Hopefully, you and baby girl make a lot of memories rocking together."

"I can't wait," I tell him, beaming. "My mom used the same rocking chair for each of us, and it now creaks after years of being used. But it always felt special."

Hunter watches me with a look of pride. "So now that you know the gender, do you have any names picked out?"

"I've narrowed it down to a few, but nothing concrete." My head falls back as I rock back and forth, the motion causing my eyes to close. "Oh shit."

"What?" Hunter's brows furrow.

"We have to do a gender reveal announcement."

"What the heck is that?"

I snort. "It's exactly as it sounds. You reveal the gender on social media basically or, in our case, the fake Instagram page. But I should call my parents first and tell them."

"How do you want to do that?" he asks. "Reveal it?"

"Hm…Maddie probably got a good picture of us today, so I'll use one of those shots and attach the sonogram picture."

"Oh, alright."

Standing, I walk toward Hunter and murmur, "There's someone else I need to tell."

He nods as if he's been thinking about it too.

"I don't know if it'll destroy them or give them some peace of mind. Either way, they deserve to know they have a grandchild on the way."

"Invite them over and we'll tell them together," he offers.

"Okay, thank you." I give him another hug, resisting the urge to stay in his arms.

An hour later, Mr. and Mrs. Locke arrive at the apartment. They're all smiles and hugs as soon as they see me. I haven't seen them since Brandon's funeral, and I feel awful for not staying in touch. We've all been grieving in our ways.

"Lennon, sweetheart. I'm so glad you called. Thank you for inviting us over," Mrs. Locke says, her wide smile giving me the courage to tell them the news. I purposely wore a loose-fitting shirt so it wouldn't be obvious right away.

"Thank you both for coming," I say. "I'm sorry it's been so long."

"Oh nonsense." Mr. Locke waves me off. "We know things have been tough."

"Are you back at work now?" Mrs. Locke asks as I lead them into the living room.

"Yes, started yesterday," I reply just as Hunter comes out of his room. He's dressed in casual clothes, the soap from his shower still lingering throughout the air.

"Hunter!" Mrs. Locke beams the moment she sees him. He gives her a big hug, tells her how pretty she looks, and soon she's chuckling at his charm. Mr. Locke gives him a handshake and side hug, telling him how good he looks.

"So glad you two stayed friends," Mrs. Locke says as the four of us sit.

"She's kinda stuck with me," Hunter teases. "Or I'm stuck with her?"

"Ha!" I burst out laughing. "It's a mutual agreement we're stuck with each other."

Hunter and I lock eyes, and he winks.

"Well, there is a reason I asked you guys over," I start, and the room goes eerily quiet. Hunter walks across the room and stands next to me. I look at him, and he gives me a nod of encouragement.

Swallowing down my nerves, I clear my throat. "After Brandon died, I found out I was pregnant."

Both of them gasp, neither saying anything, and I'm not sure if I should continue or if this announcement is too much for them.

"You're pregnant?" Mrs. Locke asks just above a whisper, and I already see the wetness in her eyes.

With a closed smile, I nod. "Yeah, I found out today that it's a girl."

"Oh my gosh." Mrs. Locke comes toward me with her arms out, and I stand to meet her. "A true miracle, Lennon." Her voice cracks as she wraps me in a hug. "I can't believe this." She pulls back slightly and looks down between us.

"I can show you pictures," I offer, then ask Hunter to grab them from my purse.

"We'd love to see them," Mr. Locke says, giving me a hug next.

"You look so tiny still," Mrs. Locke gushes.

"I don't feel that way." I laugh and press a hand to the top of my bump so they can get a better look through the baggy fabric. "Trust me, she's in there."

Hunter grins as he passes me the sonogram photos. We sit as I pass them out.

"Oh goodness." Mrs. Locke gasps, covering her mouth. "Her little nose."

"Looks just like Brandon," Hunter adds.

"She looks a lot like him already," I say with tears in my eyes.

They inform me they have a lawyer for Brandon's case and plan to sue the person who hit and killed him. It's painful to hear the details of the accident and see how this is weighing on them—on all of us. Mrs. Locke tears up when she says the civil suit could take months, if not, years, but if they can get a wrongful death win or life insurance money, they'll save it for me and the baby. It's completely unexpected, but I thank them anyway.

We chat for close to an hour before they make their way to the door. I give them a few pictures to keep, wanting them to have some. I'm so relieved by their reactions and feel bad for waiting to tell them.

"Thank you, Lennon. You have no idea how this will help us cope and give us some closure. We miss him every single day, but knowing he's going to live on through your child gives me hope that life can go on." Mrs. Locke tears up as she embraces me, and I never want to let go but, eventually, do.

Mr. Locke pulls me into a hug, and I promise to keep them updated. Once they leave, I walk to the living room where Hunter is sitting on the couch. Wrapping my arms around his waist, I rest my head on his chest as he rubs a hand over my back. I need some kind of comfort after that emotional meeting because the heartache is almost too much to deal with.

"You okay?" he asks softly.

I nod.

"That went well," he says.

I nod again, thinking about everything that was said tonight.

We stay like this for a few minutes before I pull back and look at him. My vision is blurry from the tears threatening to fall. "Thanks for being here."

"Of course." He brings his thumb to my cheek and wipes away a rogue tear. "I knew they'd be happy."

"She's probably going to be the most spoiled kid ever," I say with a halfhearted laugh. Brandon was the Lockes' only child, so this will be their only grandchild.

"Oh, I can bet on that," Hunter agrees with a laugh. "Not just them, though. She'll be spoiled and loved by everyone around her. You've impacted more people in your life than you even realize, Lennon."

My heart thuds hard in my chest, his words casting a spell that has my emotions magically suspended.

I wish I could kiss him right now.

If only things were different.

CHAPTER THIRTY-SIX
HUNTER

THE PAST TEN weeks have come and gone, and the temperature is starting to drop. The leaves are changing, and soon it'll be Halloween. The major project at work finished last month, and we were well under budget as I had hoped and planned. My boss even gave me a nice bonus and has already pre-assigned me to a few large jobs that'll kick off next year. At the moment, I've been asked to help with projects that have fallen behind. I'd much rather be in charge, but I can't complain too much because less responsibility equals less stress. It allows me more time to focus on Lennon and the baby.

As I'm sitting at my desk, getting ready to answer a few emails, I receive a call from Tracie, the lobby secretary who checks people in and out of the building.

"Someone's waiting for you up front with lunch," Tracie says in a whispered tone, which is odd.

"Who is it?"

"She won't tell me her name, but she's pregnant. She wanted it to be a surprise," she tells me.

I shake my head, wondering what Lennon is up to. I look at the clock and realize it's right around her lunchtime, so I bet she ran a quick errand and brought me something. Though I already ate one of those shitty protein bars I keep in my desk drawer, I won't refuse a hot meal. "Alright. I'll be right there."

I try to hold back a smile as I walk down the stairs and open the door that leads to the lobby. As my eyes land on Jenna, I have no words. I know Tracie is watching us, so I try to act normal even though I'm shocked as hell. I haven't spoken to her since she threatened me with her lawyer. If I act indifferent, she won't make a scene. I don't need anyone at work knowing my business.

"Hey there, Daddy!" she says loudly as if she wants the whole building to hear, and I cringe.

Keeping my voice low, I ask, "What're you doing here?"

"I remembered how much you loved Chinese food when we were together and thought I'd bring you lunch." Jenna's being overly fake as she hands me the bag. I look at it and am forced to take it from her.

"Can we talk outside, babe?" The way she speaks as if we're a couple aggravates the fuck out of me. I walk past her through the double sliding doors, and she follows me.

"Jenna. What the fuck?" I stand on the sidewalk and search her face. She's as calm as can be.

"Thought you'd like to know I found out we're having a boy. Isn't that so exciting?" She grins wide as if she's expecting to get the same reaction.

If I could shake her and tell her to wake the hell up and smell the roses, I would. "We've already been over this," I tell her between gritted teeth.

"You're scared and in denial," she says matter-of-factly, and I'm positive she believes her own lies. "I gave you enough time to process this, Hunter. It's time to deal with it."

"There's nothing to deal with. You're projecting the way *you* feel. Did you tell Craig like I told you?" I cross my arms over my chest, staring her down.

She steps closer and shakes her head. "No, because this baby is yours. I know it in my gut, and I can't allow you to deny it anymore. It's time to take responsibility for your actions and man up, Hunter."

I glare, anger simmering through my blood like I've never felt before. "You *want* it to be the truth, but it doesn't mean it is. You shouldn't be here. I'll take a paternity test when he's born to prove it to you, but don't you dare show up unannounced again." I hand the food back to her, not trusting anything she'd give me at this point. It might be poisoned. "I've already eaten, so you should have this."

"So that's it? You're going to reject me again?" she hisses. "I know your little friend is pregnant too. You'd rather take care of someone else's baby than your own?" She spews fire, knowing it'll get me worked up.

I narrow my eyes, shaking my head as I try to calm down.

"Yeah, I know all about her and your fake marriage, Hunter. It's not even your baby." Her words are venom, and I need to get out of here before I say or do something I'll regret.

"Leave, Jenna. *Now.*"

"It'd be a shame if her pastor dad found out," she says in a taunting voice that has me seeing red. My fists clench, and my jaw tightens. How the fuck does she know all this?

As if she can read my mind, she continues, "The internet is a great thing these days, Hunter. You might be able to trick two middle-aged people, but you're not fooling me."

I'm glad we took this outside even though I'm sure Tracie can hear every word Jenna spews. She's not exactly quiet.

I turn on my heels, growing more frustrated. "*Stay away from me*, Jenna." I enunciate every word.

"Do the right thing, Hunter Manning! This isn't over!"

I walk into the building, leaving her outside yelling like a crazy person. Tracie gives me a sad look and scans me in but doesn't say anything. I take the stairs two at a time, pissed Jenna has the audacity to show up at my job like we're dating. She's not going to let this go, and I'm not sure what else to do at this point.

Get a restraining order on her? If she does it again, I might
have to.

The rest of the day, I'm overly annoyed with every person who
speaks to me. I'm short and need to go work out to blow off some
steam, but instead, I drive home, trying to forget what happened.

When I walk into the apartment, everything's quiet except for
the sound of Lennon's beautiful voice. I go to her room and stand
at the door, listening to her sing in the rocking chair with her eyes
closed and her hands over her stomach.

For a moment, I watch and listen to her, and it calms me in a way
she wouldn't understand. The late-evening sun shines through,
casting a warm glow throughout the room, and I find myself smiling,
soaking in her natural beauty. I glance around, looking at how the
room's been transformed into a makeshift nursery. The crib and
changing table I helped build last month fit perfectly in the space.

To get Lennon's attention, I clear my throat, and her eyes pop
open. "How long have you been there?"

"Not long," I say. "Hungry?"

She nods, standing, and I realize how much her belly has
grown. It seems as if she started showing overnight, though it's
been gradual. She glances at me, and she's glowing. Becoming a
mom has come so naturally to her, and there's no doubt she'll love
that baby with every ounce of her body. Hell, she already does
and so do I.

"I've craved pizza all day long with extra, extra, extra, extra
cheese."

I burst out laughing. "Damn, girl." Lennon's cravings this last
trimester have been random but usually anything greasy.

She narrows her eyes, and before she can even throw sass my
way, I continue, "Whatever you say. I hope they add some sauce
and crust with your cheese." I open the app and order a pizza real
quick with four times the cheese like Lennon requested. One thing
I've learned over the past few months is not to argue with a
pregnant woman over food. It's a losing battle.

As we're waiting for the delivery, I help Lennon hang and fold more baby clothes. This has become one of our traditions, spending our time getting the apartment ready for the baby girl. The church ladies have sent so much that I've told Lennon she can use my room for storage if needed. Though we've been putting up clothes all week, there are still boxes full of onesies and dresses. I'm pretty sure Lennon won't have to buy clothes until the kid is sixteen.

"I can't believe they've sent so much," she says with a small pile of clothes in her arms. She's cleared out the top two drawers of her dresser for the baby.

"Oh my God!" Lennon yells.

"What? What is it?" I panic and stop moving.

She stands as stiff as a board. "Come here. Hurry."

I rush to her and stand beside her. "Are you okay?"

Lennon grabs my hand and places it on her belly.

"She's kicking," Lennon tells me with the sweetest smile on her face.

Right after she says it, I feel a little foot against my palm. My eyes light up. "Wow. That's amazing."

I feel it again, even harder this time.

"Keep talking," she tells me. "I think it's your voice."

I drop to my knees so I can be closer to the baby and place both hands on Lennon's belly. "Hey, little one. Just want to say hello, and we feel you in there. Can't wait for you to meet your mama. She's so pretty and nice, and I know you've already heard how beautifully she sings."

The kicking continues, and I look up at Lennon and see tears. I stand face-to-face with her, wanting to take her soft cheeks in my palms and kiss the fuck out of her, but I don't.

"She likes you," she says, and I wipe the tears away with my thumbs, knowing she has more on her mind.

"Everything okay?"

"I'm upset Brandon is missing this. The more days that pass, the more he's turning into a distant memory, and I never want to forget him."

I nod, understanding but not knowing how to console her. There are days when I wish I could bring him back, so maybe she'd be happy the same way she used to be. Then another part of me wishes I could be the man who makes her smile. Instead, I try to be there for her as much as I can.

Grabbing her hand, I place it over her heart. "He's here, Lennon. He'll always be there."

She nods, and the doorbell rings, pulling us both away. "Hope you're hungry for that pizza. There's gonna be so much cheese, you'll be chewing all night."

Lennon laughs. "You're such an ass."

"Stop cursing in front of the baby." I go to the door and give the guy a tip.

I didn't realize how hungry I was until I take my first bite.

"How was work?" she asks, holding the crust so the toppings don't slide off.

I let out a huff. "Fine. Saw Jenna today."

Lennon stops chewing and furrows her brows. "Why?"

"Trust me, not by choice."

I explain what happened, and I'm pretty sure I can see her pulse throbbing in her neck.

"Doesn't she know how to take a hint?"

"No," I say, wanting to change the subject because it's still touchy. I don't tell her about the threats she spewed either. The last thing Lennon needs is more stress added to her plate. Whatever Jenna thinks she knows, I'm not going to give in to her hissy fit. "I don't want her to think she can show up here or anywhere I'm at again. It's annoying."

Lennon sighs, closing up. "Yeah."

We finish eating in silence, and I think about everything that's happened over the past few months. We've continued to eat together every night and catch each other up on our days. She's more tired than usual after work, so I've tried to keep up with the apartment so she doesn't have to worry about it.

There have been several times I've wanted to kiss her or bring up how I feel again, but it's easier, for now, to pretend I never said anything. I've allowed her to take the lead on us because that night, things changed, though she'd deny it if I called her out. I'm pretty sure I've been friend-zoned, and that's okay because I'm not giving up hope. If that's all I can ever be, I'll be forced to accept it, though I don't think she even realizes how she sends me mixed signals all the time.

After we've finished eating, I put the remaining pizza in the fridge. Lennon's phone rings, and when she answers it, I know it's one of her sisters by how excited she sounds. The further along Lennon gets, the closer they grow, and I love how supportive they both are. Lennon looks at me, and I whisper that I'm going to take a shower, and she gives me a thumbs-up.

My shoulders are tight, and I stand under the hot water, hoping it relieves some of the stress. After seeing Jenna today, I've been on edge. She's determined to make my life hell until I can prove I'm not the father of her baby. It'll be hung over my head until the day he's born, and I know, just by her threats alone, it's not the last I'll see of her.

Once I've scrubbed the day from my body, I step out, wrap a towel around my waist, and walk to my bedroom. As soon as I enter, I turn and see Lennon behind me. Somehow, I hang onto my towel, though she startled the fuck out of me.

"Shit," I whisper, not expecting her to be there.

"Sophie wants me to go grocery shopping with her tomorrow. Anything you want me to add to the list?" Lennon's gaze lowers down my body, lingers on my bare chest and then slides lower. I've been doing most of the grocery shopping, but Sophie likes to have Lennon join her. It's a way for them to bond, and she doesn't have to go alone.

I chuckle as she continues to stare while she bites her lip. It's moments like this when I know she feels exactly the same as I do but refuses to admit it. And I won't force the issue.

"I'm gawking, aren't I? Sorry." A blush hits her cheeks, and she covers her face with her hands.

"I'm gonna get dressed now…" I taunt, and she quickly turns around and walks out of my room. Sometimes, she's so fucking adorable, and the thought of her being embarrassed has me grinning. If she wanted me, I'd give her every fucking inch. All she'd have to do is ask. Guilt be damned.

I slip on some clothes and go into the living room and grab the plastic outlet protectors I purchased to put throughout the apartment. Sitting on the couch with her feet propped up, Lennon starts giggling.

"What're you doing?" she asks as I go along the walls and plug each open socket.

I look over my shoulder and grin. "Baby proofing the apartment since she'll be here before we know it."

Lennon continues to laugh. "For the first six months, all she's going to do is eat, poop, and sleep."

"And people always talk about how their kids grow up too fast. So she'll essentially be driving in a few months." I stand and glance over to catch her rolling her head on her shoulders. "Your back hurt again?" Lately, she hasn't been able to get comfortable.

"It's the worst. If I sit too long or stand too long, it makes my back so sore," she admits.

I sit next to her on the couch. "I'm gonna schedule you one of those prenatal massages. I've heard they help a lot."

She leans her head back on the couch. "At this point, I need more than my back rubbed." Lennon closes her eyes tight. "Ignore me. Seriously. I don't know what my deal is today."

It's called *sexual frustration*, but I don't dare say that. It's not the first time she's hinted about sex, and I'm sure she'd feel better if she found some sort of relief. I think about the toy she has in her room and find myself growing hard at the thought of her using it.

Imagining her mouth falling open as she releases soft moans has me wanting to take another shower.

Fuck me.

I quickly adjust myself because I'm hard as a rock. Standing, I force the thoughts of her naked body out of my head, and I hope she doesn't notice my erection.

"I think I'm going to go to bed," I tell her, yawning.

She nods and agrees she's tired. Lennon goes into her room, and I walk into mine. Crawling under the sheets, I grab my cock and stroke myself as I think about her. I'd give her everything she could ever need. I'd take it slow, kissing and sucking her supple nipples, being as careful as I can, making sure she's completely satisfied. I'd make love to her all night, taking my time until she begs me to fuck her. It doesn't take long before the orgasm rocks through me, taking full control, and I let out a muffled grunt that I hope she doesn't hear. Considering the walls are paper-thin, I'm sure she did. After I clean up, I lie back in bed and wonder if she's thinking of me when she touches herself. The thought alone has me growing hard all over again.

CHAPTER THIRTY-SEVEN

LENNON

HUNTER'S GRUNTS and groans from his room cause heat to build between my legs. Hell, those are the hottest sounds I've ever heard. I close my eyes and picture him touching himself, then rub my thighs together to relieve the ache building inside.

Reaching for my vibrator, I imagine him on his bed, slipping into his shorts and stroking his hard cock. I angle the top of the toy over my clit, and as soon as it comes alive, I desperately search for my release. I think of Hunter in his room doing the same, throwing his head back when he comes, and wonder if he thinks of me while he pleasures himself.

The guilt creeps in again like it always does when my thoughts about Hunter turn inappropriate. After our time in Utah and these past six months, I don't know that I have any energy left to fuel the remorse.

As I push those thoughts away, I focus on my body and think of Hunter next to me—watching me, touching me, fucking me. With my belly, I can't get the angle right, but I say fuck it and try anyway. The handle on the wand isn't long enough, so I grab a pillow, stuff it under my ass, and angle my hips to push my pussy higher.

I will MacGyver my way to an orgasm if I have to.

With my legs parted, I bend my knees and close my eyes. Focusing on reaching my climax, it builds and grows more intense as I arch into the vibrator. I increase the speed, and soon, I'm screaming into my pillow, not worrying or thinking about the fact Hunter is on the other side of the wall.

It's not the best I've ever had, but until I have this baby and can find my own vagina again, it's gonna have to get me through.

Sigh. Vibrator dick has nothing on real dick.

It's been two weeks since Jenna's surprise visit to Hunter's work. He tells me not to worry, and I'm trying not to, but until it's proven with a paternity test, it'll always be in the back of my mind. The closer I get to my due date, the more anxious I get.

Since Halloween is tomorrow, Hunter and I bought loads of candy to hand out to the kids who live in the apartment complex. Last year, we ran out, so I'm hoping we have enough to last the entire time.

I'm thirty-two weeks pregnant, and the baby will be here in a blink, so I've been trying to use my spare time to prepare. Work has been great so far with no major problems, and many of my colleagues are excited for me. I've been counting down the days to meet my little miracle.

After work, I sit on the couch and prop up my swollen feet because. Standing most of the day isn't doing me any favors, and though I try to sit when I can, it's not comparable to having them elevated.

I'm so tired, I nearly fall asleep, but when I hear the door swing open, I pop up with a grin. After Hunter walks in and we greet each other, he goes to take a shower, and I start pulling items from the fridge for burgers.

On Fridays, we typically order out, but tonight, I volunteered to cook because he's been doing so much for me. Each room has been completely baby-proofed from top to bottom. Hell, it's even adult-proofed at this point.

Just as I put the hamburger patties in a skillet, Hunter walks into the kitchen wearing shorts that hang off his hips and a shirt that leaves nothing to the imagination. I try to force myself to focus on the food, but he catches me stealing glances and smirks.

"Damn, I'm hungry," he groans, leaning over me. His arm brushes against mine, causing goose bumps to form across my skin.

"Me too." My stomach grumbles, but I'm craving more than the food.

He shifts on his feet as his eyes meet mine, and I shamelessly enjoy his closeness. He lingers for a moment longer, allowing me to soak in the scent of fresh soap on his body. Hunter asks how my day was, and before I can reply, a knock echoes from the door.

Hunter raises a brow. "Expecting someone?"

"No, don't think so."

The first person who comes to mind is Jenna. At this point, I wouldn't put anything past her.

By the tone of Hunter's voice, I know it's not. I hear him laugh nervously, and then I recognize a voice that has my stomach in knots.

"Wifey, look who came to visit us," Hunter says with eyes as wide as saucers as my mother peers around him.

"Mom!" I force out, searching her face as she walks toward me. I wipe my hands on a dish towel before she pulls me into a hug.

"What a surprise!" I squeal, hoping she doesn't feel how tense I am. "What're you doing here?" I keep my tone light, though I'm silently losing my freaking mind. My mother is here, standing in my kitchen. What the hell?

She grins, stepping back into the dining room, and glances

around the apartment. I feel so vulnerable and unprepared right now. "Just wanted to visit the happily married couple and see how my grandbaby's doing."

"Everything's great." I smile, hoping she doesn't see straight through it. What if she figures out we've been lying this whole time?

"Well, you're just in time for dinner, Mrs. Corrigan. Hope you're hungry."

"We've got plenty," I add.

Hunter leans over and places a chaste kiss on my lips. "Smells good, sweetheart." It's supposed to be sweet and simple, but it has my emotions bubbling to the surface. I desperately want more of him, and when we pull away, I'm completely breathless. A meaningless fake kiss isn't supposed to do that. I suck in my lips, and my mother's eyes meet mine as she sits at the table.

"I've been following your Instagram page. Everyone loves the updates so much." She beams proudly.

Hunter distracts her while I finish dinner by talking about the last few doctor's appointments and what we've been doing to prepare for the baby. He talks about the babyproofing and shopping for things he never would've thought of before now. Though he seems to be enjoying himself, I interrupt their conversation to give him a much-needed break because he's been talking for nearly ten minutes straight.

"Hungry, Mom?" I ask, pulling the ketchup and mustard from the fridge.

"Sure, I could eat," she says.

I take my time making our plates, stalling the inevitable, but all I can think about is how she'll want to see the nursery and the rest of the apartment. When she sees we're sleeping in different rooms, our entire façade will fall apart. I didn't plan for her to show up and it wouldn't take much for her to figure it out r. The thought of losing my parents, everything I tried so hard to keep and protect, guts me. I could think of more lies, more cover-ups to help the story, but she'd see right through them.

Hunter comes into the kitchen to help me carry everything to the table.

"Relax," he whispers in my ear, and I blow out a deep breath.

My body's burning from the inside out because I know we're going to get caught. There's no getting out of it, not with her sitting at my dining room table. I glance down and realize I'm not even wearing my wedding ring. At least I can blame it on my swollen fingers, but what's Hunter's excuse?

"What would you like to drink? We've got water, milk, cranberry juice, and orange juice," I ask my mom.

"Water's fine," she replies in her overly polite tone.

I hand her a bottle, then sit in the chair next to Hunter. Mom chats about her flight, and I try to keep food in my mouth so I don't have to talk too much.

Hunter gives her his boyish grin and occasionally shoots me a wink. He's a natural at pretending to be my husband. I hate that he has to do this, especially after knowing his true feelings for me. I give him an apologetic look, a half-smile so he knows how appreciative I am. He shakes his head as if it's no big deal, but it's a big fucking deal to me. He's always saving my ass.

I've devoured half of my food and barely said a word. I'm still trying to get my thoughts together when my mother sets her napkin down on her empty plate.

"Lennon," she says, meeting my eyes. "I know the truth."

My face twists, and for a moment, I feel like I'm going to throw up.

"What?" I ask, making sure I heard her right. I look at Hunter and then back at her.

"I know you two aren't really married, so you don't have to keep pretending for my sake." She speaks so nonchalantly, but my heart races.

"Mom..." I pause, my chest squeezing with guilt as I swallow hard.

"An anonymous birdie told me," she adds before I can say another word. "They called the church after Sunday service.

Luckily, I answered the phone before your father had a chance." She gives me a pointed look, but I'm confused as hell as to who she's referring to. The only people who knew were my sisters, but as soon as I glance at Hunter and his expression hardens, I have another idea of who could've run their mouth.

"I don't know what you think you know, but—"

She waves a hand in the air and cuts me off.

"I'm not stupid enough to take a stranger's word for it. I've done my due diligence and checked for myself. Marriage records are public in the state of Nevada, and I searched for yours and Hunter's but came up empty. So I called Clark County and asked if I was doing something wrong, and the clerk told me they had no marriage license for Hunter Manning and Lennon Corrigan."

Fuck.

Silence draws on as she gives me a look of disappointment, and this time, Hunter can't save me with his effortless banter and boyish grin. This time, I'm going to have to face the lies I've told.

"You're right, Mom. We aren't married," I admit, and a weight lifts off my chest even if this whole situation is painful. I feel like a kid getting caught stealing from the cookie jar. "I'm sorry I lied."

She lets out a sigh, not accepting my apology but not dismissing it either. "Now, I've been trying to understand why you would lie about getting married, but then the realization hit me. You and Hunter are having a baby out of wedlock and—"

"No." I refuse to allow the lies to continue any further. "It's not Hunter's baby."

Her face contorts, and sadness flickers in her eyes. Sadness for Hunter or me—maybe both. "Oh."

"Mrs. Corrigan," Hunter intervenes. "I apologize for lying to you and your husband. It was never our intention to hurt you. Brandon's the dad, and it's been hard for Lennon to deal with, considering he's no longer with us. Pretending to be married was one hundred percent my idea. Lennon loves you both so much and didn't want to lose you after already losing Brandon. So we came up with this lie. I hope you can understand why we felt we had to."

My throat burns from the unshed tears I refuse to release at the mention of Brandon. Not only did I drag Hunter into this, but now my mother is probably going to lose her shit.

My mom looks back and forth between Hunter and me with a frown. "I'm sorry, Lennon," she says genuinely. "I'm sorry you don't have Brandon here anymore, but you do know all actions have consequences." Her tone went from soft to firm in two seconds flat, not that I should be that surprised.

"I don't want to hear *the talk* right now. We're past that." My tone is harsh, but she needs to know I'm not going to let her lecture me when I'm old enough to make my own decisions. The last thing I need is her telling me how sex before marriage is a sin and to be made to feel like the villain when I'm so damn thrilled about becoming a mother.

"What's done is done, Lennon. I can see that." Her eyes glance down at my stomach. "I understand why you felt like you had to lie, but now it's time to handle things correctly. I can tell by how you two acted in Utah and by your photos that you have mutual feelings for each other. Love like that can't be faked." She looks back and forth between us while my heart threatens to stop beating.

"Mom…"

"Don't worry. I'm not planning to discuss this with your father. What he doesn't know won't hurt him. But the lie is already out there, so before more people find out the truth and feel as if they were scammed by you, I'd suggest you make it right."

Make it right? What the hell does that mean?

Before I lose my cool, I stand and clear the table since we're finished eating. The apartment is small, and there's not nearly enough space to disappear like I wish I could. I walk into the kitchen, hoping to find some sort of clarity and gain control of my emotions. She's pushing my limits, and I don't want to say something I'll regret. While I don't want to lose her or my father, it might be inevitable at this point.

"Lennon…" Hunter comes into the kitchen, whispering my name. "I'm so sorry."

"For what?" I look at him confused, rinsing the plates in the sink. "This isn't your fault."

He brushes a hand through his hair, looking down at his feet before his gaze finally meets mine. "It is. I should've told you, but I didn't wanna freak you out or make you more stressed."

Considering my mother is at the table and she's only ten feet away, Hunter stands close to me, his breath whispering against my cheek. This situation is awkward, and I hate that he's stuck in the middle of it.

"Told me what?" I ask, keeping the water running so she can't overhear.

"The day Jenna came to my work, she threatened to leak our secret."

"What?" I whisper-shout. "How'd *she* know?"

"You can find almost anything on the internet, Lennon. She's a nurse and probably hacked into your medical records to find your family history, due date, and personal info. Hell, I don't know. Maybe she put two and two together. Probably found your Instagram or even stalked us. I'm speculating here, but regardless, she found out and has to be the anonymous tip."

I'm seething. My blood boils, and my heart races as I try to think of a hundred ways to get away with murder. *Temporary insanity*? Could use the hormonal card.

"Thanks for the heads-up," I deadpan.

Though I understand why he didn't say anything sooner, it would've been nice to get ahead of this and prepare for the possibility instead of being blindsided. Jenna clearly has it out for Hunter and dragged me through the mud to make her point.

She's not going to let him go that easily.

"Mom, do you want some coffee?" I ask, turning off the water and looking around Hunter with the fakest smile I can muster.

"Yes, I'd love one, but we still need to talk about this, Lennon." There's a bite in her tone, and I don't know how I'm going to get through this conversation without snapping.

Too bad I can't drink right now.

I make her a cup and bring it over to her. Hunter follows and we sit. My throat swells up, wanting to get this over with as soon as fucking possible.

My mother blows on her coffee, and I wait until she takes a sip before speaking up again. "So, Mom. How are you suggesting I *make it right*?"

She smiles over the porcelain brim. "Isn't it obvious? By getting married. For real."

My brows rise to my hairline as I look at Hunter, who doesn't react at all. His thoughts must be all over the place too, but whatever he's thinking, he's not making it noticeable to me. Turning my gaze back to my mom, I glare as if she's lost her mind. She's gone too far this time.

"That's not happening," I tell her flatly so she knows I won't entertain her ludicrous idea.

She continues as if I hadn't spoken at all. "It's easy to cover up. All we have to do is say there was an issue with the paperwork, and it had to be re-filed. A rushed job and missing signature, which explains the date change." The smile on her lips tells me she's been through this before and quite proud of it too.

"It's another lie," I hiss. "Not to mention, Hunter and I aren't dating. This isn't his baby. He was doing me a favor." The words come out like venom, and I can feel Hunter's eyes glued to the side of my head. Saying them aloud is another reminder of how things can't evolve between us.

"The last thing your father needs is a scandal, Lennon. I don't condone lying, but in this case, it seems like your only option. If you do this, it fixes everything. It negates the lie, and your father doesn't have to know you slept in a room with a man who wasn't your husband—under our roof—which is extremely disrespectful. He doesn't have to know you live with the same man you aren't married to." She pins me with her eyes as if that'll magically make me obey.

I lock my jaw so I don't say what's really going through my mind.

"You're in deep right now, Lennon, and while I believe in forgiveness, you've broken my trust. You don't want to break your father's. If he finds out you orchestrated this in front of him, me, and the church members, I'm not sure things will ever be the same, and what you feared the most—losing us and your family—could very much be your reality."

The air is too thick to breathe. I'm drowning until I look at Hunter, until I realize what my mother is actually suggesting. Forcing him to marry me to appease her is bullshit, and I won't sit idly by and allow her to play puppet master with my life anymore.

"No," I bite out, finding my courage. "It's not happening and is completely out of the question."

"Lennon…" Hunter says my name so softly, but this isn't his battle to fight. I got us into this, and I'll deal with it now—the right way.

"With all due respect, Mother, my answer is no. Ever since I was a child, all you've ever done was dictate my life. I followed your strict rules and ridiculous standards, always eager to make you and Dad proud. I had very few close friends and got made fun of all the time for being the preacher's Goody Two-shoes daughter. There were times I felt I'd never be good enough when all I ever wanted was to make you two happy." I throw my arms up and let them smack back down. "What did it do for me in life? Nothing. Because here we are, and you're looking at me like I'm a huge disappointment. Doing exactly what you want me to do, what you *expect* me to do isn't happening anymore. I love you both so much, but this is my life. Not yours. Not Dad's. Demanding we get married for the sake of old traditional values isn't fair to Hunter, and it's sure as hell not fair to me."

She scoffs. "You're overreacting, Lennon. You aren't thinking clearly."

"No, Mom. I'm thinking clearly for the first time when it comes to your demands. If you and Dad no longer want to be in my life or be in your granddaughter's life, then that's on *you*. That's something you'll be forced to live with for the rest of your lives. I'm going to be a single mother soon, and my sole responsibility will be to protect my child. What you're essentially asking me to do is total bullshit, and I'm not going to do it so you look good to the church. I don't care what they think about me. I no longer care what *you* think about me either. So if you flew all this way to give me ultimatums, then you can leave." Years' worth of frustration spill out of me, things I should've said ages ago, but I'm relieved to get them off my chest now.

Glancing at Hunter, he looks uncomfortable, but also proud. He gives me a little head nod of encouragement.

When I look at my mom, I can tell she's not happy with me. She's downright furious. "That's how you really feel?"

There are two sides to my mother. The one Hunter met, who's sweet as cherry pie, kind, and accepting. And then there's this one —critical, judgy, and condemning.

"I am not continuing the perpetual lie. I refuse. As you said, all actions have consequences, and I'll happily face mine. The baby is Brandon's. I'm not married to Hunter. My baby isn't coming into a world based on lies so everyone else feels better about my situation. It's my life, and I'll do what I please going forward. And either you'll be there to support me and the baby, or you won't. I can't force you to do anything just like you can't force me. Not anymore." I firmly shake my head, licking my lips that have gone dry.

"Excuse me one moment." Hunter slides his chair out and walks to the hallway. I hear the bathroom door shut, knowing he's purposely giving us privacy, which is the last thing I want right now. When there's an audience, she's forced to be on her best behavior because appearance is everything.

"Young lady," she hisses. "Remember you're the one who got yourself into this predicament. You're the one who had sex before marriage, who ended up pregnant, and decided to lie to me, your dad, and the congregation about being married to a man who's not even the father of your baby. You live in an apartment with him as well, which I've also discovered Brandon lived here. The internet is powerful, and all of your lies can easily be uncovered, Lennon. What I'm asking you to do is make it right, to do what your heart is telling you to do. The way you look at each other, there's nothing fake about it. Nothing. He looks at you like you're his entire world, and I see it in your eyes too. Now, you can deny it. You can say it's not true or whatever you need to because you're emotionally unstable, but that relationship you two portrayed, everyone believed. I know everything he said to me and your father was coming from his heart, and that he'd take care of you and the baby in a heartbeat. He loves you, Lennon. And you know what? You love him too."

I don't have the energy to deny her allegations or try to make sense of how she can possibly know all that even before I did, so I don't argue it. She grins and takes a sip of her coffee, but I know this is far from over.

I lower my voice so Hunter doesn't overhear. "I will deal with that in my own time when I'm ready," I snap, tired of everyone telling me how I feel and what I need to do about it. This baby is my only priority right now. Hunter and I will handle everything else when the timing is right.

"You were lucky enough to find love once in your life, Lennon. Don't let the second time slip through your fingers. All I'm asking is for you to think about it."

Her words rip straight through me. I let out a ragged breath as she finishes her coffee in silence. Once she's done, she stands and places the cup in the sink.

"Thanks for dinner and the lovely conversation." She grabs her purse and walks to the door, not giving me a second glance or a goodbye before leaving.

CHAPTER THIRTY-EIGHT

HUNTER

It's been three weeks since Lennon's mom popped in unexpectedly. There was so much I wanted to say, to do, but I knew Lennon needed to speak her mind. As much as I always want to protect her, she needed to handle this on her own.

I was so proud of the way she stood up for herself. It was a long time coming, but I know Lennon well enough to see how it's affecting her. All she's ever wanted is a family and for her parents to be proud of her. From the stories she and her sisters have told, they grew up super close, not always agreeing with their overbearing parents' rules but loving them nevertheless.

Lennon waits every day for a call from her parents, and each night when it doesn't come, I know she's disappointed. She doesn't want to admit it, but I know it weighs on her. However, today is a special day, and I want to do everything I can to cheer her up.

"You ready, Baby Mama?" I tease as I peek into the bathroom where she's still messing with her hair.

"Just about, Big Papa."

I snort at the random nickname. "That's a new one."

"Hey, you started it with One Hump Llama." She glares at me through the mirror.

Unable to hide my smile, I laugh and shrug. "Still funny."

Lennon rolls her eyes and unplugs her curling iron. "You're worse than Maddie."

"But you're a cute llama. Can't even tell you're pregnant from this view." I scan my eyes down to her ass, which still looks hot as ever.

Lennon clears her throat, forcing my attention back up before she faces me. "I'm not carrying her down there." She crosses her arms, which rest on top of her bump.

"Don't know what you're talking about." I purse my lips and lean back on my heels. "Time to go or we'll be late."

Lennon sings to the radio as I drive us to the hospital for a tour of the labor and delivery ward. I'm not quite sure we need to spend an hour to see it all before she delivers, but Lennon insisted, so here we are.

Once we're signed in, we head to the fourth floor and meet with a few other couples also taking the tour. I already know they're assuming we're a happy couple, and when one woman asks when we're expecting, neither of us bothers correcting her.

"December twenty-third," Lennon says.

"Oh, you two must be so excited for a Christmas baby!"

I wrap my arm around Lennon and pull her into my side. "We sure are."

Lennon looks up at me with a curious smile. When I wink, she relaxes against me.

A woman named Jessie introduces herself and explains how the tour will work, and if we have any questions, now is the time to ask. She talks about birth plans and how having them set up with the doctor before going into labor can be beneficial for both the mother and the baby. Even if the plans don't go as expected, it's good to know the options.

Just as she's leading us down a long hallway, she tells us we're waiting for one more couple to arrive, and she'll get started as soon as they come.

"Did you make a birth plan with Dr. Potter yet?" I ask Lennon.

"Uh…get the baby out safely?" She shrugs. "Considering I have five weeks left, I guess I better discuss it with her."

I chuckle lightly. "Mission: Get baby out."

"Easier said than done." She groans. "I know I want Sophie and Maddie in the delivery room with me. I'm also pro pump all the drugs they can into me."

Before I can respond, I see my worst nightmare behind Lennon, and everything inside me tenses. *What the fuck?*

And she's not alone.

Lennon notices. "What is it? Your jaw is about to snap."

I blink and shake my head. "Lennon, I'm so sorry." This should be a fun time for her, and now Jenna is going to ruin all of that. No way in hell she'll keep her smart-ass comments to herself.

"Oh lookie, my baby daddy decided to show up after all. Wasn't sure since you *blocked* my number." Her tone is anything but sweet, and I know the others overheard.

"Cut your shit, Jenna," I hiss between my teeth. "Quit causing a scene."

"Better watch your mouth," the guy standing next to her warns. He's a big dude, whoever he is, but not bigger than me, so I stand taller and let him know his intimidation tricks won't work.

"And who the hell are you?"

"This is my brother, Jacob," Jenna says. "Since you're here now, though—"

Lennon turns around and glares. "He's here with me."

Jenna's face hardens as her eyes gaze down to Lennon's belly. "Why? I already *know* he's not the father of your child." She folds her arms over her bump. "But I'm willing to bet you're the reason he's denying our baby boy. It's *her*, isn't it? Why you kept running…"

Lennon's eyes flick to mine. "Boy?" Her voice is just above a whisper, but everything's so quiet around us that Jenna overhears.

"That's right. It's a boy," Jenna replies smugly.

Lennon snorts. "Congrats, but Hunter's not the father. So it's time to move on and leave him alone."

"He *is* the father." Jenna takes a step forward as if to make her point and threaten me. "Sorry, *princess*. Hunter's not the guy you think he is, and I'm going to prove that as soon as the baby's born."

"Jenna." I'm ready to drag her away so half the floor doesn't hear our business.

"No, let me." Lennon holds up her hand to stop me and flashes a smug grin. "You may think you won with your detective skills involving me and my parents, but you only did me a favor. So, thank you. Your little stunt allowed me to stand up to my overbearing mother. If I've learned anything since getting pregnant, it's that I'm sick and tired of people like you thinking they can control and manipulate others. I'm about to be a mom and protecting my child is my main priority, so I know why you're acting like this—to protect your baby too—however, you need to grow up and face reality. If Hunter thought there was even the slightest chance of being the father of your baby, he *would* do the right thing and step up because that's the kind of man he is. He's done everything to help me get through my boyfriend's death. So you can try to sabotage our lives, but in the end, he'll prove to you once and for all that you have the wrong man. So I suggest you tell the right guy and let them know you're having his baby because Hunter can't have kids."

Damn. Badass Lennon is sexy as fuck.

Jenna's eyes widen as her body straightens in surprise. "What?" She shakes her head with an eye roll. "You're lying. I don't believe you."

Jacob stands next to his sister, looking at her as if he's thinking the same.

Lennon glances at me with soft eyes, and I give her a head nod to continue, knowing she's asking for permission.

"He found out years ago and has the test results to prove it, so if you want to keep wasting your time and ours, then go ahead. But in the end, don't be surprised when he says he *told you so*."

As I love watching her fight my battles for me, I grab her shoulder and pull her toward me.

"You really can't have kids?" Jenna asks. "Or is that something you tell all the girls you fuck?"

"I've been telling you since day one I'm not the father," I remind her. "I didn't feel like I needed to put my personal business out there, but now that you've been made aware, do what you gotta do once the baby's born to know for sure. But you should tell Craig since he *is* the father."

"Craig? Your ex-boyfriend?" Jacob's sharp tone snaps through the air. "Drug dealing, abusive Craig?"

Jenna grimaces and closes her eyes as if she's trying to blast herself into another timeline. "Let's go. We'll reschedule."

We watch as they walk through the double doors, and when we turn around, everyone's staring at us.

"Sorry," I say.

Then I turn to Lennon, worried she'll be embarrassed, but she surprises me by rewarding me with a smile.

"I think you dodged a bullet with that one," she teases.

Releasing a relieved sigh, I grab her hand and squeeze. "You have no idea."

After the shit with Jenna, we had a successful tour, and I could see how relieved Lennon was after her questions were answered. I know she's nervous about it all, and I want to be here for her in any way I can. If she wants me with her or in the waiting room, I'll do whatever she asks. I'd never overstep, but I won't ask her either. She'll let me know when she's ready.

Lying in bed, I think about the day and how much I selfishly wish Lennon were carrying my baby. I wish we didn't have to correct everyone who assumed I'm the father, but as soon as those thoughts hit me, the guilt of taking Brandon's place eats at me. Like clockwork.

I look up at the ceiling, lying in the bed he used to share with Lennon, and wish I could talk to him. So much has changed since he passed away, but one thing that hasn't is how much I miss him. Drinking beers, talking shit, bringing up our old college days. The days of picking up girls, frat parties, and football games. The only way I can get through the loss of him is telling myself he'd be happy and proud I'm taking care of Lennon and the baby. And hope he wouldn't find us getting closer as a betrayal.

It's that little piece of hope that I cling to.

I toss and turn for an hour before my phone vibrates on my nightstand. When I see Lennon's name on the screen, I unlock it and read her message.

LENNON

I can't sleep.

HUNTER

What's wrong?

LENNON

I'm lonely in here. Can't get comfortable. Would you mind lying with me?

It's okay if you say no.

I release a sharp breath, not expecting her to ask that. It's been a long time since she's asked me to lie with her, and truthfully, I've missed it. Though it was necessary to allow some time to pass and keep some distance between us, I can't deny her. She makes me weak in the fucking knees, and I'd do anything for her.

HUNTER

Of course I will.

I'm only in my boxer briefs but don't bother putting on extra clothes before heading into her room. It's dark except for the faint glow of the streetlights coming through the curtains. She's lying on her side and blinks up at me as I close her door, neither of us saying a word. As I walk around the bed to slip under the covers, my heart hammers in my chest, knowing how deep I already am.

But fuck it.

Lennon shouldn't have to be alone in the first place.

I wrap my body around hers and she melts into mine. With her belly, we can only spoon, so she rests her head on one arm as I wrap the other around her stomach.

"Thank you," she whispers once we're settled.

"Of course."

Swallowing, I try to relax my mind so my body can stop being so tense. I know she can feel it, and I want her to be comfortable enough to fall asleep. After a few minutes, my hand shifts, and her stomach moves.

"Was that a—"

Lennon giggles, her belly tightening as she does. "She's kicking." Then she takes me by surprise and grabs my hand, moving it lower. "She's pretty active at night. I can usually feel her moving around down here." With her hand on top of mine, I feel more kicks.

"That's the coolest thing ever," I tell her genuinely. "Doesn't it feel like she's going to pop right out of your skin?"

Lennon chuckles. "Yes. The closer it gets, the more it feels like there's no more room for her in there, and she's gonna bust out. But her little kicks reassure me."

"How so?" I ask softly.

"That she's doing okay in there, letting me know she's growing and getting ready to meet me. Maybe it sounds crazy, but—"

"It doesn't sound crazy. Especially after what you've been through."

"I can't wait to see what she looks like," she whispers. "Feels like this last trimester has dragged on, and now there are only five more weeks till my due date. Seems like I've been waiting so long, and now she could be here any day."

"She'll be here before you know it," I reassure her, glancing at the crib and rocking chair on the other side of the room.

She only nods in response, her body relaxing, melting into mine as my hand stays on her lower stomach. The kicks have stopped, but I selfishly don't want to let her go. Watching her body change these past several months has been pretty awesome, and she looks even more stunning than ever before.

My heart finally goes back to normal, and when I'm fairly certain she's fallen asleep, I press a kiss in her hair and whisper good night.

I'm half asleep when she stirs, and my eyes pop open.

"What's wrong?" I whisper when she continues to fidget.

Her breathing picks up, and I can tell she's waking up.

"Do you want me to move?" I ask, unsure what I should do.

"Hunter." Her voice is low and raspy. "Touch me."

My heart pounds, and I'm positive I heard her wrong. She must be talking in her sleep. Swallowing hard, I manage to ask, "W-what?"

"Please, Hunter." Her legs shift around. "I want you to touch me," she begs.

Hell, maybe *I'm* dreaming.

She arches, and by the way my dick hardens, I know I'm not.

I lean up on my elbow and bring my lips to her ear. "Where?" I whisper.

"Between my legs."

Jesus Christ. My heart lodges in my throat, and it takes me a second to clear it.

"Are you sure, Lennon?"

"Yes." She releases a breath. "*Please.*"

The way she's begging is what my wet dreams are made of. How the hell could I deny her, knowing how badly she wants and needs it, even if it'll fuck me up even more than I already am?

"Is that safe?" I ask. "For the baby, I mean."

I'm an idiot.

"Yes, it's completely safe."

Inhaling a deep breath before moving my hand lower and around her belly, I slide inside her panties. Leaning my forehead against the top of her head, I slide one finger up her slit, feeling how wet she is. The moment I find her clit, her breath catches, and my eyes roll to the back of my head.

Goddamn.

This is a fucking bad idea, but there's no way I can stop now.

I make small circles on her clit, adding a little pressure when she releases a whimper. My whole body reacts to that little sound, and I'm sure she can feel my cock digging into her ass cheek. There's no denying how badly I want her.

Lennon rocks her hips against my palm, encouraging me as I explore, and when I slip a finger inside her, she tightens around me as my thumb works her perfect little bud.

"Oh my God…" She moans, her hand fisting the blanket next to her. "Right there, Hunter. Don't stop."

Fuck me.

Hearing her whimper my name when all I want to do is make her mine has to be the worst kind of torture. I live for the times she says my name, but *this*—I want to do everything and anything to keep hearing her desperately say it.

My lips move to her ear. "I've got you, Lennon."

Sliding her slickness around her cunt, I press two fingertips to her swollen clit and make quick circles. Her hips buck wildly, and when I add more pressure, I know she's almost there.

"Let go, sweetheart," I whisper. Though the thought has me wanting to tell her to hold back for as long as possible. But this isn't for me. This is what she needs. I can't be selfish right now, no matter how badly I want to be, or how goddamn hard it is to resist when she's this close. "Fuck, Lennon."

"Hunter…*yes*."

I mold my body against hers, holding her tight as I continue to drive her toward the edge. She's so fucking wet, it's hard to keep my pace, but I make it my life mission to give her exactly what she needs.

"You're close," I tell her, my voice low and raspy as I try to control my breathing.

"Yes…" She nods, biting down on her lower lip. "So close." Her hips move in sync with my hand, seeking relief.

"What do you need, Lennon? Tell me." I'm pretty certain she can hear the desperation in my tone.

"Don't stop," she says between ragged breaths. "Keep talking to me."

I chuckle lightly against her ear, loving the idea of her orgasming to my voice. "Okay, I won't stop." I quickly move my fingers through her arousal and slide two inside her. "You're so tight, Lennon. Holy fuck."

She squeezes her pussy around them as I continue thrusting. Lennon's head falls back to my chest, her eyes closed as her lips part. I watch the way she responds to me, imagine how she'd look coming around my cock, and as soon as I envision it, Lennon's body erupts.

Quickly, I bring my fingers to her clit, and her eyes roll to the back of her head. I could fucking watch her all night long, kiss every inch of her, and hear her beg for more.

Lennon sinks her teeth into her bottom lip, and when she turns her face slightly toward me, our mouths are only inches apart.

Fuck it.

As I add pressure to her swollen bud, working to give her another wave of pleasure, I crash my lips to hers. I shouldn't, but right now in the darkness, we aren't two broken people who can't be together. We're Hunter and Lennon, chemically drawn to each other, neither wanting to deny the other. In the dark, we're different people who can get lost in each other, and come morning, we'll go back to the way things have to be.

She kisses me, and her back arches at the same time her hips buck, and she goes off like a train whistle. Lennon's body goes into an aftershock neither of us is prepared for.

"Holy shit…" she whispers, then licks her lips. The way her chest rises and falls, I know she was as affected by that kiss as I am.

Reluctantly, I slowly slide out of her panties, and she shifts back into position so we're spooning again. Goose bumps cover her arm as I brush my hand over her soft skin, and pride fills my ego knowing I gave them to her.

A moment passes, and Lennon's hand reaches between us.

"What're you doing?" I ask in a panic.

Her fingers brush my boxer briefs, my cock still hard from everything—touching her, kissing her, feeling her climaxing around me.

"I want to give you relief too." Her voice is so small as she turns to her back. "You need it."

Jesus fucking Christ.

Swallowing hard, I shake my head. "Lennon, no." That's a goddamn bad idea. When she starts to slip her fingers inside, I quickly grab her wrist. "This wasn't about me. It was about your pleasure."

"I don't want you thinking I used you," she says softly.

Swallowing hard, I wonder if I could plead momentary insanity if I let her touch me.

No. I know I couldn't handle her hands on me. There's no way I could stop. The moment she wrapped her delicate fingers around my dick, I'd pin her down, and everything would change.

This moment was for *her.*

"I'd never think that, Lennon. Never," I reassure her.

She looks up at me, her beautiful blue eyes that I've memorized since the night we met.

Lennon pulls her arm back and shifts to face me. "Thank you, Hunter." She brings a hand up and cups my cheek, her thumb rubbing slowly across my hot skin.

I give her a small nod, then lean down and kiss her forehead.

"You're one of the good ones," she says when I pull away. "I wish things were different in our world. You deserve someone so much better than me—"

I open my mouth to disagree, but she shakes her head not to interrupt her.

"Someone who isn't such an emotional mess and could give you everything and more the way you always give to others. And when you find her, she'll be the luckiest woman in the world."

God.

I want to say so much to her right now.

Tell her I already have.

Remind her it's *her* I want. She's who I've always wanted.

Tell her how good we'd be together, how good we already are even as just friends.

Beg her to fight for me.

But I don't say shit.

I can't.

I'm thankful we're in the dark, and she can't see the tears brimming in my eyes. When it comes to her, I'm so fucking torn. I know she feels *something* for me, yet she refuses to allow herself to do anything about it.

I know Brandon was the love of her life, and that's something I'll never be.

CHAPTER THIRTY-NINE

LENNON

AFTER THE HOSPITAL tour a month ago, I've been thinking about Hunter having a baby with Jenna and it's made me a bit stabby.

Okay, *a lot* stabby.

I know what Hunter said and that his chances of having kids are low, which I believe, but even if there's a one in a million chance that he could, what if Jenna's right, and he is the father?

That thought weighs on me, though it shouldn't, considering he's not mine to be territorial of. I still feel protective of him, though, as my best friend. Maybe it was those feelings or the fact that I keep resisting how I truly feel that had me texting him that night to lie with me.

The moment he wrapped his body around mine, I didn't care about the consequences, the guilt, or the past. All that I could think of was the present and how badly I wanted him to touch me —even if just once. I didn't think he would, though I should've known better. His hands so intimately on my body caught every nerve on fire, and I burned hot for him. I needed him—in any way he'd give me—and when my body shook, I knew my feelings poured out after holding them back.

I was lusting over him.

Or worse—*falling*.

That night with him in the dark is where things between us stayed. When I woke up the next morning, he was gone. I found him in the kitchen, making breakfast, and it was as if nothing had happened. We ate together like always, I left for work, and he texted me a couple of times to check on me. That night, we ate dinner together, watched the season's final episode of *YOU* that had us both dropping our jaws, and chatted more about baby names.

I couldn't tell if he wasn't bringing it up for my sake or if he wanted us to pretend it had never happened since I'd nearly begged him to touch me in the first place. Did he only do it to make me happy and he was now embarrassed? Was it too awkward to even discuss?

Did he wish it never happened?

The thoughts flooded my mind for days, and since he never brought it up, neither did I. Now a month has passed, and it's like we've both decided to take this secret to the grave. I'm not sure what I would say if he did mention it, especially after all this time, but I can't help thinking what it meant to him—if anything.

Did it mean as much to him as it did to me?

Why would it? He poured his heart out to me, and I turned him down. Now all I can think about is how he touched me out of pity, and the thought gives me secondhand embarrassment.

Ugh.

We managed to survive Thanksgiving together. It was the first big holiday without Brandon, which brought on bouts of sadness, but Sophie and Maddie came over, and we all feasted together. Didn't hear from my mother either, not that I expected to at this point. My sisters helped keep my mind busy enough not to dwell on my feelings, though.

Then Mason and Liam stopped over later to watch football with Hunter. We decided to make this our new *Friendsgiving* tradition and watch all the *Friends* holiday episodes.

Of course Maddie then suggested we play football with girls

versus boys. I kindly reminded her I was too pregnant to even walk to the bathroom without losing my breath.

With the baby coming any day now, everything is ready and set up. Baby items have not only taken over my bedroom and closet, but a few family friends sent us a high chair, jumper, sleeper rocker, swing, and bouncy seat, which are now in the kitchen and living room. Poor Hunter has to walk through a maze to get from one room to the other.

He hasn't complained once, though, not that I expect him to. Hunter's embraced every part of this, which makes him even more incredible. He surprised me last weekend and brought home a cute stuffed bear that we named Lil Paws, so we could "test" out all the baby gear. It was adorable to see Hunter get so excited, which makes me even more sad that he can't have kids of his own. He deserves more than anyone to find a woman who can make him happy, get married, build a life and start a family with, even if it's through adoption or another way. I can see it in his eyes that he wants that more than anything.

Now it's a week before my due date, and I've been having contractions for the past few days. I know Braxton Hicks is common, and it's my body's way of practicing, but it hurts like a bitch.

"You okay?" Hunter asks as I hunch over the couch and press a hand to my back. "More back pain?"

"Yeah, it's a stabbing sensation." I squeeze my eyes and try to breathe through it. "Is it too early to ask for drugs?" I half-tease.

"Want ice or heat?" he asks before he walks to the kitchen.

"Both," I reply. "And maybe a shot of tequila."

Hunter chuckles, and moments later, he returns with a frozen bag of veggies and a hot washcloth. "Turn a bit," he directs and sits behind me. He lifts my shirt and pulls down the band of my leggings.

"On the left side, it feels like a damn Charley horse," I tell him, fighting the pain.

Placing the ice on my lower back, he wraps the hot cloth

around my neck. I try to relax to see if the tension will ease up, and after twenty minutes, I finally feel a lot better.

"Would you mind grabbing me a bottle of my nail polish from the bathroom?" I ask before he takes a seat. He gives me a funny look in return. "I want to have pretty feet for labor."

Chuckling, he shakes his head but doesn't say anything as he walks into the hallway. A minute later, he returns with two bottles.

"Which color?" He holds up a pink color and a teal glittery one.

"Your pick," I say.

"You want me to choose?" he asks, arching a brow.

"Yeah." I shrug. "Which one do you think?"

"Hmm, okay." He holds them up and looks at them with deep consideration. "The pink one is obvious since it's a girl, but this one…" He holds up the other. "This one says I'm a badass."

"That's pretty insightful for nail polish," I mock. "Teal it is."

Hunter hands it over, and I prop one foot up on the coffee table as I shake the bottle. Once I open it, I lean over as far as I can, struggling to reach my foot. When I can't, I lean my arm around my belly and try that way.

"Well, shit." I groan.

"I think there's an error in your hypothesis," he quips, clearly holding back laughter. "Belly circumference is bigger than arm's reach."

I glare, a smug grin painted on his chiseled face. "Thank you, Einstein. I realize that now." Doesn't help that my back was hurting earlier. "I can figure this out," I say, more to myself than him.

I lean my leg slightly outward, keeping my foot planted on the edge of the table, and stretch my arm out as far as possible. Barely reaching my big toe, I manage to paint half of it. It's half-assed, but then I realize I can't reach the next one.

"Ugh." I surrender, slouching.

Hunter clears his throat, causing me to look at him. His arms cross over his broad chest and he gives me his infamous shit-eating grin.

"What?"

"Here, give me." He holds out his hand, and I furrow my brows.

"For what?"

"You want your nails painted or not?"

My shoulders fall as I hand it over. Hunter sits down on the coffee table, takes my foot, and places it on his knee. I watch as he meticulously paints my nails, one by one, and even holds up my foot and blows on my toes to dry them faster.

"What do you think?"

"Well, if the construction biz doesn't work out, you have a plan B," I tease, smiling at how pretty they turned out. "How are you so good at that?"

"Years of carefully tearing shit down, measuring things, and fine-tuning blueprints. It's not much different," he explains. "All meticulous tasks."

He motions for me to give him my other foot, so I do. Again, he focuses intensely on my nails and does a great job. Hunter blows on them, and once they're dry, I stretch my legs out and admire his work. Hunter takes his phone out and snaps a picture.

"What're you doing?"

"Sending a pic of my handiwork to Hayden," he says with a chuckle. "He's gonna give me so much shit."

I snort at the fact that he's willing to send his brother a picture, knowing he'll be teased. His phone vibrates. Hunter shakes his head with a smile after reading it.

"What'd he say?"

He gives me a side-glance and pops a brow.

"What? Tell me."

He inhales a deep breath, then chuckles. "He said I'm whipped."

"Hey! Did you tell him it was *your* idea!"

"No."

"Great. Now he probably thinks I'm a blood-sucking villain who makes you paint my toenails and wait on me hand and foot."

"Trust me, he doesn't think that." He shakes his head, slipping his phone back into his pocket.

"Thank you, Hunter," I tell him. "You're a man of many talents." *In and out of the bedroom.*

I look at him, wondering if he can read my thoughts, and when he blinks away with a nervous shiver, I fear he can.

Things go quiet, and when my phone beeps with a text message a minute later, I'm thankful for the distraction.

SOPHIE

So I met someone.

LENNON

WHAT? Tell me more.

SOPHIE

We met through that dating app I downloaded months ago. Of course I was reluctant at first, but then we had brunch last week, and *sigh* he's so dreamy. Great job, owns his own house, even has a little dog.

LENNON

Wow, really? I'm so happy for you, sis! But why is he single if he's so 'perfect'? Did you find his skeletons yet?

SOPHIE

He says he hasn't found someone he's been able to fully connect with yet. We chatted for three hours at the restaurant! It felt so natural.

This is the most I've ever heard Sophie talk about a guy before, and I want to be happy for her, but I'm also cautious. I thought my ex, Malcolm, was something special too before he cheated, tried to humiliate me, then broke my heart. Of course I got the last word, but it still affected me for a long time.

LENNON

> YAY, that's exciting! What's his name? Do you have a pic of him?

SOPHIE

> Here's his profile pic, and his name is Weston.

I look at the photo she sent and give my approval with a thumbs-up emoji.

LENNON

> He looks cute. What's his job?

SOPHIE

> He's a correctional officer. His uniform is sexy too ;)

LENNON

> LOL, good to know! Do I get to meet him?

SOPHIE

> Not yet! Hopefully soon, though. We're going on another date this weekend. I can't wait!

I can practically hear her squeals in my head, and I'm genuinely excited for her.

"What're you laughing about?" Hunter asks.

"Sophie. She met a guy, and she's gushing about him. It's pretty sweet." I set my phone down and look at him.

"She give up on Mason already?" he teases.

I snort, shrugging. "I think she was sick of waiting, and she should be. If he was interested, he had plenty of opportunities to make it known."

Hunter frowns, then looks away. "Well, Mason's had a rough past, which changed him a lot. It's not *if* Mason's interested in someone that's the problem—it's his issues that stop him. Not to mention who his father is and his family background. Let's just say, there's been a lot of drama."

"What do you mean?"

"His father is the district attorney, and I know firsthand what it's like to grow up with a father in a public position. It puts him in the spotlight, good and bad. He dated someone in college and…" He pauses and shakes his head. "Sorry, it's not my story to tell. I don't know if he'd want you or Sophie to know."

I nod, respecting his decision not to air out Mason's dirty laundry, but take the opportunity to bring up something else.

"So I heard they have a girl roommate?" I eye him and watch the corner of his mouth tilt up.

"*Had*. She moved out a while ago."

My mouth falls open. "So they've lived with some girl all this time, yet no one has ever said a word about her? Is it a big secret or something? I've never even met her or know her name or anything."

"It's complicated, and she was never home. If you wanna know, you're gonna have to ask them. I'm sure one day it will all come out," he says with a mock grin, teasing me. I don't push it any further, though curiosity has the best of me. It says a lot about how much he cares about them and keeping their trust, and I don't want to overstep.

We spend the rest of the night munching on snacks and watching TV, and at ten, we decide to head in for the night. This last week of school before Christmas break is so busy between getting everything ready for maternity leave and writing a detailed schedule for the substitute teacher who's taking over my class for the next three months.

It's three in the morning when pain shoots down my stomach to my groin. It feels like the baby is clawing her way out, and when I try to move, the pain intensifies. I manage to move onto my side and pull my knees toward my chest. The Braxton Hicks are stronger than they've ever been before, and breathing through them isn't an option. Instead, I groan, unable to hold back.

"Lennon!" Hunter whips my bedroom door open. "Oh my God. You're not okay."

"No, no, I'm fine. I just need to stand and reposition myself."

Hunter grabs my hands, pulls me to my feet, and I immediately hunch over the bed as I try to catch my breath.

"These can't just be Braxton Hicks, Lennon. You're in labor," he states matter-of-factly.

"It's too early…" I argue. "I'm not ready. I have to work tomorrow. I can hold her in. It's probably false labor."

"*What*?" he asks, startled. "You *are* ready! You're freaking out because it's really time! We have to get you to the hospital."

Not letting me argue, he goes to his room and comes back dressed thirty seconds later. He grabs my hospital bag from my closet, then asks if I want to change.

"No, they'll make me wear a gown anyway," I tell him, then he's taking my hand and leading me out the door.

Everything moves at double speed when we get to the labor and delivery floor. They admit me into a room, hook me up to the monitors, insert an IV, and I learn I'm already four centimeters dilated.

I text Sophie and Maddie, knowing they're probably sleeping and won't see my messages, but I want them to know as soon as possible. Hunter, of course, is a godsend, always asking me what I need, getting me ice chips, and rubbing my shoulders. The fact that he's never experienced this before has me wondering how he's so calm and eager to help in any way he can. I thought I'd be the one talking him through this, but instead, Hunter's keeping me relaxed.

The nurses assume Hunter's the dad, and since neither of us

corrects them, they wrap a hospital bracelet around his wrist. He might not have fathered this baby, but he's as invested in this as I am.

"I want you in here," I tell him after the fourth hour of waiting.

"I am," he says, furrowing his brows.

Tilting my head, I shoot him a look. "I mean when it's time to deliver," I clarify. "I know we haven't talked about it, considering everything, but as I've learned, plans change."

"You do? Are you sure?"

Grinning, I nod. "Well, I'm ordering you to stay above my waist, though."

Hunter cracks a smile and laughs. "Deal."

An hour later, my doctor arrives and breaks my water to speed up the progress. Dr. Potter warns me the contractions are about to get more painful, and if I want the epidural, it's now or never.

"Yes, please. It's hurting badly already." I wince. She squeezes my hand, then tells me she'll be back.

"I can't believe I'm going to meet her soon," I say to Hunter once the room clears out. "It feels surreal." He stands next to the bed, then bends down and kisses my forehead. "I'm scared," I admit. "It's so painful."

"I know." He brushes his hand across my cheek and fixes the flyaway hairs on my face. I love when he does that. It's comforting. "Brandon would be so excited. He'd be losing his damn mind," Hunter tells me with a soft smile, and tears well in my eyes.

He knows I was thinking about Brandon and always knows what to say. I wish he were here to experience this with me, and I miss him so damn much, but knowing I'm about to have his baby gives me the strength to do this without him. Though I don't always feel strong, and there are days I want to curl into a ball, I feel his presence. It gives me the comfort I need to keep moving forward.

Twenty minutes later, a crew comes in, ready to give me the epidural. I can already feel the contractions coming harder and faster. I try to catch my breath as I pant through them. Holy fuck.

As they explain the procedure, my eyes widen at the needle and the fact that I need to be completely still or I could get nerve damage or worse. I know the risks, but seeing and experiencing it is different than reading about it.

One of the nurses nearly folds me in half over the bed while I hold a pillow to my chest. Hunter's standing next to her, looking concerned as hell, and though I can't talk or move, I make eye contact with him to let him know I'm okay.

"You're doing great. Almost done," a nurse says.

I try to steady my breathing, and when the anesthesiologist tells me it's in, and she just needs to tape it up, I release a relieved sigh.

The contractions that were about an eight out of ten on the pain scale earlier are now at a zero. So I take advantage of it and try to rest.

"Take my phone in case my sisters finally wake up and text me," I say, handing it over.

"What's your passcode? Is it still 6-6-6?" he asks smugly, reminding me of the time I freaked out on him after Brandon's accident when he tried to get into my phone. I was mean as hell, but it didn't stop him from being there for me at a time when I needed him the most.

"Har, har," I mock. "It's 0318."

Hunter furrows his brows as if he's trying to figure it out. I shrug. "The night we met. When Brandon and I started dating."

"Oh." He nods but doesn't say anything else about it.

I rest my head on the pillow and enjoy the magic of drugs as another contraction hits, but I don't feel it. A chair scratches the floor, and Hunter sits in it next to me. He takes my hand and holds it while I drift off to sleep.

A nurse wakes me up an hour later, and I look over and see Hunter fell asleep too. He's hunched over, resting his head on his arm but still holding my hand. I feel bad for waking him, considering he's been up since early this morning when he rushed me here.

I'm dilated to six centimeters now, which means I'm making progress. A nurse tells me to rest, and she'll come back in a few hours, but if we need anything to push the call button.

I grab my phone from Hunter and see my sisters sent me half a dozen text messages each and called me three times.

"Hey, you were sleeping on the job," I tease when he shifts in his seat.

"Shit, sorry." He scrubs his hands over his face.

"It's fine, don't worry. Why don't you go get some coffee while I call them?"

"Are you sure?" he asks as if he doesn't want to leave me, which I find so damn sweet.

"Yes, I'll be fine," I reassure him. "She's not coming for a few more hours at least."

Though I can't feel the contractions, there is a little tightness.

Once Hunter leaves, I call Sophie first, knowing she's probably already on her way to pick up Maddie.

It rings once. "Soph is speeding, so you better be holding that baby girl inside your vagina!" Maddie says as soon as she picks up, confirming my suspicions.

"Well, tell her to slow down! I'm not even pushing the baby out yet."

"Oh, thank God. Soph, you can slow down, geez!" she shouts.

"My baby needs her aunts in one piece, please."

"We'll be there in five minutes, less if Sophie blows this red light," Maddie says.

"Oh, for fuck's sake. You two are gonna give me a heart attack. Stop freaking me out!" I shout.

I stay on the phone with them until they enter my room.

"Whew, no baby yet," Maddie says when she sees me.

Rolling my eyes at her dramatics, I give them hugs as soon as they come to me.

"Where's loverboy?" Sophie asks with a shit-eating grin.

"Don't start with me. I'm about to pop out a baby!" I scowl. "I told him to go get coffee since he was falling asleep. He should be back soon."

They sit with me as I recap everything that's happened. I sent my boss a text and let her know what was going on, and Hunter said he was taking his vacation early, which made me feel guilty as hell, but arguing with him about it was pointless. He'd do it regardless.

Hunter returns with a large hot coffee and a cup of ice chips for me. My stomach is growling, but I'm not allowed to eat until after, which is horseshit if you ask me. They probably say that so you'll work harder at pushing your baby out. Like a weird labor incentive.

My sisters and Hunter keep a conversation going, occupying me while time feels like it's dragging. Everything felt so rushed, and now that I'm situated, this waiting game is for the birds.

Finally, my doctor comes in with two nurses to see how far I'm dilated. Hunter stays by my head as they check me and announce I'm fully dilated, and they're going to get everything ready now.

"What does that mean?" Maddie asks giddily. "Is it baby time?"

"Yep, gonna have you start pushing in a minute, Lennon." The nurses move effortlessly around the room to set up for delivery. When Dr. Potter and I discussed my birth plan at my last appointment, I told her I wouldn't have my mom or the father of the baby with me, so I wanted my two sisters in here instead. I hadn't decided on asking Hunter at that point, but there's no way I want him to leave now. My chest tightens at how real and fast this is all happening.

Suddenly, I feel like I can't do this. It doesn't feel right.

"Hunter," I mutter softly, but when his gaze finds mine, I know he heard me over all the commotion.

"Yeah? Are you okay?" He leans over so we're only inches apart.

"I'm freaking out. I don't know why."

"Lennon, look at me…"

I release a short breath and stare into his intense eyes.

"You're the bravest person I've ever met, and I know deep in my heart that you can do this, you hear me? I know you wish Brandon were here with you, but you have to believe he is. He's going to be watching over you and the baby for the rest of your lives, so use that comfort to give you strength."

I steady my breathing and nod frantically, tears blurring my vision at how soothing his words are to me.

"You've got this, Lennon. I know you do," he encourages, his tone firm and confident.

"I couldn't do this without you, Hunter," I tell him with pure vulnerability. "Thank you for being here. I know this isn't easy for you."

"I'm here, Lennon." He winks, then leans down and presses his lips to my forehead. "No matter what, remember?"

Hunter's motivational chat distracted me while the nurses finished up everything, and now the doctor tells me it's time to start pushing. Dr. Potter gives directions to Sophie and Maddie, who are in charge of holding my feet up while I'm breathing through the contractions. When I'm not, I'll rest them in the stirrups for a few seconds before starting again.

"Got it?" Dr. Potter asks us. "Teamwork."

"I'm exhausted already," I quip.

"Don't say that yet, Mama. Let's do a practice push for ten seconds."

The next ninety minutes test everything inside me as I sweat, curse, and groan. When the doctor says *one more push and she'll be here*, I picture Brandon's face. Tears stream down my cheeks as the sadness of him not being here hits me harder than ever before, and I use every ounce of bitterness I have to push as hard as I can.

Then the world stops.

And my body proves it's much stronger than I ever thought possible. When I finally take a breath, I feel her little body being placed on my chest. The nurses wipe her clean as I look at her precious face looking back at me. I tear up at how much I already love her. Her arms and legs flail and stretch as she tries to cry, and I'm too in shock to know what I'm supposed to do.

"She's gorgeous, Lennon," Sophie says.

"She really is," Maddie adds.

They're both tearing up and staring at my precious girl.

"Hey, baby," I whisper, my bottom lip trembling as I brush a finger against her cheek. "You're finally here."

"Do you want to cut the cord, Daddy?" a nurse asks, and the four of us freeze.

"No, I think Mommy should," he answers without missing a beat. "She's the one who did all the work."

I look up at Hunter with tears in my eyes, and though my vision is a bit fuzzy, I see the admiration in his expression, and I want to pull him into the biggest hug for being here for me. He encouraged me nonstop, let me squeeze the shit out of his hand, and whispered in my ear not to give up when I felt I couldn't do it anymore.

He's truly one of a kind.

The next couple of hours are insane. My head spins as everything happens so fast. I cut the cord. They stitch me up as the nurses finish cleaning up the baby, then hand her back to me all wrapped up. My emotions bubble over with the realization that she's really mine. My little girl.

Doing skin to skin was important to me, so they let me unwrap her and lay her on my bare chest for an hour before they took her for shots and tests. I hate that Brandon isn't here to be with her, and as if Hunter senses my anxiety, he asks if I want him to go with her. I nod and ask him to take pictures or not let her out of his sight. For all the hospital knows, he is the dad, and if that's what it takes to give me peace of mind, then I'd scream it from the rooftops. No matter what, he'll always be someone important in her life.

Sophie and Maddie stay with me while I'm wheeled into a new room. I didn't even realize they were taking photos until I see all the pics they got, and as soon as they message them over, I send one to my mother.

LENNON

> She's here. Healthy and perfect. I hope you meet her someday.

I don't know if she'll respond or even care at this point, but I won't let her use it against me in the future that I didn't tell her.

A nurse wheels the baby into my room with Hunter on her tails, and he winks as soon as he sees me. This man never ceases to amaze me. He's been so protective of me, does whatever I need, and I know, without a doubt, he won't be any different with the baby.

"She has a good set of lungs on her," the nurse teases. "She's ready to eat."

Hunter excuses himself when the nurse starts talking about breastfeeding, and I know this is probably uncomfortable for him. I read up on it as much as I could, but I seriously have no idea what I'm doing. The nurse helps me, and within a matter of ten minutes, the baby has latched on and is sucking away.

"Try to get her to switch to the other breast in about five minutes or so," the nurse instructs before she leaves.

"Does that hurt?" Maddie asks, wrinkling her nose. "Your boobs are massive, by the way."

"Thanks." I snort. "It feels…weird. I read that it hurts after a while, though," I say, staring at this little human I'm now responsible for.

"She really is beautiful," Sophie gushes. "I can see Brandon in her."

I smile. "Me too."

"Did you choose a name?" Maddie asks.

"Yeah, I think so…" I rub the pad of my finger along her forehead. Her hair is light, like mine, but she has Brandon's nose. "I was torn between two, but after seeing her, I think she definitely looks like an Alison." I stare, captivated by her little features. "After—"

"The singer of your favorite song," Sophie interjects. "Alison Krauss."

"Yep," I say proudly.

After I manage to switch her to the other side, she proves to be an eating champ, and I'm so grateful. I've read breastfeeding horror stories, and I was worried I wouldn't be able to or she wouldn't latch on. I know we aren't out of the woods yet, but it gives me a sense of pride to be able to feed her right away.

After feeding Alison, my sisters get ready to leave, knowing I need to rest, but they promise to be back later that evening. Hunter returns just as they head out, and I tell him it's okay if he goes home to sleep. Of course he insists he's fine.

"My brother says congrats," he tells me, taking a seat in the rocking chair next to me.

"Oh, tell him thank you. You called him?"

"Yeah. Mason and Liam too. They said to let them know when they can come to visit."

I raise my brows. "They want to come to see the baby?"

"Is that so surprising?" He smirks.

I shrug. "A little."

"How'd feeding go?" he asks, changing the subject and keeping his focus on the baby. She's wrapped up like a burrito, sleeping soundly in my arms.

"Really well. Do you want to hold her?"

"I'd love to." His smirk deepens as he stands, then he leans over me and carefully picks her up. He acts like a total pro, not at all nervous about holding a newborn baby, which is surprising. "She's so tiny," he says once he sits back down.

"She was seven pounds, five ounces, and twenty inches long."

"That literally means nothing to me." He chuckles, not taking his eyes off her.

"It's pretty average. I think I was a tad bigger, but otherwise, the nurse said everything looks perfect." I beam with pride.

Even though my body is exhausted, and I hardly got any sleep before labor kicked in, I'm running on pure adrenaline right now. I could stare at her all day long or even worse—stare at *him* holding her all day long.

"That's awesome," he whispers, admiring her. "Does she have a name?"

"Alison," I respond with a proud smile. "Alison Kay Locke."

"Alison," he repeats. "From your favorite lullaby."

I'm shocked he remembered.

"Yes, and Kay after my mother. She introduced me to music and this song, so even if she doesn't want to be a part of our lives, Alison will always know where her name originated from." I can't hide the sadness in my tone, but I also won't give my mother the satisfaction of ruining this moment for me. Whether she came into this world out of wedlock doesn't matter. She's perfect and amazing, and I already feel so blessed to be her mom.

"If your mother doesn't, it's her loss. Trust me," Hunter says, meeting my eyes. "Alison's already changed my life in less than twenty-four hours, and I wouldn't have it any other way."

CHAPTER FORTY

HUNTER

Neither of us has slept very much in the past two weeks, but I've made it my mission to help Lennon with Alison as much as possible. No matter how many articles or websites I read beforehand, I still don't feel prepared. Lennon's told me several times that most new parents have no clue what the hell they're doing, and they wing it. I'm learning how true that is every day.

I know this isn't my baby, but I've helped take responsibility. Holding a tiny human is scary but also exhilarating and surreal. The nights are the hardest for Lennon because she's exhausted, and I've been trying to take turns getting up so she can sleep. We're navigating our way through this together as best as we can. As long as Alison's being held, she doesn't seem to cry.

Lennon's a natural at being a mom, and it's such a beautiful thing to watch. I worry she's not getting enough sleep or resting, but she insists she is between her yawns. Overall, though, it's not as intimidating as I thought it would be. I was a little nervous about holding her at first, but I'm nearly at a pro level now, especially after being a spit-up target a few dozen times.

Still, each time I look at Alison, a wave of guilt and sadness overcomes me. The grief of Brandon no longer being here hits me at the strangest times. Though I find myself thinking back about the stupid things we used to do in college and smiling, it doesn't hurt any less that he's no longer here. I wish he could meet his beautiful baby girl.

Mrs. Locke is over the moon in love with her and comes over to help out. I'm glad I get to see his mom more now too. It's nice to have a reason for her to drop by and still be a part of our lives. When she talks about Brandon, I notice she smiles at the memories like I do. We miss him, but I'm beyond grateful he left us a part of himself through Allie, especially for his mom and Lennon's sake.

It's early evening on New Year's Eve, and I already can't stop yawning. As I stand in the kitchen, making a pot of coffee, Lennon rounds the corner like she's on a mission.

Without saying a word, she grabs a mug from the cabinet and waits for the maker to beep. Once it's done, she pours it half-full, then fills the rest with creamer. Once it's perfectly mixed, she takes a sip and hums with a grin. I've learned not to get between her and coffee unless I want to lose a limb.

"Baby sleeping?"

"Yep. I snuck out when I smelled the coffee brewing. Also, has coffee always tasted so damn good?" She chuckles, pulling out the baby monitor from her back pocket, and sets it on the counter.

I pour some coffee and let it sit for a minute before daring to drink it. The last time I did, I burnt the fuck out of my mouth. "I think you're extra sensitive to the taste because you've been off the hard stuff for nine long months."

"Probably." She shrugs. "So did you think of your New Year's resolution yet?"

Shaking my head, I walk out of the kitchen. For the past week, she's asked each day what I plan to change in the new year. The only thing that comes to mind is wanting to change our relationship status, but I don't dare say that. I keep that buried deep inside next to the sounds of her moans as she comes. "Nope. I'm gonna be the same smart-ass I've always been. And I'm not dieting and already work out when I can. So I'm out of ideas. Did you think of yours?"

"Sleep," she says without a beat. "And have more sex."

My eyes meet hers. The air around us stills, and I clear my throat, only for her to laugh.

"Kidding. Jesus." She sits on the couch and tucks her feet under her body as she enjoys her coffee. I'm forced to adjust myself because my mind goes back to that night when she begged me to touch her. Fuck me if I'm not reliving that moment right now, wanting to lay her down on the couch and give her everything her body begs for. We still haven't talked about it, mainly because I haven't found a way to bring it up without it being awkward as hell. Maybe one day.

As I open my mouth to say something, Alison starts crying. Lennon lets out a sigh.

"I've got it," I tell her.

"Are you sure?"

"Absolutely."

When I walk into the room, I instantly know Alison needs a diaper change. The first time I changed it, I thought I was going to puke. Nothing's worse than baby shit, and I don't think anything could've prepared me for it. Or maybe I'm being dramatic about it. I watched a dozen YouTube tutorials by dads so I could learn how to do it correctly.

After Alison is changed, I carefully hold her and sit in the rocking chair. She's so precious and loved by everyone already.

"Did you think of your New Year's resolution?" I ask softly, laughing. We have chats all the time, and this little baby knows all my secrets.

"Really?" I ask as if she answered. "No more waking up in the middle of the night all year long? Wow, turning a new leaf so soon."

I hear Lennon's soft laughter in the doorway. She's smiling, and I notice the sparkle in her eye when her gaze finds mine. "See, you're the only one who's not on board with resolutions."

Lennon checks her phone. "Maybe I should go ahead and feed her since she's awake."

"Sounds good to me."

Lennon holds out her arms, and I hand Alison over. Giving her privacy as she breastfeeds, I grab the clean clothes from the hamper and throw them on the couch. Turning on the TV, I notice the New Year's Eve celebration has already begun and decide to text Hayden because I know he's having a hell of a time being in the city with all those people right now.

HUNTER

Surviving?

HAYDEN

KILL ME!

I burst out into laughter.

HUNTER

Just saw the madness on TV. Holy shit. Times Square is packed as fuck.

HAYDEN

I can't go anywhere. I'm basically trapped inside the apartment. Savannah planned a big party with all her theater people, and they're going to be singing karaoke all night long. Seriously. Kill me.

HUNTER

Better you than me. Happy New Year, bro. Next year is the wedding. Exciting things are happening.

HAYDEN

You too. Next year maybe you'll grow some balls and ask Lennon out.

I roll my eyes.

Shut the fuck up. And now I hope they sing nothing but show tunes all night.

I chuckle and lock my phone.

As I'm matching socks, I hear Lennon's angelic voice. The sound causes me to pause, and I mute the TV. Hearing her sing to Alison never gets old. There's so much passion in her voice and nearly takes my breath away. After a while, she goes quiet, and soon, she's stepping into the living room. Spit-up is on her shirt, and her hair is in a messy ponytail. She looks gorgeous as hell, but I try not to stare and bring my focus back to my clothes.

"I'm a hot-ass mess," she finally says, shaking her head. She looks at the TV and sees the countdown in the corner. "Why aren't you out having fun? There are tons of things going on downtown. I think Mason and Liam are throwing a party too. Why aren't you over there?"

"Because I'd rather be with you."

"Me in all my glory? I'm not fun. You should go," she insists.

Shaking my head, I smirk. "I know what my New Year's resolution is. I just figured it out."

"What's that?" Her breasts rise and fall as she waits for my next words.

"I'm not going to let you say anything negative about yourself anymore. News flash. I love spending time with you, Lennon. Baby poop and all."

She snorts, but I can tell she's in her head. So I grab a beer from the fridge and give her a minute. When I come back, she's playing on her phone, and I sit next to her. She moves closer, and I open my arms for her to lean on me. We watch the celebrations from the comfort of the couch, and I laugh at how miserable Hayden has to be.

Nearly every hour, Alison wakes up, and Lennon and I take

turns unless it's feeding time. We eat ramen noodles like broke-ass college students, and honestly, I wouldn't want to be anywhere else in the world other than right here with her.

By ten, we're both falling asleep. We've already watched the ball drop on the East Coast.

"I don't think I'm gonna make it another two hours," Lennon tells me, and I'm relieved because I'm exhausted as hell.

"Me neither," I admit. "Let's go to bed."

I stand, and so does she. Before taking a step, I turn and look at her. Though I want to place my lips on hers, I kiss her forehead and tell her Happy New Year. When we wake up, we'll be the same two people pretending nothing's going on between us. The unspoken words say more than we ever could.

The next morning, the smell of bacon has me crawling out of bed. Lennon is up early cooking, and I'm starving, so it's perfect timing. The coffee is already brewed, and the toast pops up as soon as I walk in. I step around Alison in her bouncer and make sure to speak to my sweet girl as I pass.

Lennon notices me and grins.

"Morning," she says, and I can't help but stare at the way her ass cheeks hang out of her little sleep shorts. Turning her head, she catches me gawking, but I'm not shy about it.

"Good morning," I tell her as I pour a cup of coffee. Before I can even take a sip, there's a knock on the door. Lennon shrugs, and I go to answer it. Thinking it will be Maddie or Sophie because they've been randomly stopping by on the weekends to visit the baby, I open the door, ready to give them shit, but find myself face-to-face with Lennon's parents. My grin falls, and I immediately build a wall, not allowing them in.

Mrs. Corrigan looks at me with hopeful eyes, but I don't move. I'm too protective of Lennon and Allie, and what she did was hurtful. Lennon hasn't talked about it much, but I know it hasn't been easy for her when she was so close to her parents.

"I can't let you in." I cross my arms over my chest and stand firmly. "Not after what happened last time."

Mrs. Corrigan's face softens. "We came"—she clears her throat—"I came to apologize. To make things right. I'm so sorry."

Lennon's dad puts his arm around her, and while I can hear her sincerity, I think he was the one who made all this happen. The man is stern and has strong family values, but he's not a monster. I knew that the first time I met him, just as I knew he loved his family more than life itself.

Before I can even reply, Lennon's voice interrupts my thoughts.

"Who is it?" Lennon asks from the kitchen. I step aside, and when she sees her parents, her eyes go wide. Shock and frustration are written all over her face. "What're you doing here?"

Her dad steps forward. "When your mother told me the truth, I wasn't happy. I expected more from you, but, Lennon, I'd *never* shut you out. I teach forgiveness and how we are not perfect creatures. My love for you and your sisters…nothing can erase that. The three of you are my pride and joy and always will be. I couldn't stand the thought of you thinking we didn't care about you or our grandbaby. So here we are."

I move out of the way, allowing her mom and dad to step inside.

Without waiting, her mother closes the gap and reaches out to Lennon. "Honey, I'm so sorry for being pushy. I know my girls are going to live their own lives, and I can't control that anymore. You'll understand one day what it's like. We've always wanted the best for you and your sisters. Ever since Maddie moved, it's been hard letting go. You girls gave me purpose," she admits. "I love you so much."

Lennon nods and gives her a small smile. "I love you too, Mom." When they hug, Lennon accepts her apology and ultimately forgives her mother's behavior. She wants her parents in their lives more than she wants to hold a grudge.

"I'm not going to lie, I was pretty disappointed when I found out you weren't married," her dad tells me. "It's not too late for you two, so I'm not giving up. But…" He looks at his wife, and they hold a silent conversation before he continues. "When you're both ready."

My heart throbs hard in my chest when he gives me an encouraging wink. They could see how I *really* feel about their daughter, and even after everything that happened—the lies we told—they're here hugging, loving, and, most importantly, accepting Lennon's life choices.

"Do you want to meet Alison?" Lennon asks with a proud grin.

"Yes, please!" Mrs. Corrigan pleads. "More than anything."

Lennon takes Allie from her bouncer and carefully places her in her mom's arms. Mr. Corrigan reaches for her little hand and holds it while they both stare at her beauty. The love they have for their grandbaby is immediate. Tears stream down Lennon's mother's face and her dad looks at Alison with so much admiration, even I choke up. All of this takes me by surprise, and I can only imagine how Lennon feels. By the tears on her cheeks, it's pure happiness.

Lennon's mom notices our breakfast on the table and tells us to eat while they hold the baby. The two of us nearly inhale our food, and I don't even mind that it's cold. Them showing up was a nice and unexpected surprise. Lennon smiles, and I can tell by the look on her face that there's so much she wants to say right now but doesn't. Occasionally, she glances at her parents with Alison and smiles wide. Once we're finished eating, we join them in the living room.

As we continue to make small talk, Lennon's mouth falls open. "Dad, you missed the first Sunday service of the new year."

"It's because I love you. We love you so much," he says.

"I love you too." Her bottom lip trembles. "Thank you."

As I look around the room, all I can do is smile. I can see the love they have for each other, and it's something that was always missing from my household growing up. Something that can't be faked. It's more than real, just as my feelings for Lennon are. Her parents see it. She knows it.

She takes Alison from her mother and smiles at me. Something streams between us, something unspoken and dangerous. That line she drew in the sand seems to be disappearing, regardless that I've tried to keep my distance and give her space.

Her dad asks if we're dating, and I'm almost certain Lennon blushes. "No, Dad. Hunter's my best friend, and we were pretending. He was my fake husband, but we are roommates."

He shrugs with a knowing grin. "For now," he confidently says with a wink.

Lennon bites her bottom lip, and pink hues hit her cheeks.

Maybe things will be different this year after all.

I haven't given up on her—on us—and neither have her parents apparently.

CHAPTER FORTY-ONE

LENNON

Tonight will be my first official night without Alison. I'm only mildly freaking out.

Okay, *a lot* freaking out.

She's only six weeks old, and it feels like it's too soon, but the longer I wait, the harder it's going to be if I don't rip off the Band-Aid and trust she'll be okay without me for one night. Plus, it's Maddie's twentieth birthday, so it's the perfect opportunity to practice for when I go back to work. I know she mostly sleeps and eats right now, but it doesn't stop the mom guilt.

I pump every day, so I know I have plenty of milk for her, but that didn't stop me from checking her diaper bag fifty times to make sure I packed everything before I dropped her off at Mrs. Locke's house.

Hunter was so sweet and encouraging, telling me it was time I got out of the house and learned to socialize again. Okay, sweet might not be the right word, rather he mocked me and said I needed to wear real clothes again.

So here I am at the bar for Maddie's birthday celebration and ordering my first alcoholic drink in almost a year.

"Better be drinking that one for me," Maddie taunts when I

return to our table. "I can't believe I have another year before I can *legally* drink."

"Don't be in such a rush to grow up," Sophie says, typing out a text. "After twenty-one, it all goes downhill anyway."

"Well, that's encouraging." Maddie chuckles.

I snort at the irony, considering neither of us has our shit together. Sophie's been dating Weston for almost two months, and things are getting serious.

"I want to be old enough to buy my own drinks and graduate college. Then time can freeze," Maddie quips. "Also, didn't we say *no texting* tonight, Soph?" she scolds her, reaching over the table for Sophie's phone.

"I'm not! Okay, wait, hold on. I'm almost done. It's Weston. He'll be mad if I don't respond," she states as if she's picking her words carefully.

"He'll get mad?" I repeat. "He knows you're out with us tonight, so why is he bothering you?"

She blinks up at us and shrugs. "Okay, you're right." She locks her phone, then shoves it into her clutch. Sophie grabs her glass and holds it up. "Time to celebrate!"

I raise my drink, and Maddie lifts her virgin piña colada. We clink our glasses together, and I take a large sip.

"Okay, time to dance!" Maddie announces and bounces out of her seat. Her roommate, Erin, and another girl show up to party too. For the next two hours, Sophie and I dance with Maddie and her friends, and I take full advantage of ordering alcoholic drinks.

"Why didn't we invite the guys out tonight?" Sophie asks when we finally take a break and head to the bar.

"Maddie said girls' night only, and Hunter had plans," I say, trying to catch my breath. I don't think I've danced that much since spring break three years ago.

"Ooh, what kind of plans?" She arches a brow.

"Some work thing. He said there was a new client he had to schmooze," I half-ass explain.

"A new client, huh? A female client?" she asks after the bartender takes our orders.

"Yeah, it's a woman." I pinch my lips together.

"Where were they going?"

"He said she's staying at The Woodlands, and they were meeting there for dinner and drinks."

Sophie pops a brow. "That sounds like a date, Lennon."

"He'd tell me if he was going on a date," I argue. At least I *think* he would.

"How long do you expect him to wait for you?" Sophie asks once we grab our glasses, then walk back to our table where it's quieter. "I know you have feelings for him." She takes a sip, keeping her eyes locked on mine over the rim. "You can't let guilt and fear control your life forever. Before you know it, he'll have moved on for good, and you'll be the one left brokenhearted."

Sophie's words are like a knife twisting in my heart. I know she's genuine and wants me to be happy, but she can't possibly know how I feel. Between losing Brandon and having his baby to kissing Hunter and feeling things for him that scare the shit out of me, I'm conflicted about what the right thing is. It feels too soon to move on, but if Brandon's tragic accident has taught me anything, it's that life is too short.

"You think he's ready to date?" I painfully ask, not sure I want the answer to that. It's something I've always considered, knowing he won't be content living with Alison and me forever. But the thought of him falling for someone else suddenly makes me want to vomit.

"I know he wants *you*, Lennon, but I also know Hunter has a big heart and a lot to offer. It wouldn't surprise me if another woman was after him," she says bluntly. "Even if he isn't on a date right now, the fact that you're scared of it being a possibility should be enough for you to realize it's time to make a decision. Are you going to keep him in the friend zone forever because you're scared, or are you going to follow your heart before it's too late? How would you feel if he was on a date right now?"

A punch right to the gut.

That's how it'd feel.

"When did you get so sentimental?" I ask, wiping away the tears in my eyes before they can fall.

"If the thought of losing him makes you this emotional, what's gonna happen when he's ready to move on with his life, and he starts dating again or gets into a serious relationship?"

"I think…" I pause, my mind spinning in both directions. "I'd be heartbroken."

Sophie nods with an *I told you so* smirk. "So why are you fighting it? Hasn't he proven to you time and time again how much he loves you? How he's always gonna be there for not only you but for Allie too. How the thought of him moving on is putting you in a panic right now. C'mon, Lennon. Say it…"

I suck in a deep breath, my heart racing as the liquor buzzes through me. "I'm in love with him."

Holy shit.

The weight of admitting that feels like a thousand bricks off my shoulders.

"There's my girl!" Sophie cheers loudly, though no one around us even seems to notice over the music of the dance floor. "Now, when are you going to tell him?"

My shoulders fall, and I slouch against my seat. "What if he's changed his mind? He confessed his feelings to me months ago. What if he feels differently now?"

Sophie snaps her fingers in front of my face as if to pull me out of a haze. "Have you lost your damn mind? I know you had a baby and all, but did your brain go to mush?"

I slap her hand away and glare, but I know she's right. It's the same thing my parents have been saying for weeks.

I can't let fear keep me from admitting what I feel because I know I'd have nobody but myself to blame if I lost him. How long can I push him away before he realizes he deserves better? Deserves to be loved? I know my insecurities are fueling my apprehension right now, but it's all I can think about. So much has changed since that night months ago, and I don't know if he's been waiting for me all this time, or if we're in friend-zone territory for good.

"What the hell? You two ditched me!" Maddie scolds the second she sits down with a glass of water and chugs it.

"Lennon is having a freak-out moment about Hunter," Sophie explains casually. "I'm talking her off the ledge."

"Ooh yes, boy talk. Keep going," she encourages with a smile. "Are you finally admitting you want to bone him six ways to Sunday?"

"Maddie!" Sophie shouts.

I surrender. "Well…she's not wrong." My heart pounds as I admit that out loud for the first time. I feel goose bumps on my arms and wonder how I'll face him later after having this conversation with my sisters.

Maddie chuckles. "About damn time. Holy shit. So when are you gonna tell him?"

"It's not that easy," I say, lowering my eyes. "So much has changed since that first night we met. I'm no longer a careless college student. My life isn't just about *me* anymore."

"And I know, without a doubt, Hunter loves you and Allie," Sophie states.

I look at both of them with a serious face. "Did you know stretch marks are forever? Those magical creams are all bullshit. My body looks like a damn road map."

Sophie's expression softens. "Is that what you're so worried about, Lennon? That he's going to judge your body or not like what he sees? You're worried he won't want you anymore?"

"Yes, kinda. It's only been six weeks since I had Alison, and things haven't exactly gone back to normal. Let's not forget the fact I haven't had sex in almost a year. My vagina would probably scare him away," I say, feeling defeated.

Sophie snorts, then chuckles.

"You know I'm right. He was attracted to sexy, tight body Lennon. Now my boobs leak, I'm in bed by eight p.m., and I'm a walking zombie between getting up with the baby and breastfeeding. He probably thinks he dodged a bullet now." I slump back, and the reality of my words hits me in full force.

"Are you done with the pity party now?" Sophie deadpans. "Hunter *loves* you," she states matter-of-factly. "You love him too, and even if you're too scared to admit how much he means to you, you two are good for each other. The question you have to ask yourself is are you willing to let your own insecurities get in the way of being happy again?"

"It hasn't even been a year since Brandon died," I say. "Alison looks so much like him. It's a constant reminder he's not here and how much I miss him every single day."

"Lennon…" Her voice softens. "I know how much you two loved each other. Everyone who knew you guys could see it. But you can't stop living your life and wondering about the what-ifs. Brandon wouldn't want that, and you can't allow yourself to think otherwise. Hunter was his best friend. Brandon would approve. I know he would."

I don't realize I'm crying until I taste the salty tears on my lips.

"A part of me knows that, Soph." I wipe my cheeks. "I feel like I can maybe accept that, but now I'm scared of rejection. What if this changes everything, and our friendship ends? I don't know that I could live with myself for ruining things between Hunter and me."

"That's a risk you're gonna have to take, but I honestly don't think you have anything to worry about. It's time. Let yourself love again, Lennon. You deserve it all."

"I know I'm not a love expert or anything," Maddie chimes in, "but if I had a guy look at me with even half the amount of longing as Hunter looks at you with, I'd propose to him in a heartbeat. You two have gone through a lot together, and no one that matters will think you're moving on too soon or shame you for following your heart."

"I think I'd be devastated if he started dating someone or

moved on because I couldn't admit how I felt, and hell, that scares the shit out of me," I concede.

"Loving someone else doesn't take away how you felt about Brandon or what you two had, Lennon. Just remember that." Sophie reaches across the table and squeezes my hand. "He would want you to move on and be happy. Now it's up to you."

I nod, wiping my cheek when another tear falls. "You're right. You both are."

"Hell yeah, we are!" Maddie is the soberest drunk I've ever met.

"Will you be upset if I leave early, Mads?"

"I'd be upset if you didn't!"

We both stand, and she hugs me.

"Please give us an update."

"Tomorrow," Sophie adds. "Not like *during* anything, okay?"

"Ew," I say with a chuckle. "You two are freaks."

I finally leave the bar and grab an Uber since I've had a few drinks. Though my adrenaline has now taken over more than the alcohol. During the ride to The Woodlands, my nerves are in overdrive, and my heart's beating hard, making me anxious. I don't want to interrupt his meeting, but this can't wait. Not while I have the courage to finally tell him.

I'm in love with Hunter.

As soon as I arrive, I make my way inside and easily find the restaurant. It's dark and romantic in the seating area, and there's a bar that wraps around. Before I left tonight, I noticed he was wearing nice clothes—black slacks and a button-up—and he'd even trimmed his facial hair.

Shit. That sounds like a guy going on a date.

No. *Push those thoughts out, Lennon.*

Blinking, I look around and start wondering if he's already left. That means he could only be in two places.

At home.

In this woman's hotel room.

My chest rises and falls as my breathing becomes erratic, and I know I'm being irrational. Hunter said this was a work thing, not a—

Scratch that. He's at the bar. With a *gorgeous* woman.

She's in a black slinky dress that fits her like a glove. Dark brown hair, straight and down to her waist. Her legs are crossed and pointed toward Hunter, who's smiling and talking as she leans into him with her hand wrapped around his bicep. I notice the way his eyes light up at whatever they're discussing, and there's no way this is work-related.

Oh my God.

I'm a fucking fool.

My stomach turns, and I walk away before I'm forced to watch them make out or something.

Idiot.

I want to hit myself in the head and knock some sense into my stupid brain for thinking he'd wait for me all this time. Smack myself for ignoring my heart.

Maybe the hangover in the morning will torture me enough to block out this entire night.

As I wait for another Uber, I send a group text to my sisters.

LENNON

I was too late.

SOPHIE

What? Are you sure?

MADDIE

No way! What happened?

LENNON

His "work thing" was a hot date. She's all over him, and he didn't look like he was hating it.

SOPHIE

Lennon, I'm so sorry. Come back to the bar so we can mend your wounds the right way.

MADDIE

Yes! Please!

LENNON

I'd rather mend them with a bottle of wine and
cry about my pathetic love life in bed.

SOPHIE

You really wanna be alone right now? Let us help
you through this.

MADDIE

I'll even let you wear the Birthday Girl crown!
C'mon!

I push back my tears and snort at Maddie's last message.

LENNON

Okay. I want SHOTS, you hear? Lots and lots.

Anything to take this fucking pain away.

It's after one when Sophie brings me home. She stopped
drinking so she could take care of me. She's such a great sister.

"Shh…the cops will call my neighbors," I whisper-shout as I
trip over my own feet.

"I think you mean the neighbors will call the cops." Sophie
chuckles. "And it's you who's being loud, not me."

She gets my door unlocked, and I stumble my way inside
behind her. "Pfft, Hunter isn't home anyway. Shocker." I groan
loudly. "How many did you let me have?"

"Believe it or not, you only had three shots," Sophie says,
setting my keys and purse on the coffee table. "You're a
lightweight who hasn't had alcohol in almost a year."

"I'll be fine after a cup of coffee," I say, walking to the kitchen.

"No, ma'am. You need to go to bed." She grabs my wrist and leads me to my room.

"Aww…I miss my baby," I say as soon as I look at the empty crib. "Oh my God. I'm such a bad mom. How could I leave my baby? I didn't even check on her. What's wrong with me?"

Sophie carefully pushes me down onto the bed and kneels to take off my shoes.

"Mrs. Locke has it under control, Lennon. It's good for Allie to get comfortable with her now since she'll be staying with her when you go back to work. It's just one night," she reminds me.

"I miss her so much!" I half-sob. "Like, it literally hurts my heart how much I miss her."

"I know." Sophie grins. "Take off your clothes, and I'll get you some water."

"Yes, ma'am," I mock, saluting her as she walks out of my bedroom. When she returns, I'm down to my undies and bra. She hands me a glass of water, and I take a long drink.

"I just texted Mrs. Locke, and she responded right away." Sophie hands me my cell.

"Oh my God, is everything okay?" I rush to check the messages.

"Everything is fine!" Sophie quickly says. "She was feeding Allie and rocking her back to sleep. She said there's nothing to worry about."

"Oh," I say with relief. "Good."

"Yes, it is. Now…you need to get some sleep, okay?" She takes the glass and sets it on my nightstand.

"Can you get me a T-shirt?" I ask, pointing at the dresser that's five feet away, knowing I probably couldn't do it myself at this moment.

She hands me an old college tee, and I quickly put it on. "Ugh. This used to fit me like a glove before. Now I'm all baby fat."

Sophie shakes her head and chuckles. "You are not. Be right back. I gotta pee before I leave."

I climb into bed, and without thinking, I type out a message to Hunter.

LENNON

> I hope she can make you happy in a way I never could. She's the luckiest woman in the world. So pretty and long legs too. I bet her nipples don't leak milk when she hears a baby cry or pees a little when she sneezes. I know this will change things, but for what it's worth, I want you to be so, so happy. You deserve it more than anyone I know. Allie and I will move out as soon as I find a new place. You don't need us invading your life anymore than we have been.

I hit send but quickly type out a second one.

LENNON

> I'm sorry, Hunter. I'm sorry I was too late to see what was right in front of me the entire time.

I put my phone on silent before tossing it on the nightstand. Tipsy Lennon has no filter, and sober Lennon will pay for it. The irony of this whole situation isn't lost on me. I saw him with another woman for two minutes while he had to see me with his best friend for two years. I don't know how he did it, honestly. This is painful shit. I might actually understand for the first time why Hunter acted the way he did and why he had to keep me at a distance. He was protecting his heart since he couldn't control it.

Only allowing myself one night to wallow in my own self-pity, I'll wake up with a new life plan and stop letting my past hold me back. Alison needs me in the right mindset, and if this pain has taught me anything in the past few hours, it's that I don't do well with heartache.

"I was too late," I mutter when Sophie returns.

"You don't know that for sure," she says, sitting on the edge of the bed. "I still think you should talk to him when your head is clear."

I shrug, unable to keep my eyes open. "I already gave him my blessing. It's over."

"Whoa, wait. Lennon." She shakes my shoulder. "What does that mean? What'd you do?"

"I texted him."

"Oh God. No." I hear the judgy tone in her voice.

"It's okay, Soph. I'll be okay. We'll be fine," I tell her as I drift off.

I feel the bed lift slightly. She mutters a few words, but sleep takes me before I can ask her what she said. It doesn't matter, though. Sleep is all I want right now.

The sound of my bedroom door slamming against the wall startles me awake. My eyes pop open, but darkness surrounds me.

"What the fuck, Lennon?" Hunter roars, and when I look toward him, the hallway light is shining into my room. I have to squint to see him through the haze. "I've been texting you for two hours."

"I fell asleep," I croak out. "Why're you here?"

"I live here." He stalks toward me until he's next to my bed.

"I meant…" I clear my throat. "Why so early? The sun isn't even up yet."

Hunter looks at me, his gaze intense and unreadable. "How drunk are you?"

"Not very. Anymore," I reply honestly. "Just tired."

His throat moves as he swallows hard. "Then do you wanna explain your messages to me?"

My eyes widen at the realization of what I did and not wanting to have this conversation with him right now. Or ever.

"Um…no." I want to sink under these covers and never come up for air.

"Lennon." He sits next to me. "Were you at The Woodlands tonight?"

I squint one eye as if I'm racking my brain. "For like half a minute…"

"Why?" he asks. "What were you doing there?"

Deciding I need to face this, I sit up until I'm resting against the headboard. "I came to talk to you but realized you were on a date, so I left."

"Why didn't you text or call me beforehand?"

"I'd had a few shots by that point and wasn't thinking clearly," I admit shamelessly. "I wasn't spying on you, but I shouldn't have gone there in the first place."

"And are you thinking clearly now?" he asks, keeping his intense gaze on mine.

"Yes. I think so."

"Good, so you can hopefully understand what I'm about to say." He shifts his body so we're face-to-face. "I wasn't on a date. I haven't wanted to take a girl out on a date since the moment I met you. I don't know what you saw, but between the end of dinner and drinking at the bar to the timing of your text messages, I'm guessing it was when Carly's husband was out on a call. Because had you come any earlier or stayed a few minutes longer, you would've seen Mr. Long kissing his wife."

I'm pretty sure my face turns red and blood stops pumping to my heart.

But that doesn't explain the touching…

"Well, she seemed pretty handsy for being a married woman," I blurt. "But you didn't look like you hated it either. You were laughing and smiling."

"You're right, I was, and you know why? I was telling her all about you and Allie. I was being *that* guy who talks about poop explosions and how spit-up is a new part of my wardrobe now."

Wait. What?

He must sense my confusion. "She leaned in and touched my arm a couple of times, but that was it. She got the hint I wasn't interested in her advances pretty quickly when all I did was talk about you two."

"So if you got my message two hours ago, why didn't you come home right away?"

"Trust me, I wanted to. Sophie texted and said you needed to sleep off the alcohol and to ignore whatever you had texted me."

"That little snitch." I growl.

"So is that how you feel, Lennon?" He frowns, inching closer. "You want to move out? Because it'd gut me to lose you two."

My chest squeezes at the raw tenderness in his voice. Hunter's pained expression nearly has me in tears. The last thing I want to do is hurt him.

"I-I thought…" I stop myself, suck in my lower lip, and start again. "I thought you were ready to move on and date someone who could offer you everything you deserved. I wouldn't blame you if you did. I just…"

"What did you have to talk to me about in the first place?" he asks when I don't finish my sentence.

"Something. *Nothing.*"

"Something, huh? And that *something* couldn't wait?"

"At the time, no." I grimace. "The alcohol was giving me a false sense of confidence."

"Well, do you wanna tell me now?" He raises his brows.

"Yes. No. I dunno."

"Which is it, Lennon?"

"Yes, but it's not something you blurt out like a shopping list."

"If it's what I hope it is, something I've been waiting a long-ass time for, then you're gonna have to be the one to say it this time because I've convinced myself you never would."

I swallow down my heart that lodged its way into my throat as butterflies settle in my stomach, but I can't get the words out.

"Are you nervous?"

"What do you think?" I snap with a teasing glare.

"Do *I* make you nervous?" he asks in all seriousness.

"Sometimes."

"When I'm close to you?"

My throat goes dry. "Yes."

Hunter cups my cheek, narrowing the gap between us, and I focus on how close his lips are to mine. "What about now? What do you feel?"

My breathing increases, and I blink to clear my vision.

"My heart's pounding," I admit. "Like it's gonna burst right out of my chest."

Hunter appears a bit surprised by that response, then looks down as if he's staring directly into my soul. "It's how I've felt since you came to the bar that night, asking for a drink, taunting me with your gorgeous blue eyes. Nothing's changed for me, Lennon. I just had to get better at disguising it."

"You mean being an asshole," I quip.

"Would you rather I said something that night I found you bent over in my kitchen?"

"No, I guess not." I already feel guilty enough for him having to go through that. Though we've already talked about it, part of me wonders what would've happened had I stayed with Hunter that night and waited for him.

Would we have been here three years later?

We'll never know.

"If you want to kiss me, you're gonna have to be the one to initiate it this time, Lennon," he tells me.

I don't know what to say or how to react, especially when my head's still throbbing.

"What am I to you?" he asks when I stay silent.

"You're my best friend. The person I trust more than anyone. The person I can't see my life without..." I smile gently, meaning every word.

Hunter leans in just enough so our lips aren't quite touching. My eyes flutter closed as I wait for him to press them to mine.

"Kiss me, Lennon," he roughly demands in a whisper. "Kiss me *for real* this time."

CHAPTER FORTY-TWO

HUNTER

JUST WHEN I'M certain she's backing out, Lennon grabs my face and crashes her mouth to mine.

Thank fucking God.

Honestly, I was two seconds away from dropping to my knees and begging her to kiss me. I've been deprived of her lips for too damn long.

Starved for them.

Lennon grabs my shirt and pulls me closer, fisting her fingers in the fabric, and when she slides her tongue against mine, I lose all my restraint. I wrap my hand around her neck and sink into her, deepening the kiss as our bodies mold together.

Holy shit.

Lennon wants this as badly as I do. *Fucking finally.*

She pulls me on top of her, eagerly fingering the buttons on my shirt, and when I lean to one side, our mouths part just long enough for me to take it off. I quickly rip off my undershirt too.

We collide as Lennon's leg wraps around my hip, and I devour her mouth the way I've imagined for the past three years.

"Fuck, Lennon," I hiss against her when I move my lips down her neck. Then she arches her hips, meeting the erection that can't be missed. "Are you sure about this?" I kiss my way back up to her mouth and pause. "I don't think I can go back to being your platonic best friend who loves watching *Friends* and pretends to understand pineapple on pizza anymore." I blurt Hayden's taunting words, of what he's mocked me for the past year.

She laughs, and the sexiest blush hits her cheeks. "I can live with that on one condition."

I pull back and look into her eyes. "Name it."

She bites down on her bottom lip as if she's too nervous to say. "You admit that Ross and Rachel were, in fact, *not* broken up." The way she keeps a straight face has me laughing—shoulders shaking, head falling back laughing.

"You, Lennon Corrigan, are impossible." I release a dramatic sigh. "But for you, I'm willing to do just about anything. So here goes…" I clear my throat as if I'm about to make the most important announcement of my life. "They were not on a break, and the bastard cheated on the hottest actress in Hollywood."

Lennon cracks the tiniest of smiles. "That's not exactly what I said, especially the hottest part, but I'll accept it."

"Thank God."

Lennon giggles, and I pull her lips back to mine. It's hard to be without them knowing how amazing she tastes and how perfect our mouths mold together.

She pulls back with an odd expression, which gives me a mild panic attack before she grins. "Actually, can you excuse me for a second? I need to go to the bathroom first."

"Of course."

She slides out, and that's when I notice she's only wearing a T-shirt and the bottom of her ass cheeks peek out beneath it.

And the willpower it takes not to haul her back to bed should be considered admirable.

Lennon looks over her shoulder as if she knew I'd be staring.

"Don't start without me now." The seduction in her voice has me groaning in agony.

As soon as the bathroom door shuts, my mind wanders like crazy.

But after ten minutes, I worry she's changed her mind.

Another five go by and that's when I tap my knuckles on the wood. "Lennon?"

There's some commotion and what sounds like her scrambling. "One sec."

"Everything okay?" When she doesn't answer, my heart races. "Lennon, can you open the door?"

I know her well enough to know she's panicking. Shaking the doorknob, she finally opens it and peeks her head out.

"Hey. Sorry. I just need another minute."

I try to read her, but a part of me wonders if it has to do with being cleared for sexual activity, but then I remember she had her six-week postpartum appointment a few days ago because I watched Allie while she went.

"Are you okay? You know nothing has to happen tonight. I hope you know by now that—"

"It's not that," she cuts me off and looks away as if she's too embarrassed to elaborate.

I tilt up her chin until her gaze meets mine again. "What is it? Tell me, please."

She releases a short breath and opens the door wider. "I haven't shaved in a month."

I hold back a laugh, trying to be sensitive, but honestly, I wasn't expecting that answer.

"So you're not internally freaking out about us right now?" I ask, studying her.

"Well, yes. But I'm also self-conscious about my body and what you'll see." There's a faint blush on her cheeks, and I hate that she feels that way.

"Why would you ever worry about that? I saw you give birth, remember?"

"Hunter!" She playfully swats at my chest, and I catch her wrist, then pull her closer until she's pressed against my chest.

"You are beautiful," I tell her slowly. "Every part of you, in and out. You don't need to worry about anything else."

Her shoulders relax as she sighs. "You deserve perfection. My stomach looks like lumpy mashed potatoes. My boobs are leaky sandbags. I still have baby weight to lose. My thighs kiss when I walk. My vagina is probably ruined. Not to mention, the stretch marks. They're hideous." Her eyes are so sad and serious. I'd do anything to make her feel as gorgeous as I see her every day.

"I know for a fact that's not true," I say, my thumb gripping her chin. "But even if it were, I'd love every lump, stretch mark, imperfection, and more because you birthed a beautiful baby girl, and that's *nothing* to be ashamed of."

She swallows, then nods. "Okay."

Her eyes scan down my bare chest as she sucks in a breath. "This would be much easier if you were covered in warts or something."

Laughing, I release my hold on her. When she reaches for the hem of her shirt and pulls it off, revealing herself to me, I'm too shocked to breathe. She's in a sexy pair of panties and a bra that leaves nothing to the imagination.

"Christ, Lennon," I growl, biting my lower lip to hold myself back. "I want to fucking *devour* you."

Her eyes light up as she nods. "Yes, *please*."

I lower my mouth and stop when our lips brush. "But first…" I pause, putting more space between us. "I need to hear you say it."

"Say what?" she whispers.

"How much you want me, this—*us*. I need to hear you say it because, after all this time, I have to know for sure you want it as much as I do."

"Okay, fair enough," she says and straightens her spine. "Hunter Manning, I can't pinpoint the exact moment my feelings changed for you or when they shifted because it happened over time. I didn't even realize I was fighting the way I felt. I thought I could happily live like this, be your friend, and have you all to myself. But that was a lie because the thought of losing you, seeing you with another woman, and watching her touch you made me want to vomit. It took a lot to finally come to terms with these feelings, but make no mistake…" Her chest rises and falls quickly, my heart pounding so hard she can probably hear it. "I am ridiculously, madly, desperately in love with you. And I want you. If you'll have me, I. Want. You."

Fuck. I'm two seconds away from getting on my knees to thank the big guy above. Never in a million years did I think Lennon would say those words to me.

I smirk, loving how vulnerable and raw she's being with me.

"Now…was that so hard?" Deciding to mess with her, I look at my wrist as if I'm checking my watch and smile. "I mean, about damn time, woman."

Lennon shakes her head and bursts out laughing, the sound going straight to my dick but easing all of my nerves. God, I want her so damn badly.

Fuck it.

Cupping her face, I pull her lips to mine and devour her mouth. This kiss is the most real kiss I've ever had—no doubts, no questions, no insecurities.

My cock presses into her stomach, and the more she rubs against me, the harder it gets. I want Lennon more than I want air, but *shit.*

When I pull back, our heavy breathing sounds between us as I lean my forehead against her.

"There's one little problem," I murmur, arching my hips.

Lennon looks down. "I wouldn't say it's little…"

That causes me to laugh. "Um, thanks? But I was talking about condoms. I-I don't have any," I say cautiously. "I tossed them out months ago and didn't think I'd need them anytime soon."

"Oh," she says, finally realizing what I'm saying. "Have you always used one?"

"Always. No exceptions," I tell her honestly.

"Okay, well…your odds of having kids are low, and I got tested after I found out my ex cheated on me. They also took a thousand blood samples during my pregnancy to test for everything under the sun." I know she started dating Brandon after that and has only had two sexual partners.

"Perfect." Brushing her hair off her face, I smile at her beauty. "Because I don't want anything between us."

"Agreed," she says. We look into each other's eyes with stupid grins on our faces. "Are you gonna kiss me now?"

Smirking, I nod. "I think I might."

I bring our mouths together, slide my hands down to her ass, and grip the back of her thighs. Picking her up, she wraps her legs around my waist, and I moan into her mouth as she rocks herself against my hard cock.

"Goddamn, don't do that," I mutter against her lips. "You're already driving me fucking crazy."

She giggles, not obeying, and when I walk us back into her room, I collapse on the bed with her underneath me.

"I should make you pay for that," I growl with a wink. "Lie in the middle of the bed for me."

This time, she listens, and as soon as she's comfortable, she leans back and smiles. "Now what, Manning?"

"Ooh, I've always loved that sassy mouth of yours." I crawl over her, keeping myself up on my hands so I don't crush her. "Tell me every part of your body that you don't like or feel insecure about and let me prove you wrong."

Lennon bites down on her lower lip as if she's nervous to say.

"Your stomach? Stretch marks?" I inquire.

She nods, hesitantly.

I give her a wink and lower my mouth to her chest. Kissing between her breasts over her bra, I make my way down to her stomach and lick over one of her faint stretch marks. Then I feather kisses over the other ones, around her belly button, and all the way down until I meet her panties. Her chest heaves as her lips part in anticipation.

"Where else?" I ask, keeping my gaze on her.

"My boobs."

She's not wearing a nursing bra tonight, which I'm grateful for because honestly when I saw it air drying in the bathroom the first time, it looked confusing as hell.

Because I can't keep my mouth off her soft skin, I kiss my way back up her body until I land on the pale flesh of her breast. I pull one of the cups down slightly until she's exposed. When I blow cold air over her rosy nipple and it hardens, Lennon's breath hitches.

"Is this okay?" I ask, worried she's too uncomfortable. I've seen her feed the baby dozens of times, but I've always respected her privacy enough not to look directly at her chest.

"Yes," she says with a whispered gasp. "Keep going."

I smile at her encouragement and wrap my lips around her nipple. Lennon arches her back, and I pull the fabric of her bra down even more and palm her breast.

"Fucking hell, Lennon," I growl before flattening my tongue against her breast, licking and kissing every inch. Her breathing picks up, and I know she's as affected as I am. I move my mouth to her other breast, pulling the cup down and giving it equal attention.

"I wouldn't squeeze too hard," Lennon says with a quiet chuckle, and when I taunt her and do it anyway, she shakes her head. "You've been warned."

"And when have you ever known me to follow the rules?"

"Good point. Should've known the second I said that, you'd do the exact opposite."

"Don't worry, I'll handle them with care." I kiss her breast once more before putting the cups of her bra back in place.

I bring my lips to hers for a quick kiss.

"You're driving me insane."

"I'm not anywhere near done with you, sweetheart." I smirk. "Tell me where else."

"My thighs," she responds, and I have her spread her legs for me. She obliges, keeping them on each side of my body, and seeing her like this has my dick groaning in agony.

I grab one of her legs and kiss up her thigh toward her pussy.

Making sure to stay away from the temptation zone, I move to the next leg and do the same. Lennon's moaning encourages me to tease and torture the hell out of her the way she's involuntarily done to me for years.

"Hunter…" She releases my name on a long, drawn-out moan.

I drag my lips along the flesh of her thigh before capturing it between my teeth, giving it a little bite, and kiss it. Lennon arches her hips as her fingers fist the blanket. Her body is fucking begging for it.

Hell, my body is ready to die.

"Not yet, sweetheart." One final kiss to her leg. "Tell me another spot."

She's panting, desperately trying to catch her breath. "My pussy."

Fuck me.

I press one soft kiss over her panties before sliding them down her legs and tossing them to the side. Once she's completely bare, I drag my tongue over her slit. Her entire body shivers as I cautiously wrap my lips around her clit and suck.

"Oh my God…" Lennon slowly enunciates each word. Her back arches, pushing her hips closer to my mouth. The fact that I've barely touched her and she's responding this way turns me on even more. My dick is so hard, I have to bring a hand down to my groin and adjust myself before it burns a hole through my damn pants.

I inhale deeply, groaning at the scent of her. Though I want to take my time, I can't deny either of us what we need. As I kiss between her legs, I coat one finger through her slickness before pushing it inside her. I want her to know how desirable and perfect she is, and that I've never wanted her more.

Lennon flails underneath me, muttering *yes* over and over, and as I struggle to hold her hips down with my free hand, I dive in and lick her. I alternate between kissing, licking, and sucking. I thrust a second finger inside, and I know she's about to explode when she rocks her hips faster.

Every part of her is beautiful, every part represents a journey or experience, and I love and crave every inch. The taste of her is what wet dreams are made of, and now I greedily want more. More of her, more of us, more *everything*.

"Hunter, I'm so close," she says between gritted teeth. I nod against her pussy, lifting one of her thighs over my shoulder, then drive my fingers deeper, faster, harder inside her. I flick her clit with my tongue, rolling and sucking it between my lips, then, like a volcano, she explodes as the sensation overtakes her.

Once she stops shaking, I place her leg down, give her pussy one final kiss, and make my way back to her lips. Her breathing steadies, and I look into her bright blue eyes that hold so much truth to the way she feels. We both spent time avoiding the way we felt at some point. But no more.

Leaning on my side next to her, I tilt her chin toward me so she can not only hear the sincerity in what I'm about to say but see it too. "Your imperfections are what make you perfect. Your vulnerability makes you human. But your heart? That's what I love most about you, Lennon. Everything you do is with purpose and heartfelt. It's why even when I wanted to hate you, I couldn't. You had me wrapped around your finger for so long, I'd forgotten what it felt like not to have you in my life in some way, but I know I never wanna go back to that. I want you. I'm just as ridiculously in love with you, Lennon Corrigan. Always. I'm yours for as long as you'll have me."

"You're mine, and I'm yours," she simply states with a sweet smile.

"You've got that right, sweetheart." Nothing could ever change that.

"Say it again," she whispers when I brush our lips together.

"Sweetheart?"

"No. That you love me." Her taunting tone makes me smirk at her bossiness. "I wanna hear you say it again."

"Are you sure you wouldn't rather I *show* you?" I kiss my way toward her ear. "Because I really, really, *really* want to show you."

Lennon slides her hand down my stomach and over my groin, rubbing her palm over my noticeable erection. "Then you better say it fast, Manning."

"Fuck." I groan loudly, my head falling back as she continues to touch me. "I can't concentrate when you do that."

"You're running out of time…" She pops the button and slowly unzips my pants.

I grab her wrist, stopping her from going any further. "I see how we're playing this game."

"What?" She looks at me innocently. "Did you think you're the only one who can get what they want from sexual favors?"

Chuckling, I shake my head at my little devil. "I've underestimated you."

Unfortunately, I've heard Brandon and her for years, being in the bedroom next to mine, and though I wish I could remove it from my brain, it's not as easy to do with all the history between us or the way I felt about her.

"Should never underestimate a Pisces." She smiles, smugly. "We may be known to be caring and loyal, but we're also very intuitive."

I want to make a smart-ass comment about how she wasn't intuitive enough to know how I felt over the past few years, but I also don't want her to stop touching my dick, so I keep my mouth shut.

"You want to hear me say it again?"

She nods with a smile.

I cup her cheek and brush my lips softly against hers before pulling back. "I'm so in love with you, Lennon, that I was willing to live the rest of my life as only your friend as long as it meant I got to be with you every day. Even as just friends. Or roommates. I would've learned to accept it. Love you proudly but silently. There was never a chance in hell I'd fall for someone else when I already had what I needed—*you*. It would've been lonely after a while, sure, but I was ready to do it. I wasn't walking away from you or Allie. I'll never walk away, which is something I've been trying to prove to you since Brandon died. You needed someone to lean on and grieve with, but I did too. Every time you pushed me away, I was determined to pull you closer. You fought me, and it only made me love you harder. You denied me, but I loved you from afar."

"Hunter…"

"Hold on." I take a second to catch my breath. "So I will tell you every single day, for the rest of our lives, night or day—I love you, Lennon. I love you so fucking much my heart goes into convulsions just thinking about it. I've never said those words to a woman before, and I don't say them lightly. Because you're it for me. You always have been."

"I don't even know how to respond, Hunter…" She licks her lips and doesn't take her glossy eyes from mine. An electric current streams between us. "The love I have for you feels incomparable, and I'm sorry I made you wait."

"God, please. Don't be. You needed to heal and get comfort more than anything. I was always here, waiting, hoping, but also healing with you. I know the guilt you feel, I feel it too, but we deserve a chance at happiness."

"You're right. After I set my guilt aside, I realized that, and I want to be happy with you."

"I'm here." I bring her lips to mine. "Yours."

"Mine."

CHAPTER FORTY-THREE

LENNON

Every nerve in my body is on fire when Hunter's lips brush against mine. Everything inside me lights up like fireworks when he says the most beautiful and heartfelt things, cherishing me like I'm his whole world.

He loves me.

I don't think I will ever get tired of hearing him say those words. He says them with every fiber of his being, so truthful and meaningful it makes my heart pound at the realization we're in love.

This whole time, I've been in denial, fighting it and refusing to allow myself to love again.

But I can't live in the past anymore.

When our mouths fuse in a heated, passionate kiss, I'm done speaking and allow our bodies to do the talking. I want this so badly every part of me aches for him.

Sinking into him, we're as close as two bodies can be, and I claw my nails down his back. Hunter rewards me with a desperate groan and reaches around to cup my ass. I feel how hard he is. I want to taste him, lick him, devour him the way he did me.

When he wraps his hand around my thigh, I use it as leverage to climb on top of him and straddle his waist. His lips consume mine, his large hands roaming over every surface of my exposed body, and for once, I don't feel insecure.

Kissing my way down, I press my lips to his bare chest, silently admiring his tattoos and muscles. Then I feather kisses across his stomach and to his very admirable V over his hips. Hunter moans when I rub a hand over his cock, teasing and desperate.

"Fuck, Lennon…" His head falls back.

Knowing he's already losing his damn mind when I've barely touched him has me smiling with pride.

I scramble to help him take off his pants and boxer briefs, and when he's fully bared to me, my breath hitches at the sight of him. I always knew Hunter was a gorgeous man, solid and muscular, but seeing him like this, exposed and hard, makes me want to kiss every damn inch of him.

Unable to wait for another second, I wrap my hand around his cock and slide my tongue up his shaft. He groans, and *oh my God*, it turns me on even more. I look up at Hunter, whose eyes are glued to me, his mouth parted as he wraps a hand in my hair and pulls it to the side.

I slide my tongue around his tip before pulling him into my mouth. His fingers tighten in my hair, so I do it again.

"Fuck yes, sweetheart. Just like that." Hunter moans as I rotate my hand over his length and suck on him, pulling him deeper into my throat. I do this over and over, before sliding my hand down to his balls to carefully massage him and then opening my mouth wider. With my ass in the air, I pull him all the way inside my mouth and suck. Hunter's hips arch as he thrusts upward, and the taste of him has me growing more anxious to have all of him.

As I come up for air, I bring both hands to his cock and stroke him hard and fast. His eyes roll to the back of his head, and I love the way he responds to everything I'm doing to him. It gives me the confidence to climb up his body and straddle his lap.

Hunter sits up, cups my face, and slams his mouth to mine. He pours so much love and passion into everything he does, and right now, in the heat of the moment, it's no different. It's always been real. I pull him closer and rock my hips to let him know *exactly* what I want.

"Hunter…" I beg against his lips. "I need you."

"Yeah?" he asks, kissing down my neck and to my ear. "How much?"

His taunting tone makes me smile as my head falls back. Hunter's mouth and hands explore, leaving goose bumps everywhere he touches.

"Please," I whimper, rocking my body. "Now."

"Fuck," he growls. "Yes."

Hunter wraps a hand around my waist and spins us around until I'm lying on the bed and he's over me. "I love hearing you beg for it." He flashes me his shit-eating grin. "Might've fantasized about it a time or two." Then he winks.

Smug bastard.

I shake my head but can't stop smiling, even when he slants his mouth over mine and kisses me.

Hunter leans back, spreads my legs wider, and aligns our bodies. I bite my lip in anticipation as he strokes his dick a few times, and when I *finally* feel him inside me, I lose all control. The way he groans, then pulls back momentarily before sliding back in is complete bliss. My hips move with his, and we easily form a rhythm. Hunter braces himself above me, and as I wrap a hand around his neck, our mouths fuse and weld together.

"You feel fucking incredible, Lennon," he whispers, his forehead pressed to mine. I wrap my legs around his waist, giving him all the access he needs. "Lennon, baby. Do you feel how amazing we fit together?" His head drops to the side, and his lips press against my ear.

"Yes…" I whisper through a moan. "Better than I could've ever imagined."

Hunter's eyes meet mine, our bodies completely in sync as he increases his pace, hitting the right spot over and over. My breathing picks up, my back arches, and I'm so damn close.

"*Yes, yes, yes,*" I mutter, feeling every inch of him and unable to control the words spewing out of my mouth.

He reaches around for my leg to bring it over his shoulder and drives impossibly deeper. The angle has my fingers clawing at his arms, wanting more, harder, faster—which he delivers.

Panting, rocking, begging for all of him.

"Oh my God, Hunter," I cry out, my body arching to meet his, and everything spins, and I see stars. The orgasm hits me so quickly and unexpectedly, I clamp my hands around his biceps and dig my nails into his skin. He releases a loud grunt, and as soon as my vision clears, he loses his fucking mind as he chases his own release.

"Fuck, fuck, fuck…" His rugged voice comes out hoarse as his jaw tightens. Damn, he looks sexy as hell when he comes, and knowing I'm the reason is so damn satisfying.

Hunter nearly collapses on top of me but holds himself up before dipping his head down to kiss me. Though we're both trying to catch our breaths, I smile against his lips as our hearts pound in a mutual rhythm.

He rests his forehead against mine. "I love you," he whispers. "I hope you don't get tired of hearing me say that. I've been waiting a while…"

His breathy confession has me chuckling. Hunter falls to the side, taking me with him so we're face-to-face.

"I know." I brush my fingers through his hair. "I love you too." My heart nearly bursts, so relieved to be able to say those words to him after denying them for so long.

"You're mine," he says with a seductive smile.

"And I'm yours," I finish.

With a smile, Hunter kisses the top of my nose. "Don't move. Be right back."

He returns with a towel, and once we're clean, we climb under the covers, and our bodies naturally mold together. My eyes flutter closed as I fall asleep next to the man I, without a doubt, have fallen recklessly in love with.

As soon as my eyes pop open, I check my phone and panic at how late it is. "Oh my God," I mutter, sit up and scan my room, then realize Alison isn't in her crib.

Hunter's hand lands on my thigh and squeezes. "She's with Mrs. Locke," he reminds me in a sleepy voice. When I look at him, his eyes are closed, but he somehow knew I was freaking out.

"Oh, right," I mutter. "I should go pick her up soon."

Hunter opens his eyes and smiles. "I sent her a text a couple of hours ago and let her know you'd be sleeping in, but we can go get her anytime you want."

I lie back down, and he wraps me in his arms. "You were up and checked on her?"

Hunter presses his lips to mine for a sweet kiss, and my face lights up at the memory of our night together. "Yep. Guess it's become a habit now." He winks, brushing his fingers over my cheek. I love his little touches and the way he's always found a reason to let me know he's close, even if it was strictly platonic at the time. But now I want his hands all over me all the time. "She sent some pictures if you wanna see. Looks like she's having a blast."

"Alison or Mrs. Locke?" I chuckle.

Hunter laughs, reaching for his phone, and clicks on the message. "Both. I doubt she's put her down since you dropped her off."

"Well, Alison is still too young to do anything except demand to be held, fed, or changed. Although she loves to kick her little legs and arms and pull my hair."

He shows me the few photos, and we both *aww* at how cute they are. Mrs. Locke loves being a grandma, and I know it doesn't erase the pain of what happened to Brandon, but it's definitely brought us closer to healing.

"Can't say I blame her for that one," Hunter taunts, grabbing a loose strand and yanking. "I might've dreamed about it a time or two."

"Oh, is that so?" I hitch a leg over his waist and pull myself on top of him. "What else have you fantasized about?"

Hunter's eyes widen as he tosses his phone, then plants his hands on my waist. His hips arch, and his dick pushes between my legs. "Fuck," he drawls the word out. "Are you about to make one of them come true?"

I smirk, leaning down to kiss him. "I might."

"Don't mess with me, woman," he growls. "I wanted to wake you up hours ago and have my way with you, but I figured you'd kick me in the dick again and tell me to fuck off."

"That was one time!" I laugh against his mouth.

"Technically, it was two," he corrects. "But I'm willing to let it go on one condition."

"Hmm…" I grind against him, knowing it's driving him crazy.

"You better stop that," he warns, holding my hips in place.

I chuckle, loving this playful side of him so damn much. "And what would that be?"

"You come on my cock right fucking now," he blurts out the words in a husky voice.

I pretend to contemplate it, and when I don't respond right away, Hunter brings his hand to my ass and smacks it.

"Fine!" I yelp, laughing.

Shifting, I take his dick in my hand, stroke him a few times, and slowly slide down on him. His face contorts, his lips part, and his head falls back when he's completely inside.

"Christ, Lennon," he moans. "Why do you feel so damn good?"

I love how much I affect him. I want to prove to him how much I want and love him, especially after everything we've been through.

With my hands braced on his chest, our bodies rock together into oblivion. Every slap to my ass encourages me to go faster, harder, and take him deeper. I love watching his face, how every move affects him, but he has no idea what he's doing to me. When I lean down to kiss his lips, he rests a hand on each side of my face gently and kisses me so damn deeply and passionately, it brings me over the edge.

I moan his name as I ride out my release, and I lean all the way back until my hands rest on his thighs and grind my hips against him as fast as possible. As soon as Hunter rubs my clit, my head falls back as we race toward another wave of pleasure. I scream out his name, begging for more, unable to control the sounds that come out of my mouth with every thrust.

Hunter grunts and growls, pushing his hips into me as he comes hard. His entire body flexes, the cords of his neck tightening while his fingers dig into my legs. God, the man is raw perfection.

I collapse on top of him, and he wraps his strong arms around me as we both pant to catch our breaths. He shifts us to our sides with our legs still tangled together.

"Not even gonna lie," he starts. "Fucking love hearing you scream my name."

I'm still trying to steady my breathing but chuckle at his admission. "Don't get used to it. Pretty sure that performance would wake up the baby. Hell, probably the entire apartment complex."

"So what you're saying is we're gonna need to put a gag in your mouth to muffle the noise?"

His naughty thoughts make me blush. "You're straight-up

dirty, aren't you?" I tease, digging my heel into his ass to bring him closer.

"You have no idea the inappropriate thoughts I've had about you." He leans in and bites my bottom lip.

"If I have to be muffled, then so do you." I wrap my hand around his neck and kiss him. "It's only fair."

"I'd be on board with that." He winks.

I look at him, wondering how I should bring it up. "What if you moved into my room with me? And we made your room into a nursery for Alison?"

Hunter's brows shoot up, causing me to panic.

"Am I moving too fast?" I ask shyly, though it feels right.

His eyes light up, and he grins so fucking wide it causes butterflies to flutter through me.

"Hell no," he tells me with a smack on the lips, then holds me tight. "Now that I'm in here, I'm not ever leaving."

When we finally make our way out of bed, I start making food while he takes a shower. I decide to text Sophie and Maddie, knowing they're going to lose their damn minds.

LENNON

I guess I have you to thank, Soph…texting Hunter to ignore my text messages and all…he came barging home at 3am demanding I explain myself!

SOPHIE

OMG… FINALLY! Tell me everything!

MADDIE

Did you two finally go to pound town?!

I snort at her bluntness.

LENNON

OMG, Maddie.

SOPHIE

WELL?

LENNON

YES OKAY! Several times. It was…

I lose myself in thoughts of him and chuckle when I read their messages.

MADDIE

What? TELL US!

SOPHIE

…hello?

LENNON

It was amazing! HE is amazing. It felt so right and being able to finally say that I love him makes my heart burst out of my chest. Is that cheesy?

MADDIE

AWWWW

SOPHIE

About damn time! Lord! I was starting to get sympathy blue balls for him!

LENNON

OMG…you two are insane. But thanks for helping me through last night. I never knew I could feel this happy again. I know it's super new and fresh, but it's Hunter. He makes me feel so loved and comfortable in my own skin.

I almost tear up thinking about how tender and loving this man is and how I can't possibly deserve a guy like him.

SOPHIE

Stop, I'm gonna cry!

LENNON

HA!

MADDIE

Liam and Mason owe me $100 now. #BOOM!

SOPHIE

Ooh me too! $100 richer!

LENNON

You two bet on if we'd hook up?

I roll my eyes, but I'm not even surprised with them.

SOPHIE

No, we bet WHEN. They lost.

MADDIE

I'm gonna make them pay up so hard!

LENNON

Okay, well you four have fun in your weird non-relationship relationships. I'm going to finish cooking breakfast so I have lots of energy for later...

MADDIE

EW

SOPHIE

Double ew

SOPHIE

But we still love you!!

MADDIE

Yes! And so, so happy for you guys!

LENNON

Love you too! Chat soon! MWAH

I hear Hunter shout my name over the water streaming, and when I walk inside, the sight slightly blinds me.

Well, fuck me. *Again.*

"Did you call me?"

"Yeah, sorry. I ran out of body wash and have an extra bottle on my dresser. Would you mind grabbing it for me?" he asks.

"Sure, one second." I tilt my head to the side, trying to sneak a look.

"You can join me if you want…" Hunter taunts with a lazy grin. "Sing to me in the shower while I fuck you from behind."

"Oh my God, you're insatiable."

His laughter echoes as I find the willpower to move my feet and walk into his room. I know the brand he uses, but I don't see anything on his dresser. Hunter isn't exactly organized, so I decide to check his drawers. Nothing. Hmm. I check his desk and closet next. Then I remembered his nightstand is basically a kitchen's version of a junk drawer and check there. I dig around, moving random things around, and when I find a black velvet box, my entire body freezes.

I know it's not from the ring he bought me since I have it in my room, but why the hell would he have this? Was he going to propose to someone before everything happened? *Jenna?*

Ugh, the thought makes me sick.

I shouldn't look, but my curiosity gets the best of me, and before I can talk myself out of it, I flip it open and see an engagement ring.

A princess cut diamond on a white gold band.

It's stunning.

My breathing increases rapidly, my heart pounds, but when I pick up the ring, I find an engraving on the inside.

03/18 the day I met my soulmate.

And then my heart stops.

The words inside the ring nearly make me choke on my emotions. We always talked about our future together and getting married, so when did he plan to propose?

Better yet, why does Hunter have it?

Kneeling on the floor, I stare at it, memories of us flooding in, and all the what-ifs burning in my mind. He died before he could ask me, before I could give him an answer, before we could ever start our forever together.

How could Hunter not tell me? I feel so fucking betrayed.

"Lennon?" he shouts from the shower.

Standing, I place the ring back in the box, slowly shut his nightstand, then walk back to the bathroom. He smiles as soon as he sees me, but it quickly falls from his face.

"What is it? Were you able to find it?"

"How could you keep this from me?" I ask, my voice brittle. Tears form in my eyes at how this changes things. I hold out my hand to show him the velvet box as my face hardens.

Hunter blinks, then looks at it, and as soon as the realization hits, he shuts off the water. "Lennon." He says my name so softly, almost as if it pains him.

I march to my bedroom and slam the door behind me. It doesn't do a damn thing because Hunter barges in.

"Lennon, wait. I know you're upset…"

"Upset?" I face him, my voice going up an octave. He's drenched, with a towel wrapped haphazardly around his waist, water droplets falling from his chest. I snap my eyes back to his. "How could you not tell me Brandon was planning to propose? How could you keep this ring and not tell me after everything we've been through?" I don't realize tears are falling until I taste salt. I hate that I get emotional so quickly and wipe them away as fast as I can.

"Lennon, please. Let me explain…" He steps toward me, but I step back.

"Hunter, don't. I should've known this was too good to be true. No wonder you suggested we pretend to be married." I'm letting my anger speak, unable to control my emotions as they spill over.

"Don't say that," he barks. "I have been here for you through everything, so don't you dare use that against me." Hunter closes the gap between us, and this time, I let him. "I did that for you and Allie."

I swallow, nodding because I know he's being sincere. "You told me to trust you," I whisper-sob. "Were you ever going to tell me?"

Hunter closes his eyes, and he shrugs his shoulders. "I honestly don't know. How do you tell someone that kind of news? Risk your emotional stress during the worst time of your life, or tell you when you're happy and watch you spiral back to those dark days? I was put between a rock and a hard place."

"Still, I had a right to know," I bite out, my chest rising and falling as quickly as my heart races.

"You have to believe me, Lennon…" He takes my hands in his, looking so defeated as he speaks. "The last thing I wanted was to hurt you. There were so many times I thought of telling you, but I didn't know what it'd do—if it'd set you back or if you'd be mad I said anything at all. I never thought this would be the situation when Brandon told me he was going to propose, and when I found the ring, you definitely weren't in the mindset to see it."

"Maybe, maybe not. But that wasn't your choice to make," I tell him softly. "My boyfriend died never being able to ask me. He died before I knew he was going to ask me to marry him. And you knew…*this whole time!*" Tears fall, and when Hunter nods and squeezes his eyes shut, I know it's because he's in tears too.

"Lennon, I'm so, so sorry," he whispers, bringing a hand to my cheek. "This is not how I wanted you to find out or for things to happen between us. I love you, and bringing you more pain is the last thing I ever wanted."

My bottom lip trembles. This man has changed my life in the best way possible. He stepped aside when I was with his best friend, and when Brandon died, he became my anchor. He's always had my best interest in mind. Always. I can't imagine how keeping a secret like this has affected him.

I try to put myself in his shoes, and the rational part of my brain knows either option would've been a shitty one. Had I known Brandon was going to propose while grieving his death, I would've been even more destroyed. If he'd told me during the pregnancy, it would've hurt more. My hormones wouldn't have been able to handle it. Soon after, shit went down with my parents, we made it through the first holidays without Brandon, and then Alison debuted. He's right. There wasn't a safe time to tell me.

I want to hold and console him for being forced to keep this secret, knowing it put him in a bad situation. But I believe him and know it wasn't held from me out of spite. He was keeping me safe from the pain it would've caused, and I understand that, as much as it hurts now.

"Please say something, sweetheart." Hunter drops to his knees, wrapping his arms around my waist and holding me. "I can't lose you, Lennon. I love you and Allie more than my own life, and I'll never forgive myself if I can't fix this."

"That's how you knew what diamond cut I'd want," I say softly. "When you bought that one at the airport."

He nods against my stomach, and my heart lodges into my throat, unable to swallow down my pain. Hunter tilts his head back and gazes into my eyes.

"I'm not going anywhere," he states confidently. "I know you're upset with me, and rightfully so, but I'm here, fighting for you, for *us*. So if it's space you need, I'll give it to you if you ask, but know that I'm not giving up."

My heart pounds so hard in my chest as I think about his words. The love Hunter has for me is so overwhelming and special, and the last thing I want is for this to screw things up. I love him, and knowing he kept this from me hurts, but it's not a deal breaker for me.

Nodding, I bring a hand to his face. "You were protecting me."

"Yes," he states. "I felt very protective of you right after he died and have only always wanted to be there for you. Once I found it, I didn't know what to do…" He closes his eyes for a moment. "But I should've told you myself instead of risking you'd find it."

"I'd like to give it to Alison one day. I think she deserves to have the ring her daddy picked out."

"Absolutely. It's yours. I never wanted to keep it from you two—"

"I know. You were put in the worst possible position." I lean down and brush my lips against his. "I believe you."

Hunter releases a long sigh. "Thank God."

I pull him up so I can wrap my arms around him. "I love you so much, Lennon. You and Allie. You're both my whole world."

With tears in my eyes and a smile on my face, I nod, feeling the truth of his words right down to my soul. "I love you too."

CHAPTER FORTY-FOUR

HUNTER

It's been a month since Lennon found the engagement ring that Brandon bought for her. We've been working through it together and trying to move past what happened. Though she's forgiven me, I regret not telling her sooner. I never wanted her to find out the way she did, but there was never a good time to mention it. Now I realize that ring just opened a tender wound, and maybe I should've told her before we went to Utah.

When Lennon was happy, I didn't want to ruin that for her because it was so fleeting in the beginning. When she was sad, I couldn't be the one to add more grief. All I've ever asked for is her trust, and I broke that, something I'm trying every day to make up for. She's told me several times that she understands why I did it, and I believe her, but it doesn't erase the fact I hurt her. I only have her best interest in mind, but in that instance, my need to protect her ended up hurting her. I'll never make that mistake again.

Before I head home, I text Lennon and let her know I'm stopping by the gym to blow off my aggravation from my work day. It's barely past three, and I feel like I've worked two full shifts.

She texts me back with a thumbs-up emoji, which means she's

probably occupied with her students. Now that her maternity leave is over, she's always on the go between taking Allie to Mrs. Locke's before work and picking her up after. I know she's exhausted from getting up with the baby and trying to stay on top of everything. I help out as much as I possibly can, offering to pick Allie up if I can get out of the office early or even doing a middle of the night diaper change. I don't know how she does it some days, but one thing's for sure: she's superwoman.

As I drive across town, I can't stop thinking about my day and how some people don't listen, no matter how many times I repeat myself. Months from now, when the project is a complete mess because they're trying to cut corners, I'm going to be the peon to help clean it up, which pisses me off. I tried to explain to the project manager why it's important to reinforce the structures with steel. Yes, it's more expensive, but it'll last longer. After I was shut down for the umpteenth time, I decided to sit in the back of the meeting and bite my tongue. I'm surprised I still have one in my mouth at this point.

After I run my ass off and lift the heaviest weights I possibly can, I get in the truck and go home. I feel better. I'm exhausted but not as tense as I was before. Allie still wakes in the middle of the night, but she's sleeping in longer stretches. We moved her to my room and transformed it into a nursery. The space is perfect, and the walls are so thin, we can still hear her little cries in the middle of the night, though Lennon is determined to keep the baby monitor by the bed. Our apartment has quickly transformed into a home for our little family, and as I park the truck, I smile when I think about it. Before I walk inside, I grab the mail and head up the stairs. Noticing I have a pink slip in my box, I go down to the office and pick up whatever the front desk signed for. The woman hands me a manila envelope, and it looks serious as fuck. I tear it open, and when I walk into the apartment and pull out the paper, I feel my balls in my throat.

Allie is in her bouncer, and I steal a quick kiss from her and blow a few raspberries on her belly. She rewards me with little baby giggles that make me forget about the letter in my hand for a few seconds. Lennon rounds the corner, looking as pretty as ever, but notices my tension. "What's wrong?"

I read over it a few more times to make sure I'm not imagining what it says, then hand it to her.

Her eyes scan over it and they widen. "She's summoning you for a paternity test? Seriously? After all this time?" Her nostrils flare, and I can see the aggravation written all over her face, which I kinda enjoy only because I know she cares.

You'd think after the hospital tour months ago when Lennon spilled the beans about how I couldn't possibly be the father, Jenna would stay away. She did for a while until she had the baby and realized after I blocked her number she'd have to find new ways to contact me. The crazy woman resorted to emailing me pictures of the baby to my work email. There's no way to block her there, so I've resorted to deleting anything with her name on it.

"Maybe she found out Craig wasn't the father after all, and she's backtracking? It's fucking ridiculous either way," I say, tempted to wad up the paper and throw it in the trash.

"You have to go," Lennon tells me. "She's desperate, and you'll need to prove to her that you're not the father. Maybe a paternity test will finally make her leave us alone."

I let out a heavy sigh, happy that I went to the gym because I might've lost it otherwise.

"You're right. I don't have any other choice." I pull Lennon close and hold her against my chest, taking in the sweet smell of her hair and skin.

She bites down on her bottom lip, and when I furrow my brows, she adds, "There's not a chance it's yours, right?" She looks up into my eyes, worry written on her face. She's seen the test results, but still, there's always that small percentage. "I mean, if you think Craig isn't the father?"

"She was probably sleeping with more guys than she admitted and has a list of men she's summoning." I press my lips against hers and smile. "And if I could have kids, I'd be knocking you up so quick, you'd want to cut off my dick."

"You're so romantic." She snorts and rolls her eyes.

"Listen, don't worry about this. I'm not going anywhere," I reassure her.

She nods and holds me close. "I know."

I pull my phone out of my pocket and look at it. It's barely past four. "They close at six. I'm going to go right now and get this shit over with."

"Do you want me to come with you? Maybe give you some positive reinforcement on the way over?" She wiggles her eyebrows, and it causes me to snort.

"I've got enough of you in my head to last me a lifetime, Lennon. They're going to swab my cheek and send me on my merry way. Shouldn't take too long."

Her lips gently slide across mine, and it takes everything I have to pull away. Lennon tends to make all the bad in the world disappear.

"I'll be right back, okay?" I steal another small kiss from her then Allie before heading to the door.

Lennon nods and smiles. "I'll be waiting for you…" She winks and slowly licks her bottom lip.

"Damn. You're a cocktease who plays dirty as hell." I leave and rush across the parking lot to my truck, hoping there's no traffic on the way to the testing center. Though I have no reason to worry or stress, I'm nervous as hell about this. I know the baby isn't mine, but what if by some crazy circumstance, he is? We used protection every single time, but what if it defied all odds? There's no fucking way. I push the thoughts out of my head when I park and walk inside.

Once I'm at the front counter, I slide my official summons document under the paned glass. While I wait for them to call my name, I find my courage and go back to the front.

"Do you do sperm count tests here as well?" I ask, hoping no one in the lobby heard me. Though I've accepted my fate, I'm still curious if anything's changed since the last time I had it checked.

"We do." She explains how it works, though I already know. She hands me a cup, and after the first test is done, they send me to another room to take care of business. After I give my sample, the nurse explains the timelines.

"Both test results will be in within two days. We'll send them by certified mail, or you can come back in the office and we can go over them with you."

"Nah, mailing it is fine." I sign a few more documents, and then I'm on my way home. I'd be lying if I said I wasn't nervous, but I'll be thrilled to fucking death to put this all to rest once and for all.

Two days pass and as promised, I get the letters in the mail. I had the front office at the apartment call me as soon as they were signed for. I left early because I'm anxious as fuck. After I park, I sit in my truck and try to get my mind right because no matter what happens, this won't change the way I feel about Lennon. Realizing I'm being a complete pussy about this, I force myself out of the truck, go to the office, and grab the envelope, but I don't open it. I can't find the strength to do it, so I text Lennon. Though I know she's in class and won't see my text, I still send it.

HUNTER

I got the results. Should I wait for you?

But then she responds right away.

I smile. I love her so fucking much it hurts. Considering I'm so goddamn antsy, I go to the gym until Lennon comes home. There's no way I can sit around the apartment and wait. I might literally go crazy. When I get to the gym, I do heavy squats until my legs feel like they're going to fall off, then finish on the treadmill. I try to get lost in the music, in the pain, in anything other than what's running through my head. Nearly two hours pass before I get a text from Lennon letting me know she's on her way home. They found a substitute to cover for her, and apparently, it wasn't a big deal at all.

The envelope nearly burns a hole in the seat where I placed it. As I pull up to the apartment, Lennon arrives at the same time. She walks toward me and holds my hand as we head down the sidewalk.

Once we're inside the apartment, we sit at the kitchen table and both stare at it.

"You open it," I say, sliding it closer to her. "Open it and tell me."

"Are you sure?" She lets out a breath and grabs it, and that's when I notice her hands are shaking.

"I'll do it," I tell her, and she hands it over to me like it's poison in her palm. Shaking my head, I rip it open and pull out the papers. On top is the paternity test result, and at the bottom, it says NO MATCH. I instantly smile.

"I knew it!" I tell her, handing her the paper. "I fucking knew it!"

Lennon reads it and crashes into my lap with tears in her eyes. Our lips melt together, and I get lost in her touch.

"I'm so relieved," she tells me, her shoulders falling.

"Me too, sweetheart. And now it's out there, and everyone knows. Even Jenna. I'm sure we won't be hearing from her ever again." I sigh.

"Better not." Lennon's nose brushes against mine. "I feel bad for her, though. I do. I hope she finds the real father and she can get the closure she needs."

"Yeah, she's not a bad person. She's just lost," I say.

She turns and notices the other papers on the table. "What's this?"

I turn her toward me, my eyes meeting hers. "I wanted to see if anything has changed with my sperm count, and they did the testing there, so I went for it." I shrug.

She frantically searches my face. "You didn't tell me."

"I'm sorry. I didn't want to get your hopes up because I'm sure nothing is different from five years ago, but now that I have you, I wanted to know for certain."

"So there's a chance?" she asks, sounding hopeful, and it nearly destroys me. She notices me swallow hard. "Hunter."

My eyes meet hers again. "I don't know."

I've been tested twice, but it's been so long I honestly don't know if it can be reversed at this point. After the initial results, I did some research about low sperm count and how men can increase it naturally with better nutrition, avoiding certain medications, drinking less alcohol, and eating less processed foods. The first test was done in college when I played football and trained hardcore year-round, which was another suggestion to avoid.

Later, I did the physical exams to make sure it wasn't cancer or a genetic disorder, which were all clear. I always figured when the time came, and I was ready to have kids, I'd do more tests and anything to increase my chances. This test will be the first step in deciding how we move forward.

Lennon presses her hands on either side of my face, cupping my cheeks so sweetly. "I've already accepted it and so have you. It doesn't change the way I feel about you. At all. But knowing will help us either way."

I let out a ragged breath. "I know."

Lennon repositions her body on my lap and grabs the stack of papers. I don't look, but instead, watch her as she reads through it. Her smile falls, and tears form in her eyes.

"I'm sorry." It's all I *can* say. Having this test done did nothing more than get her hopes up that maybe we could one day have more children, and I regret putting her through this.

"No," she croaks out. "Look." She holds the papers so tight in her hand and points at one specific reading at the bottom that says *normal*.

My mouth falls open.

Shock. Happiness.

A load of emotions streams through me.

"Normal," I whisper.

She sets the papers down on the table and turns her body until she's straddling me. With her arms around my neck, she presses her lips ever so slightly against mine. She rocks her hips against my growing cock, and I need her right now. When she pulls away, we're both shocked and breathless.

"We could add to our family, Hunter." A tear streams down her face, and I kiss it away.

"You and Alison are all I've ever needed, but the possibility is there now. I'm so fucking happy." The corner of my lips tilts so high it nearly reaches my eyes.

"Me too," she whispers. The joy on her face has my heart rapidly beating.

She stands and holds out her hand. Once I take it, she leads me to the bedroom. As soon as we cross the threshold, we can't keep our hands and mouths off one another. Taking my time, I unsnap each button of her blouse, brushing my fingertips across the tops of her breasts as they rise and fall. She helps by unzipping her skirt, then steps out of the pool of fabric around her feet.

"Fuck me," I say, admiring her curves. "You're so gorgeous."

She smirks, watching me with smoldering eyes as she removes her bra and panties. "I need to feel you, Hunter."

I love it when Lennon takes control. Within a minute, she has my clothes removed and is dropping to her knees and taking me in her mouth. I run my fingers through her hair as I let out throaty groans. Not missing an inch, she sucks and twirls her tongue along my shaft, paying extra attention to the tip as she gently plays with my balls.

"Lennon," I tell her, knowing if she keeps this up, I'll explode in her mouth, which at this rate, I think that's what she wants. She looks up at me with big blue eyes and gives me a half-smile. I pull her up, sliding my tongue into her mouth before I lead her to the bed. I grab her thighs, bringing her to the edge, and bury my head between her legs.

"You taste so fucking good." Growling, I flick and lick her clit, loving the way she writhes against me.

"Yes, yes, Hunter. God, yes…" She pants as I curl two fingers in deep.

With my free hand, I pinch her nipple between my fingers, mixing a little pain with pleasure. She's gasping, begging for more as she grabs the comforter. With an arched back, she sinks into my tongue, and I slow my movements, allowing the orgasm to build to the maximum. She moans my name, riding out her release. I stand, aligning our bodies so I can slide inside her. Then it hits me that the test results are normal, and I don't go any farther.

She searches my face. "What's wrong?"

"We don't have any condoms. Should I pull out?"

I know she's not on birth control either.

A sweet smile slides across her lips, and she shakes her head. "No."

My brows shoot to my hairline.

"I want to be the woman to give you a baby." There's

something in her eyes that has my blood pumping faster and it shakes me to the core.

"Are you sure?"

"I've never been more certain about anything in my life." The sound of her words is music to my ears. It's as sweet as her singing, and my heart is ready to explode.

As I hover above her, our mouths crash together. I'm lost in her touch, in her taste, in every inch of her as we make love. Slowly, I enter her, and she gasps as our bodies become one.

Lennon pulls me closer. Panting and moaning, we breathe each other in, and I mark her skin with my teeth and lips. She's my everything, and I can't imagine not having her in my life. We've been through so much together, and somehow, we both survived, but we couldn't have without the other.

With those thoughts roaming through my head, I lose myself inside her just as she wanted.

My eyes flutter open, and she's already looking at me with so much adoration. I can barely contain my happiness. Lennon wants to have my babies, and I want more than anything to give her that.

"I love you," she whispers as we stay connected.

I dip down, kissing the tip of her nose. "I love you more than you'll ever know."

CHAPTER FORTY-FIVE

LENNON

Hunter being able to have children is a miracle in and of itself. Not being able to expand our little family was okay, and I was completely content with it, but this changes things drastically. I want to be the woman to carry his children, and hopefully, one day I will. It's as if our jagged edges, the broken parts of us, have smoothed with time. We're still healing, but together we're whole.

My eyes flutter open before my alarm goes off, and I feel his hardness digging into my back, which makes me grin. My body aches from where he was yesterday, but I can't seem to get enough of him, not now, not ever. Considering Alison is sound asleep in the next room, I shimmy out of my panties and shorts and roll over. I take Hunter's thickness in my hand and give him a few strokes before his eyes flutter open.

"Mmm, good morning, beautiful," he hums against my lips. A beat later, I'm straddling him. His hands guide my hips, and he fucks me until I see stars. I try to keep quiet, biting my lower lip as we ride our release together. Collapsing on his chest, I let out a small laugh. "Who needs coffee in the morning when I've got you?"

A chuckle escapes him before I slide off him and clean up.

"Take a shower with me?" I ask with big puppy eyes, and he easily agrees.

Before we go to the bathroom, I check on Alison, who's sleeping soundly. I'm not sure a freight train could wake her when she's out. Grabbing the baby monitor, I take it with me.

Hunter's already waiting in the shower when I step in, and I take a moment to admire every inch of this beautiful man. My mother once told me I was lucky to find love once and not to allow the second time to slip through my fingers. Sometimes, I hate to admit it, but she was so right.

"What?" He grins as he grabs the soap, paying extra attention to my breasts and ass.

"I'm so grateful for you," I admit. "I'm not sure I would've survived without you."

He gives me a smile and leans forward to pull me close, then kisses me. "You would have. You're the strongest person I know."

I shake my head. "No. You are."

Hunter kisses my forehead as the warm water falls over my back. I wrap my arms around him, and we stand, embracing one another like it might end tomorrow. Though I know it won't, I don't take anything for granted anymore, not after losing Brandon.

Once Hunter lets me go, he washes my hair, massaging my scalp, and if my eyes weren't closed, they'd roll in the back of my head. I love showering with him because every inch of my body gets washed, and his touch feels so damn good. Returning the favor, I run my soapy hands over his abs, paying extra attention to below the waist.

"Mmm. If you keep that up, we're gonna get dirty all over again," he warns, and I giggle, knowing we don't have time.

Soon we're stepping out of the shower, and Hunter hands me a towel. We dry off quickly, then I hear Alison crying.

It's crunch time, so I'm not late for school. I still need to get her ready for Mrs. Locke, who happily watches her while I work. She says watching Alison is the highlight of her day, and I'm so grateful for her love and support. Brandon's parents have been a huge help and adore the baby so much.

I'm also glad my parents have been over the moon about their granddaughter. They FaceTime me as much as possible and have encouraged me to keep posting to Instagram for baby updates. I feel so lucky that things turned out the way they did with the pregnancy and having them in Alison's life now.

Between my parents and Brandon's, along with my sisters and Hunter, she's the most spoiled three-month-old I've ever seen, but she's also the most loved.

After she's fed and we're both dressed, I quickly double-check the diaper bag to make sure everything is inside along with fresh bottles of breast milk. I glance at the time and know I'm cutting it close. When I walk back into the kitchen, I see a shirtless Hunter standing at the coffeepot wearing a grin.

"What're you doing? You're gonna be late," I tell him, shaking my head.

"It's Friday. I don't have to be at work until ten for a meeting. I can take Allie to Mrs. Locke's so you're not late."

I release a relieved breath. "Are you sure?"

He tucks loose strands of hair behind my ear, and I melt into his touch. "I owe Mrs. Locke a visit. Plus, she gives me a bag of cookies each time I stop by."

A laugh escapes me. "Maybe I should be offended because I'm not getting any cookies." Standing on my tiptoes, I press my lips against his, and he deepens the kiss. "Love you."

"Love you too," he tells me as he slaps a hand against my ass.

"Don't forget the diaper bag and make sure Mrs. Locke doesn't need anything. Oh and—"

"Babe. I've got this."

I laugh. "Okay. I'll see you after work."

"Have a good day," he singsongs as I rush out of the apartment.

My heart is so damn full I can barely describe the way I feel. So much has happened in a year that I'm often pinching myself to make sure this is real life. Each time Hunter kisses me or holds me close, I know it is. Though I've had some horrible things happen, I'm happy where my life is now because there was a point when I didn't think I'd be able to get up in the morning. I had no purpose, and I was nothing more than a shell of myself. Time can't heal all wounds, but each day, it gets easier. I'll always love Brandon, and I'll forever be appreciative of the gift he gave me. After Alison was born, I realized that loving again doesn't mean I'm trying to replace him. He loved me and Hunter so much, so I know deep in my heart he'd want us to be together.

By the time I get to school, it's nearly time for class to start. The day is uneventful, and each grade practices the songs they'll be performing for the spring concert. The kids are so adorable, and their parents will be thrilled.

After class is done, I check my phone and see a text from Sophie and one from Hunter. My thoughts go back to the night of Maddie's birthday party and the night Hunter and I got together. After that, I knew they'd be completely over the moon when I told them about Hunter and me being official. The next morning, we did a three-way call, and when I told them about Hunter coming home and demanding I explain myself, they both said *finally*, but were definitely happy for us. Of course I skipped all the steamy details, but they got the gist.

Sitting in my car, I decide to open Sophie's text first. Ever since she moved in with Weston, I haven't seen her as much lately, and I miss our time together. Between her busy work schedule and spending her free time with her boyfriend, it's gotten harder to get together.

SOPHIE

Wanna meet at the grocery store after work? I need to pick up some things, plus I miss you!

LENNON

Yeah! When?

SOPHIE

I'll be there in about fifteen minutes. See you
soon!

I open my texts and read the one from Hunter, and I feel a ball
lodged in my throat.

HUNTER

I asked Mrs. Locke if she could keep Allie
overnight so we can go on a proper date, and
she said yes! Get ready to be wined and dined,
my love.

I immediately call him.

"Hey you," he says nonchalantly, but I know he's smirking.

"She can't stay overnight. I didn't pack everything she needs.
Hunter, she doesn't have her favorite blanket or extra bottles
or—"

"Lennon." He chuckles. "I packed all that. Plus, Mrs. Locke
knows how to take care of her. She's super attentive to everything
that little girl could possibly need. Take a deep breath, sweetheart.
She's going to be perfectly fine. And if something goes wrong,
we'll be the first ones to get a call, but trust me that nothing is
going to happen."

With a racing heart, I sit silent on the phone, thinking about
how unprepared I was for her to have a sleepover. The last time
she did, it took tons of planning. I had to make sure there was
extra breast milk, diapers, and…the list goes on and on.

"Do you trust me?" he asks, pulling me from my thoughts.

"You know I do," I say without hesitation.

"Then *trust* me. I have something fun planned for us. You
deserve a night out."

I release a breath and try to calm down. "Well, Sophie wanted
to meet me at the grocery store after work. Do I have time?"

"Yeah, I won't be home until six-ish to get you, so that works
out perfectly."

I can tell he's smiling.

"Alright. I'll see you then."

"It's going to be fine," he reminds me before we exchange I love yous.

As soon as we end the call, I head to the store. It doesn't take me long to get there, and I end up waiting for her at the entrance. As soon as I see her, my face contorts because she looks like total shit. She smiles as if nothing is wrong as we walk in. Her hair is disheveled, and she has bags under her eyes like she hasn't been getting much sleep. I'm fucking worried. Ever since she started dating Weston, her demeanor has changed. My sister isn't that happy-go-lucky girl anymore, and it's more noticeable than ever right now.

"So how's school been?" She goes straight to the vegetables, not making eye contact with me.

"It's been great. Getting ready for the spring concert next week," I say and notice bruises on her arms as she reaches for some bell peppers. I grab her hand and pull her to me to take a closer look. Her eyes meet mine as she jerks her arm back.

Lowering my voice, I stare directly at her. "What happened, Soph?"

She laughs. "It's nothing."

"That's *not* nothing." I place my hands on my hips and wait for her to explain.

"Weston was drinking a few days ago and things got out of hand. He grabbed me too hard but didn't mean to. He felt bad about it afterward."

I notice the slight bruising on her cheek too. She tried to cover it with concealer, but I can see straight through it. "Did he hit you?"

"It was an accident, Lennon," she says between gritted teeth.

Shaking my head, I'm so damn pissed that I can barely find my words. "You don't drink too much, then *accidentally* hit someone. This is not okay."

"He promised me it would never happen again, okay?" she

snaps, which takes me by surprise. She's never talked to me this way before. And why the hell is she defending him? "He loves me, Lennon. I know that's hard for you to believe because no one is allowed to be happy except for you."

My mouth falls open. "Are you serious right now? I want nothing but the best for you and Maddie. That's total bullshit that you'd say that to me."

I turn my body and head toward the exit. Sophie chases after me.

"Lennon, wait. I'm sorry. I don't want to argue with you."

I'm so pissed right now that I can barely look at her.

"I didn't mean to say that. I have a lot going on right now and shouldn't have taken it out on you. I know you only want the best for me." Her bottom lip trembles, and I know there's something she's not telling me.

"You need to be careful, Sophie. It's not okay for a man to hit a woman, no matter what, and I'm worried about you. Weston is a dickhead, and I don't care for him already, then this happens."

"I know. He promised, and I believe him." Her meek voice doesn't sound like her at all, which worries the hell out of me.

"I'm here for you. Don't let him make excuses for this behavior," I plead. "There shouldn't have been a first time."

"I won't, and yes, I know," she tells me, then quickly changes the subject. We continue shopping, and I pick out a few things for the apartment, but I can't get over the bruises on her arms.

How hard did he grab her to leave thumb and fingerprints like that? The thought makes me seethe and my heart hurts for her so damn bad. After thirty minutes, we finish shopping and check out.

After I help her load everything into her car, I pull her into a hug. "Please take care of yourself and call me if something happens or if you need to get out because he's drunk again. *Promise* me."

She nods and forces a smile. "I promise. But you have to promise me something."

"What's that?"

"You won't mention this to anyone. Not even Hunter. Please," she begs.

I narrow my eyes, not wanting to agree. "I will this time. But if I see even the tiniest of marks again, I'm not staying quiet…" I tell her. "And I will call the cops on him."

"You won't have to. He's been super stressed, and he learned his lesson about drinking too much." She swears to it and hugs me again. We say our goodbyes, and as I sit inside my car, upset and frustrated, I feel helpless. She's blinded by love, but I'm not going to let that keep me from voicing how I feel about the asshole.

As I drive home, I push the thoughts of it out of my head for now. My big sister has always been the strongest person I've ever known, so I know she can stand up for herself when needed.

By the time I make it to the apartment, it's nearly five. I bring in our groceries, excited about what Hunter has planned. Our dates consist of ordering in and watching *Friends*, which neither of us minds, but this will be a nice change of pace.

When I walk inside, pink roses are on the table and a dress hangs on the back of a chair. My mouth falls open when I find an envelope with my name on it.

> Lennon,
> Considering we never go out, I thought I'd make up for it all at once. A driver will be waiting for you downstairs at 6:30. I'll see you soon.
> Love you!
> -Hunter

"That little shit," I say with a huge smile splashed across my face.

I take another shower to freshen up, then redo my hair and

makeup. Before I get dressed, I pull some sexy lingerie from my top drawer and slip it on, then grab the dress Hunter picked out. It's a high-waisted light blue A-line party dress, fancy as hell and much different from anything I own. Just by looking at this, I have no clue what we'll be doing, but I'm excited nonetheless.

Looking in the full-length mirror, I'm amazed by how well it fits. Did Hunter take my measurements in my sleep? The thought has me giggling. I rush to my closet and grab a pair of heels, slip them on, then take a deep breath. I have ten minutes. The smile on my lips might be permanent this time. Before I walk out the door, I dial Mrs. Locke's number to check on Alison.

"Hey, Lennon. How are things going?" she asks.

I laugh at her light tone. "Just checking on you two."

She lets out a sweet chuckle. "Honey, we're doing fine. Are you doing okay?"

I realize when she asks me the question, I'm nervous. "I haven't been on a real date since—" I pause and swallow hard. *Since Brandon was alive.*

I try to think about my life right now and how Brandon would want me to be happy above all things. It's a small reminder that it's okay for me to be okay.

"I know. And it's the reason you need to have a night out on the town. So quit worrying. We're fine over here. Enjoy yourself, Lennon. You deserve to."

Her words repeat in my mind, and I grin. She was surprisingly supportive of Hunter and me being together once we told her. I was nervous at first, but she gave me a look as if she'd known it was coming or something. Apparently, our feelings were obvious to everyone around us.

"You're right. Give my girl kisses for me."

"I will. Have fun."

After we say our goodbyes, I take a deep breath and leave.

The limo waits downstairs. I get inside and see a bottle of champagne and strawberries. I laugh at how extra he's being tonight but enjoy myself, like Brandon's mom suggested, as we drive across town. Eventually, the car slows and I'm utterly speechless when I step out and realize I'm at Fairytale Town.

It's a theme park based around children's storybooks, and I'm more confused than ever when I see a man dressed as a toy soldier at Humpty Dumpty's entrance. I walk up to him, and he hands me a note and a map of the park with a smirk, then goes back into position.

I was once the boy who'd never grow up.
You could say I was a part of the lost boys until I found you.

I look at the toy soldier. "I just go inside?"

"Yes, ma'am."

"But isn't it closed?" I ask, noticing there's no one around.

"It's open for you," he ensures. I've heard about this place before but have never visited it as long as I've lived in Sacramento. I step under the archway and open the map and look for anything related to his clue. *Lost boys.* Thinking about it, I realize it's a Peter Pan reference and scan the map. My eyes land upon the pirate ship, and I follow the sidewalk to it. Upon arriving, a woman dressed like Tinker Bell is waiting. She hands me an envelope, and I hurry and rip it open.

Slow and steady wins the race. Baby, I'd wait a lifetime for you.

I bite my lower lip, grinning, then head toward the Turtle and the Hare attraction. A man is dressed as a referee and gives me another envelope. I thank him and read the next clue.

I don't need a shoe to know you're The One.

I'm smiling so big and rush toward the Cinderella coach. Upon arrival, I find a woman dressed as a fairy godmother. I glance at her hands and realize she's not holding an envelope, but she's looking at me with soft eyes and a smirk.

"Cinderella, you've made it. Now it's time for me to bring you to the ball to meet your Prince Charming," she tells me.

I burst out into laughter, realizing now why my dress is this color. I nod, giddy as hell.

"But first." She pulls a blindfold from out of nowhere. "You'll need to wear this."

"Seriously?" I ask but turn around and allow her to put it on me.

My heart pounds so hard in my chest as she slowly guides me down the sidewalk. I try to figure out what Hunter has planned, but I honestly have no clue. We walk a little farther, and she guides me up the stairs until I feel hands—*his* strong hands—grabbing mine.

"You look beautiful," Hunter whispers in my ear, and shivers run down my spine as he leads me.

"You have some explaining to do."

"I know," he says and takes off the blindfold.

My mouth falls open when I see Hunter wearing a suit that fits him perfectly. I turn to see where we are. I'm standing on the Mother Goose stage with bright lights in my eyes. I try to shield the light and see a small crowd of people out there but can't make out who it is. Looking back at Hunter with wide eyes, I have a mini freak-out because I have no clue what's going on. When the *Friends* theme song starts playing, I laugh and slightly relax.

Hunter chuckles, grabs both of my hands, and drops to one knee.

And that's when what's happening hits me like a ton of bricks.

The music softens, and Hunter looks into my eyes with so much love and adoration, I nearly collapse.

He doesn't even have to speak or ask.

The answer is already *yes*.

CHAPTER FORTY-SIX

HUNTER

WHEN I SEE Lennon walk around the corner and come up the steps, my heart pounds so damn hard, I'm sure everyone can hear it. Our family and friends are here, just as she would want it. Her parents and sisters are such a big part of her life, as well as the Lockes. Of course I wanted my brother and his fiancée, Savannah, here too. Liam and Mason as well, who flash me grins and thumbs-ups, a complete turnaround from how they acted six months ago. When I told them Lennon and I were finally together, they supported us and apologized for making conclusions beforehand. I knew they were only protective of Brandon's legacy, but they knew my feelings were real.

As I drop to one knee, Lennon's mouth falls open even though she knows she's the only woman I want to be with—the only woman I've ever wanted to be with. She tucks her lips into her mouth and squeezes my hands. My nerves get the best of me, so I suck in a ragged breath and find my words.

"Lennon," I croak out and clear my throat. "At one point in our past, you thought I was the Beast, and maybe I was. But you were always *my* Belle, the one who taught me how to love and be loved. Without you, I might've stayed a beast forever, and I will be

eternally grateful for you. Our story didn't start like a fairy tale—"
I let out a laugh as a tear falls down her cheek.

"Don't cry," I whisper, just loud enough for her to hear.

She pulls her hand from mine and wipes it away but gives me
a sweet smile to continue.

"It was far from it. But no matter what, we had each other.
When I was the loneliest I've ever been, you were a bright yellow
ray of sunshine when the days were dark and gloomy. From the
moment I met you, I knew I couldn't live without you. You're my
other half, Lennon. You're the Monica to my Chandler, the Belle to
my Beast, and the woman I want to spend the rest of my life with."

I pull the ring from my pocket, the same ring she wore when
we were pretending to be married. It's been with us through it all.
When I open the box, she sees it, and her face lights up. The
memories flash across her face, and I think back to Utah and what
we've been through.

"Lennon Corrigan, will you be *my* princess? I promise to give
you the happily ever after you and Allie deserve and to love you
with everything I have. Will you marry me and make me the
happiest fucking man alive?"

"Yes," she whispers through tears. "Yes a million times over!"
Lennon says louder.

I smile so damn wide, my body shakes as I take the ring from
the box and slip it on her finger. Standing, I pull her into a kiss.
Everyone roars and claps, and I hear Maddie's scream over it all.
"Now give her another baby!"

Everyone laughs, and Lennon pulls away and looks for her
sister, but the lights are too bright.

She wraps her arms around my neck. "I love you," she tells me
over and over.

I cup her cheeks gently. "I love you so damn much. I couldn't
wait another day to make you mine forever."

"Good. I feel the same way." Lennon is all smiles, and we walk
down the steps and meet everyone as a quartet of violinists begins

to play. Sophie wanted to help, of course, once I told her and suggested music. We're bombarded with congratulations and hugs, and I feel so damn lucky that so many people are here to support us.

Getting to this point wasn't easy, but I know nothing worth having is.

The Lockes come over, pushing Allie in her stroller. She looks adorable in the little blue dress that matches Lennon's.

"So you were in on this the entire time?" she asks them both.

Mrs. Locke shrugs and nods.

"Oh my gosh. Look at your dress," Lennon says as she grabs Allie, then realizes they're twinning.

Her sisters walk up, and Sophie suggests we need more photos. I know they probably took a ton already. Maddie takes Lennon's phone and begins snapping photos of Lennon and the baby.

"Okay, Daddy, get in too," Maddie demands, physically pushing me into the photo.

"It sounds so dirty when you call him that." Lennon gives her a pointed look and shakes her head before bursting into laughter.

Maddie wiggles her eyebrows, and I shake my head. That girl is a handful.

"Where's your boyfriend?" I ask when I notice Sophie is alone because I invited them both.

"Oh, he couldn't make it. Got caught up at work," she tells me with a smile.

Lennon glares at Sophie, and they hold a silent conversation, but I don't question it. I've tried several times to send an invite to our guys' nights so we could get to know him, but he always has *something* come up. Weston's weird as fuck. Liam and Mason both hate him with a passion, though I haven't quite figured out why yet, considering he's never around.

"Right," Mason says from behind us.

Sophie rolls her eyes, but he ignores her. Something he's good at. Their weird behavior toward each other after all this time makes me think something has happened between them—and both are hiding it. There has to be a reason, otherwise, it's just plain ridiculous at this point. Ever since Brandon died and my focus has primarily been on Lennon and the baby, the four of them have hung out, but I never ask for details. Perhaps I should have. Maybe one of them would've cracked by now.

Maddie lights up when she sees Liam even though he still pretends she doesn't exist—though I know better. The way they all act has me cracking up. Lennon notices and laughs too, but she's paying more attention to Allie than her sisters.

As they go back and forth with each other, the Corrigans come over and pull us to the side to tell us how much they love and support us. Lennon's mom takes the chance to steal Allie and hold her.

"So happy you're gonna be a part of the family…for real this time," Mr. Corrigan tells me.

"Dad," Lennon jumps in, but all he does is laugh.

They ask when we're going to get married, and Lennon has to remind them that we just got engaged. After about ten minutes of chatting, Hayden pulls me away to chat, then I'm met face-to-face with my parents. My expression drops when I see them because I didn't expect them to come. They've never wanted to be a part of my life before, so why start now?

Hayden stands guard, ready to interfere at any moment.

"Hi, son," my dad says, and my mother gives me a small, hopeful smile.

"Hello," I say, crossing my arms.

Lennon walks over and stands beside me, and she's the only thing that calms me down. Her sweet voice brings me back to reality as she introduces herself to my parents. We have no secrets between us, so she knows all about our history and my childhood.

Savannah approaches, and I finally introduce her to Lennon as well. As they're caught up in conversation, giggling like they've known each other forever, my mother looks at me.

"She's lovely, Hunter. Seems like you found your match." There's sincerity in her voice.

"I'm proud of you, son," my father finally says, leaving me speechless.

Even Hayden does a double take when the words leave his mouth.

"What?" I say, too shocked to form more words.

"I know I haven't been the best father over the years…" He trails off, and I halfway wonder if he fell and hit his head. By Hayden's expression, I know he's thinking the same thing. "But I'd like to change that. I'm sorry."

"You can't show up like this and expect all to be forgiven with an apology. You'll need to prove you mean it."

I'm not sure what the heck happened for this change of heart, but I'm still guarded when it comes to him. My mother's expression doesn't change and neither does Hayden's.

"That's fair," he says. "Maybe we can have a family dinner, like old times."

My mother nods, and I hate to disappoint her when she wants our family back together more than ever.

"Okay," I agree.

Lennon comes back over and tells them it was nice meeting them before thankfully leading me away from them.

"That was…surprising," she says, searching my eyes.

"Hayden asked if I invited our parents. He said he would, if I wanted, and I told him I didn't care. Honestly, I didn't expect them to show up, considering I've always been a disappointment to my dad."

"They're trying, Hunter. Maybe you should give them a second chance." Her lips gently touch mine, and I melt into her, allowing her calmness to wash over me. Somehow, she magically has that effect on me when I'm upset. When I'm with Lennon, nothing else even matters.

"I know. But some people don't deserve them."

"And if you truly believed that, then we wouldn't be engaged right now. It's a start at least."

I pull her into my arms, missing her closeness and how sweet she smells. "Why are you so logical?"

She grins. "Because one of us has to be."

"You look so beautiful," I whisper, my mouth grazing the shell of her ear. Lennon leans into me and hums. The curve of her body rests against mine, and all I want to do right now is get the hell out of here so we can be alone, just us.

The sun is barely setting over the horizon, and Lennon searches around for Alison. Mrs. Locke is holding her while Mr. Locke chats with the Corrigans. We walk over, and Lennon gives love and kisses to Allie, and we say our goodbyes to everyone. She wants to get out of here just as quickly as I do since Mrs. Locke is keeping the baby, and we'll have all night together.

"Leaving so soon?" Maddie asks.

"Yeah, we want to go *celebrate*." Lennon waggles her brows, which makes Maddie gag in response. Before we go, Lennon pulls her into a hug. "Take care of Sophie, okay?"

Maddie nods, and as we walk away, I look at her.

"What was that about?"

"Nothing. Just sister stuff." She shakes her head.

I wrap my arm around her, not wanting to push it, so I change the subject. "So were you surprised?"

Though she tries to pretend she wasn't, I know better. "Of course I was shocked. I think I still am. I didn't expect any of this. It's not a dream, right? Like I'm not going to wake up with your rock-hard cock in my back wishing this were real life?"

I wrap my arm around her as we walk past the Hickory Dickory Clock, and my laughter bounces through the park. "Waking up with my cock in your back sounds like a plan, but no, it's not a dream. It's real life. And we're going to spend the rest of our days together. I can't fucking wait."

"Thank you," she whispers, and for a second, she chokes up.

"No, baby. Thank you. You've made me the happiest man on the planet."

I hold her tight, never wanting to let her go as we continue through the park. I think about where we started and where we're at right now. I think about everything we've been through and how we made it together. Grateful doesn't even begin to describe how I feel about Lennon being in my life.

I take her hand as we walk over the bridge past the pirate ship and eventually pass King Arthur's castle. I look around and smile, thinking how perfect this place is. "We'll have to take Allie here when she's a little older. I think she'd love it."

Lennon lights up. "Absolutely. Now it'll always hold a special place in my heart, and I can't wait to tell her about how I met my Prince Charming when she's older."

"Just leave out the part where I was a major asshole, okay?" I chuckle, and Lennon laughs with me, agreeing. We walk to the truck, and while we make our way back to the apartment, she asks me tons of questions about planning all of this, which surprises her even more.

My heart is so goddamn full I can barely contain the way I feel. Lennon will have my last name, and we'll finally get our happily ever after.

Once we're inside, we both let out a sigh at the same time.

"People-ing is exhausting." She sighs. "But I'm so happy they were all there. My parents. The Lockes. Hayden and Savannah. Your parents. Liam and Mason. My sisters. So blessed to have them all in our lives."

"We are. And I'm so blessed to have you," I admit, and she takes two steps forward and removes the space between us. As our mouths touch, we become more ravenous for one another as the seconds tick by.

"I'm the lucky one," she says between pants and moans.

No matter how many times I have her, it's not enough, and it never will be. I've imagined being engaged to her since the moment we pretended to be married. Then I never thought it would happen.

She teases me with her mouth as she nibbles on my bottom lip. I need her but can't rush this, not tonight. We have forever, and I want to take my time and live in the moment with her, appreciating every curve of her body.

Gently, I brush my fingers across the soft skin of her neck, reaching behind her and unzipping the dress that fits her like a glove. It falls to the ground, and my eyes light up when I notice the lacy lingerie she wore for me. It's a nice surprise, and I'm ready to rip every thread from her body, but instead, I appreciate and study her as she stands confidently waiting for me.

"I love it when you look at me like that," she whispers, her breasts rising and falling.

"Like what?"

"Like I'm the only thing in the world worth looking at."

"Because you are."

Hooking my fingers in her panties, I move them to the side and discover she's already wet and ready for me.

"I can't wait any longer…" She releases a small moan when I sink a finger inside. "I need you now."

When she looks at me with so much want in her eyes as she is right now, it makes my knees weak. I lead her to the bedroom where she undresses me, taking her time undoing each button, then lightly brushes her fingertips across my stomach. Her touch drives me absolutely in-fucking-sane.

Once I'm naked, I tease her as I remove her bra and panties, touching the softness of her breasts and skin. After she lies down, I kiss up her stomach, sucking and flicking my tongue against the taut peak of her nipple, then not allowing the other to go untouched.

Lennon runs her fingers through my hair, tugging and writhing underneath me, waiting for me to enter as I tease her opening.

"Please," she begs, and I can't hold out any longer. Parting her legs and pressing her heels against my ass, she forces me inside her, and the emotions that swarm through me are so intense, I nearly see stars. We take it slow, making love, enjoying each other, completely encapsulated in the moment, in the breathlessness, in the kisses.

We're one, moving together in rhythm, and I never want this to end as she moans out my name and scratches her nails down my back. Pain mixed with pleasure, the exact definition of our relationship, the foundation of what our love was built on. But somehow, we made it together, not the same people we were when we met, different and now stronger. We're two beautifully broken people who use the other as glue to hold it all together. There is no me without her and vice versa. What we have will last a lifetime.

I remind her how much I love her and thank her for agreeing to be my wife as we lose ourselves in the moment to never be found. The orgasms shake through us, and as we come down from our high, all we can do is smile.

After we clean up, I hold her in my arms and promise never to let her go. I kiss her forehead, then gently brush my fingers against her arm as she lies across my chest, listening to my heartbeat. It's only ever felt like this with Lennon, as if my body and soul were created for this woman. From the moment I laid eyes on her, she unlocked something deep inside me, and I knew she was the one. I always knew as much as I tried to fight it.

All is quiet, and eventually, she speaks. "That night at the bar, when we first met, what were you really thinking?"

"That I didn't believe in love at first sight until I met you."

"That's sickly sweet." She smiles in a sleepy haze. "I love you."

"I love you too, sweetheart." I hold her tighter. "You have no idea how happy you make me and that you're mine."

She lifts her head and kisses me. "All yours."

EPILOGUE

LENNON

"LENNON, QUICK! HURRY!" Hunter shouts from the living room. I stumble in my high heel, one on my foot and the other in my hand. "Lennon!"

His urgent screaming has me scrambling, which makes me stub my toe on the dresser and mutter a slew of curse words.

Oh my God. This man. His face better be on fire.

"Are you coming?"

"Hold on!" I kick off my shoe, drop the other one, and run down the hallway to where he and Alison are waiting for me.

"Look! She rolled over!" Hunter's on the floor next to her lying on a blanket. "She did back to belly, then belly to back! All by herself!" The way he's gushing about her makes me beam.

"You nearly made me pee myself!" I scold, but I'm smiling because I can't be mad at him for being so excited about Alison's milestone. At only six months old, she's changing so fast.

"Sorry, babe! I didn't want you to miss it." Hunter watches her with so much love it's hard to even be mad about my throbbing toe. "Allie Kat, you're a genius!"

I snort at the nickname Maddie gave her, the one I tell her to stop saying, but it caught on anyway. Hunter loves her as his own, and as soon as we're married, we're going to make it official so he'll legally be her father. She'll keep Brandon's last name and hyphenate it with Hunter's. *Alison Kay Locke-Manning.* We talk about him any chance we can, making sure she grows up knowing that she has a daddy in heaven who watches over her every day and that Hunter is her daddy here on Earth who loves her more than anything.

At times, the sadness hits me harder than others, but then I look at Alison and think of the amazing gift Brandon gave me. I know he'd be so damn happy to know he has a little girl. I can only hope he'd be happy to know Hunter is the one who stepped up to be here for us.

Hunter looks too damn happy as he encourages and cheers her on that I don't have the heart to tell him she did this yesterday. She's been able to roll from her belly to her back for a while now but not back to belly. I was so tired by the time he got home from a late meeting that I completely forgot to mention it. He already feels like he misses too much with his crazy work schedule, so I let him believe this is the first time.

"Are you almost ready, sweetheart?" Hunter stands and presses a sweet kiss to my forehead. "You look incredible, by the way." His eyes sweep down my body, stare at my chest longer than necessary, then back at my face. "You can't look this damn good when I can't do something about it…" He wraps his arms around me, and I blush.

"Don't you even dare," I warn him. "We can't be late. Plus, I have to show you something first."

Hunter releases an animalistic groan, throwing his head back. He's being so dramatic, considering he was all over me last night, which causes me to laugh.

I have butterflies in my stomach as I pick up Alison and tell him it's a surprise from both of us. Quickly, I go to the nursery and set her in the crib, then put the bib on her I picked up at the store yesterday. I wanted to plan something special for this moment, but considering it's already going to be a busy weekend, I can't wait any longer.

"Babe?" Hunter calls.

"Coming! Just grabbing Alison's diaper bag."

"Ready?" I whisper as I put her on my hip and tickle her chunky little belly.

"Let's go show Daddy."

My entire body shakes as I walk to the living room and grab her car seat. I give her a wink as I set her in but don't buckle her just yet. "Hey, what do you think of Alison's new bib?" I casually ask over my shoulder, hoping it's enough to lure him to come over and look.

Hunter grabs his keys and wallet from the coffee table, then steps over and stands behind me. "Butterflies, cute."

I sigh, shaking my head. He glanced at it without reading the damn thing. "Yeah, I thought it was appropriate."

"For what?"

"Read. It." I adjust it, making sure it's straight and legible. Holding it between my hands, I clear my throat.

"Being promoted to big sister…" He blinks and mutters the words again. "Wait, what? Are we getting a pet?"

Oh my God. I swallow, releasing a breath. "You're lucky you're handsome," I tease, but as soon as the words come out, his eyes widen as if a light bulb went off.

"Are you pregnant?" he asks, kneeling beside me. When I suck in my lower lip and nod, he grabs me and pulls me to him. "You're having a baby?" he frantically asks, pushing us apart and nearly giving me whiplash in the process.

"Yes! I'm one hundred percent positive! Trust me, I was in shock too."

Hunter looks at Alison, then back at me. "I can't believe it."

He brings his hand to my stomach and pulls me in for a deep, heart-stopping kiss. "I didn't know if we'd be able to…" When he rests his forehead on mine, I feel his tears against our cheeks. When we found out his test came back normal three months ago, we decided not to prevent pregnancy and live with the *if it happens, it happens* mentality. He's been worried since we've been having unprotected sex for so long that we might not be able to have kids. I had to explain to him that it can take up to a year for healthy couples and, in worst-case scenarios, even longer. But as soon as I was late and my boobs felt sore, I knew. It was signs I missed the first time around, but it was impossible to ignore now. I took five tests to confirm it, and when the final test showed the pink lines, my tears were from pure joy.

I'm giving Hunter a baby, and we're growing our family.

"Did you hear that, Allie Kat? You're gonna be a big sister!" He takes her out of the car seat and squeezes her.

I watch them with pure admiration. Hunter even added to his ink collection a couple of months ago and got her name and birth date tattooed on his chest over his heart. I was stunned when he brought up the idea and then said he planned on adding our wedding date to it once we set one.

"You're gonna have to share your toys," he tells her with a pointed look.

I snort, laughing at how adorable he is with her. There's still a lot to figure out—if we'll get a bigger place, when we'll get married, and if I'll go back to work after my maternity leave. The realization that we'll have two kids under two hits me.

"We're going to have double diaper duty," I tell him. "I hope you're ready…"

He smiles so wide, blowing raspberries on Alison's cheeks. "I'm so ready. For all of it."

"I love you," I tell him, leaning over to kiss him.

He puts Alison back, then buckles her in before cupping my face and crashing our mouths together in a deep, passionate kiss. "I love you so damn much, Lennon. I can't wait to marry you, have a dozen babies, and live happily every single day with my family."

"Sounds *perfect* to me."

Ten minutes later, the three of us are packed up and on the way to the church. It's Hayden and Savannah's big day, and I couldn't be more excited about it. Ever since we got engaged a few months ago, Hunter's dad has been making an effort to repair his relationship with his two sons. I know it's been years in the making, and it won't be fixed overnight, but I respect the man for trying.

"I'll see you soon, sweetheart," Hunter says, brushing his lips against mine, then focuses on Alison. "And you too, baby girl." He kisses her cheek, and she tries to lick him.

Hunter and I go our separate ways. He's the best man, and I'm one of Savannah's bridesmaids. We've grown closer since we met, and I've enjoyed getting to know her. It was entirely unexpected when she asked me to be in her wedding party, but I appreciated being included and am honored.

Savannah introduces me to her best friend, Donny, who's the Man of Honor, and his boyfriend, William. Donny's telling us all the juicy gossip about New York and what it's like to live in the Big Apple. Everyone except William and me are theater actors. William tells me how he first met Donny and ended up moving from California to New York to be with him, which I found super adorable.

The bridesmaids sing, dance, and drink while we wait in the bridal suite, and they have me laughing my ass off. Alison gets passed around and loved on, and I spill the beans about baby number two. I know Hunter has probably told Hayden by now, but I still have to tell my sisters.

Maddie is coming to the ceremony to watch Alison for me, and then I invited Sophie and her boyfriend, but she sent me a text shortly before it started saying she'd see me at the reception. I didn't have time to ask her why.

In the past six months, I've only seen Weston a few times. They moved in together three months ago even though I begged her not to. She wanted out of her apartment that badly. Between her busy work schedule and me being in bed by nine, we barely spend time with each other now. After seeing those bruises on her arm, I don't trust Weston as far as I can throw him, and she's been distant and weird when I bring it up. I miss her so much, and I'm looking forward to seeing her tonight so I can make sure she's doing okay but also announce the baby news.

I know it's soon, considering Alison is only six months old and we aren't married yet, but this baby is a blessing and will be celebrated. Since my parents have come around and accepted that I'm going to live my life how I see fit, I'm not even nervous to tell them this time. I'm so excited for Alison to be a big sister and hopefully close to her sibling like I am with mine.

Between getting ready, helping Savannah get into her gown, feeding the baby, taking pictures, and chatting with all the other girls, time flies. I walk down with one of Hayden's friends, and as soon as Hunter spots me, he flashes me a shit-eating smirk and a wink. I can't wait for our big day, and whether we do a huge celebration like this or elope, it'll be one of the happiest moments of my life.

The ceremony is beautiful, and their vows to each other make everyone in the room tear up. They talk about soul mates, young love, finding each other again after ten years, and how when you know, you just know. They're seriously a gorgeous couple, and as soon as they kiss as husband and wife, everyone erupts in cheers and applauds.

Hunter and I are summoned for pictures after, but I know Alison is in good hands with my sister so I don't go chasing them down right away. Hayden gives me a big hug to congratulate me on the baby and then I tease him that it's his turn now. Savannah overhears us and demands we not give him any ideas until the final weekend of her show. They're so adorable together. It's impossible not to feel the love radiating off them.

After almost two hours of photos, we head to the dinner, and I'm in complete awe when I see inside the reception hall. It's a fairy tale.

"You getting wedding fever?" Hunter whispers in my ear, wrapping his arm around my waist.

"Well, considering we did everything backward, I'm not sure I want to be big and pregnant in a wedding dress."

"Maybe by society's standards, but there's no order for falling in love, is there?" He waggles his brows, causing me to laugh at his expression.

"Got me there, Manning," I mock.

One of the best parts of the evening was hearing the speeches. Donny had the entire room about to pee themselves with his entertaining story. I swear, we were all in tears from laughing so hard. He mentioned some psycho woman who tried to get between Hayden and Savannah and how she claimed she was pregnant with Hayden's love child. Turned out she *was* pregnant, but the only way it could've been his was if she was the Virgin Mary and it was an immaculate conception.

"Maybe she's related to Jenna?" I whisper to Hunter, who snorts.

"There was nothing immaculate about this conception," he says, placing his hand over my stomach.

I smirk and roll my eyes. "Yes, everyone will know your swimmers are strong and mighty from now on."

Hunter invited Mason and Liam to the reception, and once dinner was over, they showed up, wearing slick suits and all. Maddie's face lights up but morphs into a glare when a woman walks up to Liam and they head to the bar.

"How can I compete with that when I can't even drink?" She groans, pouting.

"I doubt that's why he"—I wave my hand in the air—"is the way he is."

"You mean an asshole?"

I shrug with a *maybe* expression. Liam has always been a hard guy to read. He's brooding and grumpy, and anytime I ask Hunter questions, he tells me Liam had a rough childhood when his parents split, but leaves it at that. If Liam wanted us to know, he'd tell us.

"So where's the third musketeer?" Mason asks when he returns with a beer.

The fact he's asking about Sophie is pretty adorable. Kinda late in the game, considering she chased him for a year, but I'd much prefer him over Weston any day.

I check my phone and see Sophie still hasn't messaged me back. I call her, but she doesn't answer. Ten minutes later, she finally responds.

SOPHIE

Sorry, ran late. On our way now.

LENNON

Okay, I'll meet you in the hallway! I have big news!

Something feels off when she reads my message but doesn't reply. I want to tell her and Maddie together, so I've been holding my tongue all night.

"Okay, they're finally on their way. I'm going to wait in the hall. Can you hold Alison for me?" I ask Maddie so Hunter can join me. He knows I'm not a fan of Weston, and though Sophie begged me not to say anything to anyone about the bruises, I was pissed off one day, and it slipped. Hunter was livid, and somehow, I was able to calm him down. Honestly, I need Hunter to be my buffer so I can get Sophie alone for a few minutes.

They drive up in Weston's car—quite fast, I notice—but they don't get out immediately after he parks. I start to worry, so I walk across the parking lot, and she finally opens the door.

"Hey!" I greet, coming over to hug her. Her face perks up, and when I pull back, I notice how heavy her eye makeup is. "Everything okay?"

"Yeah, we just lost track of time."

I don't buy it. Something's wrong.

Weston rounds the car and harshly grabs Sophie's hand, pulling her away from me. "I need a beer. Let's go."

I turn around and look at Hunter with a scowl on my face.

That asshole has some nerve.

"Sorry, but I'm *not* a fan," he murmurs to me as we follow them.

"Join the club."

"He better watch it before he gets his ass handed to him," Hunter says.

Once we're back inside, I carefully watch Sophie and Weston. Mason and Liam eye him pretty hard as well, the guy not making any effort to be nice to anyone. Hell, he's not even being nice to Sophie. She's not acting like herself either, which scares the shit out of me. She's timid and won't make eye contact with anyone.

"I gotta run to the bathroom and change Alison. Wanna come with me, Soph?" I ask with a smirk, daring her boyfriend to stop her.

"Sure," she says, and I motion for Maddie to come.

Before leaving, I lean down to grab the diaper bag, then whisper in Hunter's ear, "Watch him. I need time with Sophie."

He winks, crossing his arms over his broad chest. Weston would be an idiot to cross my man or, hell, any of the guys here. Mason and Liam especially.

I kiss his cheek and walk out with my sisters following.

Once we're in the ladies' room, I lock the door behind us and grab Sophie's arm so she turns toward me. "Please tell me you're not trying to cover up a black eye, Soph. I swear to God, I will murder him."

"It's not what you think," she protests weakly.

"Did he hit you?" Maddie asks, standing firmly next to me.

"He didn't mean to. Guys, stop. Please," she begs, her bottom lip trembling. The bastard has her so scared, and she's defending him.

"Please explain then," I say softly. I want to hear how him hitting her in the eye was an accident.

"Weston was punching the wall, over and over again. I tried to stop him from hurting himself by stepping in front of him, and he accidentally decked me," she explains, but I'm not buying it. "He didn't mean to, and he felt awful afterward."

Oh, as long as he feels awful…

I mentally roll my eyes.

"Why was he punching the wall?" Maddie asks.

Sophie looks down with a frown. "He lost his job a couple of days ago."

"Why?" I ask.

"Showed up to work still drunk from the night before. Instead of going home like his boss instructed, Weston started a fight and was told not to bother coming back at all."

"Was he drunk when he hit you?" I ask, deciding to check Alison's diaper while we're in here.

"Yeah, he's been drinking for days." Sophie's shoulders fall.

"So why was he driving?" Maddie asks, handing me the wipes.

"Because he wouldn't let me drive. That's why it took us so long to get here. I was trying to stall, get him to sober up, or I threatened to leave without him. He got mad and wouldn't let me go, so I said I'd wait for him if he'd stop and drink some coffee," Sophie says, looking at herself in the mirror. "It looks worse than it is."

"You can't honestly keep making excuses for him, Soph. He's a drunk, and he's hit and hurt you on more than one occasion," I tell her firmly. "Please, leave him. I'm scared for you."

She swallows as if she wants to be brave, but he's sucked all of the confidence out of her. "I don't have anywhere else to go," she explains softly. "I don't have money to get my own place, and I can't go back to my old apartment. What am I supposed to do?"

"Stay with us," I offer. "I'll get an air mattress, and we'll make it work while we find you somewhere else to live."

"It's not just that," she mutters. "He won't let me break up with him and leave."

"What?" Maddie snaps. "What does that mean?"

Sophie shrugs as if she's embarrassed. I get Alison redressed and place her on my hip.

"I tried to break up with him a few weeks ago when he slammed me against the wall," she admits, embarrassed. "He left more bruises on my already bruised arms so they're super sore now. He told me if I left him, he'd kill me."

"You need to go to the police," I demand. "You have physical evidence, Soph. Get a restraining order and start documenting it. Put his ass in jail."

"I'm *scared*, Lennon," she says with tears in her eyes.

Maddie gives her a hug, and I pull them into my arms.

"I know, Soph. We love you and will protect you, okay? Hunter, Mason, and Liam are all on your side."

"Just don't say anything yet, okay? I'd rather move my stuff out when he's sober, tell him it's over, then if he doesn't take it well, we'll get the cops involved." Sophie wipes under her eyes, careful to avoid her right eye that's swollen.

"You aren't doing it alone, though," I tell her, and we compromise.

After a few minutes, I decide to change the subject and cheer her up. "So I have some news to share…" My words get cut off by a commotion of people running and police sirens.

"What the hell is that?" Maddie says, racing toward the door.

Sophie and I follow, speed walking behind her. There's a crowd of people huddled by the exit doors. I spot Hunter and Liam. Their outfits and hair are a mess, and as soon as Hunter makes eye contact with me, his distraught look makes me panic. I've never seen him this shaken up before, which says a lot, considering the shit we've been through.

"What happened?" I ask, noticing at least a half dozen squad cars. Police officers are instructing people to stay back as they run yellow caution tape around an area.

"Your boyfriend…" Liam snaps at Sophie, his jaw twitching with anger.

"Just tell us what happened!" I shout.

"Oh my God," Maddie screams, jerking our attention to where she's looking.

Mason's in handcuffs, his face full of blood, looking like he just got thrown from a tornado.

"He's going to jail?" I shriek. "For what? Fighting?"

Mason might not be as big as Hunter and Liam, but he's fast and strong, especially since he has years of boxing experience.

"Weston started it," Hunter says to Sophie, but I can tell he's shaken up. "Things got heated, and Mason chased him outside so he'd get the hell out of here. Liam and I followed because we didn't want a scene at my brother's wedding. Then…" He shakes his head as if he's struggling to continue.

"Shit hit the fucking fan," Liam finishes, clamping his hands together behind his head. He stares out at Mason, whose eyes are glazed over, and I want to know what the hell is going on.

"Where's Weston? Is he getting arrested too?" Sophie asks, glancing around the area in a panic. Squad cars surround the parking lot, and I notice two ambulances off to the side. One of the officers says something to Mason and roughly forces him into the back of a car, cuffed.

Sophie tries to look around the crowd of people. She turns and searches my face. "Do you see Weston?"

"Maybe they're cleaning him up in one of the ambulances," I suggest, trying to calm her.

"No," Hunter and Liam say in unison, a tinge of sadness in their tone.

"Soph, he's…" Hunter pauses to suck in a deep breath. "They tried to resuscitate him, but…"

"What?" Maddie and I gasp.

Sophie grabs my arm and holds on to me as if I'm her lifeline.

Before they can explain further, one of the officers approaches us, seething. "Better get your friend a good lawyer. We're taking him in, and we're going to need some witness statements from you two."

"What's he being charged for?" I ask.

I'm so confused. So much is happening at once that I can barely comprehend any of it.

The cop deadpans, "For murder."

Find Mason and Sophie's story next in
Between Regrets and Promises!

ABOUT THE AUTHOR

Brooke Fox is the alternate pen name for Brooke Montgomery. She lives in the Midwest with her husband, teenage daughter, and four dogs. She survives on iced coffee and afternoon naps.

Find her on her website at
www.brookewritesromance.com
and follow her on social media: